LOVE AND THE LOVELESS

HENRY WILLIAMSON

LOVE AND THE LOVELESS

A Soldier's Tale

Whider thou gost, i chil with the,
And whider y go, tho schalt with me—
From the Breton lay in English called Sir Orfeo.

faber and faber

This edition first published in 2011
by Faber and Faber Ltd
Bloomsbury House, 74–77 Great Russell Street
London WC1B 3DA

A CIP record for this book is available from the British Library

ISBN 978-0-571-27525-0

To
SIR JOHN SQUIRE,
J. C. SQUIRE,
&
JACK SQUIRE,
in ever grateful memory
of past and present
Help and Kindness
this novel,
Book 7
of
A Chronicle of Ancient Sunlight
is
affectionately dedicated

CONTENTS

Part One

THE BLACK PRINCE

Part Two

'ALL WEATHER JACK' HOBART

Part Three

'SHARPSHOOTER' DOWNHAM

CONTENTS

PART FOUR

'SPECTRE' WEST

Part One

THE BLACK PRINCE

Chapter 1

NEW BEGINNING

By one of the platforms of Charing Cross station Red-cross vehicles were drawn up. Civilians were moving towards them. Phillip, walking through the ticket barrier of the suburban line, followed by a porter wheeling his valise, went with the crowd. Near the ambulances, on the asphalt, stretcher cases were lying in rows. They had the usual greyish yellow faces, weary of pain. Beyond the ambulances, peering from open windows of the train, were to be seen the optimistic faces of lightly wounded men. Heads and arms had been newly bandaged, judging by the absence of blood stains; while from the dried mud on some tunics, and khaki aprons over kilts, they were not long out of the line.

Talking with the men at one window, he learned that they had been in action on the morning of the day before, at Thiepval and the Zollern Redoubt, north of the Ancre. How quickly they had come home! The attack had been mentioned in the *communiqué* from G.H.Q. only that morning, with headlines, in *The Daily Trident*. It was now nearly October; half of the objectives of July the First immediately south of the Ancre valley had only just been taken; attack and counter-attack had crossed the chalky upheaved soil during all the intervening days and nights since that brazen sunny morning, which appeared with voiceless glassy pain in his mind at odd moments of the day and night.

Moving down the train, longing to see a known face, he spotted the Gaultshire badge on a trench cap, and asked what battalion had been in action. "The seventh! Were you, by any chance, at Carnoy on July the First? When the battalion got all its objectives?"

"That's right, sir!" There were three chevrons on the hanging sleeve belonging to the unshaven face above him.

"Then you knew Captain West, sergeant?"

"I was with 'Spectre'—beg pardon, sir—when the Captain was hit, in White Trench, sir."

"How extraordinary! I was talking to him only the other day, when he went to Buckingham Palace for his D.S.O."

"If ever a man earned a decoration that day, it was Captain West, sir, or Major, I should say."

He noticed the riband of the Military Medal on the sergeant's tunic, as he stood upright at the window to let a man pass behind him.

"I'm not with the Gaultshires any longer, sergeant. I'm with the Machine Gun Corps—in fact, I'm on my way now back to the Training Centre."

"So you've joined the Suicide Club, sir!"

"I'd say the infantry was that, sergeant."

"Give me bombers and bayonet men every time, sir, and my mobility!"

The young subaltern opened a new silver case, twenty-first birthday present, and put a cigarette in the sergeant's mouth. Pushing the wheel of his lighter upon the flint he blew the spark to smoulder on the fusee; and was offering it when a reporter with a camera called out beside him. "Now then, boys, let's show 'em—Are we down-hearted?" At the massed yell of 'No!' he pressed the shutter bulb; after which he went from window to window, asking names of regiments. A dialection of voices broke forth—Manchesters, Northumberland Fusiliers, Dorsets, Green Howards, Borderers. They were full of beans, thought Phillip, their minds saw brightly because they were out of it.

"How do you feel about going back again, sergeant?"

"When my turn comes, sir, I'll be ready."

"But is that how you *really* feel?"

The sergeant gave him a look, between surprise and caution, before replying, "Not much good thinking about it, is it, sir? Job's got to be done, we're all in it, aren't we?"

"Yes, including the *prächtig kerls* on the other side." When the sergeant looked puzzled he said, "That's what the old Alleyman in 1914 called the Crown Prince. You know, they like him as much as we like the Prince of Wales. It means 'decent fellow'. Well, goodbye, and good luck!"

He shook the uninjured hand; the sergeant came to attention; Phillip saluted him, also at attention, before turning away to the porter waiting with his valise on a trolley. Then he saw the station clock.

"My hat, I'll miss my train! Taxi to King's Cross! Drive

like hell!" as he leapt in over his valise, and gave the porter half-a-crown.

The taxi, with its modest single-cylinder engine that had thumped beside many a jeering cabbie in the early years of Edward the Peacemaker's reign, arrived with its big-end no hotter than usual, with five minutes to spare. Another half-crown changed hands, the driver touching his cap-peak on receiving so substantial a tip as a shilling. Having bought a copy of *The Times* at the bookstall for a penny, the tall young subaltern, with no ribands on his breast but two wound stripes of gold braid on his left sleeve above the cuff, followed the porter wheeling the valise to an empty carriage, wherein, having let down the window, he leaned out in the hope of discouraging others from entering. Far away beyond the end of the platform he saw the engine blowing off steam, as it waited to draw the dark carriages to the North.

The guard stood by, a large silver watch in his hand. He looked to be a kind man, elderly, the sort called Dad by his children, and not Father. Phillip was musing about him, wondering if he had any sons in the war, when he saw a figure coming through the ticket barrier that caused him immediately to withdraw his head. Downham! Hell, if he came in the carriage! He held his head down in the far corner, pretending to be looking in his haversack. Where would Downham be going? Perhaps beyond Grantham, to Catterick camp, which he had heard was as bleak as its name. Downham—one of his seniors in the office—Downham, who had been a private in the London Highlanders like himself, at the outbreak of war, but had not volunteered for foreign service— Downham, now major, never having been to the front!

Thank God, he had gone past the carriage.

Phillip returned to the window, and looked at the guard's face. A splendid fellow, tall, dutiful, a little anxious, as he waited for the last minute to pass. His zero hour—exactly to the second. Well, now he would have the carriage to himself, to think his own thoughts, to be able to rest in the presence of Lily. Yes, the guard was anxious: he showed it by the way he checked his watch with the station clock. Now he was staring at the second hand, whistle in mouth. And then—a shout from the ticket barrier made him turn his head. A latecomer was hurrying through, followed by porter with valise. At once the guard made for the carriage and pulled open the door, while Phillip stood back. "This way, sir, please!" Rapidly the valise was lifted in, the officer followed, and as the door was shut without slam a long whistle-blast and waving of green flag sent the train gliding down the platform.

"That was a close shave," remarked the newcomer, with a smile. "The taxi I bagged was running on paraffin, with a vapour-iser, and broke a piston." With a slight stutter he continued, "My God, I've had a bon time!" He went on to describe how and why he had almost missed the train, mentioning, with complete lack of reserve, incidents in a Torrington Square hotel with a girl he had met on leave. Phillip was relieved when the account was over, and he need pretend interest no more. Seeing the crossed Vickers gun badges on the other's lapels, he tried to recall the face opposite, as one among many others seen months ago at the theatre bar in Grantham.

Opening his newspaper, he found the *London Gazette*, and looked for the regiments with which he had served. One item, in the first territorial home-service battalion to which he had been attached for training after he had been commissioned, made him see again the heavy veldt-tanned face of an elderly second-lieutenant at Heathmarket, long ago in the summer of 1915. Brendon, the Boer War veteran who had snubbed him—'Maddi-son as a soldier, simply *non est*'—was in the *Gazette* seconded for duty as an Assistant Provost Marshal, with the temporary rank of Major. Portly Brendon, complaining of having to support a wife and child on second-lieutenant's pay, would be feeling pretty happy just now.

Glancing at the man opposite, he saw with relief that he was lying back, with eyes closed.

The train, beyond the cavernous darkness of King's Cross, was leaving veils of steam between drab backs of houses of the inner northern suburbs. Gradually the space cleared on either side, until they were racing through a countryside almost as meaning-less as the streets and buildings left behind. Fields, hedgerow timber, spinneys with rookeries visible in the treetops now that autumn had broken the pattern of leaves, teams of heavy horses ploughing up grass and stubble, even cock pheasants unconcerned by the rushing of the train, were equally of a flatness through the glass of the window.

Terror for a moment possessed him: every moment he was going farther from ——. But, even if he returned, she would not be there. Never, never would he see her again. If only this was the train to Folkestone, and the front.

He wondered if his wound would prevent him from re-joining the Transport Course. He must say nothing about it when he arrived, lest a slightly gammy leg, with its crater-like scar on the left buttock, disqualify him from riding. If so, he could hardly be returned to the infantry, for if he couldn't ride, he certainly couldn't march. No home-service job for him: he must get back to France, to the only life that was left.

The train rushed on. Gravelly soils changed to the heavy clays of Gaultshire. He felt his spirits lift as he thought of boyhood days —only to sink in shade once more at the thought that cousin Percy Pickering had been killed less than two weeks before.

Seeing that the other man was now awake, and looking as though he wanted to talk, he said, to forestall further details of Torrington Square, "I suppose cast-iron pistons would crack with the heat of paraffin? With too much carbon on the piston top, glowing red hot? The oil probably got thin, too, with black spots in it?"

"I don't know about that, but I do know I've got black spots in my eyes! My God, my tongue feels like the bottom of a parrot's cage. She was a damned fine girl, a Roumanian brunette——"

The speaker rubbed his eyes, which gave Phillip the opportunity to say, "I felt when you got in at King's Cross that I remembered your face. Pinnegar?. 'D' mess at Belton Park?"

"Yes. I've seen you before, too. In the bar of the theatre at Grantham? Weren't you one of that lot that got off with some of the chorus girls of Razzle Dazzle, one Sunday, and went with them to Sheffield——"

Phillip shook his head.

"No, you'd hardly be here now if you had been, now I come to think of it."

"How d'you mean?"

"You didn't hear about the court-martial? There were five of them—they got to Sheffield on a forged railway warrant, the ticket collector there suspected it was dud, and before he could get them to go with him to the R.T.O.'s office, they cleared off. They didn't like to risk returning by rail, so they pinched a taxi, but it ran out of juice near Nottingham, late at night, so they walked back, but arrived too late for parade on the Monday. They were spotted, hauled up, and put under arrest. Now I remember, it was July the First! They gave the excuse they were celebrating the opening of the Big Push! That's right; the first of July was on a Saturday! I remember now. The news came through in the afternoon, and was there a hell of a binge in the Angel and the theatre bar that night! The five fellows got on the stage from a box, and started dancing with the wimps in the chorus. Afterwards they had a party in the girls' digs, and followed them next day to Sheffield. The whole lot were court-martialled and dismissed the service."

"Yes, I remember there was quite a number of fellows like that, giving dud cheques, and being pitched out about that time. Most of the battalions were asked to send two officers to the M.G.C. when it was first formed, and I suppose sent their duds. That's how I got to the M.G.C.," laughed Phillip.

"You don't remember that Saturday?"

"No, I was in the C.C.S. at Heilly that evening, with a blighty one."

"Lucky for you! I went out in August, and had petrol-sickness when we were relieved after Flers. I went into hospital for a few days, but it was cleared out for expected casualties, so I found myself at home, with ten days' leave. I managed to get four days' extension, and was ordered to report at Grantham, and here I am. Damned lucky, too. I see there's been another push south of the Ancre."

"Yes! We've got the Schwaben at last! But tell me about Flers. It was a good show, wasn't it?"

"*Good* show? It was a bloody muck-up!" cried the other angrily. "The blasted newspapers cracked it up as a victory. The usual tripe—Beach Thomas' larks singing through the barrage, our men keen as mustard, right on top of the trembling Hun! Of course all prisoners tremble, after bombardment!"

"What was it like in September?"

"Well, if you haven't seen the Somme since July the First, you wouldn't recognise it. Everything churned up and re-churned, roads, villages—in fact, you only know where a village is because the roads, if you can call them roads, are red instead of grey, from the bricks put down. Not so much as a blade of grass anywhere, swarms of bloody flies, the woods all heaved up by the roots, dead men unburied, mixed up with mules and horses, rifles, waggons, limbers, all blown to hell, and my Christ! the ponk!"

"But Flers—didn't the tanks put the fear of God into the Alleyman?"

"A newspaper stunt! One bloody tank, left alone for a couple of minutes or so, did go down the main street, and that was all!

The bloody thing broke down just outside the village. I saw the crew crawling out, delirious with heat and fumes. One of our sections had lost some guns, so I put a team in, to work the Vickers. The Boche concentrated emma gee fire on it while they were dismantling a gun, until one armour-plate was red hot, then bullet splashes came through, and knocked out one of my gunners. Those tanks are death traps."

The speaker lay back, a fixed look on his face. There were dark grooves in his eye sockets. Phillip looked out of the window, and began to rattle his teeth to the rhythm of the wheels passing over the expansion gaps in the rails, while in his mind he sought to find, once more, the solution of a problem which had obsessed him for the past thirty-six hours: If he had behaved differently, would not Lily still be alive? Had he really betrayed his best friend by becoming friendly with her, after he had gone to ask her to let Desmond alone? If he had not interfered—if he had not —but he could think no further; and gave up the race with the wheels, and stared at the flat green countryside moving past. The carriage became a tank, scythes on the hubs of its wheels like Boadicea's chariot, slicing down telegraph poles and their loops of wires rising and dropping swiftly with the speed of the train. His teeth now kept time to the thuds of the engine, while the imaginary scythes extended to the horizon, cutting down every-thing, trees, barns, churches, houses, hedges, levelling all things in every direction. Then everything would have no purpose any longer, and the heart of the earth could rest. Or start again without mankind, thus giving every tree, bird, and animal a fair chance. Mother, Father, his sisters then could find peace. If only the bomb had fallen on his own home, when all of them were in bed——

As the train slowed before Grantham, Pinnegar said, "If we're out first, we'll stand a chance of getting a taxi, now that petrol's hard to get. If you look after my valise, I'll go outside and collar one." Phillip followed with the trolley, Pinnegar beyond the ticket barrier called out, "Our luck's in!"

Sitting side by side in the T-model Ford with its high, tarred hood open at the sides, they left for the Training Centre. There they paid off the driver with the half-a-crown demanded, a fare which Pinnegar disputed, saying to the driver that a London taxi for the same distance would have been hardly more than a shilling. The driver persisted. "I shan't give you a tip, anyway," as, with Phillip's one and threepence added to his own, he almost tossed the coins into a grimy hand.

They joined other officers in the asbestos orderly room, standing before blanket-covered trestle tables at which sergeants sat, taking particulars and checking nominal rolls. Phillip and his new friend were given a number denoting their hut—B 6—and told that batmen would be detailed for them later on.

"First parade, nine o'clock Monday. Orders will be posted in the mess this evening," said an officer with a limp and one arm missing, the assistant Adjutant.

"My God, what'll we do till then?" grumbled Pinnegar. "That's just like the Army! We could just as well have stopped in Town!"

Phillip was determined that this time he would work hard; no more fooling about. He went to B hut with Pinnegar, and together they looked in at various doors, to select the best cubicle, for most of them had cracks in the asbestos walls, while others were connected by holes.

"Someone's had a rough house here," remarked Pinnegar. Entering the end cubicle, "I say, I like this!" admiringly, for upon the walls were portraits in crayons of highly coloured and curved female figures, some clad only in high-heeled shoes and black stockings, and all with luring eyes. The friendly atmosphere of this cubicle, improved by six bullet holes in the ceiling, drew from Pinnegar a spontaneous, "My name's Teddy. What's yours? Right, how about a drink? Let's find the mess, Phillip."

"Suits me, Teddy."

Valises and haversacks having been dumped on the floor, the two friends went outside, eventually to discover a large marquee of grey canvas. Inside, scores of trestle tables were ranged beside wooden forms for seats. There was no flooring, the grass was already crushed into the damp soil. Half a dozen elderly men in long-sleeved yellow-and-black footmen's waist-coats above aprons of green baize were unpacking square wicker baskets containing table-cloths, boxes of knives, forks, spoons, and glasses. The wind flapped the loose canvas of the marquee, a sparrow flew up by one of the brown poles, seeking a way out. A man looking like the steward came forward, bowed, and said smoothly, "Tea will be at half past four, gentlemen."

"How about a drink?"

"I'm afraid not until dinner, sir."

"Who's running this show? The Temperance League?"

"Curling and Hammer, from London, sir."

"What time is dinner, d'you know?"

"Seven o'clock, sir. We hope to have everything ready by that hour."

"This is all new since I was last here," remarked Pinnegar, outside. "And to think we might have remained in London! I've got a bottle in my valise. How about a drink in the cubicle?"

"Good idea, *mein prächtig kerl!*"

"I wish they were alive, don't you?" said Teddy, eyeing the chalk figures on the walls. "You've got a hell of a fat valise. What's in it?"

"A gramophone."

"Good. Let's have some music!"

Phillip put on a record, which he had played many times to himself, *The Garden of Sleep*, sung by Sidney Coltham, a light tenor. "I like the way he sings," said Pinnegar, and Phillip felt closer to his new friend. They were listening to Kreisler playing *Caprice Viennoise* when the door opened, to reveal two subalterns standing there, with their valises. One, with the badges of a Northumberland Fusilier, was obviously a ranker officer, for he wore the riband of the Distinguished Conduct Medal.

Hiding the bottle, Pinnegar said, "How the hell do they expect us to get four camp beds down in this small space? What do they think we are, bloody hens? No wonder the walls have caved in next door!"

"'Tis better than nowt," said the Northumbrian. He had dark small eyes in a face pitted with blue specks, which gave him a badly-shaven appearance. "Th' lads would be glad of this on the Somme. D'you mind if we come in?" Phillip noticed that the back of his hands were dark-speckled, too.

"Please yourself," said Pinnegar.

"I've bagged next to the wall," said Phillip. "Under the window. I can't sleep with a window closed."

"How I agree!" said the fourth man, with a glance at Phillip's wound stripes. He, like the Northumbrian, looked newly commissioned.

Phillip offered his cigarette case.

"I don't mind if I do," said the Northumbrian.

"Awful good of you," said the other. "By the way, my name is Montfort."

Four cigarettes having been lighted, and some foxtrots listened to, Pinnegar suggested that they all go down to take a look at the town. "There might be a revue at the theatre!"

The main street was filled with officers, all apparently new arrivals like themselves. They walked down one pavement, passing by shops with the least interest, and came to a large forbidding iron-works, sombre with its own smoke-stains; and returning on the opposite pavement for variety, went down to look at the outside of the theatre. *The Man Who Stayed at Home*. A play. "I've seen it. Thank God I was tight at the time. Utter tripe!" said Pinnegar. So they visited a dull façade of ironwork, wood, and corrugated posters advertising Theda Bara and Mary Pickford, which was the local Picture Palace.

"I've seen them both," said Pinnegar. "My God, what a hell of a place to spend Saturday afternoon."

They stood on the pavement, each of them severed from the life he had known, spiritually and physically—four acquaintances casually come together, to adhere in the moment through loneliness: four among thousands of immature men with lost or withered roots recently sent into the district, yet scarcely knowing what was lacked. Where should they go? Tea at the Angel? Or one of the tea-shops? Which would be the most likely place for girls? They looked into two tea-shops. No girls there, only soldiers; so they went into the Angel.

"As I thought, a place for brass-hats," remarked Pinnegar, at the door of a long room. "And they've taken all the fire."

"They'll hear you," whispered Phillip.

"Who cares? Our money's as good as theirs, isn't it?"

Armchairs with red-tabbed figures in long shining brown boots and spurs were spoked round an open hearth. "Cavalry!" Pinnegar eyed the backs of the recumbent figures with hostility, as he sat on a hard-backed chair.

"Do you like poetry as well as music?" said Phillip, not at ease with Pinnegar's remarks.

"Some things, yes. Why?"

Phillip took from his pocket book a poem originally copied from *The Times*, which he knew by heart. It was now much frayed, having been carried in his pocket diary for nearly a year.

"Let's have a look," said Pinnegar. "I'll tell you if it's any good."

He read a few lines, and snorted. Almost angrily he read on, then throwing down the paper, exclaimed, "Absolute tripe, in my opinion! The person who wrote that had never been anywhere near the front!"

"As a matter of fact," said Phillip, hiding his disappointment, "the man who wrote this died of wounds soon after sending the poem home to his father."

"Tripe all the same," repeated Pinnegar. "All that glory of war stuff gets my goat."

"Give us a look." Phillip passed the clipping to the Northumbrian, saying, "It's not glory of war."

Pinnegar was persistent. "I still say that no-one before a battle thinks like that. I've been in two, and I damned well know what I'm talking about!"

"Aiy, that's true," said the Northumbrian, sombrely, his eyes lifting from the print after reading half-a-dozen words. "I was in attack at Glory Hole in front of La Boisselle, and I had no sich thoughts before we went over t'bags, and got coot oop by Jerry's machine guns."

"I was hit in Mash Valley, just north of the Glory Hole," said Phillip. "This is an idealist's poem, I agree, but Julian Grenfell had been in a battle, and won the D.S.O. before he wrote this."

"Yes, in the cavalry!" said Pinnegar, hotly. "And the son of a lord! With bags of decent grub sent out in hampers from Curling and Hammer's in Piccadilly! What has the cavalry done, since 1914? Even then, they covered the Retreat on horseback, while the poor bloody footsloggers wore their boots to the uppers and got court-martialled when they lost their nerve and wandered off, driven scatty by fighting all day and marching all night!"

"Steady on! Those staff wallahs may hear what you're saying."

"I don't give a damn! I'm not frightened of a bunch of gallopers! I got a bullet through my ribs during the flame attack at Hooge in 1915, and another at Arras early this year, and I never saw a cavalryman the whole time I was in France! They were sitting on their bottoms in rear areas, hunting foxes, shooting hares and pheasants, and living on the fat of the land! French was a horse soldier, so was Haig, so was Gough, and all the others at the top. What do they know of barbed wire and the front line? Sweet fanny adams!"

"Aye, that's a fact," said the Northumbrian, giving back the clipping.

"May I see it?" asked Montfort. Phillip passed it to him, saying, "Anyway, Pinnegar, I think it's a very fine poem. Though during First Ypres I must admit I didn't feel like Julian Grenfell did, when he wrote this poem."

"Of course you didn't, nor did anybody else!" Pinnegar held out his hand for the paper. "Look at this!

> *'And Life is Colour and Warmth and Light*
> *And a striving evermore for these'*

that bit's all right, I'm not objecting to that, it's the next bit that gets my goat,

> *'And he is dead who will not fight,*
> *And who dies fighting hath increase.'*

'He is dead who will not fight.' Yes, if he's a tommy, as I said just now, who loses his nerve and ends up being tied to a post, or stood up against a wall of some château pinched for Corps Headquarters, and shot by a firing squad! Otherwise he who fights is damned lucky to get a blighty one, and not an army blanket in a shell-hole! Which anyway the poor stiff has to pay for! How anyone can seriously believe that bit about having increase if he dies fighting beats me altogether! It's tripe, as I said."

"Officers are rich men, and don't think the same as t' poor man as has to work 'ard for a living," said the Northumbrian, sententiously.

"What are you, a bloody Socialist?" asked Pinnegar, hotly. "I've no time for that tripe!"

"You're middle-class, I can see that, Pinnegar. I'm a workin' man. I've 'ad to work 'ard, I 'ave, all my life, and no college education. I've lain many an hour sweatin' at craggin' lip. I got these bits of coal in t' face from a premature shot." He stared from one to another with the expression as dark as coal itself.

"Come off it, you old four-flusher," smiled Pinnegar. "How the hell did you get a commission, without any education?"

"Night School," replied the Northumbrian.

"What the hell's wrong with Night School?" exclaimed Pinnegar. "That's where Lloyd George got his education."

"And Horatio Bottomley," said the Northumbrian. "Don't forget Bottomley!"

"Bottomley my foot!" cried Pinnegar. "The biggest bloody crook unhung!"

"Hear hear," said Phillip, echoing Mr. Hollis, senior clerk in the office. Would Downham now be at Catterick?

"Then what the hell are we arguing about, Phil?" said Pinnegar, smiling suddenly.

"I don't know—Teddy!" Phillip felt warmth towards him.

"I were sergeant of machine-gun section in France, and was promoted on field when t' officer were killed," remarked the Northumbrian.

"Obviously you're a bloody good man, to get the D.C.M.," said Pinnegar. "Too good to talk Socialist guff. What's your name?"

"Fenwick. Some's call me Darky."

"Right, Darky!"

Fenwick seemed sombrely pleased to be called by this name.

Montfort, who had been listening intently to the talk, now screwed himself up to say to Phillip, "Talking about poetry, what do you think of Henry Newbolt? And *Drake's Drum*, in particular? Don't you think it's very fine?"

"'Drake is in his hammock, a hundred leagues below, and dreaming all the time of Plymouth Hoe!'" exclaimed Pinnegar. "Music Hall stuff! You'll be shouting *The Green Eye of the Little Yellow God* next. I don't care for that sort of tripe, either. Here's the waiter."

His voice dropped, and an expression, half cunning, half endearment towards the white-haired old man, came upon his face. "I suppose you couldn't manage to get us a drink?" His voice became tender, with a surprising softness. "I'll make it worth your while, you know."

In a grave voice, devoid of feeling, and audible in every part of the room, the old man replied, "This is the residential portion of the hotel, sir. Are you staying here, sir? No, sir? I must inform you that only residents may have alcoholic refreshments during the hours of the closing of the buttery. And the public tea-room is down the passage, sir. I will show you the way, sir."

"What utter tripe our licensing laws are," said Pinnegar, as they pulled armchairs to the fire in the other room.

"I like Henry Newbolt's verse," said Phillip to Montfort.

"Oh, do you? I am so glad!" Montfort seemed relieved. "Do you mind if I call you Phillip?" He seemed doubtful.

"Of course! We're all pals here!"

"You might think England was still under Oliver Cromwell, instead of in a great war!" grumbled Pinnegar. "We're supposed to be fighting for freedom, yet we can't get a drink at four o'clock on a bloody cold autumn afternoon!"

They walked back to camp in twilight, having agreed that it was not worth sporting a shilling each for a taxi. Back in the Harem, as Teddy called it, they sat on the floor, smoking, yarning and listening to Phillip's gramophone until shortly before half-past seven, when having brushed their hair, they went to the marquee, not having changed into slacks, because of the mud, and the general appearance of formlessness.

There was more criticism by Pinnegar during mess dinner. He grumbled about profiteers, and the incompetence of those responsible for the messing arrangements. Phillip enjoyed the strange scene. Hundreds of officers sat on hard forms at tables covered by cloths upon which candles in saucers guttered as draughts scored under the walls of shaken canvas. Many were returned from the war. They sat with faces made to appear gaunt and patient, or savage and impatient in the flickering light and shadow. Some talked quietly, despite knees pressed together, and elbows jogging as they drank tepid soup served in hurried relays by the half-dozen elderly imported London waiters now in tail coats with starched shirt-fronts and cuffs. Those officers who had been served first waited impatiently, some muttering, for the last to finish, when the interwaiter relay races of the Six Little Tichs, as Pinnegar called them, began all over again; the old men hurrying lugubriously through draughty candlelight with plates of cold pressed beef, ham, and tongue.

The impatient minority became the majority, as they waited for drinks that did not come. Phillip heard complaints above the canvas flapping. "What, no wine list? Damnable!"

"Waiter, bring me a large Scotch and soda!"

"Waiter! I've asked three times for a bottle of Bass' beer! Well, bring *any* beer, only bring it now!"

"Waiter!"

"Won't be a moment, sir!"

"Waiter!"

"Coming sir! Sorry sir, just for tonight it's a bit of a muddle, sir!"

Why were they so devoid of understanding? Obviously the poor old fellows were doing their best. "You're reet!" said Darky Fenwick, to whom Phillip confided his opinions. "But most on'm here's snobs, wi' no feeling for the workin' man."

Pinnegar began to sing, beating time with his fork on the table,

> "'*Waiter, waiter!*
> *Bring me a morning paper!*
> *Waiter, waiter, do you hear?*
> *Bring me half a pint of beer!*
> *It's waiter here!*
> *It's waiter there!!*
> *It's waiter all over the shop!!!*'

I heard Little Tich sing that at the Hippodrome, Birmingham, more than once," he remarked happily, oblivious of the glances he got from some of the regular-officer types at his table.

"Pinnegar, you want to watch your step," said the Northumbrian. "Some's watching you."

At last they were fed, and feeling better, deliberated what to do with themselves. In the end they walked back to the town, to drink at the theatre bar. The play was on; there was a rosy glow from the stage upon the faces lining the upper circle when Phillip peeped through the door. After several drinks he began to feel again the romance of being alive in such stirring times; this feeling led to thoughts about the immediate past.

The bar led off from the upper circle, and after awhile he slipped away; and standing under an electric light in a passage lined with dark-red wallpaper, read a few lines of the poem *Into Battle*, enough to bring back, in a moment as fleeting as it was poignant, a vision of Lily Cornford's face in the shaded gaslight under the yews of St. Mary's churchyard. There, while reciting to her some of the verses of the poem, he had dared to look at her face, to see her eyes brimming with gentleness, and compassion.

He must seek the darkness, and be alone with his thoughts. He went down the stairs and out of the theatre; and finding a narrow passage way, lit dimly by a gas lamp, he went down it, and stood still there, trying to project his thoughts to Lily, and to receive an answer. After awhile he turned back, and had gone into the street, when a voice said, "Hi! You there! Come here!"

He went towards a figure standing by a lamp-post, and saw a

red-banded cap above a British Warm with the somewhat
dreaded letters A.P.M. around one arm. It was Brendon. Would
it be the thing to congratulate him? "Good evening, sir! May
I——"

"Why are you improperly dressed? Where is your service
cap?"

"Sir——"

"What is your name and unit?"

"Lieutenant Maddison, sir, attached Machine Gun Corps,
Harrowby Camp."

"Well, don't let me see you improperly dressed again, or I'll
run you!"

"Yes, sir. May I offer my congratulations, sir? I saw the notice
in the *Gazette* this morning."

"So you know me, do you?"

"Yes, sir. At Heathmarket, the Cantuvellaunian mess, in the
summer of 1915, sir."

"What did you say your name was?"

"Maddison, sir."

"H'm. I remember you now. Where did you just come from,
the stage door?"

"No, sir, from the bar. I felt a bit faint, sir."

"Well, don't forget your cap next time."

"No, sir."

Phillip went back to the bar, conscious that Brendon was
following him upstairs.

"Cavé, chaps! A.P.M. coming up!"

Major Brendon entered a sedate atmosphere. He prowled
around, short leather-covered cane under one arm, hands behind
back. He did not speak. Nobody appeared to notice him, except
Phillip, who saw him looking at the two wound stripes on his
sleeve. The A.P.M. said, "I will see you outside." Phillip put on
his cap, and followed him out.

"You know of course that it is an offence to put up wound
stripes to which you are not entitled?"

Now that he was on safe ground, Phillip pretended innocence.
"It never really occurred to me, sir."

"You know that ignorance is no excuse?"

"You mean generally, sir?"

"I mean particularly. Now answer my questions! I want a
limited answer to a limited question! Very well. Why are you
wearing two wound stripes?"

"I was twice wounded, sir."

"Where were you hit?"

"In front of Ovillers, sir."

"I did not ask what locality, but where *you* were hit."

"In the leg, sir."

"Which leg?"

"My left leg, sir."

"What hit you?"

"Two machine-gun bullets, and shrapnel, sir."

"All at the same time?"

"No, sir, but the same morning."

"How do I know that you are not lying?"

"I cannot answer that question, sir."

"Why can't you?"

"Because I do not know your mental processes, sir."

"Are you trying to be impertinent?"

"No, sir. I was trying to give a limited answer to a limited question."

"What question?"

He wondered if his breath smelled like Major Brendon's, when he had had a drink. "You said, sir, 'How do I know that you are not lying?'"

"Well?"

"Well, sir, I cannot say."

"Splitting hairs, eh? Well, watch your step! I know all about you, and if I find you misbehaving, as you did at Heathmarket, I'll run you before the General! Understand?"

"Yes, sir."

The A.P.M. turned away. Phillip watched him down the stairs, then went back to the bar.

"What did the old bastard want you for?"

"Oh, I used to know him, he's an old C.I.V. Boer War wallah who never heard so much as a bullet whistle, so now he's the heavy martinet."

"Looked a proper twott to me," said Pinnegar. "Chin chin, old man! I say, Phil, let's try and get in the same company, shall we?" He beamed at Phillip, who said, with sudden release of warmth, "Rather, Teddy!"

On Monday, when he asked to be allowed to join the Transport Course, Phillip was directed to a hut wherein sat an officer with red tabs and Lancer buttons, who said, "Didn't I hear you

talking about Julian Grenfell in the Angel on Saturday afternoon?
I'll give you a chit. Take this to 'H' lines, Belton, and report
to the Orderly Room there."

Chapter 2

RIDING SCHOOL

Belton looked shabbier than when he had seen it in the spring.
Much of the park and the surrounding grassland was now the
colour of the soldiers' uniforms. Tens of thousands of feet and
hooves and wheels had torn and discoloured the sward. Horses,
riders, waggons, limbers, drivers, mules were daily in movement
upon the landscape.

Having reported to 'H' lines, he was sent to a troop, under a
Riding Master, which was being formed that morning. With about
a dozen other subalterns he was put in a section under a sergeant,
who led the way to a hut, where, to Phillip's disappointment,
they were told to seat themselves on forms for a lecture upon The
Saddle.

He found no interest in this, so retired into the world of
memory, hearing odd sentences across his mind-pictures.

"There are seven parts of the Saddle. They are, facing the
horse's head, the Pommel, the Seat, the Cantle, the Flaps, Sweat
Flaps, V-shape attachment, and Girth Tabs.   The saddle should
be placed in the centre of the horse's back, the front being one
hand's-breadth from the play of the shoulder. Have you all got
that down, gentlemen?"

No need to write it down, it's in the 2/- book I bought in
Grantham, *Training for Transport Officers and Horsemanship*. If
Desmond would only understand two things: that Lily had never
really been his girl, because she did not love him; that he had
never tried to get Lily for himself. Will it be any good if I write to
Eugene, who was Desmond's friend first, and ask him to explain?

"The girth should lie flat and smooth around the horse's belly.
It should admit one finger between it and the belly, the finger
being placed in from the rear to the front, so that the hair is left
lying in the right direction."

Pencils moved over note-books. Phillip sat withdrawn, mourn-
ing alone.

"If the hair is left ruffled under the girth, a girth-gall will be caused. The girth having been tightened by the straps provided, the surcingle should be placed over the saddle and girth and be as tight but no tighter than the girth. If the surcingle be tighter than the girth, the surcingle will rub and pinch the horse's skin, which would cause a most serious girth-gall."

He lived again the scene wherein Desmond had said that it would be best for everyone if he were killed. *You are too complicated a person to live.*

"The buckle of the surcingle should always be under the belly and in a direct line with the forelegs so as to escape rubbing the points of the elbows."

It would be no good writing to Eugene.

At the end of the hour a copy of *The Horse's Prayer* was given to each officer, a free issue from Our Dumb Friends League. Phillip glanced through it, and began to scoff inwardly, as he thought of the Riding School nags.

To Thee, my Master, I offer my prayer: Feed me, water and care for me, and, when the day's work is done, provide me with shelter, a dry clean bed and a stall enough for me to lie down in comfort.

Always be kind to me. Talk to me. Your voice often means as much to me as the reins. Gentle me sometimes, that I may learn to love you. Do not jerk the reins, and do not whip me when going up hill. Never strike, beat, or kick me when I do not understand what you want . . . watch me, and if I fail to do your bidding, see if something is wrong with my harness, or my feet . . . never put a frosty bit in my mouth . . . I often fall on the hard pavements which I have often prayed might not be of wood but of such a nature as to give me a safe and sure footing.

Remember that I must be ready at any moment to lose my life in your service.

He thought of the horses and mules lying beside the Harrow Road leading up to Loos: and the Dumb Friends League did not seem so funny.

And finally, O my Master, when my useful strength is gone, do not turn me out to starve or freeze, or sell me to some cruel owner, to be slowly starved and worked to death; but do Thou, my Master, take my life in the kindest way, and your God will reward you here and hereafter.

You will not consider me irreverent if I ask this in the name of Him who was born in a stable. Amen.

They left the hut and made their way to the picket lines, two long rows of horses tied to a rope and facing each other. Phillip had the same sergeant instructor as he had had during the spring: a sturdy, dark cavalryman, one of the original B.E.F. It seemed that the same old mounts were in use for the Riding School, too, a miscellaneous herd ranging between fifteen and seventeen hands high, hairies used to carrying awkward loads which usually began by patting their necks nervously, and continued the enforced relationship by speaking to them with two words only, *Whoa Back*, in tones of voice varying from confidential whisper to guttural threat. Nearly all the hairies were hard-mouthed from continual tuggings at the bits across their tongues, the curbed ends of which were chained around their lower jaws. Some horses, he knew, avoided this discomfort by working their bits forward between the teeth, so that a succession of booted rein-tuggers, their spur-rowels filed down for safety, and accustomed to handlebar steering, usually failed to elicit even a protesting shake of head, but only a continued neck-rigid boring as they sat forked, without balance, alarmingly high above the ground.

Before mounting, Phillip allowed the groom to show him what he knew already: the adjustment of stirrup leathers, by buckles under the saddle flaps, to the length of his arm from shoulder-pit to finger-tips. This equalled the length of leg, with heel well down, from boot to just above the knee.

"Prepare to mount! Mount!"

He was already familiar with the routine; and holding the reins in the approved manner through the fingers of his left hand, he pressed on the horse's withers while putting his left foot into the burnished iron. Then hopping up, he threw his right leg over the saddle and thrust the boot into the iron with one kick, thus completing mounting in one motion.

"I see you've ridden before, sir," remarked the sergeant, whose horse was standing nearby.

"You taught me, sergeant."

"I thought I recalled your face, sir."

Other pupils were still trying to mount. Phillip watched some arriving, with an appearance of being bent, upon the unfamiliar saddle level. Others clung to the near-side flanks of their horses, desperately clawing themselves up, or putting arms round horse-necks, descended to try again. One corpulent and elderly subaltern—he must have been quite thirty, Phillip thought—strove so desperately that he slid over his horse's back and fell to the ground on the other side, an action that drew from the Riding Master, who had arrived silently at a walk and was sitting, apart and motionless, regarding the scene before him, a morose comment of, "Sit your mount, sir, sit your mount, you are not a member of a Circus, sir!"

At last all in the troop were mounted. The sergeant quietly gave the order, "Section! In file, walk march!" and the cavalcade set out across the park. After watching them sombrely for a few more minutes the statuesque Riding Master—a first-class warrant officer whose face with its long rope-like moustaches was almost concealed by a flat-crowned cap held low by a strap under his chin—set off to regard another section, his long-legged chestnut mare silky in coat and action carrying him away, lightly and seemingly without effort, with a delicate action. Enviously Phillip watched what appeared to be the lightest wavy motion diminishing away behind the long tail of the chestnut. "We call that the South African triple canter," said the sergeant at his side. "It's one leg—three legs—one leg—three legs, if you watch."

"It's a lovely motion, sergeant! How much is due to the mount, and how much to the rider?"

"You'll learn, sir. Section, trot!"

It wasn't so bad as he had dreaded. While most of the others were being bumped about in body and mind, at times uttering little prayers to their mounts, he found that he could keep himself fairly upright in the up-and-down rising motion. The knowledge that his leg seemed all right enlivened him, so that he wanted to shout aloud. Round and round in a ring the trotting went, while he felt more and more sure of himself.

"Section, halt! Gentlemen, cross your irons over the pommels of your saddles! Section! Walk March! Section, trot!"

This was something quite different. Jog jog jog jog jog, discomfort, discomfort, pain pain pain. Hold breath. Jog jog jog. Oh God, I have lost my sense of balance. The muscles of my left leg are no good. Hold breath against pain. Bump, bump, bump.

"Sit down to it, sir, sit down to it! I could jump between you and the horse's back, sir. Sit down to it! Why, what's the matter with you? You want an armchair, not a horse! Grip your mount's barrel with your calves, sir, keep those heels down, those toes up." Thank God the sergeant was not talking to him, after all. And thank God when it was all over for the day.

After tea he met Teddy Pinnegar in the bar of the Angel;

life seemed good, with the marks of 'leathers' diagonal on his boots, and rubbing marks of saddle on buckskin strappings.

The next day the lecture was on the Ailments of the Horse—Curb, Capped Hock, Thorough-pin, Thrush, Bog Spavin, Bone Spavin, Capped Elbow, Ring Bone, Sprained Tendon, Splints, Wind Gall. The Yorkshire Boot for the horse that brushed. How to kill a horse humanely. In the afternoon another schooling, this time trotting bare-back round and round the endless ring, nose of wooden hairy horse following docked tail of hairy dobbin, round and round in trodden circle, hot sack-like figures hoping desperately to grip and balance on hairy barrels either too wide or too agonisingly tall with razor backs more like crags of a coral reef than a razor. Variations of *The Horse's Prayer* were groaned, sibilated, and pleaded. Go slower you brute, don't shake about so, go steady you brute! O why in hell did I say I could ride? What must the T.T.O. think of me, now that he probably knows about me? Good horse, dear old Dobbin, or whatever your bloody name is, steady now, steady old 'oss. Jog jog jog, how long will it go on, I shall fall, on on on, round and round. Try to shove down heels with toes up. No good, it hurts like hell on the base of my spine, and I can't grip at the same time with my calves, my left leg is numb, I'm a crock. I'll fall off any moment now. Jag, jag, jag, the joint of my thigh is like broken glass, perhaps a fracture is only now showing itself. Stab stab, O for a rest, how much longer, try and grip with the calves, to stop being flung up like a broken bottle grating every time this hairy brute trots. O how much longer, stop stop stop, I can't stand it any more. Jog, jog, jog, the landscape swaying at all angles. At last, at last.

"Now when I give the command to halt, each officer will draw back the reins and apply an even pressure on the bit, raising the reins as he does so, to lift the 'oss's 'ead, while the right hand is smartly raised to inform the rider be'ind of 'is intention to 'alt! Wait for it! Wait for it! Watch it now, and let me see no sloppiness this time! Kiss your 'oss's necks afterwards, give them sugar if you like but don't fall on the 'oss's neck and embrace the 'oss between the ears, in public, it isn't done, not while I'm watchin' anyway. Now wait for it! Section! 'ALT!"

Phillip's mount was waiting for it. Schooled to the sergeant's voice, it stopped so abruptly that its rider's raised right hand went forward with his body, to clutch the mount's mane for security.

"All right, dismount, gentlemen," said the instructor, quietly, all criticism forgotten. "Fall out for ten minutes."

Gaspers were soon being puffed by figures feeling themselves to be crook-backs, fossilised frogs, and sawn partly in half.

Phillip felt sure, as the days went on, that most of the horses of the riding school were duds. They had no spirit beyond that of slavery, their mouths were hardened by being pulled by the hands of Tom, Dick and Harry, their minds set in trying to avoid boring labour. Why was it that both the sergeant instructor and the Riding Master could fly the jumps, one after another, in a series of smooth wavy motions, their horses doing it with the slightest of directions? Because they had had the pick of the best horses! The sergeant rode a quiet, beautiful horse. Phillip asked about it.

"Ah, now you're talkin', sir! Blood will tell, in man and beast! Arab blood, gentlemen, is revealed in the large brown intelligent eye, the broad for'ed, in the spirit that is both dashin' and disciplined—taking the least of 'ints, controlled by intelligence holdin' fire in check!"

The feeling of Grenfell's *Into Battle*. These old cavalrymen had the right understanding——

The jumps were five in number. The first only could be approached at right angles, for the course was both short and circular.

"Now, Mr. Maddison, sir, you have been on the course before, so show the other gentlemen how to take the jumps, will you please, sir."

Phillip had named his mount, to himself and the animal, The Cocoanut. Now, with a muttered prayer to the hacked-out spirit of The Cocoanut, he approached the first fence, thinking of Mr. Facey Romford in the Surtees novel which he had read as a boy, at a jog trot. Four lengths away from the fence he banged with his heels, to urge his mount into a canter; but the only effect of rib-tapping was to cause a momentary enlivened trot, which after progress of about one length of The Cocoanut became a riding-school jog once more.

"Don't forget to 'old your 'oss back, will you, sir, we don't want to see it dashin' its knees against the obstacle, do we, sir?"

Desperately Phillip kicked again; the kicks seemed to bounce back as the animal stopped before the fence.

"Hold your mount back, sir, my word, you're on a bit of blood, sir! Never mind, try agen! This time, try not to think that you two are goin' to a funeral!"

Repeated kickings animated The Cocoanut into a walking pace past the side of the jump.

"Never mind! Try agen, sir! Third time lucky!"

Back, you brute, back, good old horse, dear old Cocoanut, be a sport. At the tone of voice, the sport turned round and began to trot amiably in the direction of the picket line. Phillip managed to pull its head round, while travelling in a wide circle.

"What are you two practisin'? Pulling a grass-cutter around a hayfield, sir?"

The instructor dismounted. He pulled a long whippy stick from the first fence. "Now put your mount to the jump, sir!"

At the sight of the long stick The Cocoanut showed some obedience; for it broke into a canter from its former amble, after which it stopped suddenly at the jump. Back again; further goading; a skittish prancing forward, a make-belief of taking-off which became a barging through the horizontal poles laced with spruce branches. Back once more; head turned round; the sergeant running behind it, whippy stick swishing, *swoosh!* on its hind-quarters, whereupon The Cocoanut gave a leap like a buck-rabbit and lifted its front legs over the poles, before stopping so abruptly that it parted from its helpless rider, who went over the jump by himself, heels following head and arms.

As he got up from his knees, he heard the impersonal mild sarcasm of the voice, "No idea, sir, no idea! Why not get inside your mount, and let 'im go on 'is own?" as Phillip picked himself up and, as though indifferent to what had happened, examined the knees of his best fawn cavalry twill breeches for mud damage. Then, as he was leading away his docile mount, he saw the sergeant loop gracefully five times as he cleared the jumps around the course.

"There you are, sir, if I can jump these five little fences, you can do it. Now try agen, sir."

"It's all very well for you, sergeant, but you've got a decent horse!"

"You're welcome to try my mount, sir."

He went to the sergeant's horse, and hoping that he would not show his nervousness, mounted, and pulled up the irons, for he did not want to be dragged. With the reins laid on the bay's neck, he turned it round. Then he clapped his heels and feeling it was all a fantasy, that he was only just remembering in time to sway forward at each jump, hands low on withers, and lean back as the horse cleared a fence, he went round somehow; and dismounted, his thighs quivering as though stretched, as he stood beside the sergeant.

"Very kind of you, sergeant. A beautiful action. It was a combination of Arab blood and your schooling that did the trick."

"We'll make a roughrider outer you yet, sir!"

It had been like sitting in an armchair, thought Phillip, with jubilation, as he tried to remount a cocoanut on four legs. He found he had no strength.

"Take it easy, sir," said the sergeant, quietly. "The muscles of your leg aren't used to it. We'll find you a more suitable mount tomorrow."

The next afternoon he was given a black gelding which the sergeant said had some blood in it, declaring that the broad brow and large brown eyes showed the Arab.

In the days that followed the section exercised beyond the confines of the domain wall, long trotting journeys into the surrounding country. Down obscure lanes they went, with stirrup irons pulled up on leathers, past fields of plough and stubble, cornstacks and ricks of hay, grazing fields and coppices. The black gelding was a high-stepper, with a tendency to pass other horses; a touch on its flanks, and it would break into a canter. Phillip was often bumped and shaken to the point of wanting to dismount, but he kept going; and one day, suddenly, he acquired a sense of balance, and with it, a feeling of mastery.

It happened when it began to rain as the section was trotting home. He was riding without stirrups, an action helped by rain having given a firmer grip between cloth and leather.

Soon his tunic and breeches were saturated; he was filled with an inner glow. When the order was given to canter, inside the park gates, the horses flung out their forelegs, eager to get back to feed-bags of oats and chaff. Passing through an avenue of beech trees, the sergeant put his horse at the gallop. Immediately his horse followed, the air behind was filled with flying clots of earth as the black strove to get ahead of the bay in front of it. He felt tremendous exhilaration as his wet breeches gripped the saddle flaps. He felt an ease of balance, so that he looked back over his shoulder at the other riders, completely confident in both himself and his horse; and letting the gelding have its head, with reins laid slightly upon its neck, he drew level with the sergeant, who thereupon gave his mount a touch of the spur. A neck-and-neck race was on through the rain, showers of sods flew behind the two leaders. Phillip had his irons drawn up and crossed over his saddle bow, he felt he was hinged to the horse's motion from the knees up. As he drew away from the sergeant, he experienced a new power upon himself, accompanied by a surging joy. It was not confined to the feeling that he could ride, but to other things in life. It was nothing to do with what he had hitherto thought of as himself; the feeling was wider, beyond the shut-in feelings, and calmer—a sure feeling, like the one Lily had, when he had met her again, after four months, and she had told him that she was going out to France to nurse the wounded. She was so calm, serene, and composed. As he fled across the park he felt that he had come through the shadow that had always lain upon his life, until now; and with a touch of the reins he brought the gelding down to a canter, then to a trot—which he found smooth and gliding, a series of little undisturbing low bumps, a mere ripple, horse and rider harmonious in joined motion. With three words, "Stand, Black Prince!" the horse stopped. He lifted his right leg over its head and slid to the ground, to find that he was quivering like the horse. If only he could buy it! The Black Prince! He stroked its nose, rubbed its cheek-bone, and the white blaze down its face. "Black Prince", he said, feeling as though he and the gelding were great friends already. The horse pressed against his hand, and gave a low whinney.

At the start of the next riding lesson, when he made for Black Prince, standing with others tied by head-ropes to the picket line, the gelding watched him approaching. Phillip saw that Black Prince's ears were erect, and when he went to its head, the gelding gave a whuffle of recognition. He had brought a carrot from the cookhouse; Black Prince saw it, the brown eyes brightened, the horse held its head ready for the unfastening of the head-stall, by which the bit was slipped from its mouth. After the carrot was eaten, the horse helped, by head movement, to slip the bit back into its mouth. Black Prince is intelligent, Phillip thought; he *knows*, as Lily had known.

The days shortened. Dusk came early. Electric-light bulbs shone behind brown army blankets that served as hutment curtains; for Zeppelins, despite the flamers, were still coming over. Grantham was now a place of darkness, which somehow lived the vaguest shadowy life of its own, peopled by civilians seen as flat surfaces, diminished in the soldiers' world because they were not in uniform, fairly useless, with unreal faces scarcely perceived. There were also many soldiers of the rank and file; these, too, were one-dimensional figures of another world, of ugly issue uniforms, heavy boots, and almost dead faces as they saluted mechanically. So much for Grantham in the eyes of Phillip, as the last of the leaves drifted down into the dampness of November.

The Angel gave forth a promising mild roar as the door into the bar was opened, to reveal scores of faces, in various shades of red and brown and varying states of animation around tables, with similar figures booted and spurred standing at the mahogany bar. The privileged stood or sat in a narrow room marked *Office* on one glass panel of the door. For Phillip the main bar was the attraction, for behind it was the centre of most young men's thoughts: two coveted figures in daring three-quarter-length skirts and black silk stockings, young women with fair hair and blue eyes, daughters of the landlord: the elder girl was, according to Teddie Pinnegar, married to the son of a peer—a khaki wedding—even so, said Teddie, she was not stuck-up over it, but helped to serve in the bar.

Where was Teddie tonight? Phillip had had a bath in a borrowed canvas trough on his cubicle floor. He felt very clean and sure of himself afterwards as he put on new shirt and slacks, polished belt and shoes, new M.G.C. badges on his tunic lapels; but now, looking about him and seeing no one he knew, he felt thin. He waited to be served at the bar, while others thrust past him, some calling cheerily to the girls. He envied the hearty ones as he gave way to the thrusters, while quietly awaiting his turn. Then with relief he saw the smiling face of Pinnegar coming in at the door, with two pips on each shoulder strap. He was with a captain whom Phillip had not seen before. The captain went into the dining room, and Pinnegar came to the bar. Phillip said, "Congratulations, *mein prächtig kerl!*"

"It was in the *London Gazette* this morning," Pinnegar beamed. "I've got two months' back pay to come, what's more. How about a drink, to christen it?" The new gilt star shone beside the old dulled one. "How are you getting on, Phil?"

"Oh, not so dusty. We're passing out next week, with any luck."

"If you'd stopped on the gun, you'd have got a company, you know, with your seniority."

"I prefer horses and mules, any day, *mein prächtig kerl!* It's the best job in France! I've had my fill of going over the top. How about you? Any chance of a company?"

"Not now. I would have had one, if I hadn't gone sick after Flers. Second loots, who've been acting as brigade machine gun officers, are coming back for refresher courses, and being given three pips. Anyway, I don't give a damn, I've palled up with a dam' fine chap, a captain, who's got a racing Mercédès, and never puts up the hood. They call him All Weather Jack, and he's a dam' fine sport. He's applied for me to be his second-in-command when he gets a company. Sort of adjutant, you know, runs orderly room and supplies. I'd prefer it to transport any day. Chance of a third pip, if he gets a crown."

"With the transport you can get a dry sleep in a camp bed every twenty-four hours. That's all I want."

The staring sleepless nights of the first battle of Ypres were still with Phillip, and the black cold rain in the flooded trenches of the winter of 1914.

"I'd like you to meet my pal Ho-bart, Phil. He's just gone through to order dinner. We're having pheasants and claret. They've got a wonderful cellar here." He lowered his voice. "Jack Ho-bart's got pots of money, from Ho-bart's boot polish. Quite a useful pal to have. Two double whiskies, please!" with a smile at the blue-eyed barmaid. "That's the Honourable's sister," he said sideways. "Marvellous blue eyes, hasn't she?"

"Yes." Lily, Lily; if only she were Lily.

"Jack's just come back from France," went on Pinnegar. "As I said, he's an awfully nice fellow. I'll see if I can wangle you dinner with us. It's his birthday. We're going on to the theatre afterwards. He's got a stage box."

"I haven't signed out." Phillip shrunk from the idea of sponging.

"What's the odds? It isn't as though it's a battalion mess, and who's to know, or care for that matter? Anyway, Ho-bart's got pots of it, so we may as well help him spend it. I'd feel the same if I were in his shoes. What's money for, but to be spent?"

Captain Hobart threaded his way to the bar. Phillip saw at a glance that he was Yeomanry, by his open genial look and hair parted in the middle and brushed back, with a whiff of eau-de-Cologne; by the cut of his well-worn breeches, washed almost white, and the buttons fastened beside and below the kneecap, the top button of each row pressing upon the little crater in the kneecap, the "button of the knee" as tailors called it; by the pale fawn stock tie, the well-boned mahogany boots, the silver spurs set high upon each ankle, with leather straps above and below. A pre-war officer, he decided. Teddie Pinnegar, by contrast, wore a pair of the much-advertised Harry Hall's breeches with a wide cut. They were horsey, and of a rather livid salmon-pink hue, fastened with laces, and kept almost formally in shape below the knee by whale-bone strips inserted beside the lace-holes. His shirt and tie were very nearly of the same hue, so was his cap, with the peak worn at an angle and the crown crushed in: rather bounderish, Phillip thought, rather a show-off; not that Teddie, he hastened to tell himself, was a bounder, not at all, only he didn't seem to know, exactly, what made up good form.

"This is Phil Maddison, Jack."

"How do you do, sir."

"Don't you call me sir, young feller! My name's Hubb't. Or Ho-bart, as some prefer to call me."

"Now don't you pretend you're not Ho-bart of Ho-bart's Boot Polish, Jack, for I've been telling Phillip all about you——"

"How about our appointment with the Widow? It's my birth-day, let's crack a bottle, shall we? In fact, I've got some on ice. Let's go into the office, what?"

Pinnegar winked at Phillip, to confirm the success of his strategy. Phillip felt uneasiness; it looked like deliberate spong-ing. He was soon reassured in the company of the two girls, and their mother, who were glad to see everyone, as was Captain Hobart. A nice fellow, he thought; so was Teddie, but he wished he would see that Hobart, under his easy manner, was bored by the continued remarks about his name.

"What tripe some pronunciations of names are! Mere snobbery, when you come to think of it. Everyone trying to be one up on the people next door! It's like fashions in women's hats at Ascot"—with an ingenuous smile at the younger blue-eyed girl who had brought in the ice bucket. Then,

"Shall I crack it for you, Jack?" he asked, as he lifted a bottle of Veuve Cliquot 1906 from the ice, and started to undo the wire over the cork.

"No, you must let me take the risk," replied Hobart, taking the bottle, and loosening the cork. *Pop!* It struck the ceiling, while Hobart managed to get most of the froth into a glass. Some fell on Pinnegar's new breeches.

"My word, now I've spoiled your new Harry Hall's, Teddie!"

"That's all right," cried Pinnegar. "I wet them myself sometimes! Well, cheero, Jack, all the best, and many happy returns!"

After the toast had been drunk, Pinnegar went on, "As I was saying, women at Ascot before the war went there solely to out-do other women in hats. Don't you agree? You'll bear me out there, I dare say, Jack?"

"I never looked at the hats, Teddie."

"I bet you didn't!" said Pinnegar, knowingly. Then, to Phillip, "You want to keep in with Jack! He's looking for a transport officer! He might ask you, if he takes a fancy to you."

While Phillip was trying to think of something to say, Captain Hobart turned to him and said, "I hear you were hit on July the First. What section?"

"Albert—before Ovillers. I got a couple of scratches, so I wasn't there long."

"I've just come back from Albert, or what's left of it. They've nearly brought the railway up, now we've got the high ground to the north and east. It was badly plastered after you left."

"I've often wondered if the Golden Virgin on the campanile was shot down."

"No, She's still there. The saying now is that when She falls, the war will end. The French engineers went up last month, and fixed her with wire. No connexion between rumour and fact!"

"Can you tell me what the 'Notre Dame de Brébières' represented?"

"'Our Lady of the Shepherdesses'. It was corn and sheep country, you know, all around there. Hence the dedication. She was also known as 'The Virgin with the Limp,' as she dragged her right foot. The French are realistic in their affairs, and bring symbolism into their everyday living."

"I never saw any shepherdesses!" said Pinnegar. "The women were a lot of old scarecrows in black clothes and sabots."

Captain Hobart continued, "It's hard to imagine it, but I knew that country before the war. I used to fish some of those Picardy streams—all spring-fed out of the chalk, you know. Do you fish?"

"I've fished in Kent, and also in Devon."

"Ah yes, small trout, but very lively, and excellent eating. Those Department du Nord rivers hold some awful good trout, you know. Two and three pounders quite common. Not quite up to the Test, perhaps, but as good as the Avon at Salisbury. Do you fish wet or dry? Wet, I suppose, in Devon?"

"Most fish wet, but I used a dry fly."

"Good man! Go after your fish, no 'chuck and chance it'. How's the transport course? Passed out yet?"

"No, we have that next week."

"I'm gettin' a company, I expect Teddie told you?"

"Yes, he did."

"Care to come along with us?"

"I'd like to, very much."

"Good man. I'll try and work it. With any luck we ought to be out in the New Year. There's a big show coming off in the spring, at Arras. When I left, Fifth Army was getting ready to clear the Ancre valley. It's no secret, of course, the old Hun knows it as well as we do. Good hunting!" He raised his glass, and they drank together. "You hunt the deer on Exmoor, don't you? I've never been so far West, I'm a fox-catcher from these parts."

"I've never hunted."

"Like to hunt?" Captain Hobart filled his glass.

"Rather!"

"We'll go out one day. There are several meets within reasonable hacking distance. We'll get hold of some gees, there are several among the remounts capable of toppin' the timber. We must foregather!"

"I've got an awful good horse in my section. It's a black gelding, sixteen hands high, some Arab blood in it. I've been wondering how to wangle it for myself, when I leave the riding school."

"Who's your Riding Master?"

"I don't know his name, but he's in the Seventeenth Lancers, with long black moustaches, and rides a chestnut gelding that lopes along with a beautiful South African triple canter."

"Sounds like 'Ropey' Griggs. A case of whiskey will grease his palm. Not a word about it to any one, of course."

"No fear. Well, thank you, Captain Hubb'rt. I ought to say goodbye now, and go back to camp. Will you have a drink with me?"

"That's awful good of you, but would you mind if we make it another time? It's my birthday, you see, and as a matter o' fact, there's another bottle coming! Won't you stay and help us make it a dead'n? And I'd be delighted if you'd join my table for dinner. I think if we're going to be in the same company in France, the sooner we get to know one another the better, don't you?"

"Well, thank you very much."

"That's settled then. I'll tell the head waiter."

When he returned, Hobart said, "Wonderful old pub this, isn't it? Where we sit now, Richard Crook-back signed the death warrant of Buckingham in 1483, his best friend, who went the way of all the rest of his pals. As you know, Richard the Third found himself alone, at the end of his life, forsaken on the field of Bosworth. Wonderful to think of history going on, isn't it, past and present all one in time? It helps one to keep this war in perspective."

"How do you mean?"

"What is happening today is all a part with what has happened before. It's the same life now as it was in the past. The means differ, that's all. War, fighting, struggles between men— it's inherent in human nature."

"Then you don't think this is a war to end war?"

"Afraid I don't. That's just a slogan, to keep people up to the mark. It's the fox promised to hounds, tear 'im and eat 'im, to keep them going."

"Yes, I discovered during the '14 Christmas truce that the Germans were being told the same sort of things as ourselves."

"You bet your life they are! They wouldn't fight, otherwise."

Hobart refilled glasses. Pinnegar was talking softly to the younger blue-eyed girl. Phillip felt balanced between them all. A bottle popped, another was shoved in the bucket and screwed round in the broken ice. The blue-eyed girl gave Phillip a smile. He smiled back. This was the life. If only Desmond——Was Lily, so soon, being forgotten——?

"You all right?" he heard Hobart saying.

"Oh yes, thanks. I was thinking what you said about Richard Crook-back betraying all his friends, one after another, until he was alone. I suppose that was his fate? Do you believe in fate?"

"I do indeed. Fate is character. A man makes the same pattern again and again. It's the pattern he's born with. He can try and alter it, but he won't succeed."

The blue-eyed girl left, with another glance at Phillip. Pinnegar slid along the oak chest they were sitting on.

"It's born in him, in other words, Captain Hobart?"

"That's what I believe."

"So Crook-back was, in a way, lucky to be killed fighting?"

"Most fortunate. He was no good at living. He was a bad type, intelligent but warped. His mode of living, or thinking, came from his twisted spine. That made his pattern of living, from the start. His mind followed the pattern of his body. That set him apart from the others. He lived entirely in his solitary feelings."

"But couldn't his feelings change?"

"He tried to change them—he had a conscience, he knew what he was doing—but couldn't change himself."

"Not like changing a name, you mean. Such as the name of Ho-bart?" Pinnegar said. "Now don't pretend you're not Ho-bart of Ho-bart's Polish, Jack. No false modesty among friends, you know!"

Phillip winced at Teddie's persistence, and was relieved when Captain Hobart laughed; but he was bored by Pinnegar's persistence, Phillip felt. "Hubb'rt or Ho-bart, it's all the same to me! You pays your money and you takes your choice! My grandfather called himself Hubb'rt, my mother and my aunts and uncles call themselves Ho-bart, to sever connexion with the generations of Cheshire peasants and small-holders going by the names of Hubbard, Hubberd, Hibberd, Hubbert, and Habbitt when they moved to London. We still call it Lund'n, by the way, and not Lon-don, but you can call it what you like, and good luck to you, you hair-splitting Brummagem counterfeiter!"

"Even so, I still maintain that you can't get away from the fact that H-O-B-A-R-T spells Ho-bart, and I defy you or anyone else to prove otherwise!"

"That's the spirit," said Captain Hobart. "You're the type who never retreats an inch, the kind of bloke we want behind the Vickers guns, so let me fill your glass, and we'll drink to the company, and the army in France, and the sooner we're out there again the better, to finish the job, and get back to normal life again!"

Back to normal life again . . . Phillip felt the shadow of his life coming upon him; he thrust it away as they clinked glasses, against a moderate roar now coming from the bar. After dinner they went in Hobart's 4·5-litre Mercédès, which had four immense

flexible exhaust pipes coiling like brass snakes out of the side
of the bonnet, to the theatre; and shattered the frosty midnight
hour by a return to camp with blue flames stabbing through the
cut-out.

Chapter 3

FRESH FIELDS

The purpose of limbers and waggons, the various woods and
metals in their construction, the harness of mules which drew
them—traces and straps by which they were tugged and the
long pole bar supported on neck, hip, and withers; grooming
by brush and curry-comb, sponging nostrils, dock, and sheath;
importance of watering before feeding, to prevent colic or stoppage when the gases of indigestion pressed against the heart and
might finally stop its beating by causing rupture; daily rations,
providing three feeds totalling 10 lb. of oats and 10 of hay for
officers' chargers and light draught horses and mules of the
section—sixty-four animals in all—and the biggest feed in the
evening, because it gave the animal more time to digest its food
and also it was injurious to work on a big feed. Chaff given with
oats, to make the animal chew; bran mash once a week to open
its bowels.

Picketing: on a hard soil, near water supply, gentle slope for
drainage, hedge or wall for shelter, hard-core standings for the
feet; watch weavers, blowers, and cribbers—neurotic animals
which disturbed the sleep of others by swinging their heads to
and fro as though with mournful thoughts, or blew sigh-
fully, or gnawed incessantly at picket post, rope, or neighbour's
rug.

March discipline: stables at least 1½ hours before moving;
the farrier, or cold-shoer, inspecting all hoofed feet; rations of
corn secured in nose-bags, canvas water buckets available;
even loading of limbers and the one G.S. waggon; forward
scrutiny to see roads were clear, to prevent blockage, fatal in
battle, when thousands of vehicles both horse-drawn and petrol-
driven were in unceasing movement amidst shell-fire, and down-
ward traffic from the battlefield was as important as upward
supplies. Phillip remembered Loos, the miles of shattered horses,
men, and vehicles by day, and the failure of the transport of over

forty battalions to get forward in the night; immobility when the enemy line was broken, and the untried reserves arrived sleepless, unfed, and thirsty upon the battlefield, and too late; so that in the morning, when they advanced, they were shot down and they broke, leaving the battlefield while the German reserves, which had come up by marches equally forced during the night, stood up and watched them go.

The day before the written exam arrived. The stout subaltern who had won fame by getting up, over, and off his mount in one unified motion, had been a salesman of women's clothes in civil life; he had a fund of smutty stories which Phillip heard with reluctance; and when he came to him with a suggestion about the forthcoming exam, Phillip did not like what he had to say.

"I say, old man, I've got an idea. The usual practice, I understand, in the sections is to give each instructor a present at the end of the course. That works both ways, naturally, with the instructor letting his class know beforehand the questions of the written paper, at half-a-crown a head. I think you'll agree that isn't altogether unreasonable? How about it? I thought I'd approach you first, old man, as you're senior officer here."

"Well, I really don't know. I don't want to go against the rest of the section, but I'm not keen on having the questions either."

"Of course, you'll pass out on your head, old man."

"You're much more likely"——began Phillip, then stopped himself. But the other man said, with a laugh, "I see what you mean!" The laugh made Phillip like the fat man. He paid up. "Thanks, old man, much obliged." The organiser collected twelve half-crowns; and that night in his cubicle Phillip studied the questions, feeling restless as he sat before the tortoise stove— one officer to a cubicle now—because he could have answered every question easily without having first seen the paper. It was too late, after mess dinner, to go down to meet Teddie, Jack and others of the group that met nightly in the Angel, and later foregathered at the theatre bar.

The written exam took place the next morning; after which the staff captain sealed the papers in a large O.H.M.S. envelope with red wax, upon which he impressed his signet. And on the following day, before the oral, when the staff sergeant was complimented for the way he had brought along his section, it was given out that all had got full marks for their papers.

The staff captain then asked questions, from a printed card in his hand. In turn each member of the class appeared before him, out of ear-shot of the others. Phillip, as senior, went first.

"What do you do when arriving at a new billet?"

"I look for nails, holes, broken bottles, and shell splinters et cetera, which might damage the animals in my care, sir."

"What is highly essential in the matter of feeding?"

"Cleanliness of nose-bags, or mangers if in permanent shelters, sir."

"If in the open?"

"I do not wait for bad weather before I make my drainage and good standing for my animals."

"What is one of the main things to avoid in stables, and why?"

"The foremost is overcrowding, which prevents horses resting and often results in dangerous kicking."

"What is better than poor ventilation?"

"A draught, sir."

"If a horse goes lame, what do you do and why?"

"I examine its feet, and look for a nail, or stone in the frog. I feel if the foot is hot, of course. I look for any swelling in the pastern joint, in front of the fetlock."

"What is the only permitted excuse for dirty lines?"

"Well, the manual says a hurried advance or retreat, sir, but in practice there wouldn't be any time to let droppings accumulate."

"That's a sound point. I see you've been out. How do you feel about your work?"

"I am very keen, sir."

"No trouble with your leg?"

"None at all, sir!"

"Right. Next officer, please!"

The riding parade was held in the afternoon. Over the jumps with and without irons, as now stirrups were spoken of; figures of eight, and the 'aids' for changing feet at each half turn; jumping with arms folded. Phillip was sorry for those on poor horses. Black Prince seemed to know what was wanted, and did it, his only fault being impetuosity. His mount, ears pricked to his rider's least intention, was off at a gallop too easily. "Bit of blood in that gelding. Nice 'oss," Phillip heard the Colonel saying to the Riding Master.

"I fancy a deposit is growing upon the off fore pastern bones, just above the coronet, sir," said the Riding Master, who had a dour look of the night-before on his face under the flattened cap.

The section passed out. A week's leave was given each officer, after which postings would be announced. Phillip was reluctant to go home, so he stayed in camp, riding into the town by day, Black Prince being available whenever he wanted a mount, said the sergeant, looking him in the eye. So he got a bottle of whiskey for six and six in the mess, and wrapping it in a towel inside his haversack, left the haversack at the sergeant's hut. When he collected the haversack, a pair of issue breeches, of the best Bedford cord, were neatly wrapped beside the towel.

The sergeant was a friend of the quarter-master sergeant, a big man of unknown age whose white hair was dyed black. He wore many campaign ribands, the first being for Riel's Rebellion, he explained, and the Red River Expedition in Canada in 1870, followed by the occupation under Lord Wolseley of Fort Garry. Retiring from the Army, time-expired, after the Chitral Relief Force in 1895, he had joined up again during the South African War, and once more in 1914. He sat at a desk inside the single cubicle of "H" lines store-room which was filled to the ceiling with boots, puttees, tunics, greatcoats, and other floggable stuff.

Talking with him and the sergeant instructor in the cubicle, over whiskey and water, Phillip felt quite the old soldier, as he spoke of the Bill Browns, the Coalies, and others with whom he had served in 1914. He took the issue breeches to the tailor in the next hut, and was measured for a tight fit around the knee, waiting while white buck-skin strappings were sewn on by the enlisted man who sat, with needle, thread and ball of wax, crossed-legged on a trestle table beside the stove. Phillip heard about his life in Whitechapel before the war: how suits from Savile Row, Sackville Street, and all the "big" tailors were collected, to be taken home and stitched together, piece-work, making sixpence and eightpence a jacket. Phillip liked him, he had brown eyes and a feeling for music and poetry; and charged only a shilling for the job, which took four hours.

From the same stores Phillip acquired a driver's coat, with large semicircular collar, which he wore into town without badges of rank. It was rather the thing, he observed: senior officers often wore burberries and British warms without rank badges. He spoke to one in a shoe shop in the High Street, taking him at first for a very new second loot, with his smooth pink face and incipient moustache; and seeing that he was buying a pair of lace-up Norwegian field boots, advised him to choose a slightly oversize pair, to wear with an extra pair of socks, loosely, to keep the feet both warm and dry in the trenches. The youth, who could not have been more than eighteen, said, "Yes, I found that to be a good idea," and went on with his purchases, which included a leather jerkin with sleeves. To try this on he removed his burberry, to reveal a major's crowns and a Military Cross riband on his tunic. At the sight Phillip, who was waiting to buy a pair of string gloves, drifted to the other end of the shop.

Now, in badgeless driver's coat, the brass buttons of which had been replaced by leather ones, booted and spurred, he mouched about the town, ending up in a bookshop. There he discovered *The Oxford Book of English Verse*, and opening it at random, read

> *The blessèd damozel lean'd out*
> *From the gold bar of Heaven;*
> *Her eyes were deeper than the depth*
> *Of water stilled at even.*

He stood there transfixed, reading stanza after stanza.

> *Alas! We two, we two, thou say'st!*
> *Yea, one wast thou with me*
> *That once of old. But shall God lift*
> *To endless unity*
> *The soul whose likeness with thy soul*
> *Was but its love for thee?*

His eyes hastened down the page to the damozel's answer:

> *There will I ask of Christ the Lord*
> *Thus much for him and me:—*
> *Only to live as once on earth*
> *With Love,—only to be,*
> *As then awhile, for ever now*
> *Together, I and he.*

But the final answer was the division between life and death.

> (*I saw her smile.*) *But soon their path*
> *Was vague in distant spheres:*
> *And then she cast her arms along*
> *The golden barriers,*
> *And laid her face between her hands,*
> *And wept. (I heard her tears).*

Black depression struck him. There was no union in the spiritual world. Lily was gone for ever. But at least he would have the poem. "I'd like to buy this book, please."

The bombazine-black girl did not smile, she had a waxen face. What had happened to her? Some Keechey betrayed her? More likely she had grown up in fear. Her avoiding eyes discouraged conversation. He went from the shop to the darkness of the picture palace, followed by tea in the Angel, and reading in an armchair before the fire. He would like to be Lily to the thin little pale girl in the bookshop.

When the bar opened, he went in. The blue-eyed girl, the younger daughter, remembered him, to his surprise. "What's the book?"

He showed her the poem by Dante Gabriel Rossetti.

"I wondered why you were so quiet!" He dared not talk about poetry; and felt himself to be bombazine-black aloof. There was only one Lily.

Other officers came in; she sparkled, laughed with them; he felt hopelessly out of it. They wore new riding boots, obviously ready made like his own, but not taken in to fit at the top; while, worst of all, the instep side of their toe-caps showed rips of spur-rowels due to clumsy walking. They were unaware of themselves laughing heartily as one mimicked the chief instructor, the Guardee colonel whose broken neck was supported in a steel cup, his one eye glaring and his spine in a steel corset; they mocked him, calling him an old dug-out, and the girl laughed with them. When she went away for a moment into the office, he swallowed his drink quickly and left before she returned.

That night, after mess dinner, he read more of the poems, and played his gramophone; and then sat down to write a long letter to Desmond. Again and again he stopped, and thrust each fresh attempt into the tortoise stove, feeling that nothing would overcome Desmond's closed mind.

He played *Liebestod*, by Wagner, unaware that the music was part of an opera, or what it was about. For Phillip it was, as in boyhood when Father had played it—insisting on absolute silence, otherwise he stopped the record and locked up the gramophone— the dying sun saying goodbye to the world. Then *The Garden of Sleep*, playing it three times. What could he do, where go? It would not be much fun going down to the theatre bar alone. He was thinking of going to bed when there came a knock on the door, and opening it, he saw 'Darky' Fenwick standing there. The thin, brooding face was welcome.

"I'm going to Sleaford to see some friends tomorrow afternoon. Would you care to come with me in the sidecar? And play billiards?"

Phillip was grateful that anyone seemed to want to be friends with him. Warmly he replied that he would like to go, very much. The next day was a Saturday, which had been a gloomy prospect, as most of the fellows in the mess went away for the week-end.

"I'm just going down to the town, would you care to come? I've got a pal who keeps a nice little boozer there. We could go in my Matchless."

It was foggy outside, but stars were visible away from the smoke-drift of the camp. The twin-cylinder engine clattered; they bumped away over the grey pot-holed road, with its slippery mud, and soon were among the dim lights of the town. Phillip wiped the drops off his eyelashes, and wondered where the driver was heading for. It turned out to be in the lower quarter of the town.

"How about a game of whist?"

"Yes, rather!"

They played with two civilians. It was a pub used by the rank and file. Phillip examined Fenwick more closely. His head seemed smaller because his hair was cut short, as though by clippers. His jaw was lean, and dark, like his eyes. Phillip filled his pipe, passed over his crocodile pouch.

"What is it? Roadside Returns?" Fenwick made the inevitable joke, as he sniffed the tobacco. "Log Cabin. Pah, it's scented! Give me Dobie's Glasgow Coarse Cut every time!" as he pushed back the pouch across the table.

"Sorry. I haven't got any." He regretted his stiffness at Fenwick's offhand manner when the other said, "Ah, but I 'ave! Help thysel'. Now let's cut for partners. Right, you and I against these two."

He shuffled dog-eared cards. They had been sitting there about an hour when the door opened and a sergeant and corporal of

Military Police came in. They stood and looked around for a minute, before leaving.

"Come on, Fenwick," said Phillip, tapping out his pipe and putting it in his pocket. "We ought to sling our hook. I know the ways of those birds. One of them got me pulled in for a deserter in France, and I thought my number was up. Come on! Sorry to spoil the game——"

"But they can't touch us, we're not doing aught wrong, Maddison! This is a free country, isn't it?"

"Come on! I want to see if someone is in the Angel. Come on!"

"But why go to that snobs' place? What's wrong wi' 'ere?"

"Come on!" Phillip stood up, and put on his cap. He did not want to meet the A.P.M. again, lest he be reported for 'conduct unbecoming an officer and gentleman', by playing cards in a pot-house. But Fenwick refused to move.

"Look, Fenwick, I must go. I've just remembered that I ought to see Captain Hobart, he'll be making up his list of officers now, for his new company. I want the transport job, and now's the time. Hobart's in the Angel most nights."

"Eh, I wouldn't mind servin' under Ho-bart. I'll come, if you think it's all reet? Sorry to break up the game, friends."

Fenwick was putting on his cap when the door opened and in walked Brendon, cane under arm, hands behind back.

"What are you two officers doing in here?"

"We were just about to leave, sir."

"Answer my question. Don't you know this place is out of bounds for officers? You don't? Ignorance is no excuse. Were you playing cards? Gambling is forbidden by King's Regulations. And why are you"—to Fenwick—"smoking in public? There may be some excuse for you," as he glanced at the D.C.M. riband, "but none for you!" to Phillip. "Follow me."

Outside the A.P.M. said, "Well, what excuse have you for being found in there?"

"Sir!" said Fenwick, "the man who keeps the place is a friend of mine, sir."

"Then you should visit him in a private room. I won't have officers going into bars reserved for the men. For one thing, the men don't like it. Do you understand?"

"Yes, sir!"

"As for you, young feller, there's no excuse! I warned you to watch your step, didn't I? Very well! Dismiss!"

They saluted, and walked away. Phillip felt constricted. Why had Fenwick been so obstinate, and slow? "I thought he would come, you know!"

"Bah, dinna' fret yoursel'! He were only chuckin' 'is weight about."

"I hope you're right."

Captain Hobart was in the Angel. Phillip was greeted like an old friend, and Fenwick with enthusiasm when he was introduced as a friend of Pinnegar's. The D.C.M. riband appeared to be unnoticed.

"Good! Got a company in mind?"

"No, sir."

"Care to join us? Maddison's in already."

"Aye!"

"That's settled then. Calls for a celebration!"

Later, when Fenwick had gone to the lavatory, Hobart said, "There's a meet five miles away at half-past ten. If you're free tomorrow morning, how about hackin' out there together?"

"I was going to play billiards, skipper."

"Billiards! In the morning?"

"I've already arranged to go out with Fenwick."

"Oh, I see. In that case you can't very well disappoint him. He looks a lonely sort of cove, doesn't he? Where are you playing, here?"

"No, at a place called Sleaford—isn't it, Fenwick?"

"That's reet," said Fenwick, sitting down. "But we won't be going till tea-time. I've got friends there, who told me I could bring along a pal."

"Couldn't be better!" exclaimed Hobart. "The meet is half-way to Sleaford. Why not come out with me in the morning, Phil, and I can run you into Sleaford afterwards in my bus?"

"What about my horse, skipper?"

"I'll take a groom, and he'll bring your hunter back. I'll see to that. You're on? Good! I'll see 'Ropey' Griggs first thing tomorrow. Be at the bottom of 'A' lines at 9.45 ack emma."

In the morning, after a restless night, in which his imagination literally ran away with him on a horse for a couple of hours over all remembered illustrations of *Handley Cross*, *Mr. Facey Romford's Hounds*, and *Mr. Sponge's Sporting Tour*, Phillip pulled on boots, well-boned by his servant, and wondered whether or not to use spurs. Supposing the rowels tore Black Prince or, worse, put the gelding out of control? He decided that, as an officer was considered to be naked without a belt, to go to a meet of foxhounds without spurs would reveal him to be 'the veriest tyro'. Anyway, riding boots looked rotten without spurs.

He was nervous when he set off on Black Prince shortly before half-past nine. But nervousness gave way to jubilation; he began to sing as he cantered on the grass, and Prince, pricking up ears, began to prance against the bit. Soon the gelding was fighting, between canter and gallop, for its head; so Phillip relaxed the reins, and let it extend itself until, seeing red around the hats of three riders in the distance, he turned to the left among the trees, thinking to take Black Prince over the Riding School jumps. Steady, Black Prince, steady! as he leaned forward and patted the gelding's neck. Steady, Prince! Then a steady pull on the reins, held low; and almost as suddenly as it had burst into speed, Prince stopped. Phillip was not ready for it, but managed to keep his seat. He remembered what Hobart had said about the possibility of Prince having come out of a mare trained to polo, the foal imitating the actions of its dam when out to paddock. Sixteen hands was high for polo; but the breeding was there.

He dismounted and adjusted girth and surcingle before going to the jumps.

"Gently, Prince! Steady, boy!" He held back the dancing horse, which shook its head as it crabbed sideways towards the first fence. Then it sprang forward, gathered itself above a dull tattoo of hooves, and flung itself and rider over. Desperately he held it from galloping away after the last fence; and keeping it to a prancing canter, brought it round again to the jumps. "Gently, Prince! Steady! Steady!" He managed to pat its neck; Black Prince responded; and went round the jumps with less dash. Involuntarily he dropped the reins on its neck, whereupon Prince stopped. He dismounted, and found that the trouble was a curb-chain hooked on too tight. "Poor Black Prince! That bloody groom! And bloody me, why didn't I check the bit?" Two fingers could be passed between chin-groove and chain only with difficulty. He released it. Prince whinnied. He felt a flow of affection for the horse, and laid his cheek against the soft bulge of skin between nostril and upper lip, feeling the warmth of Prince's breath. Playfully he breathed into the gelding's nostril, an action that was greeted by the softest whuffle; and then with fingertips stroked the bases of Prince's ears. It was like stroking his white rat, Timmy, in the old days. Dogs and cats liked it, too;

so had his kestrels, his tame jay, and jackdaws. The secret was tenderness, or kindness, as all the great poets knew. That was the secret of the world, to which the world could not trust itself, through fear.

It was time to make for 'A' lines; he must not be late. Prince took him over the grass at a gentle trotting lope, the South African triple canter. He could ride, he could ride!

After five minutes happy waiting at the bottom of 'A' lines Jack Hobart, with groom, rode up.

"It may rain, so I've brought along an extra coat," said Jack, after greetings. "Hart will strap it to the rear of your saddle."

They set off across the park, making for the south gate, where they turned east and trotted along a quiet country lane, the sun breaking through the mists of the morning lying over grass and ploughland. Jack sniffed the air.

"Makes life worth living, what? It's a good scenting day—no wind—you can smell the bullock muck in the crew-yards. Pigs, too. Some of these farmers are making their fortunes out of our camp swill. Ever seen the waste food piled behind the cook-houses? Can't blame anyone, really. Loaves arrive mouldy, sides of meat tainted. War's all waste, of course. Wonder what this country will be like afterwards? I doubt if the old routine will satisfy—even if taxation don't make it impossible—y'know, long weekends at country houses, first nights in town, all that sort of thing."

A little later he said, "By the way, I notice you ride with the reins in one hand. All right for ceremonial, but perhaps it might be better to hold two in each hand, when we get crackin' on a line and have to fly the bigger timber. It's only an idea, of course. Only, if one hasn't hunted this fairly fast country before, y' know——"

Phillip sorted out bridoon and snaffle reins, and threaded them between second and third, and third and little fingers of each hand respectively; then saw that they were untwisted, and lying flat on Prince's neck. Thus prepared for the worst, he tried to re-balance himself, feeling almost misplaced upon the saddle since now his left arm and shoulder were no longer upheld with the right arm hanging low. He felt he would not be able to keep his seat like that; but resisted the impulse to transfer the reins to his left hand. When they cantered on the grass verge of the lane, Prince following Jack's mare, he found, after a quarter of a mile, that he could sit with a new feeling of balance.

"When you go over a fence, hold your hands low, just behind your horse's withers," said Jack. "A steadying touch there makes all the difference to balance, I think you'll find."

They trotted up a drive, passing a lodge, and came through trees to a house of red brick with many windows and twisted chimney stacks, before which, on a large gravelled space, stood horses, some mounted, others held by grooms.

Phillip had seen only one meet of hounds before, when a boy staying with his cousin Willie at Rookhurst, when the scene had been pictorial, with human figures seen without discrimination. Now he wondered about the people before him. Khaki predominated, most of the officers wearing badges of cavalry regiments, and those in the yeomanry with burnished shoulder-chains. Other riders in mufti were obviously men on leave, from their soldierly appearance. Then there were elderly farmers, by the look of them. They wore dark coats with bowlers, most with breeches and long black boots, but others with ordinary trousers held within gaiters. The more rugged and elderly ones wore stiff collars, some of them celluloid, with nondescript ties; one old boy with white hair and moustaches wore long trousers and ankle boots, with a high-crowned black hat, between bowler and topper; his horse was a big chestnut animal with a Roman nose. Other, younger farmers wore stock-ties held by gold-mounted pins seemingly made from slender quill-like bones about two inches long. They were smartly dressed, in dark West-of-England skirted coats and white breeches, and had a quiet but independent manner, as they kept to themselves, touching hat-brims lightly with finger-and-thumb when addressed by one or another of the elderly gentlemen, looking like squires wearing red coats, which he must remember to call pink. Hobart seemed to know quite a number of people, among them ladies sitting side-saddle, and wearing tall silk hats. There were some children, too, on ponies, the older ones breeched, wearing bowlers and tweed jackets. Apart from them was a group of smaller children seated in wicker baskets on long-tailed Shetlands, all dressed in black velvet caps and fawn gaiters buttoned to above the knee. Their nurses stood by them, in grey uniforms and bonnets.

More riders were arriving, among them some young women dressed like men and riding astride. They had brown faces, and appeared to be unaware of the several men, apparently temporary officers like himself, who stared at them. Words are given us to conceal our thoughts. He remembered O'Connor, who had

defended him before the subalterns' court-martial at Heathmarket,
two battles ago: likewise to conceal one's glances, to observe with
the retinae of the eyes, was good manners.

The huntsman, lean red face and hawk nose, wore a coat more
pink than red with many rubbed-out weather-stains. He sat his
grey horse, apart from the pack. The hounds were in a rough
circle, squatting on their haunches apart from the riders. Two
whippers-in, one of them a boy, in red coats, were guarding them.
The hounds looked to be smaller than those he remembered at
Rookhurst, and of a uniform pale yellow and white in colour.

"Jim's hunting the lady pack today. Very fast goin'. Look at
their feet, like cats'." A howl came from beyond a group of out-
buildings, followed by other bayings. "That's the dog pack—they
know the little bitches are out today. Don't look so serious. You'll
be all right. I shouldn't try and take your own line, as you don't
know the country. Follow the rest of the field, most of 'm will go
through gates, if you have any doubt about your horse. You know,
of course, that hounds always have right of way? Never over-ride
'em. I got cussed good and proper once, by the master, for ridin'
ahead of him."

A butler, followed by three parlour-maids in dark brown uniform dresses and starched white caps with long tabs, came out of
the house and went from rider to rider with trays holding glasses.
After the serving of sherry there came a double toot on the horn,
and to the noises of hooves on gravel the pack moved off, between
the whippers-in, following the huntsman. Then the master led the
field down an extension of the gravel drive and through two
towering rhododendron clumps to an iron gate, held open by an
old gardener with dundreary whiskers and felt hat in hand. They
were now in the park. To the massed mournful singing of hounds
in kennels, and the toot-toot-toot of the horn, the huntsman ahead
began to trot, and the field behind, spreading fanwise over the
grass, started to bob, shake, and struggle with horse-heads. Steady,
Prince, steady! But Prince felt the general excitement, so did the
rooks which rose cawing out of the oaks, to flap up and float into
the pale sky, now clearing of the lower mists, and revealing
patches of blue. The colour exhilarated Phillip, and he wanted to
shout, feeling so greatly happy. Here he was, following a famous
pack, accompanied by a groom with two spare leathers worn like
bandoliers, told off by Hobart to see that he, Phillip Maddison
Esquire (since he held His Majesty's commission) was all right;
while just in front All Weather Jack, thick-peaked buff cap with

wide polished leather band set at an angle, was trotting cavalry-fashion, not rising up and down in the saddle but sitting out the bumps as though screwed to the saddle. All Weather Jack beckoned Phillip to come beside him.

"We're going to draw Galton Spinney in the middle of the plough you can see half right through the trees ahead. If there's a fox there, he'll probably come out at the far end. Anyway, I'll show you where we can stand and get a view of both sides of the spinney."

At the end of the park the field waited, while the huntsman jumped a ditch; and followed by hounds and the flanking whips, entered the ploughed field, which lay in steeply laid furrows, causing the horses to stagger at times. Some of the field were making to the left of the park, where it joined a meadow. Others were jumping the ditch. Hobart said, "Follow me." He put his horse at the ditch, it gathered itself and sprang over, while he clung like a frog. Feeling that everyone knew he was an amateur, Phillip turned Prince's head and with indecisive pressure of calves hoped he would get over all right. His horse took him over, he lost an iron, it clanged as Prince galloped after the other horse. He pulled at its mouth, loose on the slippery saddle, somehow got his balance, and kicking his boot into the iron, felt steadier. Prince slowed to a trot beside the horse it had followed.

About a dozen riders waited on a hillock immediately over-looking the hedge, and the lines of furrows seeming to converge at the oval spinney four hundred yards distant. Phillip watched hounds running into the trees: almost immediately he saw a fox loping between two furrows, coming towards them. Jack saw it at the same time, and yelled "Tally ho!" and pointed. The fox stopped, crouched down, and slunk off at right angles, crossing the furrows to get away from the rest of the field at the edge of the park. "Tally ho!" yelled many voices, as arms pointed at the fox, which began to race. There were encouraging cries from the huntsman, followed by hounds whimpering excitedly as they streamed out of the spinney. The huntsman took off his cap and scooped them on. When they got the scent of the fox they gave tongue. Huntsman blew short stuttering blasts on his horn, followed by a long note: and repeated the *Gone Away* twice, the final note being prolonged as though triumphantly.

Black Prince, said Jack afterwards, had evidently been hunted before. Fighting for its head, the gelding went off at a gallop. Cries of 'Hold your horse!' were heard in desperation by its rider, or passenger, who found himself most insecure as he pulled the reins, the effort causing him to push against the irons, which extended on the leathers at an angle of almost forty five degrees to the vertical, while he tried to balance on the base of his spine. Before him was a cut-and-laid hedge, on the farther side a ditch, and then grazing, details of which he saw clearly and impersonally as he went down face first, slowly. Without apprehension, as though it was happening apart from himself, he met the earth, harmlessly, while about him legs and bellies of horses were descending. When he got on his feet he saw riders cantering away.

"Are you all right?" asked Jack, who had turned back. "Good man! Hart will catch your 'oss."

Phillip was soon remounted and going across the meadow, and through a gate into a ploughed field, the headland of which was still stubble. Three hundred yards off he saw riders jumping a hedge. Throw your heart over first, he remembered the riding instructor saying. Hotly he held back Prince to a canter, and let him have his head two lengths from the thorn-setts. Leaning forward with hands held low by the pommel he found, to his surprise, that he was over; and with exultation followed the hoof-marks across furrows. Another fence in front, this one tall, with several years' growth sticking up blackly with thorns. Crikey, he thought: it was six feet high, though thin on the two top feet. Some of the horses in front were refusing. When he got up he saw, and heard, All Weather Jack crashing his way through, thorns scratching on leather. Give Prince his head, lean forward and low, lean forward, shut eyes, toes in. "UP, Prince!" Lean back, you fool, down, down, Prince stumbling. Hold up his head! Good boy, Prince! He galloped after the half-dozen in front. Wonderful, wonderful! Clods of earth flying from hooves in front; then sudden checkings, horses reined back. "'Ware wire! 'Ware wire!"

"'Ware wire!" he called over his shoulder, to the groom, alone following. They cantered down field, to a gate at the far corner. Beyond, he galloped down a sloping grassy field to catch up with Jack.

From the rise he saw hounds and pink coats a quarter of a mile away, running strongly; while above the meadow an aeroplane was circling.

There was a brook at the bottom of the valley. The thrusters flew this, he saw, while others turned off to a crossing place for bullocks made of railway sleepers packed with earth, where the fox had run. He hesitated: indecision tore him: desperately he decided to follow the thrusters, who were now going hard over the meadow beyond.

The aeroplane was now banking over his head. Looking up, he saw two faces. A hand waved. It was a Maurice Farman. It came down to about a hundred feet, and making a slight banking turn, headed diagonally over the meadow. He saw that hounds had also changed direction, having turned right handed; while in front the thrusters were holding back their horses. Now for it! He cantered in a semi-circle, then put Prince at the brook. Prince nearly fell at the far bank, but got up with plunging leaps, while he hung on somehow. Over anyway, water and black ooze on boots and breeches. Then seeing that the thrusters had stopped, he stopped too. A fox was running across their front two hundred yards away. Had it come back, or was it another fox? The aeroplane banked low over it. He saw the fox look up, then head towards the group of horsemen, then hesitate, before turning into a bed of rushes. Meanwhile hounds were running back, in a loop. When they came up the huntsman cheered them on. He saw, as the Farman turned over them again, the fox creeping out of a clump not fifty yards away. Cries of "Tally ho!" and yarring cries came from the group near him. He wished they could have given the fox a chance. A hound circling the clump saw it, and running round, met the fox head on. The fox stopped and looked about, then tried to run away. Its brush dragged with mud. The fox turned to meet the hound, which seized it and shook it, snarling, struggling with it while the rest of the pack came up. There was deep growling like a barrage heard some way off. Then it was over. The dismounted whips were crying to the hounds, cracking their lashes while the huntsman went among them, and bending down, lifted up the limp fox and carried it away, while the whippers-in kept hounds in a circle.

The huntsman knelt to cut off head, brush, and paws. The aeroplane passed very low overhead and made a bumpy landing two hundred yards away. Out jumped two men in leather helmets and coats, and walking forward, were greeted by the master.

"I hope we didn't head the fox, Master," Phillip heard one say. He was a captain with R.F.C. wings.

"Not at all! Very sporting effort!"

The head, or mask, was given to a lady; the brush to someone else; and a pad each to the flyers, who said they had come from Lincoln. Then the carcase, borne aloft by the huntsman, was flung to the pack, during which the Master blew his horn and everyone gave a sort of mad screaming cheer. Anyway, Phillip thought, the fox had taken many birds and rabbits, and now had copped it. He drank port from Jack's parsnip-shaped crystal flask, taken from a leather container strapped to his saddle, and ate a pork sandwich. After which they set off to draw another covert. When he tried to mount, Phillip felt his legs to be sloppy, as though they had been taken off and stretched, and put back in not quite the same way as before.

Soon it began to rain, and the afternoon went dull. Scent having failed, the huntsman blew four slow looping notes. It was the end. Phillip and Jack emptied the port flask, then hacked back to the house. Tea was waiting for them. There was a jolly party around a table, with whiskeys and sodas, as soon as tea was finished, and cigars.

"What about Fenwick? Aren't you meeting him somewhere?"

"Yes, in Sleaford, in the market square, at five."

"It's past that now. I'll run you there. My 'bus is outside. We'll say goodbye to our host and hostess, shall we? Good show you put up today, Phil."

"All thanks to you, Jack."

"A pleasure, my dear fellow. Here we are."

They said goodbye, and went out into darkness. The Mercédès stood in the rain, covered by a sort of tarpaulin. How nice to have a servant like that, thought Phillip, to bring your car to you. Jack asked the driver if he had had tea, to be told yes, Mr. Deane had looked after him well. What a fine world it was, when the butler looked after visiting servants, while their master looked after their friends in the house. Everything was done so easily, everything fitting into place. What a bore he had arranged to meet Fenwick, so different from the people with whom he had spent the day. Still, as Jack had said, it was not the thing to disappoint others.

They were soon into Sleaford. A somewhat dour Fenwick, wearing sodden leather helmet with straps loose and dripping rain, was standing by a horse trough, in the dim light of a lamp-post. The Matchless motorbike and sidecar stood near.

"Thought you were never comin'," he remarked, when Captain Hobart had driven away. "I've been out five times to look for you. My friends have kept back tea; still, better late than never."

"I thought you were going to see your friends, and then we were going to play billiards afterwards."

"Aye, thet's the idea. I've got to know two bonnie lassies, if you don't object to female company?"

"Not at all, if they play billiards!" said Phillip, facetiously.

"Aye, thet they do! Reet well! Let's get out o' t' mirk."

He led the way to a small pub down a side-street. Harry Lauder Bonnie Lassies somehow didn't go with knocking on a side-door in a dark alley. What sort of place was it? Very soon he was glad that he had not blurted out his thoughts. The place within was clean and well-kept, the people simple and homely, with two daughters. After tea they made up a four-handed game of billiards. One partnered him, but he was a rabbit, and lost the game to Fenwick, who was an expert, and his partner. He saw with some relief that the girls drank only ginger beer, while he and Fenwick had hot Irish whiskies with lemon and sugar, and glass rods to stir the steaming concoction.

After some rather thumpy music at a piano in another room, they had supper of gammon and spinach, followed by apple pudding and cream. Long before this Phillip had taken a liking to Fenwick, who was not, as at first he had imagined, a rough character, but a simple, honest-to-God decent bloke. Darky seemed to be quite keen on the elder girl, whom he had met a month before through asking a Sleaford policeman where he could get a quiet game of billiards. He explained that he wanted to keep in form, for his Oddfellows Lodge championship after the war, but didn't want any posh hotel, only a nice quiet place, homely like. The policeman had recommended the local Oddfellows Lodge, headquarters at the Silk Inn, "and here I am", said Fenwick, with quiet triumph, as he looked at the plump red shining face beside him. "Eh, lass?" She glowed with pleasure, so did the face of her father, coming in from the bar with two more steaming Irish whiskies.

On the way home, driving into the darkness of the flat and lonely countryside, Fenwick said, "What did you think of my lass?"

"Jolly nice, *mein prächtig kerl!* "

"Aiy, ah'm reet glad to hear you think she's bonny."

The two-cylinder engine clattered past trees spectral beside the beam of the acetylene lamp. After some minutes he said,

"You won't tell any of the lads aught about the Silk, will you? I mean, I don't want anyone else to come sniffin' around the Silk Inn!"

Phillip thought that few would be likely to do that, for not only had his girl a plain face, but was rather fat as well. Then, lest Fenwick interpret his silence, he exclaimed heartily, "You certainly do not, Darky old boy! By Jove, I've enjoyed my day! Only Sunday now to get through, and we'll be posted to All Weather Jack's company! A month's training, and then we'll be overseas!"

"Aye, thet's about it. Tell you what, Phil, when I came here I didn't care how long the war lasted. I've got no home to go to, I never knew father or mother, I were reared in Foundlings' Home. But now 'tis different, I'm thinkin'."

He blew two hoarse honks on the horn, because his bonny lass had kissed him good-night in the darkness. Phillip checked a slight impulse to sneer: sitting suddenly loose, he thought, why did I want to sneer? It was dreadful of him. His sister Mavis had sneered at Lily, in the same way. Was he unable to change his old self, after all? Fenwick had trusted him with his sacred thoughts. No father or mother, no known relations; now he had found his home. Home! Mother's face, so gentle and patient, giving all for her children; and he had not gone home on leave to see her, through utter selfishness. With eyes closed, he breathed deeply, releasing slowly his breath, so that he could feel dissolved and floating, nothing of himself coming into his being.

"My God," said Teddy Pinnegar, a few mornings later, "what d'you think of this, Phil. The Skipper's got jaundice! He's been sent to hospital, and they're sending another C.O. from the Training Centre to take over!"

Chapter 4

LIFE WITH THE DONKS

Hundreds of mules were walking in all directions over Belton Camp, drawing grey limbers fixed to long poles. These limbers, painted grey, rolled on artillery wheels, together with water carts, G.S. waggons, and cooks' carts. At night the vehicles were drawn up in long lines upon what was left of the grass of his Lordship's park. Companies were now going out in greater numbers. Nightly the theatre was packed with enthusiastic subalterns; so was the bar of the Angel. You had to go early to get an evening seat at the Electric Palace. Phillip forgot himself in the hilarity of a Charlie Chaplin film; but his shadowed self arose through the popular tragic actor Sessue Hayakawa —the favourite film hero of Desmond, he remembered—a Japanese actor appearing in frock coat, Indian turban, and the grief-frozen face of a hero without hope. He also saw *The Somme*, not a cinema story of any particular man or men, but of sights behind the actual fighting, guns, waggons, "plum pudding" mortar bombs on long iron rods, ambulance convoys and distant shell-bursts—sights drawing him back again to the night-world of flares, gun-flashes, and coloured rockets, far from the home he had left, in spirit at least, for ever. In that home, he thought, he had always come between Father and Mother; perhaps his death would bring them together.

There were a couple of days of cushy life, sitting around the stove in the new company headquarter hut. So far the company officers were Darky Fenwick, Montfort, Teddy Pinnegar, a subaltern who was a farmer in Lincolnshire before the war, and himself. At the other end of the hut sat the company sergeant major and quartermaster sergeant, at a trestle table covered with a brown army blanket. This cosy respite ended when the new C.O. arrived. Phillip got a shock when he saw Downham sitting at Jack Hobart's table. The same afternoon sixty gunners were marched in from the Training Centre; and next day, nearly two score drivers followed, led by a sergeant. Phillip felt that the army was indeed different from the old days when he realised that this young man, short, fresh-faced, and plump, with a snub nose was to be his right-hand man in France. For very soon he was explaining to Phillip that he had been "offered a commission", but hadn't taken it, as he had been "compelled for domestic reasons" to remain home-service.

"I've got a widowed mother, you see," he added, dropping the "sir" at which Phillip became scrupulously polite.

"Did you have to do with horses before the war, sergeant?"

"Only indirectly, in a manner of speaking."

Maintaining his attitude of aloof ease, Phillip waited for the young man to continue making the impression he hoped he was making.

"I was, owing to my father's death, following financial losses, compelled to forego education at Oxford, and to take a position with a firm of old-established country auctioneers, where I gained some experience of both riding and draught horses, waggons, harness, and fodder."

"Where was that, sergeant?"

"I followed my profession in the county of Surrey. On the outbreak of war, I joined up with the Sharpshooters. That's how I came across Major Downham, he was my company commander. We came up to the Training Centre together, in a manner of speaking."

This news Phillip received with further disquiet. He was already depressed by the thought that Downham knew the rumours about Hallo'e'n 1914, at Messines, when he had failed to get up the ammunition during the German attack on the Windmill, and so many of the London Highlanders had been bayoneted. Still, it was unlikely that Downham had discussed that with a sergeant, before he had even met him. He must act up to his part.

"Let me have a copy of the nominal role of the section as soon as you can, will you, sergeant? What have we so far?"

Sergeant Rivett had his book ready. "Twenty-two drivers, sir, including one each for cook's cart and water-cart. One stitcher; one cold shoer; seven grooms for officers' chargers. Thirty-one all told, thirty-two with myself. I have already made a copy of the nominal role, sir."

"Well done. I'm going to the company orderly room now, so come down and check your roll with that of the company sergeant major."

Events were certainly moving fast. Just before twilight that afternoon sixteen Vickers guns, with tripods and ammunition boxes, were ranged along one side of the Orderly Room hut. The next morning there was a chit from the Centre: Senior Supervising Officer (Transport) informed O.C. Company that a Mule Convoy would arrive at the station at 8.30 p.m. the following night and arrangements should be made to collect forty mules.

Phillip said to Major Downham, "We'll want head-stalls and chains, if we're going to lead our mules back, sir. With your

permission I'll try and wangle the use of a Driving School limber
to collect them in."

"Very well. Only report back when you return."

The Corporal-storeman at Ordnance was not easily persuaded.
He said that an order had come reserving all head-stalls for the
Senior Supervising Officer of Transport. But after some talk
about the Menin road in 1914, during which the corporal,
a regular soldier, took in the well-fitting driver's coat, boned
cavalry-pattern boots and fawn twill buttoned breeches, while
warming to the young officer's easy politeness of manner, he said,
"I think I can manage that little lot for you, sir."

Forty head-stalls, which had been taken from a heap set aside
by the Staff Q.M.S., were exchanged for a chit signed by P.S.T.
Maddison, Lieut., for O.C. 286 Coy; and carried back in the
"borrowed" limber for Sergeant Rivett to hang up on racks
under some covered stables Phillip had occupied in lieu of the
open standings allotted him. Then he reported to Downham
in his cubicle.

"I shall have to ask permission to sign out for mess dinner,
sir."

"All right, only report to me when you get back tonight.
And don't go and do anything stupid, such as tweaking the
Senior Supervising Officer's ears with fire-tongs, as you did to
Hollis in the office." Why did Downham want to drag up the
past?

At 7.30 p.m. the section paraded, and he led them to the town
station. The train from Liverpool was two hours late. That
meant hanging about until half-past ten. The men were allowed
away in two relays, each of half an hour, to the pubs. Closing
time was now half-past nine.

"Now be good fellows, and return promptly to time, won't
you?" A chorus of *Yes, sir!* made him feel in touch with
them.

Sergeant Rivett was with the first section, and when he
returned, Phillip went into the town, hoping to buy bread and
cheese for the men. All shops were closed, food was becoming
scarce owing to unrestricted submarine warfare. His search
produced nothing. He returned after closing time, and stood
about with the others, feeling dull and cold as time went on,
having missed mess dinner in his determination to see that
everything was done properly.

At last rosy steam of an approaching train. Soon orders and

counter-orders arose amidst hooves clattering on asphalt and sett-stone, and an occasional angry squeal and walloping of heels on wood. The mules came out, bunching, pushing, their eyes bloodshot and staring, their coats clotted. The spirit of fear ruled under arc-lamps making livid the damp night scene. "They're sods, these South American mules," said the heavy officer who had organised the mass bribery of the sergeant. "Most of 'em are only half-broken. They won't get away with it with me!"

"What will you do?"

"Put a nose twitch on any that shows resistance, and put on a pack-saddle loaded with old iron. Break its spirit."

"I don't agree with that. I believe that mules, like horses or any other animals, respond to care and kindness. Just think what these poor old donks have suffered since leaving their native pampas—sea-sickness, blows, curses, and at best indifference." Clewlee replied with one explodent word, and walked away.

Forty beasts were allotted to the company. With a start he saw that they already wore head-stalls. His drivers had extra difficulty, holding their charges, while trying to strap the spare head-stalls over their own shoulders. This delayed departure, and caused criticism from the S.S.O.

"So you're the culprit who took away my equipment from my stores, are you? And caused me to be short by the very number by which you now try and turn your men into jackasses? Who the devil d'you think you are?"

"I'm sorry, sir, I meant to help arrangements forward."

"What d'you think would happen if every trainee officer in the Centre took it upon himself to run the show? You're part of an organisation, a team. Do you understand?"

"Yes, sir!"

The days and nights that followed put all thought of evening pleasure in the town out of mind, because a staff inspection of the section was soon to be held. The drivers worked from before dawn to nearly midnight, for there was an enormous amount of work to be done. Steel hooks and chain links, by which traces and pole-bars drew the limbers, were deeply corroded by rust. Phillip bought, with his own money, paraffin and silver sand. Also cocoa and tins of biscuits. The men worked hard, rubbing with the abrasive on pieces of old puttee. On the night before the inspection they rubbed for three hours, then shook the chains in sacks containing chaff for a further two hours, but at the end only streaks of brightness shone through. They worked until shortly before 1 a.m., then stopped to lie down on their palliasses, stables having been ordered for 4 a.m.

When Phillip returned at 4.30 a.m. he found Sergeant Rivett asleep in his cubicle at the end of the hut. In his anxiety, he shook the sergeant's bed and cried, "Come on, Rivett, if you don't want to be the last on parade!" Sleepy-eyed, the sergeant stared, then he leapt up. Phillip thought that they would never be on parade by 9 a.m.

And so it turned out. Feeding and grooming so far had taken anything up to an hour and a half. The mules were half-broken, and afraid; the men afraid and half-trained. So it was this morning. The section was late for 6 a.m. breakfast, a hasty mouth-cramming of bread used to scoop up brown bacon fat in which brittle scraps of rasher were congealed, washed down by boiled bitter tea and sugar, upon which globules of oil floated from yesterday's skilly. The same dixies were used for all meals. Then to wash and shave in cold water, to scrape wet mud from puttees, breeches, tunics, and coats, ready for the next struggle in more mud with mules, many of which resisted attempts to harness them. It was chaos in darkness; but without shelling. Phillip, who had slept for two hours in his clothes, went from driver to driver, giving a hand; but the parade was half an hour late.

The inspection by the Senior Supervising Officer was swift and decisive. Forty years old, swarthy, powerful of frame and voice, giving forth the feeling that disciplinarianism was all his mind, he stared at the ingenuous, boyish face showing hesitant dejection before him, and then between pauses, each followed by a tap of short leather-bound cane upon open gloved palm, he said,

"Rusty chains." Tap. "Dirty harness." Tap. "Muddy limbers." Tap. "Mules not groomed." Tap. "Drivers imperfectly shaved." The gloved palm closed over the end of the cane, holding it stiffly, while he continued to stare into the young man's face, at the large blue eyes with their long lashes.

"We've had no time, sir——"

"I'll see your drivers' rifles."

These had lain under limber covers since leaving Ordnance. After trying, in vain, to look down the first three barrels, the S.S.O. took Phillip aside. "How long have you held your commission? Nearly two years? Then what possible excuse can you have for allowing your men to appear on parade with rifles the barrels of which are still bunged up with *store* grease?"

"I wasn't going to let the men bring them on parade, sir."

"Good God!" said the S.S.O., almost in a whisper. "I've heard some odd things in my time, but this beats them all. You know I'll have to report this, then you'll lose your job. Why shouldn't I report it? Can you give me any good reason?" He gave a sort of smile, while looking straight into Phillip's eyes. Simulating innocence, Phillip replied, "Well, sir, I thought that as we weren't going to fire the rifles yet, and as the men had more than enough to do——"

"So you thought it a sensible idea to hide them away, did you?"

"No, sir."

"And you find the work too much for you?"

"Not for me, but my men have had too much to do. Those chain links take many hours to burnish. We've been up, shaking them in chaff bags, until midnight for five nights in succession; and I've had morning stables at four o'clock in the morning."

Abruptly the S.S.O. mounted his horse and rode away to the next inspection. Two days later Phillip had a chit from Pinnegar, to report to the Orderly Room.

"Downham wants to see you about some report or other. I've tried to tell him it's all tripe. Don't let him bounce you. If it were Jack, he'd take it to the Colonel."

Downham said, "Well, I can hardly say I'm not surprised, from what I know of you. You've had a damned bad report from the Centre. Better read it."

This officer is incompetent, and reveals inability to deal even with routine duties. He should have further training.

The next day Phillip left 286 Coy. His new company commander in "B" lines was a tall upright Canadian with ginger hair and moustache, who soon told him that he had passed through Kingston Military College, Ontario. Phillip shared a cubicle with Clewlee, who snored unbearably at night, and had a habit, in the morning, of washing his face in his canvas basin after he had cleaned his teeth in the water. He also had mustard with his porridge, and bit his nails. Both were members of what was called among themselves the Punishment Squad, passing the first few days in arms drill on the square, under a sergeant-major.

On the third night Phillip cut mess dinner and made for the theatre bar, where he drank whiskey in intervals of watching the variety show. He made friends with another lonely subaltern, and they had a glittering, glassy time until the late-night reaction. With aching eyeballs and head he appeared on parade the next morning, not having been able to face breakfast. He got through the day somehow, without lunch, and at tea, sitting beside the new company commander, was asked to help him in the orderly room. This was encouraging: if he worked hard, it might lead to a second-in-command job, since apparently he had been kicked out of the transport section.

Some days later, while they were sitting there, Phillip having dealt with routine office work, Clewlee came in to say that he had gone sick, and had come to report that he was to be admitted to hospital in a few days' time. Meanwhile, he was fit for light duty.

When Phillip saw his medical report, he had a shock. Second-lieutenant Clewlee, waiting to go to Cherry Hinton hospital, was suffering from syphilis.

When Phillip told his skipper this, the Canadian said, "Sure, I knew that. He spent a week-end about two months ago in a Nottingham hotel, and slept with the receptionist girl in the office there. He's been trying to treat himself in his cubicle for some time, instead of seeing the doc. right away. Somebody told him that mustard was a cure for the complaint. But what can you expect from a man who before the war was what we in Canada call a dry-goods clerk, and you over here know as a counter-jumper?"

Phillip tried to conceal his alarm at this information. Perhaps he was already infected by the terrible disease which had killed Uncle Hugh. Before him arose a scene that Christmas afternoon when Father was asleep in the sitting room and Mother had opened the door, to see Uncle Hugh, who was forbidden the house, standing there. He had clattered in on crutches, and was sitting in the front room, and they were all laughing at his jokes when suddenly Father came in, and was distant and polite until Uncle Hugh said he knew when he wasn't wanted, and shambled away again, while Mother cried silently. When he was gone Father had been angry with Mother for crying, instead of wanting to protect her children from a possible horrible end; and Christmas had gone dark.

On the following morning, on his way to the Medical Hut in "B" lines, Phillip passed Clewlee, who had just come from the Hut. Clewlee was walking slowly, leaning heavily on his stick, his face white and pained. He had just had an intramuscular injection of salvarsan in the thigh. He did not look up as he approached Phillip, in whom such fear arose that, as he came level with the limping man, and before he could think to stop the dark phantasm of the past from release in words, heard himself saying, "You filthy beast!"

Clewlee stopped, his face contorted. He half raised his stick, words frozen in his throat. Before he could retort, Phillip walked away in a kind of daze, wondering what had made him speak like that. It might have been Father, speaking of Uncle Hugh years ago to Mother! Did the mind snap sometimes like elastic, to get rid of its fearful thoughts upon someone else? That was what Father Aloysius said was sin; hate was the absence of love. Poor devil, how awful he must feel! Ruined for life. When he saw Clewlee again, he must beg his pardon. But when he went to the cubicle to find him, after tea that day, he was told by the batman that Clewlee had left.

He went into Grantham, and bought a bottle of Lysol, which he diluted before splashing all over the floor, door handles, and lower walls. He burned his washing flannel, hair-brush, shaving-brush, tooth-brush and towel, in case Clewlee had used them, in the tortoise stove, which roared, and soon the iron pipe glowed dull red.

While sitting there, he remembered the poem which Uncle Hugh used to recite to him in his garden room, years before, when he had been seven or eight years old.

> *From the hag and the hungry goblin*
> *That into rags would rend ye,*
> *All the spirits that stand*
> *By the naked man,*
> *In the book of moons, defend ye.*
> *Beware of the black rider*
> *Through blasted dreams borne nightly;*
> *From Venus Queen*
> *Saved may you bin,*
> *And the dead that die unrightly.*

With a wench of wanton beauties
I came unto this ailing:
Her breast was strewn
Like the half o' the moon
With a cloud of gliding veiling.
In her snow-beds to couch me
I had so white a yearning,
Like a moon-struck man
Her pale breast 'gan
To set my wits a-turning.

There were other verses, all of them terrible. He read Shelley, to try and lift himself from depression; but it was no good; then an unexpected visit from Pinnegar cheered him with the news that the officer sent to replace him had had an identical report from the S.S.O.

"So I told Downham that he ought to see the Colonel and tell him that you had done your job satisfactorily. He did so, and you're to come back tomorrow, old lad."

"Thank God. May I come back tonight?"

"Sure thing. What's to stop you? My God, this hut stinks!"

He told Pinnegar about Clewlee.

"I suppose you've got the wind up! Now don't you worry! You'll be all right! I've got more good news. Jack's coming back to the company when he's better. I had it from the Colonel himself!"

No more was heard of the adverse report. The S.S.O. kept away now that the company was established. Practice made the drivers less unsure of themselves, the mules less fearful. He noticed that the ears of most of the mules were upright as they pulled their limbers around the park. The "donks", as the men called them, felt at home; they were interested. He came to know some of them as beasts of character. There was Jimmy, grey and hairy, with a mild Sunday-school expression, almost wooden in its simplicity. Others revealed the same slow and gentle temperaments as they stepped delicately, thoughtfully picking their way, while the light draught horses, which had arrived after the mules, plodded forward cheerfully, un-selfconscious. They seemed to leave things to their drivers, of which there was one to each pair, riding the near-side, and guiding the off-side animal with touch of whip-handle and rein; while the mules, though trusting, seemed primly to decide for themselves how they would step. There were two kinds of mules: the donks proper, whose dams were mares; and the jennets who took after their stallion sires, more horse than ass. The jennets were silent; the donks brayed.

"Jerusalem cuckoos, we call them," said a driver who had served in Palestine.

The more Phillip saw of the drivers, the more he liked them.

"I'm sorry to have to ask you chaps to do so much, but things will be easier in France. I've managed to get some dilute sulphuric acid for your chains, that will get the rust off, but remember, vitriol burns! Rust is tri-ferrus tetra-oxide, oxide of *ferrus*, Latin for iron. The acid will change the iron oxide into sulphate, leaving the bright iron. Wash off the acid thoroughly, then dry and oil. This will save all that boring shaking to and fro in chaff. Ask me if you want anything, won't you? That's what I'm here for—to look after you chaps."

"Will there be any leaf, sir?"

"Yes, when we come back from trekking. When Captain Hobart returns we're going on the road for a week, and then there'll be leave, half the company at a time. Four days. That's what the other companies got, before going out." As he spoke, he leaned against Jimmy, inoffensive as grey ash, and as soft in temperament, with its large brown eyes and tall hairy ears.

Splendid news came one evening. Hobart was coming back to the company.

Under Jack Hobart the company was made up to strength, with seven officers, and an attached transport officer for training. One morning they set out for a week's trek. A cold north-west wind brought an occasional touch of sleet on Phillip's cheek and eyeball as he sat Black Prince at the rear of the column. Leading the company he could see the figure of All Weather Jack, beside him Pinnegar; then 'A' section, led by gunners on foot, Darky Fenwick on the old mare, followed by his section and their limbers; then 'B', led by Montfort, who had been an actor; then 'C', led by a South African called Lukoff, a Boer who had fought against the British fifteen years before; then 'D', led by a small Cambridgeshire potato farmer named Bright, whose trudging grim walk and manner belied his name; and behind the last section rode Sergeant Rivett on a spare hairy light-draught horse, leading cook's, water, and officers' mess carts; and at the tail of the column, long legs hanging loose to boot-soles free of burnished irons, he himself lounged on Black Prince, happy in his new nickname of "Sticks".

The black gelding had been exchanged for one of the company remounts at the Riding School picket line before dawn that day.

Through country lanes the column of companies making up a battalion trudged and rolled, while flakes of snow floated down the sky, to drift through leafless elms bordering fields of plough in ridge and furrow, and low-lying grazing.

During a halt, he heard, above the mist now beginning to form over the fields, the faint cries of birds—*seek*, *seek*, they seemed to be crying. *Seek*, *seek*. He remembered other redwings, called by old labourers the wind-thrush, passing over the Seven Fields of his boyhood, flitting on south before the clacking field-fares arrived from Norway, in the sad winter months when food was so scarce upon land hard with frost. *Seek—seek!* through the foggy mist, redwings seeking the sun, flying before the cold north wind, which brought death to "colour and light and warmth". *Seek—seek*. Seek always beauty of the spirit, the beauty sought by Francis Thompson, the outcast upon the Thames Embankment, who had left forever the ways of men. Phillip, who had first heard of the poet from his Aunt Theodora, had bought the three-volume *Works*, ordered at a bookshop in Grantham, and had read most of the poetry and prose with startling awareness of his own feelings.

A fine mud creamed the iron rims of limber wheels; the men sang along the marching column, they were on their way, having done with training, the sameness of parades, the hurry and sweat of pursued living. Before them lay seven days of trekking, with good billets at night, to be followed by four days embarkation leave—then away from it all, out with the rest of the boys; and, for Phillip, the zestful thought, once again the sharpness of life against the background of death. That was the natural life!

That night they came to Newark, and warm billets. The officers had quarters in an old inn, panelled with dark oak, and my word, said All Weather Jack, this is something like a dinner, as, washed and brushed up, they sat down at a table before a roaring fire and a sideboard on which stood, under pale spirit flames of large pewter chafing dishes, a saddle of mutton, a turkey, and roast ribs of beef. Half a dozen bottles of 1892 Chateau Pape-Clement claret accompanied the feast, finished off with a Stilton under a blue and white Wedgewood cover and ivory-handled scoops to cut out the crumbly cheese, like cubby holes in the front line. Packed tight with turkey, mutton, baked potatoes, celery,

Christmas pudding with brandy butter, wine, cheese, coffee, and liqueurs, Phillip got into bed with his boots and spurs on, ready for stables in the dark of 6.30 a.m. After a breakfast as sumptuous as the dinner—the same chafing dishes now filled with devilled kidneys, grilled gammons of bacon, fried eggs, scrambled eggs, and tomatoes—washed down by coffee—the meal begun with porridge and cream—he faced the day and the future with hearty optimism, expressed by the thought, Let 'em all come!

They pulled up at a village where they were to spend three days on a firing range. Phillip and the trainee transport officer, a soft Yorkshireman a year or two older than himself, passed much of the time in the parlour of the small pub, their billet, drinking hot rum and lemon and playing games of ludo, snakes-and-ladders, draughts; and tiring of this, gambled on two-handed cut-throat bridge. After lunch, with strong Burton ale, Phillip decided to visit the company on the range, and setting off at a gallop, followed by his pupil, arrived there during the massed firing of guns. Unaware of the strength of XXX Burton, he pulled up Black Prince from the gallop to salute Captain Hobart, and found himself lying on his back upon grass, not quite knowing how he got there, his right arm still at the salute. The battalion colonel was standing about twenty yards away, watching a section firing in traversing bursts, so he neither heard nor saw what later Hobart called Sticks Turpin's ride to Burton. His only other remark was, "Prince has played some polo, I fancy." Phillip sensed an unspoken reproof, and there was no more mid-day drinking.

While staying in the village he made a deal with a farmer, exchanging a sack of oats, weighing twelve stone, for half a cartload of carrots. These were sliced up in the farmer's root-machine and fed to the animals in their nose-bags at mid-day stables. At the next feed his appearance was greeted with lifted ears, whinnies, and intelligent mule-eyes under upright range-finding ears. The farmer was pleased with the deal, too; but three weeks later he regretted it. For by that time hard winter had set in, and the price of carrots rose to five times the market price of early December.

"Bad luck we'll just miss Christmas at home," said Hobart, back in the company lines. "When d'you want to take your embarkation leave, Sticks?"

Phillip had anticipated the question, and many times had rehearsed the answer; but when the time came, he found he could not reply. Reserve had grown upon him, the habit of saying what came into his mind was broken; and the nascent personality felt reluctance to enter again the old world wherein he had been defeated. Home-life, such as it was—love, friendship—all were of the past. The present was endurable, in that activity stopped thought. Only at the front, where everything was different, even the sun and the moon, would he be able to live his new life.

"Oh, I don't think I want any leave, thanks all the same, Skipper."

Jack Hobart had suspected a youthful love-affair gone wrong, nothing more, but had asked no questions. Now he felt that he knew Phillip well enough to be of help.

"My dear fellow! All work and no play! Won't your people want to see you?" He knew that Phillip had a father, by the record of next-of-kin: though the address was 63 Haybundle Street, E.C., apparently an office.

"I don't think they particularly want to see me."

What a liar he was. Eyes directed on the floor, he felt pain as he imagined his Mother's face. But it had always been the same: under childhood love for her had been a broken-glass feeling to hurt her by running away, to be lost. Why, why had she once tried to whip him, his knickerbockers down, with Father's cane?

Hobart saw that he was twisting his signet ring.

"Do forgive my asking, Sticks, but haven't you any friends?"

"Not really."

"Well, I'm in much the same boat. Very nearly the lonely soldier. Most of my pals have gone west. How about spending an evening, or perhaps a couple, with me in town? Sergeant Rivett knows enough to carry on, doesn't he? Good! That's a deal, then! We go tomorrow! I've managed to get twenty cans of juice, so we'll go in the old Merc, what? We'll dine and do a show, and stay at Flossie Flowers' pub. Plenty of life there, Sticks, my boy!"

The journey down the Great North Road was through air on the edge of frost, but the cold was endurable because unheeded. Phillip knew the road from motor-biking days in that remote time before July the First. They had lunch at Huntington, then blinded on down Ermine Street. At the Caxton Gibbet cross-roads an aeroplane came down low and raced them. It passed over them easily, wheels six feet above them, while the pilot leaned over the cockpit to jerk with two fingers of a gloved hand challenging

insults at the driver. All Weather Jack pressed down the accelera-
tor pedal and the blue needle of the brass speedometer wavered
at 70. A mile ahead the biplane zoomed, did an Immelman
turn, and dived again, to approach with lower wings almost
touching the plashed hedges on either side of the straight road as
he ran his wheels on the macadam. The bus pulled up fifty feet
away and roared over them with a whiff of castor oil.

"That's an altogether new type of bus," shouted Jack.

"It can hop it!"

"Rotary engine. Passed us doing a hundred and ten! You
all right?"

"Rather!"

The sixteen plugs of the 4 cylinder $4\frac{1}{2}$-litre Grand Prix Mercédès
were all firing, the cut-out was open; the blue needle crept
up to 95. This was the life!

Chapter 5

EMBARKATION LEAVE

Flowers' Hotel had a narrow entrance between a hat shop and a
boot-shop. The mahogany door was reinforced with much brass,
smooth and almost featureless from polishing. The proprietor,
Miss Flora Flowers, was said to combine a sharp awareness for
social distinctions with a liking for *la vie bohème*. One of her
favourite remarks was said to have been made originally by a
young Canadian soldier from Toronto, with some pretensions to
be an opera singer—"I believe in 'the aristocracy of thought'."

Breeding, she explained in her underground boudoir, on
the second night of All Weather Jack's visit with one of his
subalterns, was vertical and not horizontal.

"My dear Flossie, is your autobiography to begin at last?"
Fixing her eyes upon the playwright who had spoken, she said in
her deep voice, "I do not mean what you mean, Freddy."

"Surely, Flossie my dear, both conditions are required? Or
should it be planes?"

Phillip listened with bewilderment to the talk of the famous.
Jack had told him that Freddy, in the uniform of a private
soldier, had written *The Maid of the Mountains*. How could he
be so entirely different? He seemed to be waiting for some-

thing, and yet not to care if it came, all pointed nose and wry
mouth, pale eyes in expressionless face.

"Certainly not! Breeding is vertical, Freddy."

"But park palings are so cold for the girl, Flossie."

Phillip felt depressed as the beautiful *Maid of the Mountains*,
which he and Jack had seen the night before, became unreal,
made-up.

"You have a common mind, Freddy. I said that breeding
is vertical, not horizontal. One is bred *after* one is born. A
terrace house in Brixton can produce an aristocrat of thought,
and a palace the most common of minds." She turned to
Phillip beside her, and patted his hand. "Such a nice boy!
Sensitive, quiet, self-possessed! I know breeding when I see
it. Do you know, you're the first friend All Weather Jack has
brought here, and I've known him nearly twelve months?
Those eyes and eyelashes should belong to a girl. Don't take
any notice of me, Boy. Here, let's have a little drink." She
clapped her hands. An aged jockey-like figure appeared, in
black stove-pipe trousers and yellow-striped waistcoat with sleeves,
a grey quiff plastered upon his brow. "Bring some good wine.
Take it from Lord Wyre's bin." To Phillip she said, "Bertie
Wyre's making a second fortune out of his camp contracts, so let's
do the right thing for him, and share his good luck. All soldier
boys who come to Flowers' are in the family. Now you're one of
the family, see? Don't forget to let me have a photo of you before
you go out, will you, dear?"

All Weather Jack had said, when he came into his bedroom
before dinner the night before, "If Flossie tells you you're one of
the family, it means she accepts you. Don't be put off by her
painted face—she's been on the stage. Flossie's the best sort in the
world. But don't call her 'Flossie' until she invites you to."

"Of course not. Is she Miss Flowers, or Mrs.?"

"*Miss* Flora Flowers. That wonderful Gaiety chorus, when
many of the fillies were entered into the stud book, y'know.
Somebody set her up here—well, one doesn't mention it. I'll see
you later, downstairs. Now I'm going to shave and bathe. I'll
show you the bathroom."

Phillip took the hint; and having shaved and had a bath, he
went downstairs, and walked down an uneven corridor covered
by a carpet as soft as sand. SMOKING ROOM. He entered an
atmosphere of cremated cigars, bald heads, chubby cheeks, and
moustaches like the tips of gull's wings. There were khaki uniforms,

some with red tabs; dark blue sailor jackets, ringed with gold above the cuffs; a grey beard and a high-lapelled jacket or two. Many pairs of hands held *Pall Mall Gazette*, *Blackwood's*, or *Strand* magazines in armchairs beside little tables with tumblers on them under green-shaded electric lamps. No head moved as he looked cautiously about him. The walls were lined with framed SPY cartoons of the famous. He sat upon a chair near the door to await Jack Hobart, wondering if he had come to the wrong room as he became aware of subterranean or intermural noises, as of hot water pushing bubbles along pipes. He listened. The noises were in the room, coming from figures fallen asleep in the heat of the broad coal fire. He tip-toed out, and went back to his bedroom, fighting back a mild frenzy. Empty, lifeless! Nothing had life. Remembering the three Francis Thompson volumes in his haversack, he read for some minutes; and finding the phrase, *I am an icicle, whose thawing is its dying*, thought that was exactly his own condition, set apart for ever from his fellows. Desperation animated him; he went downstairs again. Nothing. Nobody. But if he left, where could he go? What do? Then a porter appeared and directed him along a corridor. He went down some stairs, along a further passage, and across a covered court-yard to a room where between thirty and forty young officers of the two services were sitting at tables, having tea with their girls. A string orchestra on a raised platform at the end, among tubs of large-leaved plants, was tuning up.

Thinking that Jack had told the porter to take him there to wait until he came, he sat at a vacant table, hoping not to be noticed in his solitariness. He put on an expectant expression, as though it were only a moment before a brilliant party, coming in, would hail him as the one they were looking for. Casually, as though deeply interested in thought, he looked around when the orchestra began to play a waltz. Couples arose and glided upon the parquet floor between tables. There were a number of guardees, all looking calm, and amused. They laughed slightly with their girls, who seemed to be more than at ease, as though all their thoughts were assured, like their world. How did it feel to belong to such circles?

An elderly woman, dressed in a black skirt sweeping the floor, and fitted bodice with sleeves to her wrists, came and stood before him, smiling pleasantly. Would he like some tea? Did he prefer Indian or China tea? He stopped himself from saying that he was waiting for someone. "Oh, China! Thank you." A tray was brought by a younger waitress, who did not smile. It was the first time he had seen slices of the thinnest lemon arranged in a circle, and almost equally thin rolled bread and butter. Should he give her a tip? Before he could decide, she said, "Thank you, sir," and went away. The hot tea and lemon, the delicious bread and butter made him feel better. He became interested in the couple at the next table.

An officer, with his back to him, was facing a girl wearing a sort of military forage cap, of dark blue material with red piping and small yellow tassels. When he dared to glance at her, Phillip saw a gaze of very bright blue eyes upon himself. She sat with her chin resting in the palm of one hand, and thinking that she was smiling at someone beyond him, after awhile he turned round casually and saw no one there. He kept his eyes on his table, thinking that he must have been mistaken; she probably hadn't noticed him, thinking her own thoughts. Even so, he felt her gaze still upon him, and looking up again to watch the dancing, found himself held in her smile.

The waltz ended, there was polite clapping, through which a man and girl made for her table, and sat down. When the music began again the girl with the bright eyes got up to dance with the man who had just been dancing, leaving the man with his back turned still sitting there. Watching her, he saw that the cap she wore went with a uniform tunic of dark blue with red facings, round brass buttons, and epaulettes. A short skirt, half way between knee and shoe, completed the military effect.

"Hullo," she said, as the dance brought her past his table. "Aren't you with All Weather Jack?"

"Yes," he said, half rising.

"Ours is the next dance!" and with a flutter of fingertips she swung away to the strains of Destiny Waltz. He felt devastated. He couldn't dance. Oh hell, why hadn't he learned?

When the next dance began he got up with a feeling almost of being in no-man's-land in daylight. She opened her arms and he was for it. "I can't dance!"

She laughed. It was like a story in *Nash's Magazine*, he said to himself, rejoicingly.

"I've been driving in a Voluntary Ambulance Unit attached to the Belgian Army, and now I'm having a spell at home. I take out wounded officers from Dolly Hill-Walker's hospital in Regent's Park. Dolly is a cousin, and a neighbour of Jack H'b'rt's parents, that's how I met him. Now you know all about me!"

"My name is Phillip Maddison."

"And you're a two striper!"

"Well——"

She hugged him impulsively. "I am Sasha! And you—Phillip! What more do we need to know?"

While she was talking, he saw that the man sitting still at the table had lost both legs.

"Oh, I forgot! Of course, we are dinner partners tonight, Phillip. Ah, there's All Weather Jack. My word, isn't he smart!"

Hobart wore blues. They all sat at Sasha's table, and had a bottle of champagne, then another. It was time, she said, to take her two lambs back to Dolly in Regent's Park. An hour later—most pleasantly spent by Phillip with Jack at a downstairs cellar-bar, she returned wearing a light blue evening frock the colour of her eyes. Another girl arrived, Bobo, to make a foursome. They drank sherry. So far Phillip had not seen the fabulous Flossie; but he had found out a little more about the place, from Jack. The old boys in the room he had gone into were collectively known as The Club. They were, or had been, particular friends of Flossie at one time or another. In fact, said Jack, talking through his back teeth, Flossie at one time *was* The Club.

"Strictly between ourselves, of course. And never in the good lady's hearing it need hardly be said. You know the form—'Kiss and never tell'."

"Certainly." All the same, he thought, in the past he had told everything to Desmond, and Mrs. Neville. Jack went on, "In fact, the pass-word, I'm told, used to be 'Are you going to the Club today?' Not a word! Marvellous woman, Flossie. She's asked us to her party after the theatre tonight."

How suddenly life could change: two hours before, the place was lifeless, and now—— No, *he* had been lifeless. Friendship, or love, made all the difference. And yet—something more was needed. Poetry—the spirit of beauty—the faith that Lily had. There would never be anyone like Lily again.

"A penny for them?" Sasha smiled into his eyes. "Darling Phillip," she breathed, and took his hand when they went in to dinner.

Afterwards, four stalls at the Alhambra. *The Bing Boys Are Here.* They were, and so am I, Phillip Maddison! Marvellous, wonderful! Warmth, light, colour, *lovely* people! On the stage the funniest couple, George Robey and Alfred Lester, and adorable (Jack's word) Vi Lorraine. Jack said, "I've seen this show fifteen times!" During the interval he told a story about 'Duggie' Haig, who had come to see the show with his children.

"George Robey told me this. Saying a few words of thanks to the principal artistes afterwards, the great man said, 'I had to come and see the performance, everyone in France talks about your "Bing Bong Brothers".' 'Sir,' replied Robey, 'if we are the Bings, your men are certainly the Bongs'."

Sasha held Phillip's hand tightly during the last scene. He saw tears in her eyes. Alone with her in the taxi back to the hotel— Jack and Bobo, both in huge fur coats, returned in the 'Merc' after the show—Sasha held his hand to her bosom, saying, "Oh, I cannot help thinking of all the boys who have been there, sitting in the very same seats, laughing and clapping, who——" She wept a little, and recovered. He sat still. Peering into his face, "Phillip, darling, you *do* understand, don't you? I love them all, I *must* love everyone I see, it is *me*, it is the life in me, nothing to do with 'Sasha'! I must give, give, *give* while I can! Do you, who love poetry, understand? Tell me you do?"

"Yes, I do, Sasha. Oh God, yes——"

"You too have tears! I knew, I knew! Darling, darling, *darling* Phillip! I loved you as soon as I saw you. I felt you were dreadfully lost and unhappy. I won't ask questions, of course. What are words, anyway? It is *feelings* that matter. My husband understands, thank God. Oh, I love him so dearly! We are everything to one another. Does that shock you, darling?"

"No, I think that love creates love."

"You understand! Of course you do, with your fine feelings! Darling, darling Phillip! Kiss me if you want to. If you don't want to, then don't! What is a kiss, anyway? It is the spirit that matters. Life is a spirit, I am sure of it! One either knows, or one does not know. My sisters are shocked at the way I behave. When I was still in the schoolroom they called me 'the prostitute'! What does it matter? Love creates love, hate generates hate, which is sin, and hurts the soul. Darling, you *are* so sweet!" She kissed his hand as the taxi drew up by the brass-bound mahogany door, with its dim rows of service caps on one side, and field boots on the other.

"Look at them, Phillip! All waiting to be taken away, used, and then——! Think of them moving about, here, there, and then, one day——"

"They know the form, Sasha. Once they belonged to sheep, and to bullocks. They were taken away by men——"

"Isn't life *hell* for everything, darling? Simply hell!"

They laughed, and went in through the door.

A party was going on in Flossie's air-raid cellar, got up as a boudoir. Champagne. Smears of what looked like jellified tar on little thin "captain" biscuits turned out to be caviare, given to her, said Flossie, by the Grand Duke Nicolas on his last (incognito) visit to London. Sitting on a chair with its tall and narrow back curving over her head like a shell, among her boys in blues and her girls in their "glad rags" sitting on the floor around her, she did not so much hold court as assume matriarchal benevolence over them. To Phillip she was a slightly frightening figure behind a painted face with gummed-on eyelashes and brows and wig of auburn hair by Willie Clarkson, a theatrical outfitter whose own face, as he leaned over her squeaking a funny story, seemed to be adorned with what paint had been left over from his work upon Flossie Me Darlin', as he called her, while telling his story.

"It's every word of it true, every word, I swear it! There was the Dook of Connaught, and several Ladies of the Court invitin' me, *me* Me Darlin', to the Palace, to tell them all how to make-up for Charades at Christmas! Up and down the Throne Room we steps, the Dook and me, his arm in mine, while I try to keep step. Such big boots he wore, and spurs, my word, he'd been turnin' out the Guard, or somethin'. Well, Flossie Me Darlin', there we were, or there was I, all mixed up, the Dook holding me by the arm, like I was pinched by a copper, walking me up and down, up and then down, me knees knocking, me toes turned first in then out, the Throne Room it was, too, like an ambassador, me all the while tryin' to kip step wiv 'im in Field Marshal's costume! Me Darlin'," he quipped, "I did me best to suggest you for the part of Britannia, but the Honourable Mrs. You Know Who said 'No, Definitely No!' I could have sunk into the floor at me floater! Oh blime! I've bored you! Sorry!"

The excited, painted little doll stood beside her in bright nervous jerks, adjusting his *toupé*, false teeth, set of padded shoulders, and shooting his cuffs.

"Go on, Willie, I know it so well, you tell it differently every time. Go on, don't mind me, I want to say something to Valentine here before I forget. Go on with your lines, dear, they all want to hear."

But the marionetting enlarged doll seemed to be broken in several places. Flossie was whispering into the ear of a pink-and-white-faced young Irish peer, who had been telling her of his vain attempts to get posted to Paris, where the love of his life awaited him. Jack had told Phillip that Valentine had been wounded during the Retreat, left for dead by the Germans, and repatriated through Switzerland. His only brother Dermot had been killed at Loos, so Valentine had not been sent back to his regiment, though he had asked to be posted, because there was no other heir.

"Good lord, I saw his brother then! He thrashed some of the 24th Division men, who were leaving the battlefield on that Sunday, with a hunting whip! I was with them, and saw the advance party of Guards going up, my cousin among them!"

"Yes, the whole line gave way, I remember. I was with the Yeomanry then, waiting for the Gap."

He looked at the young Irish lord with interest. So people in high society had their problems just like anyone else. "Leave it to me, I'll talk to Max, darling," Flossie was saying. Valentine, his fresh oval face topped by raven hair, thereupon called for more Veuve Cliquot, to drink to the damnation of the Boche who had found him wounded during the Retreat, left him for dead, and kicked him when they had seen that he was alive. He and the playwright called Freddie seemed to be great friends. Here I am, thought Phillip, among the famous and the beautiful, in the very hub of the world, although I hope to God I won't revolve in this hot room, that would be too damned awful, I mustn't drink any more fizz. Has it always been like this, he thought, as the red-bearded painter he had seen in the Café Royal, and again at Albert, came in, to kiss Flossie's hand. He was in the uniform of a major, with one gold ear-ring hanging from an ear. Has it always been like this, or is it the war? What fun war is—except in the front line. But for the war, I, Phillip Maddison, would never have known such wonderful scenes and people! If only I had the power to express all this in words!

A gramophone was now blaring out a Highland reel, *The Dashing White Sergeant*, and everyone was dancing, it was a sort of kaleidoscope pattern, ever shifting like the sort of telescope he had got when a child from the Cave at Beereman's at Christmas, you turned it and bits of coloured glass made gaudy patterns like spiders' webs thick with coloured bundles and blobs of flies. They were yelling now, Highland Chieftains, a chap in a kilt was yelling in a high cutting yelp-voice. Hell, hell, the noisy kaleidoscope was revolving, he knew that fatal sign, and staggered out.

When he was better he tottered to his bedroom and lay down on the bed, leaving on the light. He awoke to feel someone taking off his shoes, very quietly and gently. A voice whispered, "Darling, you're shivering. I'm going to get a hot-water bottle and put you to bed." A hand cooled his forehead, fingers smoothed his hair. Undid his belt. He felt an eiderdown covering him. Later was vaguely aware of the door opening again, and cool fizzing. "Drink this, darling. It will make you better." He drank. Hid face under eiderdown to muffle what he hoped was only a belch. "How very polite you are, darling. But don't worry about me. I've got two sons—or one, perhaps I should say. Although Robin still comes to me, the pet."

He felt better. He looked about him. "Two sons, Sasha? They must be babies."

"Yes, always my babes, darling. Ninian was killed last September, on the Somme, bless him. His aeroplane simply stopped flying! Alex his brother is still at Eton."

"Oh, I am sorry. But—are you joking? You can't be older than I am, surely?"

"I am old enough to be your mother, darling. But what does age matter? It's how one *feels* that matters. Only the few understand. Painters, like Augustus John and Jimmy Pryde—composers like Ralph Williams and Frederick Delius—poets like your beloved Francis Thompson. Heavenly creatures, all of them! And poor Valentine, bless him. He's a poet really, such a nice boy, but so wild! And all because his mother disliked him, and loved Dermot, his brother. Poor darling Valentine, he's mad about that gel in Paris. He ought to be allowed to go to her, to be loved by her. If he had a son, I'm sure his mother would forgive herself, and love Valentine."

"Sasha!"

"Yes, darling?"

"I know it's not the thing to ask questions, but I am so puzzled about you."

"There's nothing you needn't ask me, darling. But first, let me put your pyjamas on for you. May I open your haversack?"

"I'm afraid I forgot to bring any."

"Of course, there was no room, was there, with those great big books of poems, darling. Why wear pyjamas, anyway? I'll pull off your slacks, they must be folded, ready for tomorrow. Undo your braces, and the top buttons, darling. I am a trained valet. I've done it so many times."

When he was in bed she said, "Well, good night, darling, sleep well."

He held her hand. "Don't go."

She slipped off her gown, kicked off shoes, wriggled, pulled and unbuttoned, and stood naked, as he saw in a glance, her breasts sagging from the feeding of her sons. Then the light clicked, and a sweet-scented spirit was moulding itself warmly into the shape of his body. He had no feeling of her being a woman, only of warm, child-like kindness. Damn, his mouth was beginning to run with saliva.

"Sasha, do forgive me, but I think I'll have to go outside for a moment."

"Poor darling, won't it pass when you feel warmer? I hope it's a false alarm."

"I have a hydrometer which is an infallible warning!"

"Oh, lucky you! Would you like me to hold your head?"

"Oh no, thanks all the same. I'm quite used to this sort of thing."

Cold, shivering, he crept back to her warmth, lying against her back. Her arms were crossed over her breast, like a Crusader effigy on a tomb. He did not know what to think, until, remembering Lily, it seemed to be very simple. She was what she said she was. But if she loved her husband, as she said she did, how could she go to bed with other men? Or had she really fallen in love with him? When Lily had done so, she had given up all others. But then Lily had said she had not loved them, only been sorry for them. Then fear arose—Clewlee.

"I can feel you thinking, darling."

"I'm a bit puzzled."

"What about, darling?"

"Do you mind if I'm frank?"

She turned round. "Of course not, darling! Say anything you like!"

"I was wondering if you were a sort of Club. I beg your pardon! I didn't mean to say that."

"It's a very natural question, in the circumstances, isn't it? It's a compliment in a way to be likened to Flossie, but no, I don't think I'm exactly what you'd call a sort of club. That doesn't help much, does it, my pet?"

"Well, if you're sure you don't mind my being frank?"

"Of course not, darling. I told you I didn't."

"How many men have you loved? It's awful to continue questioning you like this, I know."

"How many? Goodness knows. I was always bad at arithmetic."

He laughed. "I think you're playing with me."

"I'm so glad, darling. Play on!"

"Twenty? Thirty? Forty?"

"I honestly don't know, darling. Such things as numbers don't count with me.

"But how about having babies? Would your husband mind if you did?"

"Unfortunately I can't have another baby. Alex had a rather hard time arriving, he took three days, poor darling, and afterwards I couldn't have another," she said, hugging him.

"And your husband doesn't mind you—loving others?"

"Oh no, darling. If he were that sort, I'd be no good to him. He's my second husband—my first was killed on the Aisne, exactly two years, to the day, before Ninian was shot down over Mossy Face Wood, his friends call it. The Germans were very good. They dropped a letter giving the time of the funeral, and didn't fire or anything when Ninian's great friend flew over and dropped a wreath. He did have an idea to land on their field, to thank them personally, but thought it might not be understood when he got back, so he hedge-hopped, and got fired at, but it was his fault, for not keeping height."

"But do you tell your husband, the one you have now, about your affairs?"

"The details, you mean? Of course not. I don't even remember them myself. They are unimportant. He knows the real 'me', and did before I married him, and understands. If he had all my love, it would swamp him. I can't help loving people—I told you, didn't I, darling?"

"What would he say if he walked in now, and found you with me?"

"Well, if he could walk, he'd say hullo, darling, and feel a bit sorry for you, knowing you'd feel rather odd, and then find himself another bed somewhere."

He lay still. What a frightful bounder he was, to ask all those questions. So the man with no legs was her husband. At length he said, "Oh, I am so frightfully sorry. Yes, of course I understand. Oh, what must you think of me."

"Darling, please don't worry. Oh, you are so tired. Now you must go to sleep, darling." She could feel him lying very still. "I'm not turning you down, darling, you do what you want." After some minutes, "Don't worry, darling. If you were the aggressive sort, I would not be able to love you. The rings I have on my door bell at night, from men I've never met, who think I'm—what's your word, darling?—a club."

"Sasha."

"Yes, darling?"

"I am so ashamed I asked those questions. I didn't realise that the man at your table was your husband."

"Don't worry, darling. He thought you were very sweet. You see, he was rather badly hurt, as well as losing his legs." With a touch of her lips on his cheek, she breathed the word *darling*, and turned round, crossed her arms on her breast, and lay still.

He could not sleep. He floated down long corridors of the mind, revisiting scenes of past defeats and disasters. When he thought of Lily, he breathed deeply, and held to the steadiness of her eyes. Francis Thompson had known someone like her, in *Dream Tryst*.

> *When dusk shrunk cold, and light trod shy*
> *And dawn's grey eyes were troubled grey;*
> *And souls went palely up the sky,*
> *And mine to Lucidé . . .*

"Darling, why do you sigh so absolutely silently?"

"I didn't want to wake you. Were you asleep?"

"Yes, I was. But also I was thinking about you."

"I think you are Mother Eve. And I feel tremendous love for your husband, really."

"Darling, how sweet of you to say that. I think you understand, like God. I *felt* you did, when I saw you at the *thé dansant*, sitting alone. You have the most gentle mouth, darling. How your mother must love you."

He lay still, thinking of himself in Mother's bed when he was little, wiggling his toes to get rid of twistings in his mind, and Mother saying, *Oh Sonny, do keep still, dear, and let me sleep*. It had been torture to lie still, in the white night beyond the darkness.

Rising gradually, he dressed with prolonged quietness, then

felt his way slowly to the table, and having part-covered the electric reading lamp with a towel, turned the brass switch. In the glow he wrote on a piece of writing paper taken from the box, *Thank you, Sasha*. Then a similar note to Captain Hobart, in an envelope. He laid them on the floor, then removing the towel, crept to look at her. Her face looked quite different in repose, without the eager expression which made her so young, and her lips, parted and loose, seemed fuller, but without colour. It was a face devoid of all feeling, yet not heavy; almost she might be dead, so peacefully did she lie across the pillow. He knelt to kiss her a gentle goodbye, and without moving head or opening eye she put out a hand and touched his face, murmuring, "Goodbye darling." Was she dreaming? For she lay as before, across the pillow, curly head almost hanging over the edge.

He walked down Whitehall and along the Embankment to Vauxhall Bridge, and crossing the Thames, continued down the long tramless highway of the Camberwell New Road until, thinking to take a shorter line, turned up Rye Lane and came to a Common, which he had never seen before. It was six o'clock, and too early to make directly for home. He thought to arrive by half-past seven, by which time it would be growing light. He circled the open grassy space, braced by what he thought of as "the hard glitter of the ebon night", seen jubilantly with the delayed effects of wine. Then by the Pole Star he set off in the direction of Wakenham, and arrived at Hillside Road as the sky was showing a smoky red line low in the east, thinking that now along the Western front, from North Sea to Alps, hundreds of thousands of weary men were standing-to, or perhaps attacking across livid wastes, sharing equal fear with the attacked.

It was early yet, so he sat on the brick wall under the porch until he heard the alarm clock going off; then his mother coming downstairs. He rattled the letter box. She was in her old dressing gown, and her hair, tied by a frayed riband, hung wispy and grey over the collar. Her face lit with joy at seeing him, then showed a feeling of anxiety, despite the smile.

"Embarkation leave! We're going out soon—in about a week's time."

"Oh, Phillip——"

"Don't worry, it's a safe job this time. The chances of being hit are about equal with those in a Zeppelin raid at home."

She made him some tea, a little hurt that he had not kissed her; but he looked tired, and, like his father, was liable to sudden periods of exhaustion. While they talked, he brightening with the tea inside him, they heard Richard unlocking the door of the bathroom, to call down the passage to the end bedroom, "Mavis! I'm out. Come along, now!"

Richard, his face pale by prolonged office work on top of chilly night patrols as a sergeant of Special Constabulary, shook hands punctiliously. "So you're going out again, Phillip! My word, the authorities nowadays don't give a fellow much time to recover after wounds, do they?"

"I asked to go, Father."

"Oh!"

Rashers of streaky bacon were put before them. The flap of the front door clicked, a newspaper fell. Phillip went to get it, glanced at the big black headline. "Good lord, Lloyd George is Prime Minister! Poor old Asquith!"

"Well, my boy, all I can say is that nemesis has overtaken him, with his everlasting 'Wait and see' policy!"

"But it was *The Daily Trident* that continually said that Asquith said 'Wait and see', Father!"

"And quite right too, Phillip! Asquith is responsible for all the bungling so far."

Phillip caught his mother's eye. She was silently laughing; but frowned at once and shook her head at her son.

"As for his wife, who had the effrontery to visit German prisoners at Donnington Hall——"

"Well, as a matter of fact, Father, Margot never went there. I happen to know that from one of her great friends, Mrs. Kingsman——"

Hetty, anxious to avoid an upsetting argument, again shook her head at Phillip. "What time will you be home tonight, Dickie?"

"Oh, late as usual. About nine. I have to go on patrol duty from ten until two." He looked at his watch. "Is Mavis out of the bathroom, I wonder?"

"I don't suppose she'll be long, Dickie."

"She ought to get out of bed earlier! Morning after morning it is the same thing. She stands about, day dreaming. I've watched her from my bedroom window, just standing there. 'Pon my soul, she has not the slightest consideration for anyone at all! I shall not have time to clean my teeth, before leaving for my train!"

He was putting the watch back in its wash-leather covering when there was a rumbling noise, as of far-off gunfire. "Another daylight raider——?" he was saying, when Doris cried from upstairs, "It's Mavis, Mother!"

Pushing back his chair, Phillip strode out of the room and up the stairs three at a time.

"The door is locked! I think she's ill!" he called down the stairs.

"Oh, Mavis, Mavis!" lamented Hetty. "I told her never to touch tripe again!"

Richard came up the stairs carrying the pick with which he had sub-soiled his allotment. Using the end as a ram, he burst the lock. Phillip saw his sister, in bloomers and vest, with ashen face and froth on lips, and eyes like those of a man just shot, lying on the floor. He lifted her arms, Richard her feet, and between them the unconscious girl was carried to her bedroom.

"I'll see to things," said Phillip, looking at his father's distraught eyes. "You clean your teeth. I can put on the lock. Only the screws came out, I can plug the holes with matches. I'll do it when I've been to Cave-Browne. May I use your Sunbeam bike? Thanks."

The doctor arrived, and said she must rest. When he had gone, Phillip said, "Mother, what's the matter with her, *really*?"

"Doctor Cave-Browne says we are not to worry, it is purely functional, Phillip. Your sister is very run down."

"But is it epilepsy?"

"You must not use that word, Phillip! It is not a mental disease, but purely functional, as I said. Mavis needs a complete change. Life is not easy nowadays, for anyone. And your sister feels things very deeply."

"I remember she collapsed on the night of the Zeppelin raid. Is this the second time?"

"There was another occasion, Phillip. Please do not say anything about it, will you, when you see Mrs. Neville? Mavis is so anxious that nobody outside the family will know."

Lying back in his armchair, as of old in Mrs. Neville's flat before the fire, he felt relief that his friend and *confidante* was the same as ever. He did not like to enquire about Desmond, but hoped she would speak of him. As for Mrs. Neville, she realised the change in Phillip. In the old days he used to tell her everything about his goings-on and the people he met, usually seeing the funny side of what, she knew, had hurt him at the time. But now he was reserved, and too quiet. What could have happened? She must try and find out, indirectly. Sooner or later it would come out, if she knew her Phillip! She began primly,

"You are quite the soldier nowadays, I can see that, Phillip! Your mother has told me that you have over sixty horses and mules in your charge! And you had a day with the hounds! My word, you are coming on! Quite the gentleman! Not that I mean that you were not always one by birth, dear. How do you get on with your new captain?"

"Quite well, I think. As a matter of fact, I came up with him to town yesterday, in his racing bus."

"What fun! Does he have a flat in Town?"

"Well, in a way." He kept his eyes lowered, and she thought, So that's where he was last night! Well, as long as he's careful, that won't do him any harm. But, oh dear, could it be——?

"An older man, if he's the right sort, can help by setting a good tone. What is his name?"

"Captain H'b'rt, Mrs. Neville. He was in the Yeomanry before the war."

"Is he married, dear?"

"No, Mrs. Neville. He lives with his parents in Regent's Park."

"That's the best residential part of London, Mrs. Hudson always said. Such beautiful crescents! Didn't the Nash Brothers design them? My, what a walk you must have had! Whatever made you leave in the middle of the night?"

"Well, as a matter of fact, we didn't go to his home last night."

Oh dear, was this captain one of those, she wondered.

"Don't tell me if you'd rather not, Phillip. After all, you are grown up, and able to take care of yourself. Men with queer ways always have existed, of course——"

"Oh, nothing like that about All Weather Jack, Mrs. Neville."

"Then it's a woman!"

"Well, in a way, yes."

"Ah——!"

He told her about Sasha, starting seriously, but leaving out about her crippled husband, and ending the account as comedy. Soon they were quaking in their chairs.

"You know, Mrs. Neville, I'm not being fair, really. You see, she lost her husband, then her son. Now she's married a war cripple."

"Ah, I can understand her feelings! A woman is always a mother, you see, dear!"

Tears filled the round grey eyes. "'Come, dear lady, let us laugh, for we are for the dark'. Oh God yes, Shakespeare knew the laughter, and the tears, of the heart!" She sighed with pleasure-pain, happy that they were back on the old footing. Then her other self broke through, "As Mr. Hudson used to say, 'Every woman is at heart a rake!'"

He had heard her say that before; he was thinking, If only Mavis could die, she would cease to suffer.

Responding to his subdued mood, she reassumed her former mien, and continued, "This Sasha sounds a true, brave woman. I've heard about Flossie Flowers, of course. She was quite a figure at Monte Carlo in my young days. Not that I was ever there! Oh yes, Flossie in her young days was one of the famous courtesans! I used to hear a lot about her from Mr. Hudson— he was in Fleet Street, you know. As for Flowers' Hotel, well, I don't know enough to say, Phillip." Her voice became prim. "Desmond's father, I believe, used to go there quite a lot." Another sudden shriek of laughter. "And my son may be there before long, the way things are going!"

"How is Desmond, Mrs. Neville?"

"When I heard from him last, he was on Salisbury Plain, with the field gunners, you know. You haven't heard from him, I suppose? No, I was afraid you wouldn't. It will take time, Phillip." She sighed. Again the shriek. "Or Sasha!" She sighed again. "Don't mind my little fun, dear! Oh, what it is to be young!" She looked out of the window. "There's Gran'pa and Aunt Marian trotting off down the road together! Usually your mother goes with them. Every Tuesday they get the midday tram to the Old Vic, you know—what a good thing it is that Mother has something outside her home to interest her! A woman needs to be taken out of her worries, you know, Phillip." She saw that he was turning his signet ring. "Are you going to see Freddie? No, well, perhaps it's just as well. That phase in your life is closed." She paused in hesitation; then plunged. "What do you feel about Lily now, Phillip?"

She watched him cover his eyes with a hand, and heaving herself out of her chair, went into the kitchen to put on a kettle, feeling that she was an idiot to have asked such a direct question.

For, of course, Lily had worn his signet ring, and Dr Dashwood, coming from the hospital mortuary, had given it back to Phillip. Faithful to his memory of Lily! All the same, it would do him a world of good if he could find a really nice, experienced woman, artistic of course, who would help him to feel things a little less unhappily. He was too tense. Like his sister Mavis, poor girl, so sensitive and intelligent, but caught up in that narrow home! What Mavis wanted was a love affair, not a hole-and-corner business, which would mean only one end for the girl, but a nice, kind, older man, who would look after her—goodness, what was she thinking? Men were all *roués*, when they had the chance.

All the same—what was it Mr. Hudson used to quote, at the Highgate Sunday afternoon *salons*? Something from William Blake, how did it go? 'What is it every man and woman wants to find in the faces of others—the lineaments of gratified desire.' She wished she could remember the quotation: but Phillip, with his young ideals, would not be able to understand it. Poor young things, all of them, caught up in the same dusty cobweb, where the ruins of an earlier generation were already lying. She wept a little, and then made the tea.

Part Two

'ALL WEATHER JACK' HOBART

Chapter 6

ANCRE VALLEY

Under arc lights they entrained at Grantham station, leaving at 9.30 p.m. Phillip shared a comfortable first-class carriage with "Darky" Fenwick. The train rolled south all through the night, and arrived at Southampton at 6 a.m. The company was embarked by 7 a.m., and anchored in the harbour until 3 p.m., when the transport steamed away. No saluting whistles and sirens as in 1914, no searchlights swinging upon the ship from points on the Solent shore. He was surprised and delighted that he felt no qualms when they met the Channel swell; it was a good voyage, ending at 2 a.m. at Le Havre. By 8 a.m. they were disembarked, and marching through cobbled streets amidst trams groaning against worn rails, to a Rest Camp—one of scores spreading into the country east of the town; and next morning, down again to the railway, to entrain for the front. After the usual all-night crawl, with many joltings and horn-tootings, they arrived at Ascheux at 2 p.m. Having assembled troops and transport, they took to the road, and halted at a village of cottages and barns of lime-washed *pisé* and thatch, rather like a Devon village, except that the roads were of grey mud, not red. There, soon after arrival, Captain Hobart had a letter delivered by an R.E. dispatch rider on a Triumph motor-cycle, telling him that the company was attached to a brigade of the East Pennine division of second-line territorials which had recently arrived in the B.E.F.

After the men had had a rest, tea was prepared; meanwhile Phillip led his animals to water before feeding. They drank at a long canvas trough beside the road, the mules as usual taking their time, during which another transport officer said to Phillip, "Bad luck, isn't it, being shoved into this East Pennine lot? I hear they chucked away their rifles and Lewis guns first time coming out of the trenches."

After watering, the drivers mounted each a mule, leading the off-side animal on the right of the road, and returned to the covered stables allotted to them. There a small man with prominent front teeth below a waxed moustache, and a blue band round his cap, was waiting. He peered at first one animal, then another. He wore a badgeless driver's coat. Phillip thought he was some sort of Voluntary Ambulance Driver come to look on.

"Nice beasts, these Jerusalem cuckoos," he said, conversationally. "Most people are afraid of them. They won't kick you."

"I'm glad to hear it."

"I hear we're joining a rotten division, the second East Pennines."

"Is that so? Well, let me tell you that in the 'rotten division' your mules will be called mules when you address me in future! Moreover, they will be groomed before watering, so as not to interfere with feeding, which should take place immediately after watering!" retorted the visitor, sharply, in a North Country voice.

By this time Phillip was wondering who he was. He did not like to take a closer look at the blue-banded hat, or the badge on the front, while the dark eyes above the waxed moustache were fixed so intently upon his own.

"Furthermore, don't you know that animals taken to water are not to be ridden, but led by drivers?"

"I'm afraid I didn't. What do you represent, sir, the Dumb Friends' League?"

"Cheeky, eh? What, are you new to the army?"

"Fairly new. I only joined the B.E.F. in September '14."

"Well, Dumb Friends' League or no, don't let me catch you again lettin' your drivers ride to watering! And watch your step, young man! I'm Major Pickles, A.D.V.S. of this 'rotten division'."

"I'm very sorry, sir. I honestly had no idea who you were. Of course the 'rotten division' is rudeness on my part. I apologise, sir."

"Well, you'll know next time, won't you? And take my tip, young feller, don't go about passing cheap judgments on matters you know nowt about!" With that he strode away, spurs clinking. When Phillip gave his C.O. an account of this, Hobart remarked, "A horse doctor, what? Yes, I think it's best to be careful to whom one passes first impressions. We've all done it in our time——"

"Yes, I certainly will, skipper."

The mess was in an empty cottage, on the door of which was painted in large white letters, 6 *Officers*. A table was missing; so were some of the upstairs floorboards, obviously taken for firewood. Pinnegar set two of the drivers, carpenters by trade, to knock up a table from some planks he had come across. It was built with collapsible legs for transporting. Planed and holystoned with a brick, it was a job well done. Jack Hobart produced seven folding canvas chairs—a present to the mess, he said. A fire of floorboards was lit in the grate, and while Jules, who had been a chef in a London hotel before joining up, cooked dinner, the C.O.'s batman laid the table, from the hitherto-unseen mess box. Luxury indeed! He spread a new white tablecloth with silver spoons, forks, and ivory-handled knives, all engraved with the Hobart crest. From another box came a wire-covered siphon with sparklets, a bottle of whiskey, glasses. Phillip sent his batman to get his gramophone, and while this was playing *Chalk Farm to Camberwell Green*, sung by Gertie Millar, Hobart told them to help themselves to drinks.

After a meal of tasty rissoles made with bully beef and bacon chopped small and mixed with oatmeal and herbs, white bread, and red wine, followed by apple tart and coffee, Pinnegar spoke about future mess arrangements.

"As mess president I'll be able to buy extra grub at the Expeditionary Force Canteens. Also whiskey at three and six, or five francs, a bottle, for whoever wants it. I think it'll be more satisfactory if we use our own bottles, marked by initials; and I propose a general rate of twenty francs per head per week for the extras. All agreed? Right, I'll enter it in the Company War Diary."

Thus began Phillip's fourth adventure in France. Having sold his camp-bed before leaving Belton, he slept in his valise on the floor.

After two days' rest, during which there were various inspections, including a visit from the white-haired G.O.C. Division, who had been through the Gallipoli campaign, they left for the line by way of a gentle valley to Engelbelmer, a village damaged by gunfire but with most of its church and trees standing; and leaving by a track, followed another slight hollow under two skylines to Martinsart, passing on the way many forsaken gun-pits from which howitzers had fired before and on July the First. Gas-gongs of 18-pounder brass shell-cases were still hanging from apple trees and lintels of sand-bagged shelters.

Near one he saw a bell-tent standing, and a perforated fire-bucket. Inside the tent was a stretcher. In a couple of minutes the tent was down, pegs pulled up; pole, canvas, stretcher and bucket slung on a limber. The stretcher, with handles sawn off, would make a comfortable camp-bed.

In a drizzle of rain, they passed through Martinsart; and following beside a rusty steam-tram-line along a valley, came to the village of Mesnil, amidst many old shell-holes fringed with sere grasses. There, in a barn near the shattered church, the transport put up the picket line.

Two half-limbers had to go on at once with the company, which was relieving another company in a brigade in the line at Bois d'Hollande, a nasty place, at the apex of a salient east of Beaucourt. This village had been taken, with its garrison, a month previously, Hobart told Phillip, by the initiative of a wounded temporary colonel of the Naval Division, said to have been a dentist in New Zealand before the war, who had taken charge of the remnants of various battalions when the attack had been held up, re-organised the assault, and won the Victoria Cross.

Phillip went with the limbers, riding Black Prince. The road lay beside the old railway line. After passing through another shattered village, he saw more clearly beyond the embankment the flooded marshes of the Ancre. Across the swamps, palely grey in moonlight filtering through the valley mists, was the dark mass of Thiepval wood and the skyline beyond which lay Ovillers and the ground over which his battalion, nearly half a year previously, had been cut to pieces by machine-gun fire. Guns flashing and sending up their spinning shells lit the charred trunks of branchless trees standing in water. The road was thick with mud. Flashes in the eastern sky before them were from German guns; shells droned down across the river, and burst with ruddy fans and crashes. Although they fell three hundred yards off he winced, and saliva came into his mouth. Troops coming out of the line shuffled past unspeaking. Machine-gun bullets whined and plopped into the marsh, at the end of their trajectories, he knew. There were many halts. The word came back that Station Road, in front, was being crumped.

In rain the column moved on, halted, moved on again. He was wet and cold. A racket of machine-gun fire broke out in front, among a haze of distant flares. A red rocket soared up; the British guns behind and on either side—he knew they

were eighteen-pounders—stabbed whitely, each flash recording
a photograph around him. At last they halted at some ruins,
where guides were waiting. This was Beaucourt, he learned.
Guns, ammunition boxes, water cans, rations in sandbags were
unloaded; a few whispered words with Hobart, the mules turned
round in knee-deep mud, and quickened their pace on the way
back. It was two o'clock when he reached the picket line, to
find the tent erected; and looking in there, expecting to find
his stretcher-bed set up, with his flea-bag, he saw in the light of
his torch Sergeant Rivett lying on a ground-sheet, gently snoring.
Closing the tent, he went to the picket where a smell instantly
brought back a scene in the Brown Wood Line in 1914. The
guard was crouching over the fire-bucket flickering with yellow
flames of ration biscuits, a tin of which he had found in a cellar.

"I haven't seen biscuits burning like that since First Ypres.
I see you've been out before," said Phillip.

"Yes, sir." To Phillip's delight, he learned that the man had
been with the second battalion of the Gaultshires, at the first
battle of Ypres. "Did you ever know Captain West?"

"I did, sir. He was my company officer at Neuve Chapelle.
He was hit just before me, sir."

"We must have a talk sometime! What's your name? Well,
Nolan, give the drivers a hand at unharnessing, will you?" He
unsaddled Prince, and tied him next to the chestnut mare, the
gelding's usual neighbour on the rope.

When the mules were tied up and their rugs fastened, and
Prince also was rugged-up, he asked Nolan where the two drivers
were to sleep.

"I don't know, sir."

"Didn't the sergeant tell you?"

"No, sir."

"Come with me," said Phillip to the drivers, who wore their
ground-sheets over their shoulders, against the rain. He led
them to the tent. There he awakened the sergeant, who sat
up, rubbing his eyes. "Where do Smith and Miller sleep,
sergeant?"

"Eh? Oh! It's Mr. Maddison. I'll get up right away, sir,
and find a place for them."

"Isn't there a place already allocated for them?"

"No, sir. I understood that drivers usually make their own
bivouacs of their ground-sheets." The sergeant began to pull on
his long driver's boots.

"Well, these men are tired. They'd better come in the tent."

"Very good, sir."

"Do you know where my servant Barrow is?"

"I've no idea, sir."

Phillip turned away, and sought the picket. "Have you got your bivvy put up?"

"Yes, sir."

"I'll relieve you."

"Very good, sir. Lewis comes on at three o'clock, sir."

He had felt contempt at Sergeant Rivett's selfish, or un-imaginative attitude; but brooding over the fire-pail, he thought that his unawakened selfishness came from being the only son of a widow'd mother. He had not yet broken out of the soft-shelled maternal egg. He himself had been like that, until he had had the raggings which had cracked his conceit, or self-conception; and later been lucky to meet men like "Spectre" West and Jasper Kingsman. He would speak quietly to the sergeant in the morning; but after sleeping under the tarpaulin covering the baled hay, where he crept at the suggestion of Lewis, the ex-gipsy and cold shoer, and waking fresh into day-light, he thought it best to say nothing further. Besides, he himself should have seen that all the men were properly housed, before he had gone up the line.

That afternoon Barrow, his batman, helped by Nolan, built a sand-bagged shelter against a few square yards of standing wall. It was roofed with corrugated iron and covered with sandbags, and was finished by the time Phillip returned from exploring the British old front line and Noman's-land across to the German front line. He brought back a very small, beautifully made German portable stove. It was simplicity itself: a cylinder of sheet iron welded eight inches in diameter and eighteen inches high. There were fire-bars below and a door, a lid on top, and six feet of flexible piping. It was light to carry, weighing about ten pounds. With the pipe passing through a hole made in the sandbag wall, it was soon pouring out smoke, and radiating heat in the shelter, which was just long enough to take the stretcher-bed, which rested on old bomb boxes. There, until the company was relieved six days later, he lived warmly, enjoying the thought of being on active service, while his bank-balance was mounting up at home.

They went back to huts in Colincamps, where the rest was spent in gun drill by the sections, and by the transport in carting cases of bombs and trench-mortar shells to forward dumps. After three days they returned to the line. Serious fighting was over; the weather was now the enemy. It was December, and the dark of the year. Snow fell on the 19th. A gale followed, with chilling rain. The company came out of the line on Christmas Eve, reaching Colincamps in the small hours of Christmas Day. There had been talk of an extra special Christmas dinner for the men; really good rations were to be issued this year, said the A.S.C., with a surprise for each man. The good ration turned out to be frozen pork and dried vegetables. These, boiled up together, were followed by a small slice of gritty Christmas pudding, and then the surprise—a ration cracker bonbon for each man, containing a paper cap.

In the afternoon Phillip rode down to Albert. The leaning Virgin upon the campanile of the ruined red-brick basilica brought many memories, among them one of Father Aloysius, who had explained so much to him, and helped him to see life clearly against a background of death. But O, how lonely was life, after all.

Through the cleared streets of the town's square he passed, coming to the Bapaume road, a rising riband of grey mud red in patches from shell-holes filled by bricks, and ground by wheels and feet of men and beasts into liquid. Mules and horses were moving where once it would have been death to be seen in daylight. The transport animals had come across the battle-field tracks, their bellies looked as though swallows had been building nests under them, their ears were dejected, as slowly they walked back home to picket line and stable. He came to the old front line, now flattened and dragged about; littered, like the verges of the road, with rusty rifles, Lewis guns, helmets, shells, and other *débris*. Dismounting, and giving the reins to his groom, he walked, with clogs of loam clinging to his feet, about the old Noman's-land of Mash Valley, where he and his platoon had gone over in July. Little was recognisable. Lips of the mine craters were trodden down, paths wandered among thin stems of weeds which had sprung up during the past summer. Many of the dead still lay where they had fallen, each an almost level suggestion of something wasted into the soil, with relict bone and fragment of uniform covered with little heapings of earth thrown out by tunnelling rats. A few runs were still in use, judging by the smoothness of entry and exit.

A brass buckle; fragment of leather; skull with curls matted upon it; puttee coiled about leg bone; broken helmet from which sandbag covering had fretted away, leaving only the faded paint of divisional colours—everywhere the dead had merged with the ground. Where was Rose Avenue? He was lost, helplessly, in chalky waste. Ovillers was a disturbed whiteness, a frozen sea with thin, black masts. He moved on, searching. Pimm—Howells—Sergeant Jones—Marsh—Clodd—Hammond—Smith—Rybell—Johnson—the summer print of faces and places faded in the cold ruin of winter. Was this litter of burst and broken sandbags, collapsed and spilled, the trench where he had clambered out on that summer morning? This the wicker pigeon cage carried by Pimm, lying near a scatter of ribs, and, immediately by the handle, a cluster of tiny white finger and knuckle bones? Was that the torn-open petrol tin of water Pimm had been carrying when it seemed that a shell had burst near and thrown scalding water upon his own thigh? Was that his pelvis bone, in which three small coins, a franc and two 10-centime pieces, had been embedded by the shell explosion? He felt the scar in his buttock tingling as he stood beside what was left of Pimm; and closing his eyes, gave the emptiness of himself to prayer. Poor little terrified Howells, would he be identifiable by his bullet-proof vest, or had the phosphorus bombs which had caught fire while he carried them consumed bones and all to ash?

Thousands upon thousands of helmets lay among the grass bents and thistle stalks. Anguish rose in him; wherever he looked, to whatever horizon—eastwards, to north and south from where he stood, the grey wilderness extended an arc of sky-line fretted by stumps of trees, soil and subsoil burst up, to fall and be tossed up and down again, abandoned, fossilised under the cold shearing of wind, and the helpless pity of the rain. His mother's face came to him, while he thought that the spirit of a million unhappy homes had found its final devastation in this land of the loveless. He went back the way he had come, riding into a low purple sunset down to the valley of the Ancre, and up the track again to Colincamps.

It was freezing hard two days after Christmas, with ice an inch thick in shell-holes. Sergeant Rivett was reported by a military policeman when he was seen with his drivers trying to break the ice in order to water the mules. A chit from Division followed: *This practice is contrary to General Routine Orders and must cease forthwith.* The nearest drinking point, by canvas trough, was at Albert. It took some time to go there and return, thrice daily, on hard corrugated roads; while half the drivers faced an average of eight hours daily on fatigues. Then there were the nightly journeys with rations and S.A.A. which Phillip led, leaving the routine work of stables, forage-fetching, detailing of drivers, etc., to Rivett.

Two men were admitted to hospital during this period, one driver with pneumonia, the other with a ruptured appendix. One replacement driver came, a loose, uneasy fellow of about twenty-four, named Cutts. He had a bad history, according to Teddy Pinnegar. Cutts had run away in the division's first attack, and been sentenced to death by a General Court Martial. The sentence had been commuted to penal servitude for life, with suspension for the duration of the war. Good conduct might, it was understood, mitigate part of the sentence, perhaps reducing it to twelve years. Cutts had served in one of the territorial battalions, before being sent to a new unit.

The word *flabbergasted* came into Phillip's mind as he spoke to Cutts, with his staring brown eyes, curly forelock over forehead, large nose and loose mouth. He had about him the instinctive fear of a bullock entering the shambles. He spoke in jerks. Presumably he had no people: letters never came for him, and he wrote none.

Sergeant Rivett, at the other extreme, seemed to spend his time writing letters, apparently to everyone he had ever known. Phillip, censoring letters, came to know more about the men's backgrounds than about the men themselves. Rivett appeared to have imagination; he was, according to what he wrote, having a desperate war. Every "screed" was "penned" to the roar of guns (one, referring to a French attack "down south", spoke of the "sullen mutter of Creusot's seventy-fives"). Apparently Rivett saw daily what others missed: thrilling dog-fighting overhead. "Knights of the air" spun down in flames, far above the terrible conditions of trench warfare. One letter began, *Dear Sir,* and looking at the envelope, Phillip was startled to see that it was addressed to Major Anthony Downham, "A" Mess, Machine Gun Training Centre, Grantham. It gave a description of the burden of his work, then stated, somewhat mysteriously, "things out here have to be seen to be believed", before concluding with respectful good wishes for the New Year.

Most of the drivers' letters were simple, laconic, uninformative.

The war and wintry conditions were accepted mentally; no
writer expressed his inner thoughts. Like himself in 1914, they
did not dare to form their real thoughts into coherency, any more
than they dared to think of death. Their letters home were
almost bare, ending with the phrase, *in the pink*. "Here's hoping
you're in the pink, as I am." How did it originate, *in the pink*?
Of course, the pink of condition.

Even when the hard weather had turned drivers' faces and
hands blue, they were still in the pink.

Frost, turning mud to stone, brought different anxieties.
Apart from the extreme slowness of the mules picking their
way upon miniature Alpine ranges and frozen lakes, and despite
the strenuous work by Lewis, the company shoer, in roughing
the shoes of the animals, there was always the chance of one
slipping and breaking a leg. Also, howitzer shells would burst
on impact instead of boring deep into mud.

The strange thing was that, with the coming of frost, no heavy
stuff fell in the valley. Except for whizzbangs, all that came over
was an occasional armour-piercing naval shell, searching for the
British 15-inch naval gun on its multiple-bogey carriage. About
the course of this shell there was some speculation. The scoring
sound of its passage high overhead arrived simultaneously with
a brown and yellow fountain in Albert; immediately afterwards
there was a little *pop*, followed later by the crash of the shell
exploding. There were several theories about the little *pop*
which came down from the sky, followed by the scoring sound
heard at the very moment the shell exploded a mile away. One
was that the air above opened before the shell, and then clapped
back, as when a bullet, passing by one's head, cracked in the air.
Others said that the report of the gun firing in Bapaume station
arrived behind the shell, carried by suction. Or, the shell
travelled faster than sound, it arrived before it was heard passing
over. Phillip wondered if the report of the gun firing was dragged
in the swirling air behind the shell; but no-one seemed to know
the answer.

What was certain was that Fritz was pulling out his heavies
and going north to Arras, where Third Army was said to be
preparing a push against the Vimy Ridge.

A thaw set in at the end of the month. A full moon shone over
the marshes, where the cries of wildfowl came eerily, in that it
seemed strange that any life could remain among the charred
poplar stumps. Rain fell heavily, prisoners with blue circles of

cloth let into their *feld grau* uniforms daily scraped tons of mud off Station Road. They saluted smartly all British officers. Soon the mud was embanked six feet high beside the road, embedding dead mules and horses, shattered limbers, rifles, the rubbish of uniform and equipment. Snow fell out of the north-east, whirling over the wastes of the Somme battlefield, covering all with its white shroud, endusked in places by the black bursts of German shells searching for batteries. After the snow it was a world of clear sky, white earth, and austere sunshine. For a while desolation was shrouded. Up-ended mules were white mounds marked by four posts with tiny frost-glitters. Black was white—burnt poplar stumps, charred aeroplane frames, old corpses with faces like pickled walnuts were clowns, with caps of snow covering frozen hair. White was also black, where shells had burst and left small craters bordered with stains of smoke.

The snow had melted when frost struck hard, solidifying earth and water. Drivers crouched over their mules, beating icy mitten'd hands, with fingers annealed blue to crystallised reins. Phillip scrounged a roll of new cocoanut netting, one of a pile on a dump in Englebelmer, wondering what it was for. Back at the picket line, they cut it up to provide extra bedding for the drivers. Then, noticing that some donks had lowered an ear, sign of exhaustion, he scrounged another roll, making of it extra blankets for them; only to find that most of the mules had spent the small hours in eating one another's coverings. Some already had the habit of gnawing the rugs of their neighbours, in the nervous misery of the nights.

Sergeant Rivett told him that the cocoanut screens were for concealment from view. They were to be strung on posts, to hide traffic movement on roads under observation.

"The French have been doing it, I hear. They call it camouflage, sir. I did hear that enquiries have been made about the two missing rolls from the dump."

Without warning, as before, the Assistant Director of Veterinary Services appeared. Phillip saw him, from his tent, looking at the ragged remains of what Nolan had called the Donks Spring Suitings.

"What are your mules doing?" asked Major Pickles.

"Resting, at the moment, sir."

"Where did that camouflage screening come from?"

"It's in case of aircraft spotting them, sir."

"I said, where did it come from?"

"I found it on Station Road, sir."

At that moment Jimmy let out a bray, and began to eat its neighbour's tattered shawl. "I think they like the oil in the cocoanut fibre, sir."

"You don't say?"

"Sir, about the rations. We can draw only six pounds of oats per day for our mules and horses. We're down on hay, too. I can't guarantee to keep them in condition——"

"Who asked you to guarantee anything? In any case, the rations are short because a ship hit a mine and blocked Boulogne harbour. You'll have to do the best you can with what you've got. No, that screening won't hurt them. As you say, there's oil in it. But that's no authority for stealing from dumps, mind!"

"Sir, nothing was further from my mind!"

"Eh? Well, watch your step, young man!"

When a mule lowered both ears, it had given up. It stood awhile in dejection, nosebag and net of hay unwanted. In the black night it sank down, its eyes in the morning were glazed. He shot three prone mules above the eyes with his revolver, while the drivers stood by, mute with their own dejected life.

Later he wondered how this had got to the ears of the A.D.V.S., who appeared in the afternoon and demanded to know why the sick animals had not been sent to the Mobile Veterinary Station at Albert. Phillip said he had not heard of the Mobile Station. The A.D.V.S. then rated him for allowing his mules to develop mud rash. When he had gone, Phillip looked up the causes of mud-rash in his book: "Debility following on over-work and generally poor conditions, such as prolonged exposure to inclement weather." The cure—rest, warmth, bran mashes, linseed in feeds, dry covered standings. Where could he buy linseed? Dare he try a lorry-hop to Amiens? And incidentally get a decent dinner at the Godbert?

When a temporary thaw came a loaded limber stuck fast. Several dismounted drivers failed to shift it, heaving at wheel-spokes, with two pairs of mules tugging. Pushing behind, Phillip added a hundredweight or so of mud to his person. Extra pairs were hooked in: eventually ten pairs failed to move it, now sunk to the axles, as a concerted pull by the weak animals was imposs-ible. The limber had to be abandoned.

The next day, a company runner came down with a written

message from Captain Hobart, telling Phillip to go up and see him. He took his groom with him. Morris was an undersized Cockney youth who looked as he did because he had been starved in childhood—projecting teeth, prematurely set bones, slight curvature of spine and bandiness from rickets—large head on narrow shoulders, permanently reflective eyes. He had been a carter's lad before the war, sleeping with the horses for warmth and love of them. In spite of his nut-like brittleness, Morris was strong, his spirit urging him on where others might hang back.

With Morris following on Jimmy the mule, Phillip trotted up Railway Road, passing its junction with Station Road from Beaumont Hamel. From here the road rose to higher ground which had been the second line of German resistance in the recent battle. It led through the ruins of Beaucourt, and past the track, once a country lane, leading through a valley to Pusieux-au-Mont. The way, now open to observing eyes in the east, led to the Baillescourt Farm line. Here Phillip handed over his horse to Morris, telling him to return and wait for him in the Pusieux Road valley. Alone, he walked up a narrow sunken track which he imagined had formerly been used by farm imple-ments and waggons coming out of Baillescourt Farm, the ruins of which lay on the edge of the slope leading, on the other side of Railway Road, down to the former water-meadows of the Ancre.

The track climbed away at right angles to Station Road, its western bank showing, every ten yards or so, the rectangular entrances of dug-outs, each about three feet wide by five high. As he came to the skyline, Phillip saw a group of figures wearing cap comforters and woollen scarves above greatcoats standing hands in pockets in a sand-bagged emplacement dug out from the gulley. "Darky" Fenwick greeted him, his dark eyes lighting up with pleasure.

"The skipper's gone to see the brigade major, and Teddy's visiting the sections. He'll be back about three. Come and see my Love Nest."

Down into clumsy narrow darkness, where a struck match and a candle flame seemed to make the close stale atmosphere a thicker fluid black. "I thought mebbe thee'd like a wee drap, Sticks." They drank whiskey and chlorinated soda-water. Tiers of beds, wooden-posted and with mattresses of wire-netting, took dim shape around him. Outlines of galleries were seen but to dissolve at once in solid blackness, which seemed to give off a smell of rancid fat and something else he could not determine.

"Aye, 'tis in all the German dug-outs," explained Fenwick. "All Weather Jack says 'tis from Jerry eating sausages and smoking too many damp Dutch cigars."

"Well, thanks for the drink, Darky. While I'm waiting for the skipper, I think I'll do a bit of exploring."

"Look around Pimple, 'tis an interesting sight. Some war artist ought to paint it."

He walked to the highest point of the plateau, for the view. Here the waterless shell-craters looked to be as fresh as when they had burst out of the dark brown soil, except for one difference. Lying lip to lip, the holes, six to eight feet deep and with sloping sides, each held its relic of privacy and meditation. Here had come solitary man to escape from the world as he knew it, to be alone for a while, and ease himself of constricting thought. Here each shell-hole had its offering, with an appearance of having been placed precisely as pollen in the cells of a bees-comb. A few moments of freedom, of dissolved self-in-servitude, for the private soldier who had none of the comforts of the officer, or of the officer's escape from his private self through responsibility.

As the contour line descended, so did water begin to lie in the craters. He saw in front of him a slight mound, a stalkless mushroom of earth, which might have been the part-levelled tumulus of some ancient chieftain. A score of dead Germans lay sprawled around The Pimple, down into which went the shaft of a dug-out. Others lay in shell-craters half-filled with crimson water. He decided the colour was not due to blood, for other craters, without corpses, held water of the same hue. Every pocket of trouser and jacket had been either pulled out or razor cuts made to get at the contents. None wore equipment or had carried rifles: a massacre of surrendered prisoners had taken place. All had young faces. When he got back he asked what had happened. Fenwick said it was done before they came up, but as the Guards, who never took prisoners, hadn't been in the line there, it must have been the work of rookies enjoying their first taste of heroism.

"We're fighting a system, which keeps down the working man, an' I believe t' working man everywhere in the world should have a proper chance. We must smash militarism," he said sombrely, as he puffed his pipe. "I don't believe in injustice to

prisoners. Such acts prolong 'atred. 'All Weather Jack' agrees
with me. He's a real gentleman, money or no money. Ah, here
he comes." Footfalls echoed down the steep wooden steps.

Captain Hobart said, "I'm afraid the horse doctor's got it in
for you, Sticks. The Brigadier wants to see you about those three
mules you had to destroy. Fortunately the report forwarded
to Brigade by Division was couched in pretty strong terms, which
reveal well that the A.D.V.S. is no friend of yours. I've done
what I could to put things right with the brigade major. You
know where he hangs out? About a hundred yards up the
Pusieux road, on the left in an old Boche dug-out at the foot of
the steep escarpment you'll see there. Let's have a spot before
you go."

Escarpment, it sounded like a brown cliff of sandstone. He
asked what it meant.

"A precipitous side of a hill or valley. You see a natural escarpment on the Wiltshire downs, where weather has eroded a cattle
path, and chalk and flints have fallen. Keep smilin', and tell the
General what happened. They were goners when you gave them
the *coup de grâce*."

On the way back whizzbangs shrieked down and spirted up
earth beside the road. He walked on. The general was sitting at a
table just behind a blanket hung over a door-frame with broken
hinges. Someone had taken the door for firewood. The room had
been the telephonists' room in a German brigade head-quarters,
judging by the panel on one wall. White-haired, quiet-voiced,
ruddy of face, with impersonal blue eyes, the fifty-five-year-old
Brigadier pushed the report across the table. He himself had been
up before the Corps Commander, when one of his battalions, in
the line for the first time a fortnight before the machine-gun
company had joined his brigade, had left in so disillusioned, otherwise exhausted a condition that some of the feebler troops had
thrown away their rifles, Lewis guns, and equipment. The battalion commander had already gone home "sick"; the brigadier
wondered when he would be "stellenbosched". He was what
was called by younger men a Dugout: a colonel in the Boer War,
he had retired in 1912. As for the Major-General commanding
division, he had come from Gallipoli, which had been a "poor
show"; while, senior to the Divisional General, the Corps Commander felt that his Army Commander, a thrusting cavalryman
who in two years had advanced from a brigade to an army, might
at any moment render him *degommé* for lack of aggressive spirit.

Phillip's eyes skated over the typed page.

This officer has repeatedly ignored General Routine Orders, culminating in arbitrary and unnecessary destruction of miltary property at a time when submarine sinkings of mule boats——

He read no further, but waited with lowered eyes for what was coming, trying to appear calm. Was it to be a court martial? The Brigadier barely looked at him.

"What is your side of the matter?"

"Sir?"

"Why did you shoot three of your mules?"

"If I hadn't shot them, sir, they would have been dead in half an hour. They were beat, sir. We tried to get them up, but they wouldn't move. I think they had pneumonia, sir."

"You should report sickness or wounds without delay to your officer commanding, so that the appropriate action can be taken in time." He was dismissed.

Followed by the thin figure of Morris, peaky upon Jimmy the mule, Phillip walked his horse down Railway Road, feeling jubilant. The mud was hardening. A purple sun went down upon a scene soon to become rock.

That night the boots of Cutts, the first man on picket duty, froze to the ground as he tried to fan with his helmet yellow heatless flames from sodden poplar logs picked up in the marsh. Phillip, returning from taking rations, fell asleep before his stove and found on awakening that the toecaps of his boots were brittle and cracked.

The next day the drivers' red-rimmed eyes ran with tears that glazed upon their cheek-bones. Iron leggings of wheel-drivers—those nearest the limber whose right legs were protected from being crushed against the pole—caused some pain; finger-tips stuck to the iron when touched. Through the opaque valley air the rolling wheels came loud and continuous under the pall of frost, which dulled the glitter of stars and made milky the distant flares. It was Sergeant Rivett's turn to take up rations. Phillip could not keep warm on his camp bed; there was not enough fuel for his stove and the picket's fire-bucket, so his sand-bag shelter was cold. He spent an hour walking about to keep warm, and then, seeing a light on the hillside—he had walked to Station Road—he went up, to find a party of Canadian railway engineers in a hut with a roaring fire, drinking rum. Soon he was sitting

among smiling faces; some time later he staggered home, and had
the luck to meet the ration limber returning from the line. He got
in and lay in the back of the vehicle, on what seemed to be an
endless bumpy journey, careless and happy.

Sergeant Rivett brought to him, one morning after the post
had arrived, a driver with fixed staring eyes. A letter from home
had told him that his wife and two small children had been killed
in the explosion at Silvertown, the Thames-side chemical factory
of Brunner, Mond & Co. Acres of small houses had been
flattened. Driver Tallis had one son, of five years, left; and the
little boy was crying all the time for his father. Would Mr.
Maddison, sir, forward his application for compassionate leave to
the Officer Commanding?

"I'll go right away. I am very sorry, Tallis. Of course the
police will have to verify this, you know. It is the usual rule."

"I have already advised Driver Tallis to write to the police at
Silvertown, and ask them to send verification at once to Captain
Ho-bart," said Rivett.

"Well done. Good man. But I think it would be as well for it to
come officially to the Officer Commanding, sergeant. Anyway,
I'll go at once to the orderly room, and see that a wire is sent
off."

Three days later Driver Tallis left for home—or what was left of
it—on six days' compassionate leave.

Paper orders arrived every day. The most important was that
mules were to be used as pack animals wherever possible, over
unmetalled tracks. Thereafter was some easement for the donks,
and warmth for dismounted drivers, one leading an animal. Mule
robberies occurred; lines were raided by other units, to make good
losses and so avoid strafing by the Blue-banded Dogsbody, as the
A.D.V.S. was called. Two mules were lost one night, one of them
Jimmy. But the tall and very hairy grey Jimmy was not easily
concealed; and four evenings later he was seen to be walking
contentedly in an R.F.A. string of mixed mules and horses, with a
wooden box containing four 18-pounder shells strung through
each stirrup leather—improvised pack equipment. Phillip
stopped the man leading Jimmy, saying, "That's my mule! That's
Jimmy! Hand him over." The man was embarrassed: what
would he do with the shell boxes? Phillip said he didn't care;
Jimmy had been scrounged, the company mark, HO, was clipped

on his flank. So the big grey mule came back to the company, as quietly as he had left it, and as though with complete indifference to what unit he worked with.

A stray dog came into the lines, to accept many caresses and lumps of bully beef. The men said it was a German dog, because it had one blue and one brown eye. Little Willie was as un-demonstrative as Jimmy the Mule, and remained on the stretcher-bed before the stove until a thaw came. Then, apparently seeking nicer food, it was next seen riding in an A.S.C. lorry in Albert, looking out of the window beside the driver, and licking its chops. It rode there for a week or so, and then, according to the driver, transferred itself to the Canadian Railway Engineers, for a diet of tinned salmon.

About this time an order was sent that transport officers were to supervise the making and planting of vegetable gardens adjacent to their lines.

"What do you think we could plant in this mud, Nolan?"

"Well, sir, I hardly know. We might try rice in the swamps down there, or watercress."

"How about toadstools? We can present then to the Blue-banded Dogsbody."

Pinnegar's comment was, "That's the sort of tripe you'd expect, after they've given the Master-baker at Rouen the Military Cross!"

One morning he took two limbers to Englebelmer, for the task of moving boxes of bombs and small ammunition from the dump at Vitemont to another beside the cemetery at Auchonvillers. They passed a windmill on the right of the road, where the ground stood high. It was now the fourth week of February. The frost having lifted, in places the wind had dried out patches of metalling on the road. At twilight, having delivered the load, and when he was about to turn round, M'Kinnell, an old and steady Scots driver with two sons serving in the B.E.F., pointed his whip to the east, where the new moon was rising over the old battlefield, and said, "Yon fires, have you seen them?" Nolan, the other driver, remarked, "Jerry seems to be having some fun over there, sir." Three fires were visible in the far distance.

When they reached Englebelmer more fires were speckling the country lying to the east under the night; and on returning to the transport lines in Mesnil, lit by the flashes of a bombardment, he found Teddy Pinnegar waiting with the news that the Germans were evacuating their forward trenches, and the transport must be ready to pull out at four hours' notice.

M'Kinnell and Nolan had brought back a good load of firewood. Phillip and Teddy sat before the stove, and had a drink or two of whiskey before they went up the line together, both on foot, leading the limbers with rations and ammunition. The road was lit by blue and white flashes.

"The gunners are pooping off all the shells they can, before the move forward," said Teddy.

The next morning the transport lines were advanced about a mile to beyond Hamel. The new camp was in a gully which had lain in Noman's-land until the battle of 13 November. There a tank was stuck, bellied in the ground, its guns taken away. Phillip moved in with his stove, the carpenter making a frame to take his bed. There he slept, beside the stove, which burned dull red near a rack of 6-pounder shells, which, however, did not explode. He found them there after a week; and deciding that they were by now acclimatised, left them alone.

About this time he began to wonder if it was poverty and suffering which brought out character, and made fine men. There was Daddy M'Kinnell, as the drivers called him. Upright, faithful, dutiful, polite but never obsequious: a man nearer fifty than forty, who had once done him the honour of showing him a photograph of himself and family—in two rows; himself and "Mother" almost deadly serious; the three boys grinning, wearing their Sunday best suits with celluloid collars and elastic bow ties, their heads close-cropped against nits. The boys having grown up, Daddy M'Kinnell had joined the Army.

At the beginning of March heavy howitzers were being pulled along Railway Road by tractors. On the 10th there was a dawn bombardment; towards noon prisoners came back, hatless and helmetless, in loose grey uniforms and knee boots, shorn heads, some with beards and spectacles, shuffling along covered with mud, looking (except for beards, spectacles, and cropped heads) like the unemployed he remembered at home, about 1906.

Rations and ammunition that night were taken up by twelve pack mules, to a mile beyond Baillescourt farm, where stood the remains of a village of shattered walls and rubble heaps which already had its own mysterious life underground in cellars, judging by the candle rays which twinkled at road level, and the tinkle of a gramophone heard as they halted awhile amidst other strings of pack animals waiting anxiously lest shells fall upon the con-gestion. At last they could move on, and following the guide, turned left-handed to Beauregard Dovecote, an abandoned strong point on the edge of rising ground, as he saw from the occasional gun-flashes on low clouds. A guide led them past a fork in the lane, when gas shells began to pass over with soft noises of *whooe-er whoo-er, pop pop*, to fall into what the guide said was the Brickfield. They sounded like phosgene, which had a delayed action on the heart. Should he order box-respirators, hanging at the alert across greatcoat chests, to be put on? Seeing was already difficult; there were no Very lights. He wished he had not brought Prince, whom he was leading, when 4.2s began to spout smoky-red fans two hundred yards across the Brickfield. Where was the ration party meeting them? The guide then said he thought he had lost the way. Rifle bullets cracked past. Phillip put the pack animals under Nolan and telling him to wait there went on with the guide to find the front line. They came suddenly upon a post. "Who are yer?"

"Ration party."

It was one of the company guns. They had overshot the dump by a quarter of a mile, where Beauregard Alley began at the northern horn of Miraumont. He apologised to Teddy Pinnegar, who said, "That's all very well, but where the hell have you been all the time?"

The shelling began again. He thrust himself forward into it, with a sort of sneer. Who cared? The men followed. The shelling stopped. At 1 a.m. they were back, without loss, at the picket line, three miles down Railway Road. Entering Tank Hotel, as the men called it, he found that his shirt and tunic were soaked with sweat. His servant had kept the stove going, and the heat, together with hot tea containing rum, soon hung down the old eye-lids.

Three days later the Germans had abandoned their second position on rising ground covering Loupart Wood to Achiet-le-Petit. A further bombardment lit the dawn. More prisoners shuffled back, as the transport moved forward in daylight through Miraumont while bearded, turban'd, dark-skinned cavalrymen passed them, pennons on lances scarcely fluttering in the windless air. The Bengal Lancers! He felt the romance of the scene: perhaps it was open warfare at last!

In a hollow of the road where the Ancre stream had been diverted to flood the village cellars, railway sleepers had been laid. As he rode over the moving baulks, he saw a hand sticking up between two sleepers. A Yorkshire soldier among others repairing the road laughingly put the handle of a broken spade between the waxen fingers, saying, "Now then, Jerry, get on wi' it; no bluudy skrimshankin' 'ere!"

The road went on up rising ground beyond the village, and passing a culvert in the railway embankment, Phillip saw where the stream had been dammed. "I don't care for that!" remarked Hobart. "Think of the trout that will be left high and dry!" It was strange to see green fields again, torn by only a few shell-craters. They passed through the brick-and-rafter heaps of Achiet-le-Petit, and he slept that night near the blown-up railway station, sharing a bell tent with Jack Hobart, warmed by the German stove, its pipe sticking out of the door flap.

Before going to sleep, he wrote in his *Charles Lett's Self-Opening Pocket Diary and Note Book for 1917* by candle-light, *Heard a chiff-chaff in Miraumont, among some willows.*

"Here's *Comic Cuts*," said Hobart, tossing over the latest CORPS SUMMARY OF INTELLIGENCE, which had just come in, marked *CONFIDENTIAL: Not to be issued to Commanders of lower rank than Battalion, Battery, and Field Company Commanders, and not to be taken into Front Line trenches.*

1. The enemy continued his withdrawal throughout the night of 17/18th March, evacuating COURCELLES, DOUCHY, AYETTE, GOMIECOURT, and ERVILLERS. These villages are now occupied by our troops. The Corps on our right have now extended their line from FREMICOURT . . . to SAPIGNIES, and have reached MORY. The Corps on our left . . . ADINFER WOOD . . . to FICHEUX . . . no opposition. . . . See attached map.

2. Owing to the rapidity of the enemy's retreat, it has been difficult to keep touch . . . no information to hand of the dispositions of his main troops, but his nearest line is part of the HINDENBURG LINE or SIEGFRIED STELLUNG, running in a S.E. direction East of St. MARTIN-sur-COJEUL and CROISELLES through BULLECOURT. Mobile cavalry patrols have been seen on the road between ERVILLERS and ST. LEGER.

3. A very severely wounded prisoner of the 3rd Coy. 55th R.I.R. (220 Division) was taken at QUESNOY FARM early this morning. From his statements it appears that the 220th Div. came into RANSART area on 28th February. He was ignorant of the order of battle, but said the 207th Regt. was on his left. As this

prisoner was in a dying condition and half unconscious from
morphia, his statements should be taken with reserve.

But a dying man would instinctively tell the truth: it is all he
has to hold on to, thought Phillip.

4. Fires are reported this afternoon in scores of villages in the East.
    Practically all cross-roads, level crossings, entrances to and exits
    from villages have been blown up.
    The rails of all railways have been torn from the sleepers.
    A prisoner states that orders were given to poison all wells.
    The well at BARLEUX was found to be poisoned with arsenic.
5. LATE INFORMATION. ALL villages west of SIEGFRIED
    STELLUNG are in flames.

Jack was asleep, and snoring gently. He turned down the wick
of the lamp. The night was quiet. He could not sleep in the
rushing silence. Then through the moonless dark came the cries of
flighting mallard, flying west to the peaceful marshes of the Ancre.
They would be nesting soon, he thought. For birds, the spring
meant love—for men, the spring offensive, and the kiss of bullets.

Chapter 7

HINDENBURG LINE

In a drift of sleet they arrived next day upon wide and gently
rolling downland east of the Arras-Bapaume road. Jack Hobart
asked Phillip where he would like to put up his picket line, saying
that the guns were to cover the Brigade front, behind the infantry
screens now about a mile and a half to the east.

"About here, d'you think, Sticks? The guns will be eight
hundred yards in front of you, then. Right, carry on, old boy."

They pitched tents near the source of a small brook, which
Phillip saw from his map to be the headwater of the Sensée river.
Each officer had been given half a dozen cloth-back Trench Maps,
with all German positions, and wire, meticulously marked on
them in red. They were printed in sections of large rectangles
marked by capital letters. Each rectangle was divided into
squares of 1,000 yards, and numbered; and each square was sub-
divided into four smaller squares, about the size of postage stamps,

marked *a*, *b*, *c*, and *d*. Thus a position could be pin-pointed to within a few yards, and found by cross-reference.

The sleet which had fallen as they were leaving Achiet-le-Grand gave way to rain; they sat dry and happy in a shelter made of posts and rails and covered by a large black tarpaulin "won" by Phillip from the A.S.C. forage dump in Achiet station yard. The mess table made at Ascheux was still a home comfort, with the canvas armchairs. As usual, Jules made good use of the rations. Initialled whiskey bottles stood on the table with the gramophone, while everyone read letters just arrived from the post-dump at Sapignies.

When the rain stopped, Phillip told Sergeant Rivett to let the drivers and grooms graze their animals in pairs upon the grass and clover all around them. By the look of it, the place had been grazed by sheep, before the withdrawal of the Germans. But a short bite, as Jack called it, had grown since; and by the way the mules and horses cropped, they were enjoying the smell and taste of their new surroundings.

Phillip accompanied Hobart when the guns were sited.

They were placed under the higher contour lines, so that the gunners would have their targets against the skyline, should the Germans make a surprise attack. Also, being placed lower than the skyline, they would not come under direct observation from the Germans, before such an attack. He marked the gun positions on his map 57C N–W, on which was printed in the right top corner, *Trenches corrected to 5–2–17.* There was a later edition, *corrected to 4–2–17,* of the country to the east, which took in the Siegfried Stellung, the complicated trench systems threading red through it, like the wandering veins on an inflamed eyeball under a magnifying glass.

Phillip had an idea that the Germans might sally forth from their great new underground fortress, in a series of lightning raiding columns, to destroy with gun-cotton slabs all the many batteries of guns and ammunition dumps which were coming into position before the Hindenburg Line; they might even drive through and take thousands of prisoners. If anything happened to Hobart, Pinnegar would be in command, and he did not trust Teddy, he was too easy-going, damning the staff as "Spectre" West had done, but in general, not particular, terms. If the Germans had prepared a huge trap, and open warfare began, backwards across the old Somme battlefield, of which they knew every inch . . . their submarines were sinking ships faster than they could be built, Russia was just about out of the war, so it might be a case of one terrific burst to win the war, of another British retreat from Mons, but this time to the coast.

The gun-sites having been marked, he felt his mind to be neater, and returned with Hobart to camp, to write up his diary, and enter up his pay for March—£13-3-6 @ 11/6 a day, plus £3-17-6 field allowance @ 2/6 a day; add to this £10 half-quarterly pay from the office. Not bad, £27-1-0 in one month!

Under a shining sun, he began to feel that the war was remote, that life was enjoyable, that he wouldn't have missed any of it, the war was a tremendous adventure! The Ancre Valley was a remote memory. Green downland extended all around; the mules and horses had the run of fine, open pasture, unmarked by war. They grazed eagerly upon the growing grass, their ears upright, eyes clear, coats smoothing to glossiness, no longer staring. Patches of grey skin eroded by mud rash were growing new hair. The drivers, too, had lost the haggard, pinched look which had seemed normal in the mud.

"Have ye seen yon Alleyman graveyard?" said M'Kinnell one morning, as he groomed a mule. "'Tis a bonny sight, I'm thinking."

Phillip went over to look at it. The small cemetery was laid out with gravel paths lined by low box-wood hedges in an intricate pattern, with beds of pansies, red daisies, and other low plants which later would flower. About this time *The Daily Trident*, which arrived four days late, was making much of a story, with the aid of a Belgian cartoonist named Raemaekers, of German dead being collected from the battlefields and tied "in bundles of four", to be sent in open trucks to German factories, the fat of the cadavers being used in the manufacture of high explosive. Here in the wide and shallow bowl of upland grazing was a cemetery with half a dozen carved headstones, five of them for Germans and one for an Englishman who had died of wounds. Looking around, he saw a solitary grave about a quarter of a mile away. Walking there, he saw that it was enclosed within posts and wire. A broken four-bladed wooden propeller stood at its head. Flowers bloomed on the mound. *Here rests in God a brave unknown English flier who fell in battle July 14, 1916.*

Another afternoon, riding around the countryside, he came across a large cemetery at Ablaizanville. It had wrought-iron gates, behind which, set in turf, were cream-coloured stones and carved monuments, both Germans and British lying together. A still larger cemetery at the edge of the village was set with wooden crosses, and some of the British shells had fallen among them, disclosing long leather boots and grey tunics, and what they contained. Father ought to see it; then he might cease to be held in the mental barbed wire of armchair hate. He thought to write a letter to *The Daily Trident*: but would they allow it, as they had started the Corpse Factory stuff?

He picked a few pansies from the graves, and sent some home to his mother in a letter, others to Mrs. Neville.

During a further exploration, he came to a sandy escarpment above a sunken road. Seeing that a tunnel had been made in the face of the cliff, which was only a few feet high, and obviously filled in, he dug with his hands and pulled out a wooden box about thirty inches square and ten deep. It had rope handles and a clip fastener. Inside were small black bombs, each in its compartment, like packed eggs. In another rack were the detonators, which could be screwed in place of a cap holding in black grains of ammonal. He filled up one, pulled the ring, and flung the bomb away. It burst after a few seconds. The box would be the very thing in which to carry souvenirs, so he put the bombs, together with the detonators, in one heap, fitted up one, pulled it, and after placing it on the heap, lay down in the sunken road. Explosion after explosion cracked unseen; when he looked up again, he saw the A.D.V.S. approaching, followed by a groom.

"What's the game now, eh?" asked the Blue-banded Dogsbody.

"Destroying a booby trap, sir."

When they had gone by, he hid the box, lest someone pinch it for firewood. He would pick it up later, when passing with a limber.

Life in Clover Valley, as All Weather Jack called it, continued into April. On the 3rd news came, via Brigade, that the United States of America had entered the war. They heard it with little interest. "About time, too," remarked Pinnegar. "The Yanks have made a lot of money out of the war, lent a lot all round as well, and don't want to lose it."

Life went on evenly: fetching and delivering rations, ammunition, and fodder; carrying out divisional transporting jobs; inspecting the feet, mouths, and general condition ("top-hole") of animals; harness, saddlery, boots and equipment of drivers daily to be oiled, soaped, polished; metal-work burnished. He left the routine work to Sergeant Rivett, and went farther afield on Black Prince, followed by Morris riding Jimmy the grey mule.

Once, after passing a cross-roads, on sudden impulse he set off at a gallop over the grass, followed by the groom who had managed to kick Jimmy into a canter; they had gone about two hundred yards when there was a tremendous explosion, and looking back, he saw a yellow-brown mushroom-shaped cloud rising behind them. A time-action mine had blown a deep crater at the cross-roads which later was railed around, lest waggons, limbers, and guns skirting its edge, topple over. It added to the spice of living.

"Look at this newspaper tripe," said Pinnegar. "Here's the *Trident* talking about the 'Hun-like barbaric destruction' of evacuated villages and 'spiteful' cutting-down of trees; but all the Germans have done is to make a *glacis* in front of their new fortress-line, to give clear observation for their balloons, and to cause us to expend labour and material on the building of new billets, storehouses, divisional and corps headquarters, railways, and the boring of artesian wells, which is being done everywhere. Utter bilge!"

Phillip thought that poor old Father would believe every word of it; newspapers were a kind of poisoning of the mind. After the war he would damn-well clear off, and avoid getting into the same rut, even if it meant never seeing England again: but his heart quailed at the idea.

There were some plots of coppice-wood growing in places upon the downland, planted as covert for pheasants, Hobart told him. Some wrecked huts lay about in one coppice, and among them stood what appeared to be a splendid sentry-box painted in broad diagonal bands of the German imperial colours, white, black, and red. He approached this gingerly: there were stories of all kinds of booby-traps in the area, pianos in dugouts with a particular key wired to buried explosives—someone playing *If I were the only boy in the world, and*—roa-ar!—it would be a world entirely of girls henceforward! The sentry box looked to be an obvious booby-trap. Probably opening the door would set off a stick bomb. The door was a-jar; he pushed it with a long stick, while crouching down. Nothing happened. It was a private latrine box, let into the ground by four legs. While he and Morris were pulling it out of the ground, the dog with eyes of two colours appeared casually out of the scrub, and allowed itself to be greeted as an old friend. It followed them back to camp, returning with Potts driving a half-limber to fetch the privy, which was much admired when set up near the officers' tents. It must have

belonged to an *oberst* at least, said Hobart—"And a very useful
addition it is, especially now that these blasted north-west winds
have brought back the sleet!"

During the fetching of the magnificent privy, Phillip had sat
on the grass and smoked a cigarette with Tallis, asking him about
his little boy. Apparently the child doted on his father, the more
so for the terror of having seen his mother and sisters killed in the
Silvertown explosion. "I don't mind going west for myself, sir, it's
the little lad that worries me, if anything 'appens to me."

"I might try to get you posted to home service, Tallis."

"Please, sir, I didn't mean that. I'm all right with the boys
here, sir. Only if my Phil——"

"I understand. If anything happens to you, I'll look after him,
Tallis."

It was strange to realise, when he looked in his note-book, that it
was nearly Easter. That afternoon the company moved its transport line forward. Following the course of the brook, descending
under the skyline, they came to Mory. There, to Phillip's uneasiness, Pinnegar put up the tents on a grassy field at the highest
level, the 110 contour on the map. Surely that would be visible to
the Alleyman?

The afternoon turned out sunny, and the mess table was laid
for tea in the open. While they were sitting there a rattle came
down from the sky, and looking up, Phillip saw a lumbering
B.E.2c, which had been droning in wide circles as it spotted for a
howitzer battery, dropping away as a small biplane dived past it.
The biplane zoomed, and climbed away into the sun, obviously
to try again. Meanwhile the slow old art-obs bus seemed to be
gliding down in a straight line. Then across the sky flew a small
sturdy plane, which began circling as it climbed away from the
scout biplane which had fired. "It's got black crosses!" said
Hobart, looking through his binoculars. The enemy plane, now
above the gliding machine, turned over and dived upon it,
whereupon the other scout came down vertically in pursuit.
Phillip saw the hair-like smoke of tracer bullets. The machine, a
Sopwith Triplane, missed the German scout, and falling fast, just
managed to pull out of its dive, while almost touching the earth.
The German pulled up also, but a hundred yards above, so that
they saw the black crosses at the end of its wings. Rifles were being
fired at it; it turned over and came down at the row of tents,
firing at them with its machine gun. It passed over the tea-party

at the table so close that Phillip could see the black leather helmet
of the pilot, and his face looking down. He waved a gloved hand,
then flew away east, about ten feet above the ground. The
B.E.2c meanwhile had continued its glide, and struck the ground,
turning on its nose. There it remained, soon to be surrounded by
soldiers. Word arrived, by way of Jules the chef, that the observer
had been killed while in the air, and the pilot hit through the
neck.

Having assured himself that they were being taken care of,
Hobart went on talking to Phillip about the day's foxhunting they
had had with the Brownlow. Phillip felt anxious, but concealed it,
even when there came the drone of a descending shell. It burst a
hundred yards from the tents. Phillip wondered what Jack
would do. He went on talking. Another shell—a 4.2 like the first
—groaned down and exploded. Two more followed at intervals,
the fourth fifty yards from the picket lines. Showing no concern,
Hobart went on talking. Splinters, thought Phillip, could do
some damage at fifty yards. The mules were bundling together,
some of the drivers were trying to calm them.

"I think I'll go and see if I'm wanted, skipper."

No animal had been hit. Sergeant Rivett was not to be seen.
Cutts, the driver who had replaced the one gone to hospital with
pneumonia, was standing about twenty yards away, held by the
arm of Nolan. Going to find out what was the matter, Phillip saw
he was slobbering at the lips. At that moment Sergeant Rivett
hurried up, his face staring with fear.

"I saw you slinking off, Cutts! You did that once before!"
he cried. "I know all about you, and if you don't take care
you won't be so lucky next time!"

Anger arose in Phillip: and with it the thought or self-portrait
of himself uttering involuntarily the words *Filthy beast* to the
Canadian's scornful 'dry goods clerk' who had got syphilis.
He checked himself; remained still within himself, impersonal,
as Sergeant Rivett turned to him, saluting, to say, "Sir, I wish
to report Cutts for dereliction of duty. I saw him leaving the
line when the first shell burst. I consider he was deserting his
post, sir, in the face of the enemy!"

"If you please, sir——" began Nolan, but Sergeant Rivett
cut him short. "Speak to the officer only when you are addressed!
Have I your permission to dismiss Nolan, sir?"

"Very well, Sergeant Rivett."

When Nolan had saluted and gone, Phillip said, "How did

you know that Cutts had been sentenced to death before he
came to us?''

"He told me himself, sir, when he came. He has told many
of the drivers, too, sir. If you ask them, they'll corroborate my
word."

"Why do you think Cutts was sent to another branch of the
service?''

"I suppose to give him another chance, sir."

"Exactly! So we must give him another chance, don't you
think?''

"Do I take that to mean, sir, that I as Sergeant am to take no
notice if one of my men deserts his post in the face of the enemy?''

"Everyone gets wind up at times. I was so jumpy when I
came out first that I was almost out of my mind."

"I am responsible for discipline, sir. Almost solely so, if I
may say so."

"You're windy, too, you know, Rivett."

"Sir!—I ask to see the commanding officer, with your permission, with a view to handing my stripes!''

"Look at it from Cutts' point of view. We ought to try and
help him. Something's broken his nerve. A shell, perhaps; or,
from the look of him, he probably had hell as a child. He hasn't
had your advantages, coming from a good home."

This reference to his social superiority seemed to satisfy Rivett,
for he said, "Very good, sir, I'll say no more about it."

The sergeant came to see him before dinner. He asked if
he might detail Cutts for limber duty that night. "I feel sure
he's trying to work his ticket, sir. There's nothing wrong with him.
He's a lead-swinger."

"I think not. Put him on picket duty until further orders."

"Then who will look after his mules, sir?''

"He can. But not take them up the line."

Half an hour after sunset Phillip set out, four fighting limbers
with eight pairs of mules. A full moon shone above the track
following the course of the brook, and along the bottom of a
shallow valley leading to the embankment below the Hindenburg
outpost line. Great white clouds were now passing over the
moon, a cold wind blew from the north-west. The Hindenburg
Line was dissolved in a dusky pallor; not a shot was fired. The
silence was strange. Saying goodbye to Jack and the others,
he led the empty limbers back at a trot, with a moonlit feeling
of having a highwayman's shadow.

When they had unlimbered, and the mules were rugged up at the picket line, Phillip went to have a word with Cutts. He found him sitting by the fire, one arm round Little Willie, the German dog. Little Willie was paying the company a visit. According to Nolan, Little Willie had been on leave in the Hindenburg Line, as his coat smelled of stale sausage and cigar smoke.

Phillip sat on an empty shell-box opposite Cutts. Since the shelling that afternoon, a tarpaulin shelter had been rigged up, to conceal the light from the east. He warmed his hands over the coloured flames of the coke fire, in which could be seen dull-red *boulets*. These egg-shaped objects of compressed clay and coal-dust had been scrounged from the remains of an old German dump beside the railway line at Achiet by Sergeant Rivett, who had brought back a couple of filled sandbags that morning.

"I was blown up by a shell, Cutts. It was at Messines, in the first year of the war, when I was a tommy like you. I was buried, and when an old sweat who had befriended me dug me out, my eyes flickered with electric snakes for some time afterwards. When we came out of the battle I couldn't sleep, for fear of going back again. So I understand anyone else who feels like that."

The driver said nothing. His teeth began to chatter. When he opened his mouth to speak he gulped. Phillip saw that his hands were tightly clenched.

"It's a bad old war, Cutts. The only thing to do is to try and stick it out. Nolan and I will help you. So when you feel awful, or terribly afraid, come and see me, will you? An officer is the soldier's friend you know."

"T-t-thank you, sir!"

"I am like you. I can't get used to shells. It's the *noise* which frightens me. It's such an absolutely final, brutal noise, isn't it? Well, goodnight, Cutts, and don't worry. Don't fight yourself in your brain. That's the worst thing to do. I know, I used to do it. Still do, in fact. Prayer does help, you know. Goodnight, old fellow."

Cutts gulped thanks.

Some hours later Sergeant Rivett came to Phillip's tent. "Sorry to disturb you, sir, but it's Cutts again. He's wounded in the hand. I've put on a dressing. I think you should see him, sir."

Phillip pulled on his long rubber thigh boots, which he had "won" from an R.E. dump in Albert after his boot-caps had been burnt by the stove. Worn with thick woollen stockings, over socks, they had kept his feet dry and warm. It had made a great difference to his outlook, he found.

"What happened?"

"The fire bucket exploded, sir. I think someone must have put a Mills bomb in it."

"Who can have done that?"

"Well, sir, I won't go so far as to say that it comes within the category of a self-inflicted wound, but it cannot be ruled out——"

"Just a moment, Sergeant Rivett! Didn't you scrounge some coal from the Achiet dump? German coal? And you know the orders about looting, surely? Moreover, that was a booby-trap —their egg-bombs look just like the French *boulets*. I expect we'll be able to find fragments lying about in the morning. If any *are* found, it will look like dereliction of duty—isn't that what you said—on our part, won't it? You for taking the coal, I for not running you in for looting. However, Cutts is the one who matters."

The wounded man was lying back, wrapped in a blanket. Nolan was with him. Phillip lifted up his arm, with the bandage on the hand.

"I don't trouble!" exclaimed Cutts, as though proud of his power to bear pain. "I can git up. Look!" as he struggled on his feet, revealing in the light of a torch the dripping of blood.

"Take it easy, Cutts. How did it happen?"

"Bookit blowed up sudden like, sir, after I'd put on coal to keep it goin' for next picket, sir. It caught Little Willie, sir. I'm very sorry, sir."

"Is the dog hurt?"

"I don't know, sir. He cleared at the clap."

"He can't be very hurt, if he could run. Well, I think it's a straightforward case of egg bombs being mixed in with the coal we got, another booby trap. Call it gunshot wound due to Enemy Action. Or do you think it's a case for a Court of Enquiry, Sergeant Rivett?"

"That's for you to decide, sir."

"Now let Nolan take him down to the Aid Post. Best of luck, and let me know how you get on, won't you, Cutts? Write me a letter. I'll help you in any way I can—remember!" He shook the uninjured hand and, having said goodnight to Nolan and Sergeant Rivett, went back to his tent, which he had to himself, having got it the same time as the boots from Albert.

But there was not much sleep: a battery of 60-pounders during the day had taken up position in a sunken road a hundred yards away, and was firing over the tents. Every white stab buffeted the canvas. He lit a candle, and read the Oxford Book.

Every time a gun fired it snuffed out the flame, so he gave up reading; and lying back, was soon asleep.

He awoke at first light, and lay motionless in his flea-bag, listening. The ground seemed to be bubbling. A prolonged bombardment was taking place somewhere. Was it falling on the front line, in the valley below the Hindenburg Line? Had the Germans retired only to lure on the Fifth Army, to cut it off by driving into the flanks of its untrenched positions? In contour'd chalky country sound acoustics behaved oddly; it was not possible always to determine how far away a bombardment was taking place.

He got up, and roused the sergeant, ordering all animals to be saddled, and hooked into limbers, all stores and officers' valises to be loaded, ready for emergency. When it was light he mounted Prince and rode east, crossing the Arras-Bapaume road, seeking the highest ground where he could use his field-glasses. From the crest of a field of young wheat he saw the Hindenburg Line across intervening folds in the ground as a bluish-grey riband of new barbed wire against grass. The trenches were on the reverse slope, out of view. All was quiet, no shell-spoutings of counter-barrage upon the horizon. While he sat upon his black horse, looking east, a drift of wind, or some eddy in the strata of heavy dark clouds, amplified a roll of gunfire from the north. He remembered the rumoured attack on the Vimy Ridge, near Arras. The spring push had begun!

Heavy cold rain fell, with intervals of sleet, all the morning. The news in the afternoon, at the Brigade forage dump in Achiet-le-Grand—where already new railway lines were being laid by Canadian engineers—was that the First and Third Armies had gone over at dawn, and taken thousands of prisoners and hundreds of guns. But the attack made by the Australians near Bullecourt had failed.

"Who's windy now?" said Sergeant Rivett, to the lance-corporal in charge of the grooms. "We had to load up all the stores, now we've got to put them all back again."

The next morning a message came from Brigade to stand by to move forward in the event of the Germans evacuating the

Hindenburg Line opposite Fifth Army. Allenby's Third Army up north had got through the last line of the Hindenburg System, and now before them was only the Drocourt-Quéant Switch, still under construction. Rumours late at night, via the post-corporal from Sapignies, were of a cavalry massacre at Monchy-le-Preux, when a charge had come up against uncut barbed-wire and machine-gun fire. Hundreds of riderless horses were running about the countryside, said the corporal. Phillip thought about going there the next morning, to see if he could pick up one or two; but orders came to stand by to move forward at half an hour's notice. Hobart told his officers, in confidence, that if the Hindenburg Line was not evacuated, the division was to take part in an attack at the hinge by Croiselle-les-Fontaines. The French, too, under a new General, Nivelle, who had re-placed that old dud Joffre, were about to open a very big attack down in Champagne. So it looked as though, at last, the old Hun might crack! That night, under the tarpaulin roof of the mess, the levels of initialled whiskey bottles were lowered.

The next morning there was another casualty among the drivers. All the military telegraph poles had been cut down by the Germans, the wires lay tangled and spread about. Driver Tallis, walking through them, tripped on a wire, there was a sharp brittle explosion, and he dropped, writhing with pain in one leg, into the flesh and bone of which small white fragments of porcelain had cut deep. One piece went through his ankle, penetrating boot leather twice. He was congratulated on his luck. Just in time, he was told: for while he was being carried away a Special Duty Squad of the R.E.s came and dismantled all the telephone insulators, finding that several had been removed from the cross-pieces and detonators fixed into the hollows before being tied on again with wire. Phillip saw him before he went away to hospital. "Write to me, Tallis, and tell me how young Phil is getting on."

The company moved a mile and a half away, to lower ground near the piles of bricks and rafters called Ervillers, a village through which passed the neatly swept road from Bapaume to Arras. They camped on a pasture field a couple of hundred yards from the village. Phillip thought how much cleaner and finer was the country than that of Belgium. It was so open and wide. Enemy aircraft were often flying over; one shot up the camp, approaching suddenly with a roar fifty feet above the grass. It was gone before the sentry could fire his rifle. So Phillip, finding a cart-wheel in the village, with the axle, had it fixed to a post put in the earth, so that the wheel revolved horizontally. Upon this a Vickers gun was mounted, to fire into the sky. Late one afternoon, when the sun was dipping to spill golden light upon an otherwise peaceful scene—the ground was being prepared for a gymkhana—an aircraft dived through the luminous haze from about twelve thousand feet, firing tracer and incendiary bullets. One of the observation balloons tethered in a line a couple of thousand feet up showed a lick of flame, while a tiny figure jumped from the basket below; and as the balloon broke raggedly, issuing black smoke and redder flames, the aeroplane zoomed up, fell over at the turn, and dived, firing upon a second. This, too, caught fire. Both were falling when the zoom and turn was once more repeated. A third caught fire. Down dived the Hun scout, to flatten at twenty feet and roar over the camp, while the Vickers gun shook the wheel as it fired but the aeroplane, its black crosses quite large, tore away east. By this time the balloons had shed their crews who floated down on parachutes, fortunately away from the burning ruins which dragged down at the end of their cables, in shreds and flaming tatters.

The next day, while he was censoring mail, Phillip read an account of what had happened in a letter by Sergeant Rivett to Downham, still apparently at the Training Centre. He considered that, if it fell into enemy hands, Rivett's letter would give away the whereabouts of the company. So he blacked out about the raid on the Fifth Army balloons, laughing while he did so as he imagined bloody old Downham trying to make out what it was all about.

April 23rd, 1917.   286 Company M.G.C. B.E.F.

Dear Sir,

It is with the greatest pleasure that I take up my pen in reply to your most welcome letter. I sincerely hope, Sir, that a brief account of my doings since last I wrote will be interesting to you. Things are happening fast out here, as the following account may convey. This afternoon, while I was in the act of supervising the putting up of jumps for the forthcoming company sports, suddenly an —— ———— appeared and in a trice it —— —— —— a ——, then it —— ———— —— —— ——. And as if that wasn't enough for the blighter, he pooped —— —— in full view of the entire camp!

The sports were held the next day. The main event, devised
by Phillip, was a bit complicated. It was called the Inter-
Section Relay Jerusalem Cuckoo Leapfrog race. Four riders,
one representing each section, set off, to jump each fence: and
having done this, each was to await the arrival, if any, of his No.
2 jockey, over the same fence. There they were to exchange
mules, and the "Number Ones" to set off for the second fence,
on the other side of which each would dismount again, await
to exchange with his Number Two, and so on round the course.
Mules would not as a rule jump; it was hard to make them go at
more than an obliging trot, so, as Sergeant Rivett wrote again
a few days later to Major Downham, 'the fun was fast and furious'.
So was the Sergeant's style, thought Phillip.

I wish, Sir, that I had the pen of an artist to describe to you the
mulish amble to the first jump, the complete stoppage of all con-
testants there, while the entire cohort of racemules waited for their
struggling riders to choose another way forward! Then, of course,
the expert had to show us how to do it! Mounting the greyest of
grey 'donks', as we call them out here, Sir, he clapped spurs in
vain upon the extremities of hollow ribs. He had no more success
than if he had mounted the lions in Trafalgar Square for a similar
purpose! This old grey long-eared chum showed what he felt about
the whole performance when he began to eat the catkins on the
hazel sticks with which the jump was erected. Our C.O. was heard
to remark *sotto voce*, as though to the aforesaid sticks, "Who says a
mule hasn't got a sense of humour?"

SECRET 13.4.17

EAST PENNINE DIVISION ORDER NO. 36

———————— (words erased) ———————— the attack on the
HINDENBURG LINE ordered in E.P. Divisional Order No.
31 of 8.4.17, will take place at a date (not before April 16th) and
at an hour to be notified later, unless the enemy withdraw previously on account of the attack of the Third Army.

His eye skated down the blue roneographed foolscap page . . .
responsible for the capture of BULLECOURT . . . will jump
off at two minutes before Zero hour and will advance at rate
of 100 yards in 2 minutes . . . strong bombing party will push
Eastwards . . . before the barrage lifts . . . special attention being
paid to the Sunken Roads running N.E. in U. 22, where strong

parties of the enemy are liable to be met with . . . One battalion
and two companies of the Brigade will push forward at Zero
hour plus 2 hours and 15 minutes under an artillery barrage to
the 3rd Objective . . . 1 Brigade will be in reserve in the valley
North West of MORY . . . Order re Tanks will be issued later
. . . Tanks will follow the Infantry as closely as possible, but the
Infantry will not wait for the Tanks . . . The 2nd Australian
Division will attack on the right—boundaries as shown on the
attached sketch.

"That's a bloody fine way, I don't think, to send out Battle
Orders, 'Provided the wire is sufficiently cut' scratched out in
pencil so bloody carelessly that anyone can read the words!
I bet that's the work of some fat little rotter from Eton sitting on
his bottom and living off the fat of the land. The staff all over!"
said Pinnegar. "There've been half a dozen attacks on Fontaine-
les-Croiselles already, and local assaults on Bullecourt, and every
one a wash-out!"

"How deep are those belts of wire, Teddy?"

"Anything up to a hundred yards."

"What part do the sections play?"

"Overhead covering fire from the railway embankment, then
move forward with the third wave. Stay in the first objective,
under Brigade order. *If* we get there."

"Where do you go ?"

"Remain with Jack at company headquarters, under the
railway embankment."

"Where's Brigade battle headquarters?"

"At l'Homme Mort. What's the idea of all the questions?"

"I just want to know."

"I said, What's the idea?"

"Oh, just in case you're all knocked out."

"You're a bloody fine Job's comforter! Anyway, you're only
the transport wallah. You do damn-all in the attack. A.T.O.
doesn't count in seniority for command, you know."

"Of course I know. But it's just as well to know, Teddy."

A yellowhammer was building a nest in the bank near the
cookhouse. He went to see how it was getting on. But with no
real interest, because, while quite content with life, he was not in
English country.

The new leaves on the hedgerow bushes, the pricking green of barley and oats in the fields, swallows flittering about broken barn walls, twittering happily—everything was seen a little apart, as though through thin glass. The war did not worry him, the coming attack gave a feeling of excitement, as something to be felt apart from himself. It was a comfortable feeling that he was out of the actual fighting, an interested spectator. Everyone seemed to be enjoying the fine spring weather.

By May Day there were three eggs in the rootlet cup lined with hair from mules' tails. Jules the chef came out of his cooking shelter and smiled at Phillip. He, too, was watching the nest. "We call the yellowhammer a scribbling lark in Gaultshire, Jules. See, the eggs are all scribbled on, as by a wet copying ink pencil."

"Very pretty, sir. Dinky little bird. I love it!"

Phillip saw a new Jules. He was kind. "Many fellows come to see it, sir. They wouldn't think of hurting it. Nice boys!"

Back at company headquarters, Pinnegar was huffing at a paper just come in. "Same old tripe," he said.

"May I see?"

"I don't care what you do."

(SECOND) EAST PENNINE DIVISION
ORDER OF THE DAY

As the Division will shortly be going into action to take part in its first great battle, the Divisional Commander desires to assure all ranks of his complete confidence in their ability to defeat the German troops opposed to them.

That the East Pennine Division will maintain its reputation for staunchness and grit—qualities for which Yorkshiremen have ever been famed—that they will gain all objectives and hold them against the most determined counter-attacks, is the firm conviction of the General Officer who is proud to be their Commander.

May 1st 1917.

At 3.10 hours two days later the servant pulled at Phillip's leg under the camel-hair bag and said, "Get up, sir," quietly. He was awake at once, and after a cup of gun-fire tea, thick and sugary, went to the wheatfield on the 110-metre line enclosed within a single strand of wire against trespass. Zero hour was at 3.45 a.m. About 3.44 a.m., in the hush of darkness beginning to give way to a spectral pallor in which he could see the wire of the reserve line across the sunken road as a blackish mass, a lark rose in song above him. It was followed by another, and a third; and he waited, with the stillness of expectation, while the singing grew faint and shrill as the birds flew towards the paling stars. There was a great ragged orange flash, oval and instant, from the four 9.2 howitzers in the chalk quarry on his right, and while the flash went through his eyes into his mind the sky became one great raging sea of light. Hundreds of batteries were firing. The 18-pounders were far in front, in the shallow open valley through which he had passed many times while taking limbers, in the dusk, to the railway embankment; 60-pounder counter-battery guns stabbed whitely beyond the sunken road, merging into the orange belches of howitzers—6-inch, 9.2, and 12-inch behind him, under the crest. Thousands of great fingers of light were flickering to the zenith, while the earth shook and rumbled with one continuous drumming reverberation. And through the intense exhilaration of this massive light and sound, while red, green and golden rockets arose from the ragged line of fire where shells were bursting, he heard, faint and high and thin, seeming to him to be like the jingling of frailest silver chains, the songs of larks.

Then it was over; and he heard, through the comparative silence, the solid hammering of machine guns. He went back to the lines; and shortly after 9 a.m., returning to the battery in the chalk pit, was told, 'Back on the first objective', and thought, *Provided the wire is sufficiently cut* . . . higher authority must have overruled the divisional general, who must have seen enough of uncut wire at Gallipoli.

Later in the morning, walking wounded began to limp back. They said the attack had failed halfway to the first objective, and no reinforcements were to go up. There was the usual black pessimism of shocked troops who had gone over for the first time. One man who arrived, with a shrapnel ball through his left calf, while lying down, said that Mr. Montfort had been killed, while Mr. Fenwick had been hit while going to help Sergeant Butler. It was on the edge of the sunken lane. Mr. Fenwick had a leg blown off. Sergeant Butler had been hit in the throat. Mr. Fenwick was in a shell-hole. He had helped him put a twister above it, to stop the bleeding.

"Where was Mr. Fenwick when you saw him last?"

"In the shell-hole, sir, near Sergeant Butler, on the edge of the sunken road. And our dog, Little Willie, was wiv 'im, sir."

"Did Little Willie go over with you?"

"I don't know, sir. I only found 'im beside Mr. Fenwick."

"Where exactly is the sunken road? Wait a moment, I'll get my map. Have a cigarette. Tea's coming. I won't be gone very long."

He returned with 51 b S.W. It showed part of the Hindenburg Line which had been captured ESE of Arras, below the main Arras-Cambrai road running straight as an arrow, and below the arrow, three downland tracks, scarcely roads, by which farm produce looked to have been taken to the cathedral market town. One of the lower roads, in peacetime, had passed through Neuville Vitasse, Henin, and Croiselles on the way to St. Quentin, and a railway had served the same country, keeping to lower levels but passing by Croiselles. He knew his way about that village, because he had explored it, and part of the glacis in front of the Hindenburg Line, at the beginning of April. It had been blown up by the Germans retreating to their *Siegfried Stellung*.

During that April exploration the Germans had been dropping a few shells into the ruins, searching for 18-pounders hidden in it. A battery commander had cursed him for showing himself; he had wandered on down to the embankment, looking at the skyline of the Hindenburg Line, apparently peaceful, but strong with invisible fear and steel. To test himself, he had walked across a road, where British troops were hidden, with the intention of getting as close as he could without being fired upon. A strange lightness of spirit possessed him, as though his body existed no more. He had felt that no harm would come to him; but being shouted at, had turned back, to be cursed by a major, dirty and angry, who asked him what the hell he thought he was doing? Didn't he bloody well know he'd draw fire upon the men in the front line?

"Exactly where was Mr. Fenwick lying when you last saw him? Can you pin-point the place on this map? Croiselles is there. There's the Sensée brook going under the road. Further along is the sugar factory, or what's left of it. Now the land begins to rise, see? Those lines mark the heights. That's the seventy-metre line, that's a track branching off towards the Hindenburg Line, up a gentle slope, seventy-five metres—eighty metres. Now do you see that darkish mark, looking like a wire-worm? That's where the waggon track has been worn down, making a sunken lane."

"That's the place, sir! Almost on the top of the rise! I just saw Jerry's wire three hundred yards away, before we had to get into the prone position, sir. Jerry's fire was real terrible, coming from all directions. But we was all right while we lay down. So Mr. Fenwick shouted to us to crawl into the sunken lane. When we got there, we saw it was swep' by indirect emma gee fire from Bullecourt, a mile east from where we was. Bullets wasn't cracking like, but going pss-pss, four or five guns together, like 'ail the bullets was goin' past! From a distance, you see, sir. They was all on a droppin' tra-jectory."

"I don't expect they'll be firing, now the attack's stopped. Ah, the cook's brought us some tea! Well done, Cookie. I'll see if I can get some rum from the quarter bloke." He poured two spoonfuls into the tea, then gave the jar back to the C.Q.M.S.

Soon afterwards, having seen that particulars of the walking wounded had been taken for the company War Diary, he left the C.Q.M.S. in charge, and followed by Morris, rode through St. Leger and down towards Croiselles. Poor old "Darky" must be found, and if possible brought back later on by stretcher bearers. The thing to do was to find the place where he was in daylight, and then organise and lead up stretcher bearers to arrive in the village as soon as dusk fell, before the German patrols went out. Even then, like as not they wouldn't fire. He remembered their decency at Loos, on the Sunday when the line broke and the New Army divisions left the battlefield, and he, lying with some of the wounded, had been told he could go back by a German colonel, after some of the men had been given brandy, and their wounds bandaged. Also on July the First, in front of Ovillers, the same decency had been shown.

With a haversack full of field dressings, and feeling light-hearted, he left Prince with Morris, and walked down the valley. Here the railway followed the stream on the edge of Croiselles. He walked on beside the shallow flow of water, remotely wondering if any trout were left alive in it. He scoffed at himself for the very idea. Trout fishing in the midst of such world-accepted madness! Yet some people in England might be fishing at that very moment; in England it was *May*, and most things still going on as usual. Thinking of England unsteadied him. Why was he risking his life like that? To appear as a hero? Did he *really* care for Darky so much? They had never really been friends. Not close friends, anyway. Fenwick had seemed to think they were pals after the visit to Sleaford, and the Silk Inn, so he had played up to it. In

a way it was true, but to be quite truthful, he—— It was the same
with Pinnegar, who seemed to regard him as a great friend, ever
since they had ridden together in the same carriage from King's
Cross. He did not *really* like Teddy, nor Fenwick, much. Why
then was he going beyond his job to find him? Was he showing off
—even to himself? Was it because Fenwick had told him he was
a foundling, and had been so happy to have someone to care for
him at last, the girl in the pub? It was *easy* to go to the rescue of a
wounded man—it made one feel fine, and free. Had Father
Aloysius felt as he felt now, led on by something, outside the
"little ego", as he had called it? To be truthful, it was rather fun,
walking on grass up the slope, with the sun behind him now, and
his shadow moving before him, under German eyes.

He came to an uneven line of dead men. Some lay face down,
as though asleep; others were on their backs; a few seemed to be
hiding their faces. He stared at them, and knew one reason why
he had come: to have the feeling of being quite clear, in the
presence of the dead. What were their spirits, if still about,
thinking? Or had they gone home. One had a face the colour
of the terracotta carpet in the front room at home, and a hole
through his neck. Now the rough grass was torn with shell holes,
lipped with chalk. Near the final skyline he sat down, and looked
at his map. He must find Fenwick. No more idling. If only he
had a prismatic compass, which he had despised as home-service
nonsense when attached to the Cantuvellaunians, two years ago
to the month, he would be able to set the map and find the
sunken track. He tried to set it by the sun. Oh hell, get on and
see where Bullecourt lay, then judge the position by the fact that
Croiselles and Bullecourt lay almost in an east-west line, the
sunken track with it.

He walked on up the slope, passing an occasional dead man
in the grass. Already their tunic pockets were slit, their haversacks open and the contents pulled about for the cigarettes and
chocolate they might have contained—usual sight on a battlefield,
for the dead didn't want anything more, and why waste what
might help their pals?

A few thorns were visible a couple of hundred yards ahead, and
as he got near them he saw a magpie sloping away and thought it
had a nest there. The bushes were on the brow of the hill. Many
more dead lay in the grass there, they must have been seen in
silhouette as they advanced, or had to cross the pre-arranged
criss-cross streams of machine-gun bullets. He got to the thorn

clump without drawing fire, though now Bullecourt, dark brown with the colour of a crab-shell—he remembered thinking that of Messines in 1914—lay directly in front, less than a mile away, in rack and ruin externally, but strong with the power of death in the thoughts behind many thousands of invisible eyes. Sure enough, there was a magpie's nest in one of the thorns, and only about six feet from the ground. It was just as he had read of in books: a dome of thorns on top, to keep off other egg-suckers. The magpie did not want to be done by as it did to other birds! While he was gingerly putting his hand through the spines to the side of the nest, a Yorkshire voice said, "It were too 'igh for me to get at th' eggs, ulse I'd 'v sooked 'em meself." Turning, he saw a cheerful face grinning from the ground a few yards away. The speaker was lying in a slight chalky hollow, with several water-bottles and bayonet-stabbed bully beef tins around him. Other tins had been hacked and beaten almost flat, and when he saw that the man had an arm missing Phillip knew why the tins were battered.

"I didn't want these eggs to eat. I used to collect one egg from each different nest. I think I'll take this one back with me."

"Aye," said the wounded man. "It takes all sorts t'make world."

He explained that he had been one of a patrol which had set out eight nights previously, to report on the enemy wire. The patrol had been surprised and dispersed by hand grenades and light machine guns. His left arm had been blown off, and he had lain down that night, weak with loss of blood, and all the next day, having crawled to the cover of the thorn brake. There he had stopped, "knowing the boys would be back", keeping himself alive on iron rations and water taken from his dead mates. He held up his arm, off below the elbow. Maggots were on the discoloured and liquefying flesh of the stump. "They fookin' maggits 'ave kep' meat from gettin' too proud." Phillip gave him a cigarette, and seeing the miniature cloth stars on his tommy's tunic, the man said he was sorry for using bad language.

"But they are just what you said they are, or will be, when they've got wings!" replied Phillip. "Anyway, I'm glad I came across you. Perhaps you can direct me to a sunken lane near here."

"That's just over brow of yon hill, sir. That's where my mates copped it, the Jerry patrol wor' lying there, when they chooked their stick-bombs."

"I'm looking for a friend, who was hit there this morning. I think I'll go on, and have a look."

"Aye, 'tis quiet now, sir. Jerry's 'avin' a coop'r tea now."

"I'll come back for you."

He found the dog, rasping with excitement and thirst, lying beside Fenwick, whose dark eyes were burning in a taut face. He was feeble of voice. Near him lay Sergeant Butler, dead. Butler, time-expired after many years in India, had survived several attacks; he had seemed to be the hard core of his section, but one night, when he had come to sit round the picket fire, he had spoken hardly at all, but kept touching the fire with a stick, burning the end into flame and then knocking it out again, until the stick was small, when he thrust it into the glowing coke, staring at it with lifeless eyes as it changed from flame to ember and finally to ash. Then without a word he had got up, saluted, and gone away, leaving the impression with Nolan that he had already made up his mind that he was going to be killed.

The long afternoon turned to twilight. Phillip helped the Yorkshireman to the line of outposts, where he handed him over to the first-aid post, and waited to lead the stretcher-bearer party that was going out. Asked who he was, he explained about Fenwick; back he went, and helped to bring him in, then returned up the valley, followed by Little Willie, as the moon was rising over Bullecourt. Morris was waiting with the horses. From the echoing ruins of Croiselles white flashes of field-guns seemed to increase the singing of two nightingales on the hillside.

When they got back to camp, Phillip heard from the picket that the company had come out of the line, and were asleep; so he did not report to Captain Hobart until the next morning, by which time news had come from the Dressing Station in Ervillers that Fenwick had passed through to the C.C.S. at Achiet-le-Grand.

"Good effort, Sticks! You've got plenty of guts, to go out there alone, in full view of the Boche."

"Honestly, skipper, it was no more than going for a walk on Blackheath, on an August Bank Holiday evening. With all the bodies lying about; only there weren't any females."

"Talking of home, there's a possibility of leave coming up again soon. The division is going out to rest and refit, I hear." Hobart shoved over an Order of the Day, which said that the General Officer Commanding Fifth Army congratulated the Second East Pennine Division on its performance in its first great Battle.

Phillip kept his own War Diary in the pocket note-book.

May 4 *Fri*	The Fox pleased with division, God knows why. 7th Div. badly cut up. H. Line too damned strong for us at present. Another attack at night failed.
5 *Sat*	Early morning H.A.C. and Warwicks attack again. Failed. Evening, Warwicks and Welch went over. Barrage at 10 p.m. Raining. German counter-attack smashed.
6 *Sun*	Awful rot in Daily Trident about our attack. Fine day. Took two sick mules to Mobile A.V.C. at Achiet. Had bottle of champagne with Teddy in E.F.C. marquee there.
7 *Mon*	French take 5,800 prisoners at Chemin des Dames. Raining at night. 2nd Gordons take Bullecourt. Full moon.
8 *Tues*	Intense barrage fire at 9.35 p.m. German counter-attack and re-take Bullecourt.
9 *Wed*	Half quarter day. £10 from M.F.O. Two new officers arrive. Wind-up at midnight, Strombos horns wailing, gas attack. Still at Ervillers. Wrote many letters.
10 *Thur*	Parcel from home. Heard from Eugene. Raining in evening. Intelligence says Germans in bad way over raw materials.
12 *Sat*	Letter from Darky Fenwick at Trouville. Thanked me for saving his life. Rot. Colossal bombardment at 3.45 this morning. 91 Brigade over top at Bullecourt.
13 *Sun*	Raining.
14 *Mon*	Company going into line Bullecourt tonight. Took up guns etc. Shelled a bit, including about 200 phosgene. Got back midnight.
15 *Tues*	Weather threatening. News of German retiring to DROCOURT-QUEANT line. Very quiet at night.
16 *Wed*	Went to A.S.C. mule races in afternoon. Got second place on Jimmy. Weather breaking.
17 *Thur*	Rations to Bullecourt at night. Bloody time, much shelling on track. Sweated greatly.
18 *Fri*	Tired and fed up all day. Many Ger planes over.
19 *Sat*	Great artillery strafe at night. Heard from R.F.C. pilot at E.F.C. Achiet that French had mutinied down south. Two Army Corps set out to march to Paris.
20 *Sun*	Drum fire in morning. Rumours of big attack up north by Third Army.
21 *Mon*	Took limbers to Bullecourt. Strafed. Shot wounded mule. New moon arose just after midnight.
22 *Tues*	Raining heavily. Went to Achiet-le-Grand cinema in evening. Fine show. Many letters: Mother, Father,

		Doris, Eugene, Mrs. Neville, Tom Ching, now in Artists Rifles.
23	*Wed*	Two new officers killed. All Weather Jack awarded M.C. this morning.
24	*Thur*	Fine day. Went to picture palace Achiet, good show, electric lights, fans, pukka plush seats etc.
25	*Fri*	Corps H.Q. at Achiet shelled by 13.5-inch railway gun from Cambrai.
26	*Sat*	Brigade out of line, to Bihucourt. Jack Hobart went on leave. Address for emergency, Flowers' Hotel. Teddy P. i/c.
27	*Sun*	Division going north tomorrow.

The company, marching south from the green expanse of chalk country, passed through the brick-heap villages. Phillip saw one maimed fruit tree in leaf, momentarily a startling sight. So they re-entered the crater-zone, green with young grass, at the head of the Ancre valley. It would take a hundred years, he thought, looking around from the saddle, to clear up the ruin and desolation. Magpies were back, and kestrels; a relief.

All that morning, and part of the afternoon, the short column moved, easily, down the road from the high ground to the low ground, into the valley of the Ancre, Phillip at the tail, behind the last limber with its red, white, and black German privy. Many faces turned to it, many remarks made. "Some souvenir!" said the R.T.O. at Albert.

Little Willie the German dog trotted with them, sometimes leaping on a limber to rest. At Beaucourt they were passing a stationary lorry convoy, when Little Willie, looking up from his couch, began to whine. He had come upon his lorry-driver pal, who whistled to him from a cab.

"Go on, Willie!" said Nolan. "You belong to the Mud-balled Fox," the Fifth Army sign stencilled on the cab-door. Little Willie gave a yelp, and sprang off the limber; the lorry cab-door opened, and he jumped in, to sit happily beside the driver.

The company halted under the leaning Virgin at Albert. At 5 p.m. they entrained for Amiens; thence to Abbeville, for the Flanders front.

Chapter 8

MESSINES RIDGE

They detrained at a new military station called Duke of York
outside Bailleul. Phillip had seen this countryside in 1914, when
it was all wide fields of grass or under the plough, with plashes of
water along brown furrows reflecting a wintry sky. Now, nearly
three years later, as far as one could see were rows of elephant-iron
hutments, marquees flying the Red Cross flag, new roads leading
through acres of massive dumps—shells, balls of barbed wire,
wooden duckboards, guns, waggons, and ammunition boxes
piled seven feet high.

The dust in the air seemed to be part of the reverberation of
the guns. Upon the roads was constant mechanised movement
—hundreds of lorries, motorcars and motorcycles passing in two
streams. There were guns, too, trundling along. Among them
was a 15-inch howitzer, hauled by a tracked vehicle, with steaming radiator. Its slow forward movement was surrounded by
many attendant Heavy Group gunners.

> 30 *Wed*   The great Whore of Death on the way to challenge her
>   rival, Krupp's Iron Virgin. Hung with black veils, she
>   is lugged to the bridal chamber, served by her pollinat-
>   ing dupes. This monster from the dark side of the moon.

New heavy railway lines had been laid close to the front, in
concealed territory. From the railheads ran out light railway
tracks, with small steam-engines pulling trucks loaded with
shells, mortars, wire, screw-picket stakes, all the materials of attack.
Where the light railways ended, narrower-gauge tram-lines began,
the shallow trucks hauled by petrol-driven engines. Fatigues,
latterly called working parties, once "supplied" to the sappers by
infantry in reserve, were now provided by the new Labour Corps
units, so that the fighting soldier's renascent spirit was not dragged
out of him in all weathers when "resting" in the back-areas.

They were now in the Second Army, a Master-gunner's Army
—"Old Plum and Apple"—a play on the invariable jam issue,
the General's name, short figure, and chubby cheeks. It was known
that an attack had long been prepared against the Messines—St.

Eloi—Hill 60 ridge, from which the Germans looked down upon the British trenches, guns, and transport routes. For nearly a thousand days, from many points, German observers at the telephone had gazed through telescopes resting on ground-level splayed slits in the western walls of massive concrete-and-steel forts, called Mebus, built within the ruins of farm-cellars and other shattered buildings, behind belts of barbed wire, some of them a hundred yards thick. It was a war of attrition, in which all the skill, bravery, patriotism, and belief in rightness of cause was identical in the deadlocked armies.

The name, White Rose Camp, seemed to be ironical, with the dominating smells of horse-dung, chloride of lime and fat of smoking incinerators; but one morning, passing the Commandant's office, he saw a white-washed brick wall, and a garden of various flowers growing below bushes of large white tea roses. All was beautifully kept by a German prisoner with the usual blue circles let into his tunic and trousers.

Nightingales were still singing; gun-flashes in the warm brief nights seemed to stimulate them. The company sections had special training as barrage gunners. They were under the command of Group at Division. Thirty, forty, fifty divisional guns would be firing together during the bombardment.

There was a wood near the camp, and wandering in it he saw that acres of ground between the trees were covered by layers of sandbags filled with blue-grey clay. The blue gault clay of Gaultshire! What was its purpose? Why was a dump of it made there? And why had the sandbags been allowed to rot? Did they cover an underground magazine? The dumps at Achicourt near Arras had gone up before the battle for Vimy, set on fire by a German airman: perhaps now they were underground, for safety. But why no sentry? Or engine house to pump out water in this low-lying country?

Captain Hobart supplied the answer when he dined with Phillip at the *Faucon d'Or* in Bailleul that night, in the room where the mirrors along the walls still remained smashed from September 1914, when drunken Uhlan officers, enjoying an after-dinner spree, had thrown empty bottles about.

"Well, strictly *entre nous*, Sticks, we've got some very deep mines under the Messines-Wytschaete ridge, been diggin' 'em since 1915, tunnels a hundred feet down, below the wet sand and slurry and into the blue gault clay. That's what you saw in the wood. The stuff is dumped there and elsewhere under cover to prevent it being spotted by the Boche airmen. There's been a hell of an underground war goin' on among the tunnellers, ours and theirs, for years. Listenin' apparatus, blowin' in one another's tunnels with camouflets, and other jolly little habits. However, we've been one up on the old Hun, I hear, with our silent pumps for air and water. Also, we've got deep dug-outs big enough to hold two battalions at once, and space to sleep a thousand men at a time. We've learned the lesson of the Somme, Sticks. Let's have a brandy, shall we? Though I suppose those damned Uhlans drank all the real old stuff, what?"

All Weather Jack usually spoke in that jaunty, polished sort of way, so unlike pukka regular soldiers. Phillip wondered if he had assumed this manner, a sort of shining boot-polish manner, because he felt he wasn't really "out of the top drawer".

The next morning Captain Hobart held a conference of his officers.

"As you know, we are soon taking part in the opening phase of a battle which will lead, it is hoped, to the end of the war this year. The part the M.G.C. will play is twofold. One, before the infantry go over and during the actual assault, when batteries of massed Vickers will pour curtain fire 400 yards ahead of the creeping 18-pounder shrapnel barrage, which will move ahead of our infantry. Vickers guns will be emplaced well behind our front line, to sweep the crest and beyond. A stop to each gun will be fitted, to prevent the barrel being depressed to below the safety arc of fire over the heads of the infantry. This lattice fire, as it might be called, is to prevent enemy reinforcements coming up, and to catch those retreating.

"The second part we play is when we move forward and meet the counter-attack while it is forming up, breaking it, before it can become effective, by firing on all tracks, routes, and roads on the other side of the hill.

"Now for the enemy tactics. The old Hun has a new plan of elastic defence against our assaults. It consists, broadly speaking, of lines of concrete forts, fairly massive, about 200 yards apart in their second line. They are low, 4 or 5 feet above ground at the most, and strong enough to resist a direct hit of anything under an 8-inch how. The concrete is made of the finest water-worn gravel of the Rhine, brought in barges through Holland, and reinforced with steel rods, about an inch thick, to absorb the shock of shells on impact.

"The garrisons of these forts wear white arm-bands, and don't retreat. On the other hand, the Germans in the trenches of the foremost positions aren't supposed to stay and fight there, but to do what damage they can, and then clear off away back behind the *Allgemeine überstellenbau*, the line of forts, and fight from crater to crater, returning with reinforcements according to how our advance goes. It's an elastic defence, you see.

"Now for other main aspects. This time there's going to be no mistakes of uncut wire, as we met with at Bullecourt. We're under Plumer now. As you know, he's a Shop man, a gunner. And what's more, we've got the advantage, very much so, in numbers of guns, over the old Hun. And I think there will be more surprises for him. Now, cheer up your men with what I've told you."

Leaving the routine work to Sergeant Rivett, Phillip rode about the countryside, deeply interested in everything he saw—new wire cages, sign-posted from the front, *Prisoners this way*; tracks *For Walking Wounded*, leading to underground dressing stations; other tracks marked by black arrows pointing towards the Ridge, scores of them, all lettered and numbered. It appeared that every brigade, battalion, company, platoon, section, and man of the assault had a special job, learnt, practised and rehearsed many times. He began to appreciate the enormous amount of work the Staff had to do. Large models of the Ridge had been made, railed off, and surrounded by duck-board walks, so that every private soldier, gunner, driver, sapper, airman, and hospital orderly could see what was to happen. That was, he thought, a splendid idea, probably devised by some junior officer of 1914, who had risen up to be a G.S.O. Suddenly the idea came, I could do a job like that.

The models gave everyone an idea of the whole thing: this knowledge would help to open up the mind, he said, of the private soldier, hitherto treated more or less as though he were a bullock, having no intellectual life at all, because he had never been allowed to know what was to happen, like a convict in prison.

"I'm with you all the way there, Sticks. Why not give a talk to the company, on the difference between 1914, 1915, the First of July? You know, how we all have to learn by experience."

Before the talk, Phillip bought from the E.F.C. two tins of mixed biscuits, which he distributed to the men, through their section sergeants. "Good old Sticks," he heard—"He's a lad, is Sticks"—and felt a fraud.

2 Sat Gave a lecture, felt feeble. Contrast today with old days,
Loos, etc. Nothing left to chance this time. Objectives
are limited. The guns will blast away, troops advance;
pause for more blasting; then advance further. Everything is foreseen, from our side at any rate: the bones
of Loos have become chalk, the Somme dead are soil
again: their sacrifices were not all in vain. Almost the
fear of death is overcome, certainly depression. The
lonely soldier is a rarity, as far as one can see. New
Zealand and Australian troops, who never salute, give
out feelings of zest and power. Even so, I am still a
stranger in this land of 1914, which haunts me.
Widow-making guns and howitzers hung with black bast
netting. Flight after flight of scout planes passes over.

The fine weather of early summer continued. Everywhere in
fields of rising corn poppies grew, whole fields as though red
with blood. On the afternoon of Sunday, June 3, the King's
birthday, there was a trial barrage, which broke with thunderous
suddenness. Over rising country to the east arose palls of dust
and smoke, hiding the line of earth and sky. Phillip watched with
fascination almost sexual as he recalled the terrors of that sky-line
on the morning of Hallo'e'n, 1914, when, with ammunition which
did not fit the magazines of rifles, the London Highlanders
advanced against the unknown terrors of war. He felt ghost-like;
almost regretted that the war might end; for it was said that
over 2,000 guns were massed below the slope of ground from Hill
60 in the north to Plugstreet Wood in the south, along twelve
thousand yards of front. There were mines, too, all along the
German front position. Some ran half a mile underground, a
hundred feet deep, packed with up to ninety-five thousand pounds
of ammonal, blastine, and gun-cotton. Their deep shafts were
often lined with steel cylinders, and all had notice boards with
DEEP WELL painted on them. They had strange names mixed
up with English ones, Hollandscheschuur, Maedelstede Farm,
Peckham, Kruisstraate, Spanbroekmolen, Ontario Farm. He had
heard about them in conversation with all sorts of junior officers
in the crowded back areas, as he rode north and west, interested in
all he saw, followed by Morris on the grey mule. Everything his
eyes saw held interest and wonder, as he moved among tunic-
shoulders embroidered with many divisional devices—green
shamrock of the 16th (Irish), lilac butterfly of the 19th (Western),
red circle and Maltese Cross of the 23rd, red-and-white check on

waggons and limbers of the 25th, the bloody hand of the 36th
(Ulster), the white bar across various coloured squares of brigades
of the 41st, the 8-pointed white star on a black square bordered by
blue of the 47th (London) Division, mobilised in August 1914—
his division of long, long ago—where were the old faces of
Wimbledon, Bisley, and Crowborough? The red little, dead little
army was no more. The Empire was now in France—the silver
fern of New Zealand, the black triangle of the Australians; down
south the maple leaf of Canada, and the springbok of South
Africa. This was the life! In the everlasting movement of wheel,
hoof and foot raising the dust of the greatest occasion the world
had ever known—and yet——

And yet, underneath all the sun-burn and the laughter—
hundreds of thousands of secret thoughts passing to and from
England, Scotland, Ireland, Wales, Canada, South Africa, New
Zealand, Australia—the sea between the young condemned and
the old. But the old were condemned, too, as he thought that he
would never go home again. Here in Flanders, where the poppies
grew in Noman's-land, was *The Garden of Sleep*.

It was afternoon when he arrived back at camp to find the
limbers packed by a complacent Sergeant Rivett.

"Where have you been, Sticks?" asked Hobart. "Damn it,
man, this is Y day, and no time to go joy riding!"

Watches had been synchronised during his absence, at noon.

At twilight he led the limbers to their emplacements, and
returned without incident to the picket line. The summer evening
shaded into dusk. Small moths fluttered in his tent, tenuous as a
parent's thoughts. Except for an occasional flash and boom,
quietness settled over the level land below the Ridge.

The night seemed to be fecund with death-thoughts: a hundred
thousand minds dreading goodbye. Thunder clouds loured;
twilight went heavy, lightning repeatedly shattered the dark
glass of heaven, rain lashed down, to make each man waiting in
the assault trenches more lonely than before.

Drinking the third mugful of whiskey and chlorinated water
alone in his tent, he felt a longing to lift, suddenly, all fears and
sadness from them—release them—cry that a miracle of thought
had happened, that all could go home. How easy to feel like
that, cushy in a tent, with damn-all to face! Like Father, lying
back in his armchair, and killing Germans with his mind. While
he sat in a tent, saving them all with his mind! Vain feeling,

soft feeling, coward feeling, whiskey feeling! What did anything matter?

Carrying the Decca and box of records, he went to visit a
neighbouring transport officer with whom, the day before, he had
split a bottle of champagne outside the Expeditionary Force
Canteen below Neuve Église, beside the light railway, while sitting
on the grass.

It was now after midnight. The moon climbed a clear sky.
The Germans were searching back areas; British counter-batteries
were replying. As he walked towards his friend's tent, the sky
flushed over the Ridge, there was a rumbling roar—a German
ammunition dump going up somewhere.

He found his friend in a camouflaged tent, playing Patience
by the light of a candle. At once the two began to enliven one
another with thoughts of their present happy life. Phillip was
shown an item in *Comic Cuts*, the Corps news-sheet.

"Read that, old boy! And then ask yourself if this isn't
Fred Karno's Army!"

Reading it, he imagined an old professor with flat service hat,
tie awry, spectacles, grey hair fringing collar, at work in an
attempt to brighten up the war.

> There is evidence that Flanders has been, in prehistoric times, the
> scene of other engagements. In one area the fossil remains of a
> mammoth have been uncovered, together with flint implements used
> either to kill the beast or to cut it up. Unfortunately the entire
> skeleton could not be excavated, but enough has been salvaged to
> show that it was an unusually good specimen. The district where
> it was found is rich in remains of prehistoric man.

"Well, *mein prächtig kerl*," said Phillip, feeling himself to
be like All Weather Jack as he poured from a bottle he had
brought along with him. "They'll be diggin' up the remains of
some of our poor old donks in a thousand years' time, what?
Findin' oxidised Mills bombs and bits of guns and limbers, and
wonder who we were, and what we were scrappin' about. Cheer
ho! Knock that back, we mustn't let the talkin' stop the drinkin'!"

After half a bottle had disappeared, the following dialogue
took place.

"Did you hear that Broncho Bill's back?"

"Who's he when he's at home, *mein prächtig kerl?*"

"Haven't you heard of Broncho Bill?"

"Would I bloody well ask if I had?"

"All right, all right, keep your hair on! Cheerio!"

"Chin chin. Who's Broncho Bill?"

"I'll tell you if you'll listen!"

"I *am* bloody well listening! Get on with it."

"I will, if you'll give me a chance. Right! Cheerio!"

"Cheerho!"

"Fancy not having heard of Broncho Bill! I can't get over it!"

"Would you like to hear my gramophone for a change?"

"What'jer mean?"

"Change from Broncho Bill, *mein prächtig kerl.*"

"But I haven't told you yet!"

"Well, go on, then! I won't say a word. Continuez, mon ami!"

"Right. Broncho Bill's an Australian deserter, who's been playing merry hell with the Area Commandant, the A.P.M., and the Military Police for over a year. They say he was an actor before the war. His first known exploit was breaking into some officers' quarters, and pinching a uniform and some blank chit books and a rubber stamp. He went to various Field Cashiers' officers, and drew monthly advances for half a dozen books, each with its forged name, saying he was the second-in-command of his battalion. Then he pinched a car and went to other paymasters, and did the same thing again, several times, in fact."

"Wasn't he caught?"

"Yes, with some other deserters he'd palled up with, having a tremendous binge in Hazebrouck. They were put under arrest, but Broncho Bill escaped, leaving his pals in the prisoners' cage. The M.P.'s looked everywhere for him, but he'd vanished. Wait a mo'! Three days afterwards a hell of a poshed up redcap sergeant with a black Kaiser moustache reported to the R.S.M. at the cage, and showed an order to take the prisoners away to court-martial. The warrant was in order, so the R.S.M. handed them over, and they were never seen again. The M.P. sergeant was Broncho Bill disguised!"

"Good lord! What a lad!"

"I know! Well, not long afterwards there were mysterious fires in houses in Bailleul, and robberies. The M.P.'s have agents, you know, or informers—it's a dirty job being a cop—and through them they learned that it was the work of Broncho Bill and his gang. An informer tipped them off on the next job. The A.P.M., you may remember him at Grantham, Brendon——"

"Brendon! My God, I know him! He was in my battalion at Heathmarket in 'fifteen!'"

"Well, as I was saying, Brendon went in his car, and a lot of redcaps, and surrounded Baloo. All exits guarded. In the square, where he stopped, there was a smart squad under a sergeant with ginger eyebrows and Charlie Chaplin moustache. Terrific Guardsman salute, old Brendon returning it. Then the search for Broncho Bill began. When Brendon returned to the square, his motorcar was missing, and the driver sitting on the *pavé* with a whack over the head, minus his revolver, cartridge pouch, armlet, and cap. You've guessed it. Broncho Bill was the bloke with the false eyebrows and moustache."

"Where did he go?"

"God knows, and he won't split. I've heard that he has a hide-out on the old Somme battlefield. He travels about, been known at Amiens. A month ago he was at Pop. He got hold of a room and started a crown-and-anchor board. Also 'one up', you know tossing heads-or-tails, with coins with two heads. He was rumbled at that, but whipped out a revolver and threatened to shoot the first bloke who tried to stop him. Now he's back here."

"How d'you know?"

"A pal o' mine works in the office of the Area Commandant, and told me that his chief was rung up by the A.P.M., saying he'd had a chap who'd done five years' hard labour in a Dartmoor prison, and was sending him as a camp warden. He suggested that he be put in a dug-out next to the Area Commandant's staff dug-out, so's they could—keep an eye—on him. Hell, I'm blotto."

"What happened?"

"Christ knows, and he won't split."

The story-teller pushed past him, and stumbled out of the tent. Phillip put on *The Garden of Sleep*, which, Hobart said, had been written in Norfolk, near Sheringham, among fields red with poppies. Poppies—opium—sleep. The flowers of death, of Francis Thompson's "after-sleeping". How strange that they could be blooming everywhere, on the eve of a great battle.

After the record, he put on Kipling's *Mother o' Mine*.

> *If I were drowned in the deepest sea*
> *I know whose thoughts would come down to me,*
> > *Mother o' Mine——*

When his host came back, saying that the fug in the tent had turned him up, Phillip waited to hear what the gaol-bird had to do with Broncho Bill.

"Well, he cleared off after a bit, and was caught, and brought back. Here's the point. As he was being taken along the village street, to the cage, a redcap overheard an A.S.C. corporal coming out of an estaminet say, 'That's the bloke that's been harbouring the Australian deserters.' So the redcap reported it to my pal in the Area Commandant's office, whose chief rang up Brendon. That night a ring was made round the dug-outs' entrances in the field, and the redcaps went through the tunnels, checking every man in every platoon with their company officers. And caught Broncho Bill and two of his gang. They were handcuffed and taken to the M.P. Camp on the Dickebush road."

"Were they shot?"

"What, Broncho Bill? Don't be silly! He's still at large! He had been a day in the camp when he knocked out the sentry sent to look after the three of them when they went to wash, got his rifle and went to a hut; his mates each got a rifle, and made for the gate, saying they'd let the daylight into anyone who tried to stop them."

"Did he get away?"

"He got away, but not his pals. They got as far as the Poperinghe road, there was some shooting, one was hit in the arm and again in the leg, and the second gave up while trying to cross a muddy field. Broncho Bill got clear. A day or two later he pinched Brendon's best breeches hanging out on a line, right outside his office. Then while they were all out looking for him, he came back and pinched Brendon's horse, after knocking out the groom in charge of it."

"Good lord, what a nerve! How long ago was that?"

"Last week."

"What a lad! What a lad!" cried Phillip, and finding a record of Emmy Destinn singing *Ritorna Vincitore*, put it on the turn-table and, kneeling down, listened to the deep, tender, and passionate notes of the singer. All yearning, all hope, all rest was in the music. When he looked up, the other chap was lying back on his camp-bed, his eyes closed.

He finished the bottle alone. The funny thing was the stuff didn't make him swirl as in the old days. It was a food, and went very well with riding. Perhaps the shaking of the liver got rid of the poison. "Cheer-ho, *mein prächtig kerl!* " he toasted the recumbent one. "I heard that phrase on Christmas Day, 'fourteen, when we made friends with the Alleyman, as we called 'em then, and one showed me a meerschaum pipe with Little Willie's face on it. Their Prince of Wales, y' know. I can't bear the kind of chap who sneers at their Kronprinz, they don't sneer at our Pragger Wagger." He felt the tent swirling about him. Christ, he was blotto. Getting up, he walked back to his transport lines, feeling better in the fresh air. Black Prince jet black in moonlight. Dear old Blacker Pragger, to whinny at him! Faithful Black Prince! He felt he loved him, and put his arms round the warm neck.

Beside the gelding stood, uneasily, the stocky bay mare once ridden by Fenwick. She was named Betty, after Darky's girl at Sleaford. Good old Darky, back in England, safe with a nice wooden leg, soon to marry his girl of silk, and lie warm every night against the terrible softness of her body. He thought of Sasha, and how she must really despise him for being nothing. He felt twisted up, and gave a shout. *Bloody fool!* Never, never would he go back to Flossie Flowers' again.

"Did you call me, sir?"

"No, no, Sergeant Rivett. I was thinking of something, a long time ago. Goodnight."

"Goodnight, sir." The sergeant walked away in dissolving moonlight.

For a long time, it seemed, he stood with his cheek against the warm silk of Prince's neck, vaguely aware that the bay mare was turning her hindquarters, dumbly, to Prince. Perhaps all the light and flame had disturbed her: but how stupid he was, she was in season. Poor brown mare. As he imagined her feelings, sympathy flowed in him. Pushing between the mare and gelding, he put his arms round her neck, and talked to her, feeling her warmth flowing into him through his face. He felt to be nobody, to be of the moon. Was she appealing to him for relief, or sympathy? God, I'm tight, he thought: no matter, why shouldn't I help the poor creature. With slight erotism, and thrusting aside a feeling of being seen, swiftly he took off his jacket, and baring an arm, prepared to ease the mare. She turned her head as though with understanding, while Prince, whose ears were alert, uttered a happy little sound, huf-huf-huf. I believe they understand, he thought. How superior animals were to men who raped, with daggers in their minds.

He put on his tunic, and was buttoning it up when he saw the short figure of Sergeant Rivett a few yards away. Had he been there all the time, camouflaged by the moonlight? Had he seen him? He spoke to Prince, pretending not to have seen the sergeant. Then he changed his mind.

"What's the time, sergeant?"

"Nearly two o'clock, sir. I am about to change the picket."

"I thought of going for a short ride, it's such a beautiful night. And there's nothing doing now until five ack emma."

"Very good, sir. Shall I warn Morris?"

"Oh, don't wake him."

"He's still up, sir. None of us can sleep in this moonlight."

"Right ho, I'll take him with me."

Supposing something did come in, while he was absent? Rivett could deal with it. But supposing it was a job of taking ammunition up, and there was shelling? Rivett was windy, he might behave as he did to Cutts when a few 4.2's had come over at Mory. Rivett had his mother with him all the time, thinking of her and what she would feel if he were killed, just as he himself had felt in 1914. It was fatal to have your mother with you at war; thank God he himself had broken away. And yet, was that only why he could keep his feelings down, when shells came over? No: it was Lily helping him. If he hadn't the thought of Lily to keep him going, he would be windy himself: if he were going to be killed, he would be killed, and that was that. Rivett was where he had been, before he had been able to yield himself to Lily. So it was best to keep Rivett away from the line; he was very good for the routine work.

Hell, nothing could possibly come in. Only an attack from the Alleyman, what was called a spoiling attack, to catch our chaps on the hop, all ready for the advance, and so unready for defence. In which case he could soon get back. Even so, how would the limbers be needed? But what a schemozzle it would be if the Alleyman had decided to attack ten minutes before zero! It would be hell let loose. Would the order to blow the mines, prematurely, be given? That would scupper them all right! If not, our chaps and Germans would all be mixed up, and what would our machine guns do?

Hell, why worry. It wouldn't happen. The attack would go according to plan. The sections were not going over with the first waves. They were to squat still at their emplacements, sixteen among seven hundred Vickers machine guns helping with the barrage. The rate per gun was three hundred rounds per minute, fired in bursts . . . twenty odd thousand empty brass cartridge cases being flicked out by the extractors per minute, the bullets swishing up and over the Ridge. Poor bloody Alleymans! He imagined himself in *feld-grau* uniform, bringing up ammunition, water, and rations, and having to pass through one of the seven hundred lattice-curtains of nickel. Fourteen million bullets, spinning, three feet above the ground, over the Ridge and down the reverse slopes. Each one a whisper, a cry, a moan, a buzz, unheard in smoke, dust, and roar-rendings of more than two thousand shells from guns and howitzers, and nearly as many again from Stokes mortars and short-ranged torpedoes—the "flying pigs" of the heavy trench-mortars.

This vision momentarily spoiled his ambition to see the grandeur of the opening bombardment from Hill 73, behind Ploegsteert Wood, between two and three miles away. There was a ruined chateau, La Hutte, on its top. He remembered it had yellow walls seen in the distance when bicycling down from Messines on Christmas Day, 1914, during the truce, to try and find cousin Willie at Plug Street.

How tight was he? Holding hands before him, he shut his eyes and stood on one leg. He stumbled; still, it was difficult in the moonlight. He tried again, and kept upright while he counted three, slowly. Good, he was all right. Very well, check. It was 2 a.m. He was free for a least three hours. Pack mules, loaded with water and ammunition, were to be at the emplacements at 5 a.m., together with pack mules to carry the Vickers guns to the Second Line just below the Crest. There was to be a two-hour pause, in which to consolidate. Then the second assault, to be followed by a five-hour pause, to await the counter-attack, smash it, and then advance to the sixth objective, the Oosttaverne Line.

Zero hour was at 3.10 a.m.: if he left at 2 a.m. he would get to La Hutte Hill in plenty of time to see the start of the show. With no transport on the roads, he would be able to trot all the way back, taking from fifteen to twenty minutes.

"I'll be back well before five o'clock," he told Sergeant Rivett. "You'll know what to do if anything comes in, won't you?"

"I'll do my best, sir."

"Not that anything is likely to come in, but anyway—I'll not be gone for long. Back about four ack emma."

"Very good, sir."

When his officer had left, Rivett said to the man on picket duty, "There he goes, joy-riding again! Leaving everything to me!"

The driver said, "Yes, sergeant," but he thought that the sergeant had it as cushy as the A.S.C., for Sticks always took the convoy up the line, while Rivett stayed back and had a good kip every night.

Followed by Morris, Phillip took the road to Wulverghem, with its faraway memories of the grey morning after the defeat at Messines on that never-to-be-forgotten night of Hall'o'en. As he trotted beside his shadow, aeroplanes began to fly over, at about a thousand feet. Surely that would tell the Germans quite clearly that they were flying to and fro in order to drown the sounds of tank engines, as they moved up to their starting points? Then, before him, was a misty movement, which he saw as he went on to be a column of marching men. They were the reserves, and carried much equipment, spades, extra bandoliers, canvas buckets of bombs, and Lewis-gun ammunition—and oranges. He stood still as they passed, faces turned curiously towards him. They seemed endless, so he walked on, followed by Morris. Other columns were moving across the fields, all in silence. No red point of cigarette.

By the time he got to La Hutte Hill the guns, which had been firing intermittently, were silent. He left Morris with Prince, and walked up a slope. Somewhere inside the hill was a very big dugout, called the Catacombs, rumoured big enough to hold a brigade. He was aware of faces suddenly appearing, as he came upon groups of men talking in quiet voices, some sitting, others standing, all waiting like himself for the start.

He found an 18-pounder shell-box, and settled himself comfortably elbows on knees and face in hands, while thinking that the Bible phrase of bowels turning to water could not be bettered.

The aircraft flew back towards Bailleul and Hazebrouck. Time dragged at the moon. At last it was three o'clock. His heart began to thump. It was so quiet that he could hear nightingales singing far away. They were surely very late in singing, the eggs must be hatched by now, and normally the cockbird ceased to sing when the hen began to sit. Perhaps the unnatural noise of the guns had strained their nervous systems. Some birds, notably wrens, uttered nervous little trilling bursts of song when alarmed at night. Perhaps all beauty, whether of sound or colour or shape, came out of pain, or suppression of life, as poetry came from suffering. Then he thought, How *can* any species evolve without fear, or dread of pain? Life on earth was obviously a series of experiments. And behind fear and pain was the spirit of life, which was love. Of course! He felt calm, and happy. Life must endure all things.

Low voices were audible. He stood up and moved towards a group, drawn by the feeling of their excitement which showed itself in all their faces turned one way; but in time saw the dark old-blood colour of their hatbands, and moved away to a safe distance. Then hearing their voices, he knew them for Australians, and felt at ease, though still keeping his distance.

What were the Germans feeling in their pill-boxes, so white in the sun after the bombardments had blown away the covering earth around them? Had they evacuated their forward positions, knowing of the attack, as they had Y Sap before La Boisselle on July the First? Their detector-sets had picked up the Fourth Army's telephone messages then, perhaps they had better instruments now? He felt the being-drawn feeling between his legs, and his mouth was dry—he looked at his watch—nine minutes past three.

Before he was ready for it a great tongue of deep yellow flame arose slowly into the moonlight. It went up silently and was followed by another and another, curling up away in the distance, slowly turning red and broadening upon his stopped breath, until each became in shape like an enormous rose, opening its petals and shedding them slowly in fire and smoke. He could not breathe; then the entire world seemed to split; terrific explosions bumped against him. He did not know if it was his legs shaking or the earth. Smoke arose blackly, tarnishing the moon, which seemed to tumble and twirl. He found himself thrown down upon the grass, while figures of staff-officers, their red bands clearly seen in the fiery light, were clutching one another and calling out among themselves.

But it was not over; now yellow chrysanthemums were rising on broad ruddy stalks, to burst and rock the earth. Staggering reports echoed in thunder all around the night, suddenly to be joined by a mixed massiveness of light quenching moonlight. More than two thousand gun-flashes fluttered to the zenith; thunders rolled; and through them running sparkles of three necklaces appeared low in the night—three zones of barrage fire upon the western slope of the Ridge. Now seven hundred Vickers guns would be heating their water-jackets, and more than a hundred battalions of infantry advancing up the slope.

From above, white and green rockets burst almost imperceptibly. How pathetic, he thought: SOS, SOS, SOS, the German rockets were saying, help us, help us, help us, to their smothered artillery.

As he rode back, in the light of the guns and a dawn of lurid pink, he saw the camouflage netting of a howitzer battery, 9.2 guns almost track to track, flare up as one gun fired. Even Jimmy the mule broke into a canter, to get away from that. The sun was behind the Ridge, now clear against the sky, when he got back to the picket line, feeling grey and emptied out. There was no time to sleep, so he had some tea from his batman, who came into his tent with the German dog on a leash.

"What's the idea, Barrow?"

"Precaution, sir, as you might say. I don't want to git Little Willie half-inched, not wiv all them Horsetrailians about, proper scroungers they are, sir. They nick anyfing from a dorg to a mule if they could git away wiv it."

When he had gone, Phillip poured whiskey into his tea, and soon felt more cheerful. And when the sun rose up, and all firing ceased, and he knew it was successful, he drank another quartern to celebrate. They were moving up, said Barrow, coming into the tent, to the tune of *Destiny* waltz.

"I shan't want any breakfast, thanks."

"Come on, sir, you must stoke up! I've got some nice rashers fried, wiv a bit o' fat bread. I know just what you want, sir. They say it's a walkover this time. I reckon Ole Indenburg's copped it good an' proper. Abaht time too. This new General Plumer 'as put paid to 'is little game. Not like at Bullecourt, sir."

A minute later he returned. "The guide 'as come from the capting, and Sergeant Rivett says the pack mules will be ready in ten minutes, sir. I brought you some fresh tea, and here's your lunch. Jules packed it special, sir. He says he's got all the orfficers done the same. There's a ration of oranges, too. Very different from the Fifth Army style, sir. Shall you want me to come, sir?"

"Would you like to?"

"I would very much, sir."

Visions of souvenirs from dead Jerries animated the batman.

By the time the pack mules reached what had been the German front line, the battle was halted beyond the skyline. In the crater-area not one green blade of grass was visible. Everywhere brown earth was overturned and pocked. Broken fragments of concrete lay about. Rusty steel wires clawed the air above split and shattered mebus, called pill-boxes. Barbed-wire belts were buried among corpses in torn *feld-grau* with blackened faces, flopped about in all positions. Some of them wore white arm-bands. They had stayed in the unbroken pill-boxes and been bayoneted. There was hardly a dead man in khaki to be seen. Already the pockets of the dead Germans had been slit or pulled out, and rings cut off fingers.

They passed by the ragged mine crater at Spanbroekmolen. It was about a hundred and fifty yards from lip to lip, and deeper than the German dugouts, for one was exposed at the edge, with its occupants. Looking through his field-glasses, Phillip saw what was like something at Madame Tussaud's: a boarded room with one side open, revealing four German officers seated at a table, with waxen faces. They looked as though they had been playing cards. Glasses and bottles on the table were still upright. Apparently they had been killed by concussion. In the pit below were ragged lumps of blue clay each big enough to fill a G.S. waggon.

"I reckon they're between two and three yards each," said Barrow, who had worked on roads in civvy street.

"Yards long, you mean?"

"In a way, yes, sir. All through, solid like. You know, sir."

"Oh, cubic yards?"

"That's what I mean, sir."

The guide led them past tanks, their tracks churning as they tried to get over the loose and undulating ground. Sitting on a box near the crest, was Captain Hobart writing a report. "Hullo, Sticks. Got everything? The post too! Good man. Better get back fairly soon, the second barrage is due to drop in about forty minutes, so you'll have to look slippy. You haven't forgotten water for the guns? Good man!"

The contents of the Vickers' water-jackets had boiled away, despite the steam being led through water-buckets, for conceal-ment and condensation. Soon everything was off-mule'd, and he went back. The new lines of infantry, all extremely cheerful at the success of the attack, were among the tanks in position for the second phase. Hardly had he passed the Spanbroekmolen mine

hole when the guns started up. 18-pounder shells seemed to be
screaming a foot or two over his head, making him crouch, until
he remembered the drivers, and walked on as though unconcerned. It was 7 a.m. The barrage was falling beyond the unseen
crest.

Two hours later he went up again with more water, oil, ammunition, food. Each pack mule carried six boxes of belted ammunition, and a petrol tin of water. The second objective had been
taken. The sun was now hot. Captain Hobart was sitting in
shirt-sleeves, soft fawn stock-tie around neck, leather braces over
shoulders. "Hullo, Sticks, my boy, we've done it again!" he
said, as he buried, Phillip noticed, the peel of his ration orange.
The forward crest was crowded with troops, most of them with
tin-hats and tunics off. Some were naked above the waist, lying
back to get the joy of the sun. Orange peel was chucked about
everywhere, and the congestion of troops added to the illusion of a
Bank Holiday on the Hill. The reason was, of course, the small-
ness of casualties.

"Will it be all right if I go forward a bit, Skipper?"

"Another of your Cook's tours, Sticks? Don't go too far. This
picnic is too dam' good to last, if you ask me."

"I rather want to see where I was, nearly three years ago,
Skipper."

"Well, don't be long. As I said, this pause is too good to last.
Reminds me too much of Loos, Sticks."

"Yes. I'll be quick."

He looked in vain for the old road along the crest, with its rusty
steam-tramlines embedded in cobbles, along which he had
bicycled on Christmas afternoon, 1914. But where was the road?
Had he crossed it, before meeting Hobart? Of course, the bombardment had dug it up. He felt lost. Then looking east, he saw
green country stretching away to the far horizon. That was the
same. There were the trees beside the river Lys, no longer bare,
but in full leaf, untouched by shell-fire. He thought back to the
sunlit winter scene, resting himself in thought.

Then, back in the present, he wondered why the attack was
not pressing on. Was it going to be another Loos—the line unexpectedly broken, and no pursuit? Or was the plan to await the
counter-attack, smash it, and then advance, having exhausted the
local enemy reserves? But the heavy guns could not get up over
such ground. Perhaps that was why the push was stopped.

Looking through his field-glasses he saw a column of troops

marching along the road from Wervicq, near the canal. The counter-attack was late: but it was coming. He hurried back to report, to be told that it had already been spotted.

"Well, so long, dear boy."

When he got back to the picket line, he went for a ride on Prince. There was a spirit of optimism everywhere, especially in the Casualty Clearing Station, where the number of wards had been doubled, with the staff of doctors and orderlies; they had nothing to do.

But something now had gone wrong, judging by the remote crackle of small arms and machine-gun fire on the Ridge later in the afternoon, after the British barrage and attack at 3.10 p.m. Rumour said that the Germans had recaptured the position. Many wounded began to arrive. Rumours spread: some units had retired in panic. At 5.30 p.m., as he was waiting to go up again with the pack-mules, red SOS rockets arose into the sky. When going up, he heard that the British barrage had fallen upon an Australian brigade, in advance of the Oosttaverne line, having been mistaken for Germans. They had retired; the Germans had come forward again.

Phillip lost two mules, and a driver wounded, that night. On the return, green cross and yellow cross gas shells—phosgene and lachrymatory—made the wearing of box-respirators necessary. Despite the special anti-dimming paste, it was hard to see, with the mask over one's face, and stifling hot. He had swallowed some tea, with rum, and had hardly got down for a bit of shut-eye when a runner came with the news that Captain Hobart had been killed, and that Mr. Pinnegar was in command.

Part Three

'SHARPSHOOTER' DOWNHAM

Chapter 9

BASE WALLAHS

A week later, when the battle was over, the company went to
rest and refit at Nieppe, behind Armentières. Pinnegar was still
acting C.O., but, he grumbled, there were rumours of a new
major coming from Wisques, the Machine Gun School near St.
Omer. A draft to replace casualties arrived, among them Cutts,
from whom Phillip had heard nothing since he had been wounded
by the egg-bomb in the fire-bucket.

On the third day out, an inspection was ordered by Lt.-Col.
Wilmott, the divisional Machine Gun Officer, who accompanied
the Brigadier-General of Group, from Corps. The Brigade Major
came, too, with a second-lieutenant who was the Brigade
Transport Officer and galloper to the Brigadier—both positions
unofficial and honorary. Phillip had seen this junior subaltern
only on one occasion, during the A.S.C. gymkhana at Ervillers: a
graceful, willowy figure on a horse, son of a considerable Yorkshire
landowner, and a winner of several point-to-point races in the
Brigadier's country before the war. One other figure approached
with the visitors, the blue-hat-banded Assistant Director of
Veterinary Services.

The day before the inspection, and again on the morning,
Pinnegar urged everyone in the company to give a first-class turn-
out, hoping thereby to be given permanent command of the
company. In the transport section chains were swung and shaken
to-and-fro within bags of chaff, limbers were washed and oiled,
saddlery soaped and polished.

Round the sections the inspectorate passed, the Brigadier once
asking to see a Vickers gun stripped by its team. He wanted to look
at the barrel. This took some time; a certain spanner was missing.
The barrel rifling was seen to be worn. Why had it not been
replaced, the General asked Col. Wilmott, who passed the query
on to Pinnegar.

"Spares indented for have not yet come to hand, sir," replied
Pinnegar. "We are waiting for them."

"Why haven't you gone yourself to draw them?"

Pinnegar turned to his quartermaster sergeant. "You indented for them, Bowles?"

"Yes, sir. Immediately we came out of the line."

Pinnegar passed this on; and was asked, "Why not before you came out of the line?"

"We had spare barrels then, sir."

"Then why aren't they fitted?"

"We used them in the later barrages, sir."

"Then you had no spares when you came out of the line?"

"If you put it that way, no!" retorted Pinnegar, flushing.

The inspectorate passed down the lines of guns on their tripods, each crew stiffly at attention.

"Action!" said the General, suddenly.

Nobody moved.

"Don't your men recognise an emergency order?" cried Colonel Wilmott.

"Well, what d'you expect me to do?" replied Pinnegar.

"I want to see how quickly your men can go into action," said the General. "Target six hundred yards, between clump of trees at eleven o'clock!"

"Come on, jump to it!" yelled the section sergeant. "You 'eard! Action!"

The crew dashed themselves upon the ground, No. 1 at the spade grip, No. 2 at the belt, No. 3 observing, No. 4 writhing to grab spare belt-box, etc. Pushing the belt tab through the feeding porte, No. 1 grabbed it, jerked it twice, thus feeding a round into the breech; and in the excitement raised the safety bar, pressed the thumb-piece, and a dozen rounds kicked up the dust between the tents and the picket line, where Phillip was waiting, dismounted, wearing a new pair of silver-plated racing spurs he had bought for 10/6 from an advertisement in *The Tatler*.

A hoarse cry from Driver Cutts, sitting on a trace mule, made him realise that he had not been cured.

When it was the turn of the transport another demonstration was being given overhead. Several anti-aircraft batteries were pooping off at an old 2-seater Cody-Wright Birdcage sent over, said Phillip afterwards, to take photographs for *The Birmingham Smoke Trumpet* in anticipation of Teddy Pinnegar's appointment. Little white balls of smoke were bursting ten thousand feet up, in irregular chains, following a tiny pale midge-like object. Splinters began to sing and hum around the camp, their notes of descent varying with the size and pattern of fragmentation. Drivers looked to their front during the inspection; they knew that "Vinegar" was on trial, and anyway the shelling by archie of an aeroplane was a common sight. Col. Wilmott, accompanied by Pinnegar wearing his best Harry Hall's salmon-pink breeches, and Phillip, was passing the tall grey mule when Jimmy gave a tremendous double kick with its hind legs and threw its forty-five-year-old driver, M'Kinnell, at the feet of the General, who said, "What's this?"

"Can't your drivers control their mounts?" asked Col. Wilmott, sharply.

"I've never known this mule kick before, sir," said Phillip.

"Your drivers should anticipate what their mounts are likely to do."

Phillip knew enough to keep silent; he saw a thin red weal near the mule's off point of hip, but said nothing. When the inspection was over, he pointed out the wound to Pinnegar.

"Driver M'Kinnell was lucky not to have his head bashed into his shoulders."

"What is it?"

"A nose-cap of an archie shell. Poor old Jimmy."

The mule was led away to the Mobile Veterinary Station, and the casualty recorded without comment in the return that night to Brigade.

"That bloody fool Wilmott told me that the General said he'd never seen such a poor turn-out!" grumbled Pinnegar. "What does he expect, with a third of the men, and three officers, casualties? I'm fed up. I'm quite happy to go back to my regiment. After all we've been through together, to have some bloody stranger from the C.O.'s pool at Wisques planted upon us! Probably only just come out from England, and never been in action! It would be just our luck to have someone like your pal Downham again."

"Oh God. But I suppose anyone can apply to go to a particular company?"

"Why not? It's all done off a roster in some orderly room at the base. You've got to grease the orderly room sergeant's palm, of course."

"Oh hell. Sergeant Rivett's been corresponding with Downham. It might very well give him an idea to try and get here, to someone he knows."

When Phillip returned from a visit to Jack Hobart's grave

in Kandahar Farm Cemetery, he had a shock when Nolan, on picket duty, said, "The new C.O.'s arrived, sir, the one we 'ad temporary in H Lines when Capt'n Ho-bart got jaundice."

"What?"

Devastated by his premonition having come true, Phillip went to his tent, where he drank a tooth-mug of one part of whiskey and two of water. Then he put on a record of Destinn singing in *Tosca*, and lay on his bed, while passionate and tender contralto tones brought back poignantly an awareness of Hobart, whose favourite opera it was. Why had it happened to Jack like that— a chance in a million: a dud howitzer shell passing within a few inches of his head had sucked out his breath and broken the tissues of his lungs, so that he had been drowned in his own blood. He felt weary and hopeless. All the decent people seemed to get killed, just as life was beginning to have possibilities. Now it would be the same old muck-up all over again.

He lay on his bed, thinking of old days, and fortifying himself with more whiskey.

He was lying back, with some sort of interior comfort, and resolution not to care a damn, when Downham's lean ruddy face looked in at the tent flap.

"Hullo, you young blighter! Why the hell didn't you come and see me when you returned from wherever you'd been joy-riding?"

Phillip got up. "I was just coming, sir—I felt a bit tired——"

"Sit down. And don't bother to pretend."

"Would you care for a spot, sir?"

"Subalterns don't ask field officers to have a drink, at least not where I've come from. Well, how are you?" He held out his hand, and gave Phillip a crushing grip. Jack's handshake had been gentle, not the hearty stuff.

"Very well thank you—sir."

"Drop the sir, man, we're not on parade! What I came to tell you is that a chit has come in, about sending an officer to the Divisional Signalling Course. I don't see how we can spare a section officer, so it'll have to be you. Sergeant Rivett can look after the transport while you are away. No need to look so depressed. It will probably be your turn to go on leave by the time you come back."

After four days Phillip was sent back from the course. Returning to the picket line, he learned from Sergeant Rivett that Black Prince was "now the charger of the Officer Commanding".

"Which horse am I supposed to have, d'you know?"

"It's beyond me to say," replied Rivett, buoyantly.

"But I've had Prince since October! The Riding Master at Grantham made a point of letting me have him, at Captain Hobart's special request! Didn't you tell Major Downham that, sergeant?"

"Sir, I consider it to be outside my duties to question the decisions of the Officer Commanding." Phillip went to see Downham about it, to find that he already wanted to see him about the report that had come in from the Divisional Signalling School.

This officer shows no interest in his work, is inattentive, and appears to spend his time writing personal entries in Army Book 136 provided for the purpose of taking notes on the material of lectures.

"Well, my young friend of a Christian bloody fool, still true to form, I see! Who the hell d'you think you are? What sort of a fool d'you think you're making of me, when I've just taken over the company, to have the first officer I send on a course kicked out for sheer damned laziness? You always did dodge all the work you could! And a fine reputation your transport has got with Division! The A.D.V.S. was here this morning. I had to take him round, since you'd gone off on a joy-ride, leaving all the work, as usual, to your sergeant! And there's another matter, over which you'd better watch your step! I don't know what sort of a pervert you are inside, but take my tip, young Maddison, and watch your step when you come back! Here's your leave ticket. Your leave starts at midnight tonight. Well, what is it?"

"Sir, may I have permission to leave camp for one hour this afternoon."

"What for?"

"Urgent private affairs, sir."

"What are they?"

"I want to go to Kandahar Farm Cemetery, sir, to see Captain Hobart's grave."

"Very well. But you can't take the black gelding."

"I understand, sir. May I take any other horse, not in use?"

"I should have thought that the brown mare would be more in your line."

He knew then that Sergeant Rivett had reported what he had seen on the night before the Messines show to Downham.

He rode the bay mare to Kandahar Farm Cemetery, and planted some pansies, taken from the Commandant's garden during the darkness of the previous night, on All Weather Jack's grave, now set with a plain wooden cross.

Chapter 10

TEN DAYS' LEAVE

HE went to rail-head with Bright, the rather grim silt-lands farmer, whom he managed to lose at Boulogne. They had nothing to talk about. A few days later he was to realise what had been wrong with Bright; meanwhile he was glad to be on his own in a bunk among unknown others, crossing the Channel in darkness. There was an escort of three destroyers. To his surprise and satisfaction, he felt no qualm of sickness.

Taking a taxicab from Victoria, he looked about him eagerly for a manifestation of his own feelings, but saw none. Trafalgar Square was but a place in memory of the many occasions shared with Desmond, Eugene, Jack Hobart and others, including Aunt Dora and cousin Willie. He told himself that he must expect nothing: all scenes had an existence but in the mind, and would fade with a man's death. Away with personal desires; only poetry endured. What time did the War Office open? He thought to see Colonel Orlebar, to ask for a transfer back to the Gaultshire Regiment.

It was half-past eight. The Strand was crowded with soldiers and sailors, all going somewhere. Many had wives or sweethearts with them, and carried full kit and rifle; they were returning from leave. What could he do to kill time, until ten o'clock? It was a Saturday, too, and perhaps Orlebar would be away for the weekend. The weekend! How to face it at Wakenham? Should he go to Flowers' hotel? On the excuse to tell Miss Flowers how All Weather Jack had died? Would it be the thing to go there for breakfast only? Hardly. He went into the Strand Apex House, and had eggs and bacon, while reading in *The Daily Trident* of the successful offensive in Russia; about Kerensky, "the new strong man"; 122 British ships had been sunk in June by German submarines, totalling 417,925 tons. He thought it odd that the May figures, which he remembered reading in the *Trident* in White

Rose Camp, had also been 122 ships. Perhaps they made up any odd figures to deceive the enemy, or someone in the Admiralty had muddled them.

Outside in the Strand he saw a team of Boys' Brigade nippers hauling a sort of limber by ropes, with a board on it saying *Prince of Wales Waste Paper Fund.* He added *The Daily Trident*, thinking of Father. Why not go and see the old fellow after his visit to the War House?

He filled up a form, and was led along passages by a much smaller Boy Scout than before, to the M.S. department. To his pleasure he was greeted by Colonel Orlebar, who remembered him, but said nothing of the last meeting in the Café Royal, at the luncheon for "Spectre" West's gong, when he had drunk too much wine and had to go out.

"If you'd been here this time yesterday you'd have seen 'im. He crossed over last night, to take up a special appointment. Perhaps in the circumstances you might care to consider going down to see the Militia Battalion on the East Coast, and have an interview with the Colonel there, and get him to apply for you. Is your present Commanding Officer willing to release you?"

"I am fairly certain that he is, sir."

"In that case the better course would be to go down to Felixstowe, and see the Colonel; and if you get his approval, to forward your papers through your C.O. in France. If and when the transfer goes through, you may be posted to a line battalion, or more probably, be sent home to Felixstowe, and then take your turn."

"I suppose, sir, there's no chance of my going direct to a line battalion of the Regiment in France, without coming home first?"

Colonel Orlebar looked shrewdly at the young man before him. "You're pretty keen, aren't you? How many times have you been out so far?"

"Four, Colonel. But I have only done fourteen months in all."

"That's a fair stint. Well, the best of luck!" He half rose across the table, and held out his hand. Phillip thanked him, saluted, and left; with a glance at the clock on the wall. It was a quarter to eleven.

Should he go to Flossie Flowers'? Sasha, would she be there? The image of her winsome face drew him, her breasts slightly repelled. He felt a cad, and said of his mean self "Damn you!", then was discomposed because a man in a seedy purple velour hat and mackintosh walking the same way heard, and gave him a quick, as though alarmed, look. Phillip drew on his gloves, assuming an easy expression; but for some reason the man in the old mackintosh abruptly crossed the road, dodging between the two streams of taxis and buses, and then walked in the opposite direction. Had he dodged the call-up, and thought he had been spotted?

Phillip walked to the City along the Embankment. He was already used to women bus-conductors, in short skirts, black button'd leggings and cocked hats, but the sight of a woman in trousers pulling on the long sweep of an empty barge beside a terrier dog seemed a bit queer. He watched her go under Blackfriars Bridge with relief, then wondered why she was looking up at the sky, over the north bank and the City. Other people were looking up, too, and following their gaze, he saw a V-formation of what to him was a new type of aeroplane, bombers by the size. They were fairly low. He watched them coming nearer, they made quite a heavy growling. They turned in some sort of formation above the gilt cross of St. Paul's, shining in the summer sun, and he saw four others behind the V-formation, and was wondering why they flew so raggedly when a gun went off behind him, from the direction of Whitehall.

People began to cry out and run. Traffic was stopping. The aircraft broke formation, and he heard the whine of a bomb. It exploded with a deep *crum-m-p*. Others followed.

He felt rough and angry, and yelled "Bastards!" The policeman on point duty was waving his arms and yelling, "Take cover! Take cover!" Phillip shouted, "Keep calm! No wind up!" as men and women ran to shelter, some screaming. He stood calmly, feeling scorn. Waitresses from a tea-shop ran out, also screaming, then ran back into the shop. Where the hell were our guns, he thought angrily. Then shrapnel began to burst in the air overhead. More bombs. Splinters hissed and whined down, rattling on paving stones. *Plop!* That was a nose-cap, which had cracked a stone ten yards away. He thought of Jimmy the mule, and found he was trembling when the biplanes had flown away; but not with fear, he told himself.

As he hurried up Ludgate Hill, making for Haybundle Street where Father and Mavis worked, an omnibus stopped at the corner of Old Bailey. It was covered with sawdust. Blood, he thought; then, why no glass broken? He crossed over to hear what the conductress was saying, again and again. "Sawdust, I ask you! They dropped sawdust all over us! A dark cloud come down! Sawdust! I ask you! They dropped sawdust on us! What if it's poisoned, like their gas? Oh Gawd, isn't it awful? Don't touch it! It may be poisoned!" A man said angrily, "Where's our Flying Corps, that's what I want to know! *John Bull* will want to know the answer! No flies on Horatio Bottomley!"

"No flies on sawdust," said Phillip, walking away.

Later, he heard that a bomb falling on the Central Telegraph Office of the G.P.O. in Newgate Street had blown up the wooden huts on the roof, which were dry in the heat, and up they had gone in dust, just as the Zeppelin bomb which had killed Lily had blown glass to powder over poor old Father. How interesting all these details were; but they never got into the papers. He would put them in his diary.

"Well, old chap," said Father, in the Moon Fire Office, "you've arrived at a queer time! It just proves what I've said from the start, that the Germans will stop at nothing! Nothing!" he repeated, pale and agitated. "You saw what happened? You heard it?" He stopped himself from adding, Now perhaps you'll believe what these Prussians really are. After a pause, "Well, how are matters out there? On leave, are you? For eight days, well——Still with the same Corps? Well—this is quite a surprise!" He was relieved that his son seemed to be settled down. "Your sister is upstairs, but no doubt you'll be seeing her at home. I mustn't keep you. You'll be wanting to go down to see your mother, I'll be bound." He had not the power in him to ask if his son would be staying at home. The boy had his own plans, no doubt; and he himself was quite an old stager now having turned of fifty. He wanted to say, 'You are always welcome, you know', but the words would not come. Rather than risk a rebuff he turned away, with a wave of his hand, to his desk in the Town Department.

Phillip went on to Wine Vaults Lane, where the news of Downham having command of the company was already known.

"It's the same everywhere," remarked Hollis, the head clerk. "Downham stays in England nearly three years and rises to field rank, and others do all the real work. It's exactly the same here in this office. As you know, I got most of the new business before the war, and Howlett got all the credit for it. He's been out for the past two hours, while I've been here with Phillpots, doing the work. Now tell me, when's the war going to finish? This year? Or next, when the Americans come over in force?"

"I think it will be next year, Mr. Hollis."

"Have you got any particular reason for your assessment of the situation?"

"Oh yes. We've got the stuff now. It's bound to be a slogging match, you know."

"So you think it'll be all over in 1918, do you? Even with Downham in command of your company?"

"Oh, we've got a good sergeant major, and the men know their jobs, Mr. Hollis."

"Good. Then I'll try and hold the fort here until you come back, although I suppose you'll both be too big for your boots by then, what?"

Phillip thought that he would never want to go back to that dreadfully tame life.

It was Saturday, he suddenly realised; soon offices and warehouses would be closing; so saying goodbye he hurried away to Houndsditch, hoping to see Eugene at the C.M. Corset factory. He caught his Brazilian friend as he was drawing on his chamois gloves, boater on head, nosegay in button-hole, attaché case and silver-topped ebony stick ready to hand. His face showed great pleasure when he saw Phillip.

"I'm on leave, Gene! How lovely to see you. What about a spot of lunch with me in Piccadilly? And a theatre afterwards? Or are you doing something?"

"I've arranged to go with a bird to Brighton for the week-end."

"Oh, I see."

"I can't very well get out of it, because such an opportunity may not occur again."

"How d'you mean?"

"Her husband's gone to Dublin on business, and will be back by next week-end."

"I see."

"Otherwise I'd come with you, like a shot, you know that. How about next week?"

"I'll be going back next Sunday, and ought to spend Saturday with my people."

Eugene's sallow face showed indecision. His eyes narrowed as he weighed up the idea of a week-end with dear old Phil, in

uniform as a full lieutenant and two wound stripes, on leave from
the front, against the pleasures to be had with someone ten
years older than himself, whom he had already taken to his
attic flat opposite Paddington station. She had offered to pay
for everything—first-class fares, oysters and white wine at the
Old Chain Pier Bar, dinner at the Ship, and suite at the
Metropole. At the same time, he wanted to keep in with Harry
Spero, who might take him in partnership in his scheme for
after the war, he told Phillip, for cheap suitings for soldiers
returning to civilian life. Hence the visit to Dublin, to buy up
hundreds, thousands of bolts of cloth, before prices rose any
further.

"Harry's in army contracts for uniforms for the WAACS now,
also omnibus conductresses and police-women, and it would be
all u.p. with me if he found out about Leonora. So I'll call it
off. Where shall we go? Piccadilly Grill? Then how about the
Lilac Domino? I've seen it six times already, and still think it's
the best show in Town. Here's my new card, by the way. My
mother's father was General Goulart, you know. Would you like
to see his photograph?"

"You showed it to me, Gene."

"Oh, did I?" He was a little disappointed.

Having arranged to meet at 7 p.m. outside Swan & Edgar's
in Piccadilly they said goodbye. Gene went to telephone his
regrets that, owing to a sudden attack of *grippe*, he would not
be able to go to Brighton. He longed to say that an officer friend
had just returned from the front, his great friend Major Maddison,
of the Staff; but he did not want to offend Leonora, and through
her, his business acquaintance Jack Spero.

Phillip walked to Pimms' in Old Broad Street, where he bought
some smoked salmon and ham at a stout-and-sandwich bar to
take home. Then a taxicab to Charing Cross.

In the train he looked at Gene's flowery new card, obviously
not printed from an engraved copper plate, like his own cards,
which had been done properly by Gran'pa Turney's firm. *Mr.
Eugene Franco Goulart-Bolivar*, with flourishes and twirls—rather
vulgar, he considered. After all, Gene was a foreigner.

He got out at St. John's station, meaning to walk over the Hill,
and so avoid letting all of Hillside Road, on the other side of the
Crest, as he thought of it, know that he was back on leave.

He imagined a battle for the Hill, as he walked up the long
flag-stoned road, rising gradually until green slopes extended

before him, and the gravel path beyond the spiked iron gate and railings. No hope for the 1st Guard Reserve Division, hastily entrained from the Arras front to Wervique, marching up that way. A nickel lattice curtain would hiss sixteen-fold over the Crest, and catch the column in *feld-grau.*

On the grassy Hill, with its keepers' huts, shelters, and band-stand, somehow all looking so much smaller, he walked between the two armies of his imagination, thinking to hang about until the imagined figure of Father appeared, straw boater in hand, swinging along as he had seen him a hundred times, and always with a feeling of life stopping abruptly, in the summers of boyhood. How strange that the damping feeling was still in him, despite the war. Of course! That feeling underlay the war! It was the war! The war was different view-points upon the same thing, each view-point felt to be the truth, and so believed by Germans, English, French, Belgians, Russians, Roumanians, and among all people in the entire world. And because each fighting nation believed in its feelings, or ideas, the same feelings and ideas, the war would not end until one side was broken by the other. If only people would try to under-stand the points of view of others, and not strive to force their own exclusively. When he got back, he must try and help Downham, who must feel rather nervous, having a command when he had known no action.

Walking up and down upon the summit of the Hill, warm and sunny, the new leaves on the trees shining in the gentle breeze, he felt extraordinarily happy. He saw himself as a boy again, in dark blue jersey which rolled round his neck, blue serge knickerbockers below the knee, black stockings and shoes, and his new cricket bat, stumps, and ball. Giving a treat to poor boys, and so anxious that his new bat shouldn't be used for sky-ing stones, and a small girl smiling as she looked on, obviously longing to be allowed to join in. She wore ragged clothes and her yellow hair hung down thickly from under a big floppy grown-up hat, hiding nearly all her big blue eyes, but not their shine. He had let her play, quite unaware that this was Lily, the darling girl who had known him all the time, but whom he had not seen clear and plain, as she was, until the night of her death. O Lily, he said to himself, as he walked on the grass, to and fro with his shadow, sometimes passing under the tall young lime-trees near the bandstand, with its sparrow nest hanging raggedly from the inverted pinnacle cage of iron under its roof, O Lily, are you in the sunlight and the blue sky, calm and smiling with the love of God?

While he walked up and down, levitated by his feelings in the fine summer weather, seeing the Hill again as he had seen it in boyhood, a party of girls came along the crest, linked arm in arm, and singing a song that he had heard Gertie Gitana sing at the Hippodrome, years before; a sad and haunting song of a girl who had nothing to leave when she died, no money or property, but only happiness in nature.

> *I'll leave the sunshine to the flowers*
> *I'll leave the songbirds to the trees,*
> *And to the old folks I'll leave the memory*
> *Of a baby about their knees.*
> *I'll leave the stars to the night-time,*
> *And the quiet hills to the breeze,*
> *And to those in love I'll leave the moon above,*
> *When I leave the world behind.*

The faces of the eight advancing girls looked most peculiar as the singing line approached; they were yellow, and he realised they were munition workers from Woolwich, probably having the day off from packing bombs or shells with picric acid. They were happy, two were graceful, their breasts under their white silk blouses moved up and down in unison as they walked in step, the arms of these two being linked crosswise behind them. Their yellow faces gave them a Chinese look, rather attractive, he thought. Mrs. Neville had said that they treated soldiers, the only way they could get off; but they must have worn overalls, hiding their breasts, if private soldiers noticed such things. Perhaps such men cared only for one thing—the soul in them was not awakened.

He sat on a seat, pretending not to have noticed them, waiting for them to pass, so that he could see their breasts moving and feed on the movement in his mind with longing that was almost an ache through his being. But the girls passed behind the seat, and he did not like to turn his head, but sat there, leaning forward, poking the gravel with his short cane, as though absorbed in some problem.

When they did not go on, but stayed by the bandstand, twenty or thirty yards behind him, he looked round. They seemed to be discussing something; there was a mixture of directions in eager cockney voices. "You go there, Ireen, that's right, you cross with Dot, and you, May, you take the first round with Vi!" He shifted on the seat and rested his leg along it, to enjoy what they were doing. They began to dance, in pairs, weaving in and out of a circle, then all but two of them forming into pairs of arches, a couple passing under with bobbing heads; then they formed into two lines of four each, advancing and bowing and swinging back again, before breaking into couples and dancing in and out of their changing formations. He thought that girls in ancient Greece must have danced like this; and how well they looked, in spite of their canary-coloured faces, and what good clothes they wore. But for the war, these who had been poor urchins, screaming in nervous excitement around the bandstand on Thursday nights when the band played—dirty-faced children, pallid, thin, clad in rags—many without boots or shoes or stockings—but for the war they would now be white-faced girls, subdued, probably raped before adolescence, driven to inner hopelessness, or the streets; lost to love in unawakened homes. Now the war had brought, under its sacrifices, some kind of freedom, and hope for the future. He wanted to speak to them, but could not rise above his voiceless inner self.

He got up from the warm oak seat, thinking that perhaps Father had already gone home by the path switching from the row of elms, which led in front of the Grammar School, a path invisible behind the plantation of hawthorn bushes. It was sad to leave the happy girls; the moment of their summery joy was over; they sat or lay upon the grass—"Blime, I'm puffed!" said one—and were silent when he walked away. Had they noticed him, he wondered; and turning by the shelter at the top of the gully leading down to his home, saw them looking his way; he waved, and at once eight arms waved back. Perhaps they had been feeling as he had been feeling: I love them, he thought, I love them: the moment is gone for ever, it will never be the same again.

The spirit of the summer day prevailed. Mrs. Feeney, as always, had left the rooms dustless, polished, spotless, the steel fire-arms on the hearth shining bright.

Not a cross word at lunch: Richard was released by his son's open manner, for Phillip concealed his thoughts, and strove only to appear interested in Father's allotment, the "considerable damage" done in the raid—"the second daylight raid upon London by those beastly Gothas". He showed interest in his parent's description of the explosion at Silvertown, seen from London Bridge, as he was coming home from the office one January night.

"It was an awful sight, Phillip, really awful! I was crossing over London Bridge, it was a pitch dark night—you know the authorities are now very keen, and quite rightly, about exposed lights. These German beggars up above follow the streets, you know, and particularly the railway lines leading into London. Well, as I was saying, I was crossing the Bridge, in utter darkness, keeping close to the parapet, when all in a moment everything was as clear as day! Much brighter than when the Schütte-Lanz burned, you remember, old chap? The light came from down river, a great uprushing of yellow flames. The queer thing was these died down, but only for an instant was it dark again, for immediately afterwards the sky was a mass of rainbow colours—I can't tell you the effect! It had to be seen to be believed! I don't exaggerate in the very least, I assure you! All the colours of the spectrum run riot—green, red, violet, blue. They filled the entire sky, making the Tower Bridge black!"

"Rather like the Aurora Borealis, I suppose, Father?"

"Oh, much more vivid than that, Phillip! It was like a vast kaleidoscope, all the colours swirling and mingling together. Heaven knows what was the cause of the explosion."

"German spies, I bet," said Doris.

"No," replied Phillip. "Five tons of T.N.T. were set off by a fire in one of the top-storey rooms at Brünner Mond, then the various chemicals for S.O.S. rockets—barium, strontium, magnesium et cetera caught fire, in the air."

"What?" said Richard. "You know all about it, do you?"

"Only a little, Father. Please go on. It is most interesting. I haven't heard what it looked like, until now."

"Oh well. Where was I? Oh yes. As I was saying, it was a wonderful sight, but that was not all! In a few moments the whole Bridge was vibrating with the effects of an enormous explosion! Then, when it had rolled and rumbled away, the sky began to glow with burning buildings. I had my own ideas of what had happened, but kept them to myself, for obvious reasons. But now, it appears, you know all about it!"

"What was it, Phillip?" asked Doris.

"Well, as it never got into the papers, and as one can't be too careful, perhaps——"

"Now you're pulling my leg, old chap!" said Richard. "Come on, tell us——"

"Well, Father, the little bit I heard fits in with your very vivid description. I got my information from a driver in my section whose home was blown up, so he was given compassionate leave. Lost everything except one small boy—his wife, two young children, his parents. Everything flat, for hundreds of yards."

"Oh, how very sad! And his poor little son, left all alone!" Hetty was nearly in tears.

"Luckily Tallis was wounded, and got home with it. I heard from him the other day. He's going to work in a munitions factory."

Richard laughed with relief. "So he'll be able to take care of his little boy, won't he? Well now, tell us about what you have been doing, old man."

"Yes, do, Phillip! We know almost nothing from the paper."

"There isn't much to tell. All Weather Jack, the C.O., copped it, and now Downham's in command of the company. I want to go back to the Gaultshires, if I can."

"What, another change?" asked Richard.

"Won't that mean giving up your riding work, Phillip?"

"I might get a battalion transport. Anyway, in the infantry things are much better now. Messines was a good show."

"Yes, we thought you might be there, when you mentioned your bike ride on Christmas Day. Mother and I read between the lines, didn't we, Mother?"

"Yes, Dickie."

"So things are going well out there, are they, old man?"

"Unfortunately the French are out of it. Nivelle's a wash-out. He lost hundreds of thousands of his men in one day in Champagne. The troops mutinied, and some set out to march on Paris."

"Oh!" said Richard, glancing from one face to another. Incredulity and amazement gave him a partially helpless look. "But I have seen no mention of what you say in *The Daily Trident*!" Then with a pang of disappointment he remembered his son's habit of—well—drawing the long bow.

"*Mutiny*, you say, my boy?"

"Yes, Father."

"That's a most serious charge to make, you know!"

"I am not making any charge, Father."

"Well, I can only hope you will not go about talking like that, outside this house. That's all I can say. No doubt you remember what happened last time."

This was a reference to Phillip's abrupt recall when on sick leave in June of the previous year, after he had been talking in Freddy's bar, and Det.-Sgt. Keechey from Randiswell police station had reported his words.

Phillip hesitated between a desire to speak out and another to avoid his father and all he might say. The hesitation gave a third feeling of acute discomposure. He stabbed a slice of smoked salmon with his fork, and put it clumsily in his mouth and chewed without tasting, while keeping his gaze on the plate.

He put down his fork. "I'm sorry I spoke," he said, to the tablecloth. Why had he come on leave?

"Are you sure of your facts?" went on Richard.

"No, Father. It was a rumour. You are quite right, I shouldn't have mentioned it."

"Well, we'll say no more about it, old chap," said Richard; but his anxiety, increased by inferior food, overwork, and habitual loneliness, was not to be suppressed. "All the same, it is most disturbing to hear what you say, considering the gravity of the submarine sinkings. It only goes to show that the warnings of *The Daily Trident* have some foundation in fact—provided, of course, that what you tell me is the situation with our Ally."

"But Phillip has said that he only heard it——" began Hetty, but she stopped when Phillip frowned at her.

"Well, 'the least said, the soonest mended'," said Richard, wiping his bearded lips with his table napkin. "It's a lovely afternoon, I think I'll do some work on my allotment. The fashion has spread!" he went on, genially, looking at his son, "since you were so very kind as to provide me with some cabbage plants—let me see, it was just about a year ago, wasn't it? Well, Phillip," as he put the rolled napkin in its ring, "I'd like to thank you for providing an excellent lunch. What do you say, Hetty?" He manoeuvred a few crumbs on the cloth beside him to a knife blade, and tipped them into an envelope.

"Yes, it was very thoughtful of Phillip." At that moment a sharp *rat-tattat* sounded on the knocker of the front door. "There's Mavis! Open the door, will you, Doris?"

"Mother!" said Doris, in warning voice. "Remember what you said—'Elizabeth'!"

"Ah yes!" exclaimed Richard, jocularly. "You must prime Phillip about that new departure! Well, I will leave you to enjoy yourselves," and putting his napkin in its especial place in the drawer below the mahogany bookcase, he went through the open french windows into the garden, to put the crumbs on his bird-tray under the elm, followed down the lawn by Zippy the cat, mewing unhappily at the memory of tomtits well out of reach of its chattering teeth. For Zippy ground, or rather chopped its teeth at birds that remained selfishly out of reach so that it could not catch them. Sometimes the neuter appealed to the birds with faint mewings; but they never came down, to be kind to Zippy.

"Bastard!" said Phillip, looking through the open doors.

"Really, dear! Your father——!"

"Oh, I only meant the cat. What's all this about 'Elizabeth'?"

"Your sister," said Hetty, "has asked particularly not to be called by her first name any more. She wants to be known by her second name—Elizabeth. So you will be careful, won't you, dear."

"All right, I'll call her Liz. And now we're on the subject, would you mind not calling me 'dear', in future? Now please!" —seeing her face—"it doesn't mean that I'm callous, or indifferent—but I'd much rather be called Phillip—if my name can be pronounced with one 'l'!" he went on jokingly. "I'm rather fed up by people asking me why it is spelt with two 'l's. It's too late to alter your spellin' on my birth certificate, but you will be careful to pronounce it with one 'l' in future, will you, Hetty?"

Doris considered this in puzzlement for a few moments; then she cried, "Aren't you funny! How can you pronounce it with one 'l', I'd like to know?"

"Easy! One 'l' makes it quicker to say with a flip of the tongue. No lingering echoes. Actually, I'd much rather be called by my second name—Sidney. Call Father by his second name, too, why not? 'Yes, of course, naturally Teddy.' Say it jauntily, as though you had a cloth cap on your head, and Teddy had just asked you to have a pint of thick in Freddy's. Why laugh? I'm perfectly serious! One gets rid of old clothes, one washes off the stains of the day, one cleans one's teeth, or should do. The effect is renovating. So let's all go the whole hog in our family circle!" he said, as Mavis' footfalls came from the bedroom above.

"Phillip," said Hetty, quietly, "be kind to your sister; she isn't very happy just now. Don't make jokes about her wish to be called Elizabeth, will you?"

"And don't call her 'Liz'," said Doris. "She thinks that's vulgar. Anyway, Mother had her christened Eliza, but she doesn't like that either."

"Really, Hetty!" said Phillip. "Calling your gel 'Eliza the Thrush'. And you a Shakespearean lover!"

Hetty could not help laughing: he seemed to be his old self again.

Mavis was making a desperate effort to become a new person. Mavis was the name for the song-thrush, heard long ago in the Surrey lavender and herb fields of Hetty's childhood. That time had been such a happy one for her, with her brothers and sisters, that the thrush had been for her a symbol of happiness and joy. Mavis—a word spoken with love and tenderness by the mother at her baby's christening, had become, for the twenty-year-old girl filled with ruinous thoughts, a sound almost of horror. Desperately she sought to escape from herself—but how, how? She must change utterly—by will-power alone could she cure herself. Prayer was no good. Everyone must depend upon themselves, alone. Her attacks were not inevitable, they were not inherited. They were functional. The doctor said so. If she did not change herself, which meant her thoughts, she was doomed—done for! O, she would die, for very shame, if anyone in the office were to see her fall down and twist about in one of her 'attacks' (as she and her mother, dreading the shorter, usual word, spoke of them). If only she could live away from home, and not see Father! But then, what about Mother? Poor little Mother needed her, to help her against Father. There had been a gleam of hope, of going to live with Nina, her great friend, and to see Mother once a day, in the evenings, perhaps at Gran'pa's next door—but when it was all arranged, the change to take place at Easter—Doris had spoilt it all by announcing that during her holidays from school she was going to work on a farm in East Anglia, with some other senior girls under a mistress. When Doris returned, with bright eyes, and full of eager talk about rank-harrows and seed-harrows, littering bullock yards, and pail-feeding calves, she announced that she was going to join the Women's Land Army when she left school at the end of the summer term. When she was gone, who would Mother have to stand up for her against Father's beastliness? So the move to Nina's was off.

Phillip lay in a deckchair in the garden, under the elm. Doris knitted on a rug. Zippy the cat found consolation by what the girl called hurdy-gurdying—purring loudly while extending its clawed toes on her lap. Mavis was eating her lunch in the sitting room. When she finished, she called through the open french windows, "Come on, Doris, come and help Mother to wash up." Then having taken a tray of plates and cutlery as far as the kitchen, she said, "I've asked Doris to help you. I must get ready for Nina. She'll be here any minute now!" and went on upstairs to her bedroom. Doris lifted off Zippy, dumped the cat on Phillip's lap, and went in to dry for her mother. Phillip got up, dripped Zippy over the wooden fence into the next-door garden, and went into the sitting room to play his father's gramophone.

Nina arrived. Doris opened the door to her.

"I won't be long!" the voice of Mavis called down. The bathroom door was shut again. "Phillip's in the garden, go and talk to him," said Doris.

Nina blushed when she saw Phillip. He thought she was much prettier than when he had seen her last. She was fair, with blue eyes, a straight brow and nose, and firm chin.

"How are you getting on, Nina?"

"Very well, thank you, Phillip. And you?" He told her of his wish to transfer to the Gaultshires.

"But will you be able to stand it again, Phillip? I don't mean to interfere, but won't it be too much to go through, again?"

"You mean I'm a funk? Well, I am! Anyway, one can only be killed once."

"Please don't talk like that, Phil!" She blushed, and changed the subject. "Tom Ching called here last night, did your mother tell you? He said he was on his final leave before going to the front. Of course he was hoping to see Mavis, but she was unexpectedly kept late at the office." After a pause she said, "I wonder if you can give me some advice. Only please don't let Elizabeth know that I've spoken to you about it. I've been thinking for some time about joining the Women's Legion, and perhaps learning to drive a motor for an ambulance, or something. Today in the paper there's an announcement about a new Corps, the

Women's Army Auxiliary, it's to be called. I've got it here." She gave him *The Daily News.*

"'Army Council Instruction'," read Phillip. "Substitution of women for soldiers in certain employments, at home and at the bases and on Lines of Communication Overseas. Sounds pretty good, Nina! They want clerks, typists, cooks, wine waitresses, butlers. You'd make a grand butler, Nina! You'd have to dress like Vesta Tilly, Nina!" He saw that she was blushing, and went on quickly, "Ah here we are, Motor transport services!— 'Technical women will be employed with the R.F.C. and A.S.C. Motor transport! I'd go like a shot, if I were you!"

"I *do* want to go, Phillip, but don't you see, there's Ma— Elizabeth. She depends on me so much. You won't tell her I told you, will you?"

"Trust me! I suppose she wouldn't pass the medical board?"

"I'm afraid not, Phil. You know about Doris, and the Land Army, I suppose? I did think that it might be the very thing for Mavis—oh dear, I must try and remember!—Elizabeth, but she says she wouldn't like the rough work. Also, there is your mother."

"Rough work would be the making of her!"

Mavis came through the french windows and down the steps into the garden. She was dressed in a new frock. "What do you think of it, eh? Oh, hullo, Phil; you home, eh?"

"It looks awfully well on you, Elizabeth! Don't you think so, Phillip?"

Before he could agree, Mavis said, "It's no good asking him! He'll only criticise it."

"Yes, I think it looks awfully well on you, Elizabeth."

"There, he's being sarcastic! I know him of old!"

"I'll leave you to it." He went to talk to his mother, but found he could say nothing. "I think I'll go and see Gran'pa and Aunt Marian next door, then go down to Mrs. Neville. Then I may go on the Hill." The Canary Girls, dancing and singing—but it was Saturday afternoon. Other people would be about: it wouldn't do to be seen talking to them in daylight. He imagined darkness, the pretty one coming to him, on her rather sweet Chinese-yellow face an expression like Sasha's. But what was he thinking? There would never be anyone like Lily.

"You be careful!" said Mrs. Neville, when he had told her about Nina, and the Canary Girls. "Baby Week's beginning next week, so you mind what you're up to this time!"

He left, without having asked about Desmond.

What was there to do?

Nina looked unhappy when he returned from seeing Mrs. Neville.

"Had another quarrel?"

"Not exactly, Phillip. But Elizabeth *is* difficult, you know."

"I suppose she's never got over Father's turning against her, when she ran away from home that time. Hearts do break, you know," he said, unsteadily, to recover immediately. "Have you told her about your plans?"

"It's that which caused the trouble. She feels that nobody wants her. Well, I've done my best, honestly!"

"You sound like poor old Mother, after one of Father's cross moods. If only we could all see each other's point-of-view! Or better still, have none of our own. But to do that, one has to— well, sink down, I suppose, like a saint."

"Elizabeth now wonders what you and I were talking about in here when she came in." Nina blushed again at the thought of Phillip knowing about Mavis' accusing, *I believe you're beginning to like Phillip more than you like me!* At the very thought—which she shied away from at once—she felt her face burning.

Phillip knew what she was feeling, and why. He felt drawn towards her, but held himself back by thinking that he would feel awful afterwards if he behaved with her as he had with Polly. God, what a hypocrite he was, faithfully to Lily and yet—almost wanting to get hold of Nina.

As though having considered the problem of Nina exclusively, he said, "I think you're wise to join up. The war won't last for ever, and it's a tremendous chance to widen one's ideas of things. You might go to India, or France, or Gibraltar—anywhere! The friends you might make! Yes, Nina, you get out of the rut! That's my advice. Now I'd like to ask yours. Do you think it a good idea for me to ask Mavilabeth and Doris to dine in Town with me tonight, and do a theatre? You must come, too, of course! Good! I'll go and ask the girls now."

Mavis said, "I suppose you ask me to come as an afterthought? You really want Nina to go with you, don't you? Come now, be honest! I saw you two talking together, from my bedroom window."

"Very well, she needn't come if you don't want her!"

"How do you know I don't want her? She's my friend, isn't

she? Of course I'd like her to come! Only why are you asking us three, all of a sudden? What's behind it, eh?"

"Well, I'm on leave."

"And can't get anyone else to go with you, is that it? I know *you*, you see! What's happened to Desmond, with whom you used to be so thick?"

"I've no idea."

"I bet!"

"Oh dear. Anyway, Eugene's coming. How about it?"

"Did Nina say she would come?"

"Only if you came too."

There was a ring at the front door bell. Hetty said, "I expect that's Gran'pa!" and went away. When she returned, it was with Tom Ching. As though knowing that he was unwanted, the caller hastened across the lawn, his hand held out in greeting, saying that it was just his luck to find Phillip at home. He seemed so glad to see him, that Phillip had not the heart to go to the station leaving Ching behind, although he knew that Ching's interest in him was only a reflection from his hopeless love for Mavis; but knowing what he must be feeling, he said to the old school-fellow he had never liked, "We're all going up to a theatre. Why not join us?"

The party went out of the house, except Phillip, who had dashed upstairs for his cigarette case.

"You will bring the girls safely back, won't you, dear, I mean Phillip—oh dear, Sidney!" she laughed.

"Yes, dear; I will, dear. Leave it to me, dear. In fact, why not come too, dear, and have some fun for once, dear?"

"Oh, I'd love to!" cried Hetty, clasping her hands. "But there's Father, you see, Phillip. He never feels easy when I go out and leave him."

"He never appears to feel easy when you're with him, either. Still, we're all like that in our family. Each one has a battle of the brain going on all the time. That's one reason why I like being in France. It's peaceful there!"

"Perhaps we can go to the Old Vic, and see Shakespeare—one day before you go back, Phillip?"

Five first-class tickets to Charing Cross, a taxi to Piccadilly. It stopped beside the winged Archer on top of the fountain, and they got out beside the flower girls standing there with their great baskets of tulips, carnations, and roses. Across the wood-block

road, Eugene could be seen, standing by the Piccadilly corner-
stone of Swan and Edgar's. Watching him from the kerb was one
of the new policewomen. She was dressed in a plain blue coat and
skirt, blue armlet with the letters WP in white and a hard type
bowler hat with a wide brim. She was new to the job, but knew
Piccadilly for what it was. She had been watching Gene, with an
idea that he, an obvious foreigner, was waiting for an assignation.

"How funny he looks, doesn't he? Isn't he conceited? That
eyeglass is sheer swank! Phillip gave it to him, because it kept
dropping out of his eye, ha ha!"

"Please don't say that to him, will you? Apart from anything
else, Eugene is very sensitive."

"He can't be very sensitive, otherwise he would realise how
ridiculous he is. Who is he trying to look like, Max Linder?"

The taximan was waiting for his money, the flag being down.
"Let me pay," said Ching.

"No no, really." Phillip gave the driver a ten-shilling note and,
seeing his disabled soldier's badge, told him to keep the change.
Gratefully the driver drove away.

"Ten shillings!" said Mavis. "What do you want to do that
for? The fare was a shilling on the meter, with one and sixpence
extra. That's half a crown! Three shillings would have been
ample!"

She was near to tears. In the train her brother had spoken
nearly all the time to Nina. And why had he asked Ching to
come, when he knew how she disliked him? He disliked Ching,
too; he had always said so. Then why, except to spite her? It
wasn't fair. He had always done things like that. He knew very
well that Ching was a pest, calling at the house whenever he came
on leave, and staying there, making sheep's eyes at her. She
wished she had not come. Poor Mother, left all alone at
home."

"Come, Elizabeth, we're all going to enjoy ourselves," whispered Nina.

"But ten shillings, don't you see it would have helped Mother
quite a lot. Father gives her precious little housekeeping money,
as it is."

Ching had an inspiration. He bought two bunches of flowers
—the largest in the basket—and offered the first to Mavis.

"No thank you. I really couldn't."

"I'll carry them for you until you get back home, Mavis."

The use of that awful name made her say shortly, "No thanks."

"Oh well," said Ching. "How about you, Doris? You can have the two bunches, if you like."

Loyal to her sister, Doris promptly said, "No thank you!"

"Lovely wallflowers, lady," said the flower girl.

"How about you, Nina? Wouldn't you like them?"

"Well, its awfully kind of you, but really——"

"All right. I don't want these, after all," he said, to the young woman in the straw boater held on by a long hat pin, and a shawl over her shoulders.

"Such lovely flowers, too, ducks! Do you want y'r money back?" The affection in the woman's voice caused something to break in Ching. "No. I'd like you to have them."

"Tell you what, love, I'll give you y'r money back, and you can treat me to this lovely bunch of lavender. It'll keep, see. Go on, take the money, ducks. I can sell my flowers many times over, 'tisn't like before the war." She gave Ching back his florin. "Now the lavender'll be tuppence, ducks. Ta! And good luck, dear!"

Phillip looked across the road at Eugene, who had not seen them yet. The Brazilian was looking at himself in the shop-window glass, as he adjusted bow tie, angle of straw boater, and set of grey herring-bone jacket with its hand-stitched lapels. Unaware of being watched, Eugene admired his own good looks, particularly his mouth, lips, fine white teeth, and almond eyes, which had been praised by many girls and women.

Led by Phillip, the five "Wakenhamites" left the island, to cross in a gap of the traffic. Eugene saw them coming, and waited with some satisfaction to meet Mavis, whose looks and figure he had long admired.

Eugene lifted his boater, letting fall the eyeglass.

After introductions, Phillip suggested their old haunt, The Popular, before Eugene could ask about the Piccadilly Grill. He remembered the last time he had been there with Desmond and Gene—and the bill, nearly five pounds, which, as usual, he had paid.

"Take the girls there, will you, you two, and order what you and they want while I slip away to book seats for the show."

When he rejoined them he noted with satisfaction that Gene and Mavis were getting on well. Leaning over the table, he was telling the girls the story of *Madame Butterfly*, his eyes returning again and again to the face of Mavis. A bottle of "Popular Huzzar" sherry stood on the table, with five unsipped glasses.

"Come on, knock this back!" said Phillip, emptying his glass.
"It's quite harmless. Where's Ching?"

"He's gone, Phillip."

"Why, Nina?"

"He said he knew when he wasn't wanted," said Doris.

"The truth at last!" said Mavis.

"Poor old Ching. However, don't let the talking stop the
drinking!"

The orchestra, by special request, struck up *Butterfly*. Soup
arrived; the empty bottle was taken away with the plates, to be
replaced by fish and a bottle of Chablis. Claret with the chicken,
but no potatoes—"Sorry, sir, a Ministry of Food order—
no potatoes on Saturday!" However, the salad seemed to
give the second bottle of claret a better taste than the first.
By the time coffee was served, with kümmel, the party was a
success. Why was it, Phillip wondered, that whenever he had
a few drinks and others didn't, it always seemed as though others
had had as much as he had? He ordered brandy and cigars—for
dear old Gene and himself. Damme, Mavis was jolly pretty;
at moments, she had a gentle beauty, she seemed to glow. He
felt pride that Gene was obviously impressed by her. She
laughed gaily at times, her eyes were bright, they had lost their
dark and remote look.

The seats were in the tenth row of the stalls: nearly a week's
pay, but what did it matter? He had over a hundred pounds in
the bank now. What should he do if Gene wanted to borrow
money afterwards? Gene still owed him quite a lot; so did
Desmond.

The orchestra was playing the familiar gay theme of the
heroine, who wore the lilac mask, or domino. He knew all the
names of the cast, having seen *The Lilac Domino* several times
before. How lovely it was to see and to hear Clara Butterworth
and Jameson Dodds again! It was very sad when estrangement
came between the lovers, but life was like that. The audience
was half khaki, wives and sweethearts sitting close to their men,
some on leave like himself, others soon to go out. Here was the
world of dream, blossoming before them on the stage as a flower.
Soft eyes, moist eyes, deep red plush seats, darkness glowing with
romance and the yearning of the heart. Then, during a scene
outside the ballroom, when it seemed that the lovers must be
estranged by misunderstandings, and that Nina was sending
towards him the same feelings that he had for the hero and

heroine, he turned his head involuntarily and saw her misty
blue eyes opened wide, as though by the swelling of her heart.
Fear made him withdraw his feelings into himself. His flow
towards the stage interrupted, he looked at Doris on the other
side of him. How her face was set! Was she thinking of Percy,
buried near Flers? She was the one of the family who had real
guts. Then from the corner of his eye he saw Gene's hand moving
towards the hand of Mavis, watched her take her hand away,
rather roughly; and was half sorry, half relieved, because Gene
was a sort of *roué*.

Only when he was lying in bed that night did it occur to
Phillip that the term he had applied in his mind to Eugene
might have been applied to himself, and that his friend, of whose
amours he privately disapproved, was natural. At the same time,
was it natural to want to ravish a girl, if you did not love her?
Was deception natural? No, it was treachery to tell the tale to
a girl, to deceive her in order to possess her, without caring for
her as a person. How serious was Gene? He had asked Mavis
to go with him to the pictures. Would that mean taking her to
his flat afterwards? Anyway, he wasn't likely to get much change
out of Mavis. She was too selfish—or rather too involved in
herself to have true sympathy for anyone else. Again, ought
he to tell Gene of her attacks? As usual, he could not make up
his mind about anything, as he strayed into memories of old
scenes, all disastrous, reducing him to thin nothingness, a state
of mind in which Lily did not enter, for she was dead, and gone
for ever. He wished he hadn't drunk so much wine at dinner.

One morning, idly looking at *The Daily Trident*, he was surprised to see a photograph of Bright, looking grimmer than ever,
beside two of his brothers. He got up and ran in to show his
mother, and to read to her the account, under the headline,
TARRED AND FEATHERED. Bright's wife had been
"receiving attentions" from a young man who was "in a reserved
occupation under the Ministry of Munitions", and having been
warned by the brothers to stop seeing her, had refused. The
three brothers had kidnapped the lover, taken him to a barn on
the farm, stripped him, tarred him, rolled him in white Leghorn
feathers, driven him into the market town in a motorcar, and
there turned him loose.

"Oh dear," said Hetty. "Of course it was very very wrong of
his wife to encourage the young man, she must have been terribly

unhappy, I think. Still, her husband was at the front—and yet, we must not judge. I feel sorry for all of them, Phillip——"

He lay about in the garden during the sunny days, thinking of France which, hour by hour, was drawing him darkly nearer to feelings of return. In quietness of spirit he went to the Old Vic with his mother and grandfather, in plain clothes, pretending it was the old days as he rode with them in a tram through the Old Kent Road to the New Cut, where on a corner stood the dingy little theatre. They were early for the matinée, and went down some stone steps into a coffee house, marked GOOD PULL UP FOR CARMEN. That was part of the old days, and welcome. He pretended it was a dug-out, with much-worn American cloth on the tables, sand on the floor, steaming tea-urns, thick horse-flesh sandwiches. They sat at a table where the attendant wiped away tea-stains while lifting up a scallop shell of mustard in which was stuck a bone spoon looking thoroughly sodden.

"Shakespeare knew places like this," said Thomas Turney, getting a grip on the sanded floor with the soles of his boots.

"I was thinking, Gran'pa, if only we had places like this to go to in the trenches! They say the Hindenburg Line dug-outs have canteens in them, and also electric light."

"Very clever, the Germans. However"—with lowered voice and looking over his gold spectacle frame—"'guard well thy tongue', m'boy." Three mugs of tea came. "Gunfire!" said Phillip, sniffing it. "Gunfire tea. Early morning char. Thick, rank, and sweet. Cheerho!" He played a game with himself, pretending that he was glad he had come.

"This theatre where we are going," said Thomas Turney, "was built on what originally was a swamp. The foundation stones were taken from the old Savoy Palace in the Strand, when that building was cleared away to build Lancaster Place. It was called after Prince Leopold of Saxe-Coburg——"

"Gran'pa!" smiled Phillip, raising warning finger. "'Guard well thy tongue'!"

"Well done! But as I was saying, it is now the Victoria Hall, so we're quite safe, he-he-he!"

He went on to say that, although it was in a squalid neighbourhood, the best roses grew out of a clay soil heavily larded with muck.

"Famous actors have played here, like Edmund Kean, Booth, and Buckstone. And Paganini, the violinist."

Then, the doors being opened, they crossed the street and bought tickets for the dress circle. It was *The Tempest*, and soon Phillip was transported. The innocence and faith of Miranda and her "Brave new world!" when she met the ship-wrecked sailors! Poor Caliban, bad because he didn't know any better! The magnanimity of Prospero towards lesser men who had injured him! The farewell to Ariel, the final decision to break his wand, and sink his book into the sea, lest goodness in the wrong hands be changed to badness! And, above all, Miranda and her young lover playing chess under a tree, so calmly and happily, while the older men discussed their affairs. How wonderful to live among such people! But they lived only in the mind. He sighed as the curtain went down. Mother was clapping, smiling and with shining eyes.

He said goodbye to them outside in the street, and went by bus over Waterloo Bridge, and so to Charing Cross, to walk up the Haymarket to Flowers' Hotel. There he had tea, and, seeing no-one he knew, left soon afterwards and went by bus to Reynard's Common, to wander in places once known, and the heather where he had sat with Lily. Could it have been more than a year ago when he had brought her on his motor-cycle, and they had wandered by the lakes, on his last afternoon before going out to France for the opening of the battle of the Somme? Ariel, Prospero, Miranda, Lily—from afar, faintly shivering the calm evening air, came the sound of guns in Flanders.

Chapter 11

PROVEN

On the way up from Boulogne the weather was dull and cloudy. A slow journey added to his depression, with the morose Bright, among others, for company; the carriage was full. When the train gave its final jolting stop at Steenwercke there were no grooms with horses awaiting the train.

"We're in Downham's bad books all right," he said to Bright, who merely grunted. The two reported at the orderly room. To Phillip's relief Downham was not there, but only Pinnegar, sitting back in a canvas chair, moodily trying to enclose, within smoke-rings from his cigar, various flies clustering inside the walls of the tent. When Bright had left, Pinnegar said, after glancing around, in a lowered voice, "Did you read about that tar and feather business? I can just imagine him doing a thing like that, can't you? Rough-looking chap, isn't he? It's all over the B.E.F. Still, that slacker deserved what he got."

After awhile Phillip said, "Did my telegram from Boulogne about Black Prince get through, Teddy?"

"Yes. I was going to tell your sergeant to see to it, but Downham stopped it."

"I see."

"I should worry! The windy bastard is like that to all of us. Calls himself a Sharpshooter! The only thing he shoots sharply is his precious carcase into a dug-out!"

Pinnegar went on to ask what London was like, what he did, what shows he saw, was there a shortage of food, were prices up, was London very windy over the daylight Gotha raid, and (eagerly) personal questions about any girls; and seemingly disappointed about the last item, relapsed into pessimism.

"The old feeling in the company is gone. I'm fed up. The bloody Sharpshooter's all spit and polish. And is he windy! We had a few bombs dropped the other night, and you'd think, by the way he carried on, that the old Hun had broken through our lines! Blowing a whistle, yelling to everyone to scatter, telling Rivett to get the drivers to disperse the mules. And all because Jerry's hickaboo dropped three twelve-kilogram eggs a hundred yards off!"

"Where's Downham now?"

"Gone to Pop. We're under orders to move at twelve hours' notice. We're transferred back to Fifth Army."

"What, going south again?"

"No. Gough's come up here. He's in command of the Ypres push."

"What's happened to Plumer? Stellenbosched?"

"Damned if I know. Old Plum's been here for two years, and knows the Salient like the palm of his hand. I suppose he's got the sack because he didn't push on at once when we got on the crest of Messines. If Gough had been in command, he'd have put the cavalry through."

"So we're back under the old mud-balled fox!"

This was a reference to the dragging brush of the fox which was Fifth Army sign. All the Armies, with Corps and Divisions, had their stencilled devices. Fourth Army sign was a boar's head,

adopted by General Rawlinson after a leave spent in the South
of France boar hunting. It was rumoured that the General had
brought a young boar back with him, as a pet. It lived at Army
Headquarters, with the name of Rawly. The Fifth Army had
been formed after July the First, and had soon gone into the
mud of the Ancre Valley.

"Any idea where we're going?"

"Brigade says Proven."

"Where's that?"

"Other side of Poperinghe. Now there's a bon town! Ever
been to 'La Poupée'? You get a dam' fine dinner there for five
francs, or did, when I was there at the beginning of 'sixteen."

"I see. Well, have you got anything for me to do?"

"Damn all."

"I'd rather like to see Armentières, while I've got the chance."

"What the hell d'you want to go to a place like that for? Oh,
another Cook's tour! I've never been able to understand what
you find to interest you when you go off by yourself."

"It's all right if I have a horse?"

"I don't care what you do."

He went to the picket line. There Morris told him that he had
had the bay mare saddled up, but Sergeant Rivett's orders were
that it was to stay on the line.

"That's right, sir!" said Rivett, cheerfully. "Major's orders,
sir!"

"That I'm not to have a horse?"

"The major's orders were that no charger was to be sent to
railhead. Your servant Barrow has gone back to a gun section."

"Oh." After awhile he asked how things had been during his
absence.

"Oh, we've managed pretty well, I think, sir."

"Good. No casualties, or anything?"

"We did have some trouble with air-raids at night. However,
we scattered in time."

"I want Morris to bring the bay mare to my tent in ten
minutes. And to accompany me on a mule."

"Very good, sir. Oh, by the way, Driver Nolan is absent
without leave."

"Nolan?"

"That's right, sir. Since mid-day stables, in fact."

"Perhaps he's about somewhere."

"He left the lines without my permission, sir. He and Cutts."

Phillip realised what Rivett was thinking: almost hoping, to judge by his alert expression. Surely Nolan wouldn't be such a fool as to desert? And with Cutts, of all people!

"I'll be away about an hour, sergeant. Don't do anything about it, should they come back while I'm away, will you?"

He rode north along a lane, past fields where hay had been cut and was now being carted from cocks, to Oosthove farm, turning right-handed over the small Warnave river, in the direction of the ruins of the deserted industrial town of Armentières, lying grimly to the east. The land in front of him was low-lying, consisting of water-meadows beside and within an ox-bend of the river Lys, where old peasants in sabots and dark clothes, the men in peaked caps, worked slowly with horses and long carts like shallow boats on wheels almost up to the sites of batteries and other congestions of war. How they must hate their land being mucked up, he thought, as he saluted one old man with a long white moustache walking as slowly as his horse on the worn grass beside a thorn hedge. He got no response.

Following the bend of the river, he came to what was apparently the Corps laundry, with women hanging out greyback shirts and vests and long woollen pants on wire lines. Near the building some soldiers were arguing with a screeching old woman, and going nearer, he saw what the trouble was. Several lengths of screw-pickets had been lashed together to clear drains choked with shirts and pants. A sergeant told him that the women had done it, "as an underhand means of demanding higher wages". Inside a shed adjoining was a large and heavy machine which, his informant said, was a Foden Disinjector. Asked what it was, he replied that it was to destroy parasites in uniforms.

"Oh, a delousing machine, sergeant? What a queer name. Wonder what it means. Does it chuck out the crumbs?"

"I don't follow you, sir."

"Don't you know the army slang for lice?"

"I was the manager of a West End laundry before I joined up, so I'm afraid I am not entirely conversant with army parlance, sir."

Phillip felt a little scornful of his superiority, akin to that of Rivett. "Well, your Disinjector is better than the fizzing sticks of cordite we used in the crutch of our trousers in 'fourteen, sergeant."

He rode on towards the town, stopping next at some sheds, outside which men of the Labour Corps were making mats of old bean-stalks and wire. He asked if it was for camouflage, and was told that they were Malay mats, to cover duckboards, and deaden the noise of footfalls. This made him wonder if the coming attack was to be made at night.

He was now in Belgium, having crossed the frontier; and reaching the Ypres-Messines-Armentières road at Le Bizet, went on into the town. Many of its buildings were in ruins. Walls everywhere were pocked by shell fragments. Evacuated by the civilian population, many of the houses were locked up. Notices against house-breaking and looting were tacked on every door. Lean dogs and cats slunk about. Looking through a barred, basement window, he saw mildewed furniture stored there, and on one table a box of matches which had fallen open with damp.

There was an observation post of a howitzer battery up a factory chimney beside the Lys, with a lift to the top. The lift was a wooden platform suspended on wires to pulleys, and worked by ropes. After talking with the gunner officer, he was invited to go up with him. The lift was without sides or rails, it swayed, jolted, jarred, and at one place it stuck in the chimney. At the top, just below the rim, where the wind passed gently roaring, a couple of bricks had been removed; and resting field glasses in the small space, he looked across many lines of trenches and belts of rusty wire stretching over a flat green country threaded with dykes and streams, and small clumps of trees about farms. In the farther distance chimneys and buildings half dissolved in haze were the towns of Commines and Wervique, connected by the river wandering into the east; and beyond them, to the north, across rising ground made dark by woods and forests, lay the ridge dominating the Ypres Salient, from Zonnebeke to Passchendaele and Staden, the first objective, said the gunner, of the coming campaign to push the old Hun out of Belgium. The plan was to reach Thielt, Bruges, and the submarine base at Zeebrugge, and then, with the right flank guarded by the river Lys with the towns of Menin, Courtrai, and Ghent on its banks, to let the cavalry through to the Dutch border.

"We won't 'ave no more trouble over our swingle-tree chains not being burnished for inspection, not now, sir," said Morris, on the way back. "Driver Nolan's been an' gone an' won a special set from one of the Fred Karno's lot recently come from 'ome. They was so shiny they looked almost nickel-plated."

"How did he manage it, Morris?"

"It was during the wind-up in the hick-aboo, when them Goothers come over an' dropped their eggs. Twelve pair 'e snatched, the 'ole caboodle, sir. The other lot kep' them for inspections, a spare set like. Nolan's idea is to use 'em for our transport, and also to 'ire 'em out to others, at a franc the chain. 'E's flogged 'em to the section. Each driver put a franc in the kitty, so's the section owns 'em, and will git the rhino for 'iring. So Nolan's pouched twenty francs. Wiv that sum innisat fer safety, like, he slings 'is 'ook ter ther Free Pipes at Romarin wiv' 'is China, Cutts. Sergeant Rivett's ravin', sir, says 'e'll get 'em both court-martial'd, sir."

"What's a China, Morris?"

"What we calls a mixing chum, sir."

On his return Phillip read *General Instructions* for the Courts-Martial Section in his copy of General Routine Orders; then he went to see Pinnegar, saying that he ought to get Nolan and Cutts back before the military police got hold of them. Pinnegar, who was mess president, suggested that he take the Maltese cart and buy some stores at the Expeditionary Force Canteen at the Duke of Connaught Camp, on the Leinster Road leading to Neuve Église. Some tinned chicken, tongue, pork sausages, and *pâté de fois gras*, as well as vegetables, bread, and a dozen of whiskey. The absentees at the Three Pipes could be brought back, hidden in the cart.

Phillip thought that the Maltese cart was too small, so he took a limber as well; and the two roysterers, hidden under the canvas cover, were brought back a few minutes before Major Downham, riding Prince, whose mouth was flecked with froth, returned to camp. By that time Cutts and Nolan, less their driver's-boots, which had been stolen, lay side by side in a spare tent put up near the baled hay at one end of the picket line.

"I think you ought to put Drivers Nolan and Cutts under arrest, sir!"

"I *beg* your pardon, Sergeant Rivett?"

"I would have done so, had you not expressly ordered me not to do so, sir."

Phillip replied quietly, "I think I'll be able to deal with them, without any fuss, Sergeant Rivett."

"I mean to say, sir, it is within my province to maintain discipline, since most of the burden of administrating the transport personnel so far has fallen upon me. Therefore, sir, I consider that they should be put on charge, and brought before the Officer Commanding."

"That will mean a court-martial, possibly, Sergeant Rivett."

"I still think that they should be put on charge, sir. I can't accept responsibility for them."

"Now I'm back, I take the matter out of your hands, Sergeant Rivett." When the man standing before him did not reply, Phillip went on, "Cutts has been badly shell-shocked, or had the guts knocked out of him in childhood, spiritually the same thing, as I told you. Nolan was through First Ypres in my regiment, the Gaultshires. He's been out here for nearly three years, without leave. Also he has bouts of malaria. He was in South Africa with the Seventh division before the war."

Sergeant Rivett pursed his lips. "It seems to me that the 'old soldier' excuse can get away with anything!" There was partial challenge in his manner as he looked straight at his officer. "I mean to say, sir, just because a man happened to be in the Army before the war, the 'refuge of the destitute', I think was how they were regarded——"

Phillip walked away. What was it Father Aloysius had said, "Objects of our own hate arise from wounds within us". If Rivett had been through hell he would be at least sympathetic to others who had suffered more than he had. By God, Downham too! He hesitated: he must not feel scorn of Rivett because he was inexperienced; and returned to where the sergeant was still standing, to say quietly, "I appreciate that you have the well-being of this section at heart, Sergeant Rivett, so I will speak to Nolan and Cutts first thing in the morning. Will you bring them to me immediately after early stables."

A spruced-up, almost jaunty Nolan was marched up behind Cutts by the sergeant. It was a fine summer morning. Caps off: attention.

"Drivers Nolan and Cutts, sir."

Nolan had on a new pair of driver's boots; Cutts wore a down-at-heel pair of marching boots, obviously thrown away by somebody, with puttees. His heavy clean-shaven brown face had a sagged and mournful appearance, his dark brown eyes were heavy with fear; in contrast to Nolan, who had cut the ends of his moustache and waxed the stubs into little upstanding points.

"At my request, Sergeant Rivett is not bringing a charge, at the moment. So I'll get to the point. You know the possible penalty, don't you, Nolan?"

"Well, sir——"

"Do you, or don't you?"

"I do, sir."

"What have you to say?"

"I knew what I was doing, sir. Permission to say something more, sir."

"Well?"

"I wouldn't have gone off had we been in the line, sir."

"What else?"

"Nothing, sir."

"Cutts?"

Wretched eyes lifted a moment to officer-face; Adam's apple jerked about; jaws silently champed; hands clasped tightly; full lips wobbled; mouth opened, no words came.

"I don't think you've been fair to Sergeant Rivett, you two men. He looks after you in the section very well, and has never crimed a man in all the time we've been out here. So you take advantage. If we don't take you before the C.O., what happens when it gets about? The sergeant may lose his stripes. I may get sent back to the base as incompetent, and perhaps lose my commission. But this is a volunteer citizen army, or was when you joined up. I think you both ought to apologise to Sergeant Rivett. But let it be understood that if it happens again, you'll be for it."

"Yes, sir! Sergeant Rivett, I ask pardon."

Cutts began to tremble, then to shake. Sobs broke from him. Phillip walked away, saying to Nolan, "Look after your China."

Early one morning of threatening rain the company moved north, by way of Neuve Église and Dranoutre, to the area of the Monts de Flandres which dominated the plain around them. Once again the red, black, and white striped wooden privy was a sight remarked by many, as it was borne on the last limber through Locre, lying between the Scherpenberg and Mont Rouge. These low flat hills of gravel and sand topped by a scrub of various thin trees, hid powerful telescopes trained upon the almost imperceptibly sloping ground of the Salient rising to the Flanders Ridge seven miles away to the east.

"I bet the Germans will recognise this *schissen-hausen,*" said Pinnegar, riding beside Phillip. "They know where they left it, near Achiet-le-Grand, and that we've come from there."

"Are you serious?"

"Of course I am! The Germans know more about us, than we know about ourselves!"

By taking minor farm roads and lanes they arrived in the late evening west of Poperinghe. Remained three final, weary, dusty miles along the road to Dunkerque, before they came to their destination, the oakwoods about Proven. Here were hundreds of acres of tents and semi-circular iron huts, arranged in camps with names like Portland, Putney, Pimlico, Piccadilly, Partridge, Paddington, and Pardon.

"Piffle and Putrid would be more like it," remarked Pinnegar, for the congested sight added to the spirit of weariness. The air of summer, which as the column passed through fields of ripening corn, beet sugar, and flax, surrounding old red-brick farmhouses among barns, middens, and moats, had given an illusion of freedom, but now it was tainted by the smell of incinerators. Everywhere the undergrowth was trodden flat, the place made barren.

They were billeted in Parkhurst, the name of a prison in the Isle of Wight, and just about as appropriate, said Pinnegar, who with Lucky Lukoff, the elderly South African, was off on a binge to Poperinghe.

Downham had discovered in the Camp Commandant an old schoolfellow, and had invited him to dinner, so the remaining officers were not given leave. Jules did his best with an omelette made of ducks' eggs, followed by tinned chicken, tinned cream, and tinned peaches. Downham and the staff-captain shared a bottle of champagne, the other four drank whiskey and chlorinated water. Gunfire buffeted the air within the iron shelter.

After dinner, bridge was proposed. They would cut for the two odd-men-out. At once Bright said he didn't want to play, got up, pushed back his chair and left the hut without a word.

The others cut for odd man out. Phillip lost, and went quietly to a far corner of the hut, where his servant had put up his camp bed, undressed, got into his sleeping bag, and turned his face to the corrugated iron wall.

But not to sleep. Hopeless thoughts passed through his mind. At last, seeking relief, he turned over and watched the players in the light of several candles stuck in bottles. The flames were shimmering, gunfire must be vibrating them, not a draught, otherwise they would be flickering. At last the game was over, the Sparklet siphon hissed, the staff captain had a final drink, then Downham went through the door with him and the two others, new men whose names he did not know. They had joined while he was on leave. It was good to be alone again. He was about to hop out and blow out the candles when the door opened again, and Downham strode furiously towards him, chain-spurs jingling.

"You and Bright are a couple of yobs. Bloody manners, both of you. Dammit, man, haven't you learned anything during the time you've been in the Army? The Camp Commandant was our guest!"

"I was feeling pretty dull, and didn't want to affect the party. I've been up since four this morning, and have not felt very well all day."

"Even so, why didn't you ask permission to go to bed, instead of slinking off? You had no idea of how to behave when you first came to the office, and you've learned nothing since, that's fairly obvious! You're slack, you leave everything to your sergeant; if you don't make an immediate improvement, I shall get rid of you. Now take this as a final warning!"

"Excuse me," mumbled Phillip. He ran to the door, and was sick outside. The feeling of relief was great. "I think it was those ducks' eggs, they seemed suspicious to me. Ducks feed in all the filthy drains out here."

"Too much whiskey, more like it. That reminds me. I understand that two of your drivers got drunk the day before yesterday, after absenting themselves without leave. Why didn't you bring them up to my Orderly Room?"

"I didn't want to bother you, sir."

Major Downham stared at him. Then he burst out, "Who the hell d'you think you are?"

"Well, sir, they're my men, after all, and I'm responsible for them. They do their job, and surely that's what matters?"

"I like your bloody nerve! My God, you take the biscuit! It's like your damned cheek to assume powers that you don't possess! Why, it's a case for the Colonel. Or do you consider yourself superior to him?" concluded Downham, sarcastically.

"Well, as a matter of fact I looked it up in General Routine Orders, No. 585, where it states that the Court must carefully consider the circumstances in which a man absented himself with a view to avoiding any special or dangerous duty; also this should be borne in mind when considering what charge should be brought, at the discretion of the Convening Officer."

"Really! Do you happen to know what a Convening Officer is, by any chance?"

"I didn't think it necessary to go so far as that, sir. After all, I was in the best position to judge. I know the two men concerned fairly well."

"A Convening Officer, let me tell you, is a senior officer on the Adjutant-General's staff!"

"Well, sir, I can only say again that they were my men, and I'm looking after them. Both have been under considerable strain, one ever since 1914."

"Like you, I suppose, at Messines?"

Phillip took a deep breath, and trying to overcome the quaver in his voice, appealed to his senior. "Look here, Downham, as I used to call you, can't we drop this sort of thing? You've had it in for me, ever since I romanced to you, that first morning at the office, when I said I'd been wildfowling in the Blackwater estuary, when I hadn't. I know I was a damned fool over that. I'd read about it, and longed so much to go, and suddenly found myself saying that I had. And there's another thing"—he was near to tears—"did you have to sneer at me when I came home wounded, when you said to Mr. Howlett and Hollis that no doubt I'd been running away, because a bullet happened to pass through the front of my leg and tear away most of my behind, as bullets often do! Can't we let bygones be bygones? I apologise for my lapse in not asking you if I might withdraw from the mess, but honestly, I thought dinner was over, when cards were suggested. Shall we shake hands on it?"

Downham seemed as surprised as Phillip felt about this outburst.

"All right," he said, at length. "Only why can't you be like other fellows? You're such an ass, somehow. I can never quite make you out. Anyway, you must pull your socks up and stop leaving all the work to your sergeant. Do your job, and stop miking; and no one will be better pleased than I."

"Very well, sir, I'll do my best!"

They shook hands on it.

Phillip slept soundly until Morris awakened him with a cup of tea at five o'clock next morning, in time for early stables. Later in the morning, he was given permission by Downham to accompany Pinnegar into Poperinghe to draw company pay from the Field Cashier. The first thing they did after dismounting and handing over reins to grooms was to go into the Aigle d'Or for a drink. Hardly had they entered when Phillip exclaimed, "Good God! I know that man!"

A staff officer, whose wooden hand was covered by a black glove and fastened by a swivel to his belt, and one eye covered by a black patch, was talking to three colonels at the bar.

"Perhaps this place is reserved for the Staff, Teddy," he said, hesitating at the door.

"We've as much right to be here as any staff wallah! I'm thirsty."

"I'll find out if it's their mess."

He asked a hatless sergeant, a smooth man with well-tailor'd jacket, non-regulation brown shoes, and knife-edged creases to his trousers. The sergeant was impersonally genial, in the manner of his master. He was the sergeant-servant of the Corps General. "'B' mess is here, sir, for which the dining room is reserved. The public restaurant is down the passage."

"That is Major West, isn't it, sergeant?"

"Yes, sir. Major H. J. West, from G.H.Q. Giving a lecture, here in the town this afternoon, sir."

"Where, d'you know?"

"In the Convent School, west of the church."

"Is it only for the Staff, d'you know?"

"I think it's for battalion commanders downwards, sir."

The sergeant bowed and smiled slightly, before moving away on the Phillips soles of his highly polished shoes. He had his own valet, or batman, who gave both the general's, and the sergeant's, boots and shoes the real, much-boned Sir Garnett shine.

"Yes, it's 'Spectre' West all right, but I hardly like to speak to him, Teddy. I can't barge in——"

This feeling of diffidence was not lessened by Phillip's awareness that Pinnegar's appearance was a little on the loud side. He was wearing his non-regulation wide-cut salmon-pink breeches, floppy cap of thin material of very nearly the same shade, matching his shirt and tie. This kit somehow emphasised his I-don't-give-a-damn-for-anyone manner. What a cad he was to think such thoughts about dear old Teddy . . .

"Anyway, I don't like the look of the place. Let's go to La Poupée."

They went to a small street off the Square. It was crowded. They had to wait ten minutes, constantly being shoved as more and more officers tried to get in behind them. Pinnegar expressed his disapproval of the conditions in a grumbling voice.

"The bloody place has been commercialised."

Phillip thought this rather funny, since the real name was Café de la Commerce.

"Listen to that bloody bell every time the door opens. You'd have thought they'd have had the sense to take it down."

The bell rattled again. "They've got far too many tables in here. If anyone took a deep breath, they'd all tip up, one after the other."

Phillip laughed; and thus encouraged, Pinnegar went on, "But if anyone sneezed, fifty bloody wine glasses would ring a carillon and people'd think the war was over!" Gazing mordantly around, "Look at that waitress, I bet she gets a cheap thrill squeezing between the tables!"

"Steady on, old boy!"

"What the hell? They don't understand our language, except napoo, san fairy ann and, of course, jigajig."

Thank heaven there was such a row going on, no-one was likely to hear. At last they could sit down.

"Two Bifteks mit Bombardier Fritz. Vin rosé, une bouteille" —he held up one finger—"to commencer avec. Comprit, ma fille?" The girl went away nose in air. "See what I mean, Phil?"

"You offended her, Teddy. It should be jeune fille, or mademoiselle."

"What the hell's the difference? Why the puritan attitude? You don't understand girls. They're just like men, only the other way round—receivers, not transmitters. The little girl here has probably slept with half the fellows in the room." When the girl came with the steaks and fried potatoes, he said, "My friend here thinks you ought to be called a jeune fille. I told him—you know your way about, eh?"

"S'il vous plaît, m'sieu?" She smiled down at Phillip. "We have a ver' nice cherry patisserie to follow. May I reserve slices for you?"

"You speak very good English, ma'mselle," ventured Pinnegar, winningly. "You are far too pretty to think only about cooking, eh? Am I right?"

"Pleas', m'sieu? Two patisseries—cherry?"

"That's right. Vous make up for it trés chérie, ma'mselle, ma chérie." He patted her hand.

"Two pieces of cherry tart, m'sieu, oui?"

"Oui! And une autre bouteille, comme ça, vin rosé. Merci

beaucoup, ma chérie! I—I think I've clicked," he said to Phillip, when she had gone.

I don't, thought Phillip. And twenty minutes later, Pinnegar's optimism had gone with the wine. The steak, he said, as he tried to detach fibrous wedges from between his teeth, was nothing but old cow. "I knew by the yellow fat, as soon as I saw it. Deux cognacs, fine, comprennez?"

"C'est triste, m'sieu, il n'y ena plus! Fini! C'est la guerre, m'sieu!"

So they had calvados, which Pinnegar said was made from apples. It was fiery, and burnt a way down the gullet. "Hell," he said, "I feel as though I've swallowed a lot of shrapnel bullets." He took another sip. "Tastes more like potato alcohol to me. You know, they distil any bloody thing nowadays. This is probably made from petrol."

"Have a cigar with me, Teddy?"

"I don't mind if I do."

Two rather yellow cigars arrived in a wine glass. Pinnegar made a wry joke. "Even the bloody cigars are in khaki! Look at them, the colour of——" Phillip coughed loudly to hide the word. He wished Teddy would damn-well shut up. "Like bloody trench mortars, aren't they? What the hell you see to laugh at, beats me!" Pinnegar, after sniffing, rolled one near his ear. "If it crackles faintly, it's fit to smoke." He listened. "Only just made, by the way it keeps silent!" He began to laugh. "These Belgians are bigger robbers than the French." He bit off an end, spat it out, and tried to light it on Phillip's fusee. He sucked for some time.

"You're smoking my fusee, Teddy!"

"What did I tell you! Damp as a bloody midden!"

Phillip flicked the wheel once more, blowing on the spark which instantly changed the black fusee head to crimson. Vigorous puffs transferred the rose to the cigar end. "How's that, Teddy?"

Pinnegar let out rasping coughs. "Tastes of phosgene, if you ask me!" He tore it open. "If that isn't a cabbage leaf, I'm a Dutchman!" he cried, sticking the fuming end into his coffee. "What bloody awful coffee," he went on. "It's chicory ground up with dandelion roots, you know. Waitress! Ma'ms'el, l'addition, sivvouplay!"

"I'm sorry, Teddy, we ought to have stopped at the Eagle, as you said. Let me pay."

"Not on your life. I asked you to have lunch with me."

"Well, thanks very much. I'll do the same for you next time."

"Not here!" exclaimed Pinnegar, swallowing several soda-mints. "Not in this bloody awful Poopy!"

Chapter 12

PHILLIP MEETS AN OLD FRIEND

Outside in the cobbled street they parted, and Phillip made his way to the convent school. Several hundred officers were already assembled in the main room. Those behind followed the example of their seniors in the front rows and stood up as the lecturer walked on from the side of the platform. There was a scraping of chairs as three hundred sat down again, trying to fit themselves into the least uncomfortable positions, to relax as far as possible amidst other legs, arms, elbows, and knees. Those in the rear half of the hall were already smoking when Major West, standing white-faced and still, said quietly, "Do smoke if you want to, gentle-men," whereupon, Phillip noticed, the front row began to fill their pipes. He wondered if Westy felt nervous. It must be awful to face hundreds of ordinary officers, when you were on the Staff.

"I am asked to speak about the past, present, and future of Ypres. It is first heard of in history as a small fortress originally built on an island in the tenth century. The monastery of St. Martin was already there, apparently. The town grew fast, it had a charter in 1073, with two parishes, St. Martin and St. Peter.

"Sheep, otherwise wool, made the wealth of England, and it made Ypres rich, too. Cloth-weaving was patronised by the Counts of Flanders. After the first two decades of the twelfth century, Ypres market was known throughout Europe, being a centre of much trade. During the fourteenth century the human population was nearly a quarter of a million. One can imagine the fields around the town, grazed by flocks, the pastures drained and irrigated by water taken off and leading back into the brooks, or beeks, whose names are familiar to many of you today—the Belleward, Reutel, Zonne, Steen, Stroom, Loo, Haan, Groot

Kemmel, and so on. Sinister or apocryphal places today, but once of pastoral quietude. And will be so again, sooner than perhaps many of us can grasp at the moment.

"But to our brief history of Ypres. Trade enriches a country, which means usually one particular class. There followed civil strife, a revolt of the traders against those who had been enriched by them. Ypres burgesses, with those of the sister-towns of Ghent and Bruges, took up arms against the Counts of Flanders, who tried to restrict their privileges. They had to fight, too, against the Kings of France, always enemies of the Flemish. Wars benefit only mushroom growths, profiteers and opportunists. True industry is paralysed, foreign merchants depart. The celebrated cloth trade of Ypres declined, city life with it. The weavers left. Some went to England, and established their craft there. By this time the Burgundians had taken the city, and destroyed its charters. By the sixteenth century, the Spanish were overlords. Under the despotic rule of the Dukes of Alba, the population was less than five thousand, and most of the city in ruins.

"During the seventeenth century the French occupied the town and surrounding country. Louis XIV fortified it, making it one of the strongest towns in the conquered territory. In 1715 the Dutch garrisoned it, making the Belgians pay for their upkeep. A usual procedure in war, gentlemen, though it has been known to be worked the other way round."

This dry remark caused laughter: it was generally said throughout the British Expeditionary Force that the British paid both French and Belgian governments rent for the land they occupied, including the trenches.

"During two hundred years the city had suffered siege, bombardment, plunder, fire, hangings, and heavy taxation to enable its Spanish and Austrian masters to fight against France. Flanders, you will recall from the classroom, is the Cockpit of Europe. Human nature does not change, nor does the nature of the wolf and the sheep. The moral seems to be that of Cromwell, 'Trust in God and keep your powder dry'.

"By a decree of 1792, the French Revolutionary Convention made new laws for Belgium. Ypres was powerless against the Jacobins, and lost under their rule what the town had managed to keep under all previous rulers, its municipal autonomy. The Concordat of 1801 removed the power of the bishops. The Dutch returned, to fortify the ramparts once more. Fifty years later, in 1855, under Leopold the First, the fortifications were once again torn down.

"In October 1914, when the finest small army the continent has ever seen entered Ypres, the population was seventeen and a half thousand. The people were chiefly tradesmen and artisans, with what we would call a comfortable middle class of old burgher families and property owners. There was also a limited society of the old nobility living in hereditary mansions in the town, and old châteaux in the surrounding country of farms. A sleepy town, 'a rose-red city, half as old as time', with little ambition, small culture, her artistic minority living in the past, and caring for the town's historical relics, mainly architectural. A town like any old English market town, its economy maintained by farming, which had taken on new cultivations of hops, tobacco, beet sugar, corn, and fruit, in addition to the classic products of beef, mutton, and butter. The butter market was indeed, until the summer of 1914, one of the most important in Belgium. I myself have an affection for the town——"

Laughter and cries interrupted the speaker. He stood motionless, the laughter ceased. "I am perfectly serious, gentlemen. I came here with some friends in a reading party between Trinity and Michaelmas terms in 1906. Among other pleasures, we were offered some duck-shooting by the Baron of a very finely ordered château in a quiet pastoral hamlet. The Baron's keeper fed grain to flighting mallard in the little brook which ran out of Bellewaarde Lake. Afterwards, we had an excellent game of billiards, I remember."

This information created a stir, followed by odd noises of laughter beyond derision. The contrast was too great—the familiar rubble and earth heap of Hooge Château beside the Menin road, scene of innumerable flammenwerfer, bayonet, and bombing attacks over a totally upheaved and detonated soil saturated with gas, odours of the dead, and chloride of lime, on the one hand; and someone shooting duck and then playing billiards with a Baron, on the other. Everybody seemed to be laughing: why, Phillip wondered. Hadn't Cranmer shot a pheasant in the woods, and cooked it for both of them, in November 1914? Of course: that was in the time of the "red little, dead little army".

"Yes, gentlemen, I am indebted to the Baron de Vinck for some very good sport. So ends a brief outline of the past. Now we come to the present, and to the not so far distant future.

The Salient, and the country extending to the gentle rises—
one can hardly call them ridges, in the sense of our downs at
home, and particularly what we know as the chalk ridges of
Sussex, Surrey, Kent and Buckinghamshire—the almost imperceptibly rising ground to the east, from the Gheluvelt plateau
on the south to the Passchendaele–Broodseinde–Westroosebeek–
Stadenberg hillock on the north—the Salient is like the palm
of one's hand, when held out stiff and flat before one,
thus——"

'Spectre' West extended his right hand, horizontal to the
ground. "The ball of the thumb and the thumb are the Monts
de Flandres, lying west of the Salient. The palm of the hand is
the lower ground of the Salient. The lines crossing the palm are
the Steenbeek and its tributary watercourses, Haanebeek,
Stroombeek, Lekkerboterbeek, and other threads. They rise
about the watershed of the Gravenstafel ridge, flowing south and
west, and then north. Other streamlets flow east, having their
sources in the same sort of sandy, gravelly soils which overlay
yellow and blue clays of the subsoil. This gault clay resists the
percolation of water. So that's our country, from which it is
intended to dispossess the present squatters, on our way to the
Flanders plain lying below the sky-line to the east.

"Before I pass on to a description of the Flanders plain, I
will speak briefly of the terrain of the battle to be fought before
the breaking out of the forces of pursuit. The battlefield of the
first phase is the palm of the hand. There are valleys, or more
correctly depressions, between the fingers, whose tips end the
rising ground. These depressions, to us, are dead ground, providing hidden routes for the enemy counter-attack divisions, and
cover for their field-gun and howitzer batteries. Both the counter-
attacking divisions and the batteries are therefore mobile. The
reserve divisions will lie out of range of our barrage, awaiting
the moment to advance; the batteries each have several alternative emplacements, to which they can move at night. Now for
the *Eingreif Divisionen*. The German word *eingreif* is more than
our word *grappling*. Rather is it *interlocking*, or as they say in
East Anglia, *cogging-in*, fitting-in-with. The *eingreif* divisions, one
behind every division in the line, function by hastening forward,
under cover of dead ground, at the psychological moment when
the attackers, having arrived at their limited objectives, after an
expense of courage, have not yet got into shape for defence.

"Each *eingreif* division, arriving behind the enemy division already in line, comes at once under command of the general officer of the fighting division, regardless of seniority. The man on the spot knows the form, as it were, and so the fresh troops are placed at his disposal.

"That, broadly speaking, is the tactical form for the enemy. We shall deal with it as it deserves, before the break-out. Our job is to bring these *eingreif divisionen* forward into our cockpit, and break them there, by the combined fire-power of our infantry, gunners, and machine gunners, while our fresh divisions prepare for the next detonating bite into the palm of the unclenched mailed fist."

The lecturer drank from a glass of chlorinated water, and shuddered.

"After the lecture, we shall be going to a model of the battle-field. It covers two acres. There we shall be able to see, to scale, the lie of the land. I am indebted to a French colleague, Capitaine Delvert, for this description of the country lying south of the Moeres, reclaimed fen land, which lies east and north-east of the Fôret d'Houthulst, in the French sector. This is a rough translation,

"'It is a vast plain of grazing and arable, now in high summer a Joseph's coat of green and of yellow hectares of corn. It is traversed by many lines of hedges and rows of trees, plantations of oak and fir, amidst which stand, half hidden, red roofs, church spires, and windmills turning to the breezes from the sea. In this land the water-table is a metre below the surface, sometimes less. As it is not practicable to dig dug-outs as in a terrain of chalk, it is to be expected that under the farmhouses and other buildings the cellars have been used as bases for blockhouses of steel and concrete massively laid and therefore hidden within the shuttering of brick walls'."

The notes were put in a tunic pocket, almost leisurely. Every eye watched the marmoreal face, with its high forehead covered by short, unbrushed hair. Phillip, elbows on knees, felt inspired to some wild and unformulated heroic action. Even so, he could not think, even, of himself wearing above his heart one of the ribands worn by his hero.

"Now with your permission I shall deal shortly with the second phase of the battle, the break-out. So far in this war neither side has been able to make a wide enough breach in what in former times was the square of resistance, and in mediaeval history the armour, to enable its own armour to pass through, with supplies and all subsidiary services. Supplies and services need railways and main roads, so the breach must be wide. Since the war became static, every battle undertaken and prepared to make a breach in the opponent's armour has failed—the Germans at First and Second Ypres, the British at Loos, the Somme, and Arras; the French in Champagne. Now, at what is likely to be known as Third Ypres the question may well be asked: Will our men be able to push through five fortified lines of enemy wire and concrete, having neutralised the enemy artillery, and reach that distant skyline overlooking the Plain of Flanders to Bruges and Ghent, and beyond the mist, Antwerp and the Dutch frontier?"

There was complete silence in the audience. *Five fortified lines of enemy wire and concrete* . . . shades of Loos, Hindenburg Line, and the Somme!

"We know our enemy. We have no illusions about his ability and courage. But we do know that he is nearing the point of exhaustion, after the wastage of his 'blood bath' of the Somme, which caused his Higher Command to ask for peace terms six months ago. What will be his position when we have blasted him off the last point of observation upon the Salient, whence, for nearly three years now, he has looked down on our every movement of horse and waggon, every puff of steam at railhead, every shovelful of earth thrown up below him? So confident has he sat in his security, that he has used the Salient as a training school for his gunner cadets, using not targets of canvas as our cadets have on Salisbury Plain at home, but living soldiers who never wanted to be where they were, but who through sheer guts and if you like stupidity, never knowing when they were beaten, have remained in the Salient during more than a thousand days and nights of hell, showing such metal that in the end they cannot but win the war."

There were murmurs of approval in the front rows; but impassivity among the regimental officers behind. They'd had some, thought Phillip, looking at 'Spectre' standing straight and still and impassive.

"The Flanders plain behind and below the Passchendaele–Staden rise is only a little more than thirty-three miles in width, from the sea-coast to the Dutch frontier. There are only two main-line railway systems crossing the plain laterally. When we have broken out of the Salient, gentlemen, a day's march will bring the Ypres-Roulers-Thourout railway under howitzer fire, leaving the enemy only the lines through Ghent and Bruges. Once the railway junction at Bruges is dominated by our guns, Zeebrugge with the rest of the Belgian coast will be untenable, and the end of the war will be in sight.''

The lecturer clicked his heels, bowed to the senior officers in the front row, and walked off the platform.

Studying the model of the terrain to be fought over, in a field outside the town, Phillip suddenly realised why certain points of high ground were so important. If you were seen by a sniper, you were shot. If your platoon was seen, it was machine-gunned. If your company or battalion advance was in full view of a hidden man with telescope, map with co-ordinated references, and telephone with direct line to a battery concealed in a fold of ground behind—out of sight of your own observers—he could ring up and give the code reference from his photograph-map, and your company, or battalion, or transport would be blown to hell, out of the blue.

But even if you advanced safely and yet one of your flanks was not secure—the enemy there not destroyed or neutralised—the enemy could shoot you from the side, or if you went on, in the back. This meant that your flank was turned: you would have to re-align your men at least forty-five degrees, to be able to shoot at the enemy on your flank. Meanwhile the advance would peter out: and the angled lines of stoppage would form a salient. But if your flanks were secured, and you could advance through the enemy's position, you would turn his flank, and to save his formation he would have to retire. But once his line was breached, his scattered soldiers would not be able to protect the soft, almost civilian organisation of supply behind his line. And if the enemy had no reserves to come up and form a new line, the war would be over for him.

"So you 'decided you'd go to' a Staff lecture, did you?"
"Yes, sir."
"But that was hours ago. Why are you back so late?"
"I had a talk with the lecturer afterwards, sir."
"Just like your cheek! You 'had a talk with the lecturer afterwards'. Who do you think you are, going up to a Staff Officer?"
"He came up to me, sir. He's an old friend of mine."

"How do I know you're not telling lies again?"

Phillip did not reply. He felt steely towards the red-face: but also he wanted permission to return to Poperinghe.

"Who is he, anyway?"

"Major West, of the Gaultshires, now attached to G.H.Q."

"How did you come to know him?"

"I met him first at Loos. Later he was my C.O. on the Somme. Also, I've met him in London, when I came back. By the way, he's asked me to dine with him at the Aigle d'Or."

"How do I know you don't just want to get hold of a tart?"

"Well, sir, I'd hardly come back all the way just to ask your permission for that, would I?"

Downham laughed. "You're a bit of a card, aren't you? All right, only mind you're back tonight. There's the Army Commander's inspection tomorrow. No more rusty chains, or you're for it!"

"We've got the brightest chains in the division!"

"I hope so. Well, if you can't be good, be careful!"

"Many thanks, *mein prächtig kerl!*" replied Phillip, with a quick salute, and quicker exit.

The two friends sat before the fire in a room in the Aigle d'Or after dinner, a bottle of whiskey on the table before them. They were talking about war correspondents, and the difference between reality and appearances.

"It will take years to see what's happening now, in perspective, Phillip. It takes a long time for the truth to get into the history books, you know."

"Yes, that's what I mean——" Phillip felt riven by chaotic ideas. "I mean, take 'Sapper's' stuff——"

"Oh, that's for milksops at home, who haven't the slightest idea of what's happening. How can they? Even we see only a fractional aspect of the war. It will take thirty years before anyone taking part in this war, or age, will be able to settle down enough to write truly about the human beings involved in this war, let alone what really happened on the battlefield, and in the council chambers."

He helped himself to whiskey.

"I once had ambitions to write a *War and Peace* for this age. But I shall not live to write it. Have you read Tolstoi? Then you haven't begun to live clear of the crowd. Listen to me, and remember, in years to come, what I'm going to tell you. On this earth, every action produces its own reaction, every movement generates friction. Take the War Cabinet in London. There's a constant struggle going on, a struggle of ideas between the soldiers and the politicians. All life is struggle, frustration, and pain—in all strata of life, from the crystals in cooling volcanic flows to the divisions within the highest minds and intellects among men. It's the pattern of life. You told me just now that you can't hit it off with your present C.O. I don't want to hear any details. You may think that your experience is unique—so it is, in a way— but it is also only a part of the general struggle. Every man wants his own way. The Chief has a hell of a time with Lloyd George, who wants more effort, which means troops, for the side-shows, while 'Wullie' Robertson and the Chief think that the Boche can only be beaten here. So the P.M. invariably qualifies what the Chief wants to do. It was the same with Joffre, and later, with Nivelle.''

'Spectre' West refilled Phillip's glass, then his own. "Lloyd George doesn't want another Somme, quite understandably.''

"Do you think we'll break through this time?"

"What a question!"

"Sorry, I shouldn't have asked."

"Why not? I know damn-all, anyway. It's bound to be a hard fight first, to destroy the German reserves. The element of surprise is gone, you see. The enemy knows, generally, what's going to happen. One of our objects is to prevent his reserves from being used in an attack on the French, who had such a pasting in Champagne that they're virtually broken for the time being. It's no secret.''

"Yes, I heard that two army corps had set out to march to Paris——''

"Two! A moderate estimate! But reverting to what you told me about your feeling of inability to be yourself with your present C.O. I'm afraid such clashes of temperament, or mental patterns, are inherent in human nature. Don't make the mistake of thinking that you're an isolated case! It happens all the way up to the top. There's Holland, Third Army's M.G.R.A., for example. Holland was stellenbosched last spring for advocating that the preliminary bombardment should be in the nature of a surprise, with only two days pooping off before the assault. He wasn't popular with G.H.Q. for that. Nor was his master, Allenby, who was shunted off to Palestine. As for the mute inglorious Napoleons in the lower levels, such as corps and division, they drop off like little green apples. It's all a question of the lines of thought getting crossed. I remember Stanhope, G.S.O.2 Second Corps, telling me how he was rung up during the hard frost of January last, when the Corps heavies were ordered to the Arras front. Stanhope was asked why the devil he hadn't got a move on. He explained that each 60-pounder gun required a double team of horses to pull it out, and after the exertion the horses were beat for twenty-four hours. He said what the guns really needed was to be dragged by a caterpillar tractor to a metalled road. To which the reply came from Army, 'I don't understand what you're talking about'."

"Good lord!"

"One man's problem can be completely unrealised by another."

"Why was Major-General Holland stellenbosched? Surely surprise is essential for success in an attack?"

"Yes, but Holland's idea involved the masking of batteries until forty-eight hours before the assault; and masking means no registration of targets. And to shoot off the map accurately requires maps of meticulous accuracy. If the thickness of the linen backing of a map were to vary by so much as one-hundredth of an inch it might mean a hundred yards over, or under. Then there are such things as air temperature, wind, and barometric pressure, all affecting the flight or parabola of a shell."

Later he said, "War is not all bad, you know. Through necessity, the war has got the nation on its feet—literally and metaphorically. Think of the advance in medical knowledge. When my hand was chopped off, the surgeon made a neat little job of it, leaving a symmetrical stump, tucking in the flaps of skin and sewing them up, like the end of a parcel. The result was that it suppurated, and in the old days I would have died of blood-poisoning, as it was called. But a young surgeon saw it in time, opened the wound and drained it, leaving the tissue to wither away in the open. In the same way, war opens up *caches* of ignorance. Of course all knowledge has to be paid for. It's the privilege of our generation to help provide knowledge for the next generation. What more can a man ask than that sacrifice be asked of him for the well-being of his own sort? Personally, I should be sorry to think I'd survive the war."

Phillip wondered how much of Westy's bitterness was due to being in love with his cousin Frances, when she did not love him. If only he could have met someone else, how quickly he would cast off his obsession, as he himself had done with the image of Helena Rolls. He stopped his thoughts, lest they be picked up.

"Do you think the war will be over this year?"

"Possibly. But next year we'll have a better chance. Our opposite numbers across no-man's-land are equally clever, or ignorant, as ourselves. They're as determined as we are at reciprocal frustration and destruction. It's a precarious balance, you know, a war of attrition. Who has the last platoon will win. Even then, the winner can only take over ruin. The French are very pessimistic, after the shock of their frightful beating in Champagne. Fifty-three French divisions were cut to pieces in the first twelve hours. Pétain told the Chief that he couldn't count on his troops going over to the offensive. At the Paris conference last May, Lloyd George said, in effect, that the Somme mustn't be repeated. Pétain backed him up. No advance in depth, he said, but only in breadth. Let the Boche come forward in counter-attack into the storm of steel from our guns. Don't bite off more than you can chew, in other words. Hold on and destroy each bite into the Boche until the Americans arrive in 1918. Then break through the last crust and so to the Rhine."

"But I thought, from what you said at the lecture, that we'd get through to the Scheldt in no time——"

"What else d'you think I could say? And d'you think I liked saying what I said? To chaps like yourself, who've been through a battle, and know what it really is like? Anyway, I know damn-all. Nobody knows anything. Even the Chief knows very little," went on 'Spectre' West, pouring himself whiskey. "The trouble with his job is that he has to consider every conflicting opinion, its virtue and the defect of that virtue. Do you know that in the spring Lloyd George nearly succeeded in getting him placed under the orders of Nivelle? Nivelle had all the arrogance of his own peculiar ideas, the more so because he was without experience. All he had done so far was to get back from the Boche at Verdun, in two days against tired divisions sent down for a rest from the Somme, what the Boche had taken months to get. He sent in a plan to the Paris 'Comité de Guerre, officieusement', telling them how he could win the war! 'The German Army will run away; they only want to be off,' was his theme. For that he was promoted over the heads of Foch and other Army Group commanders, and Joffre was sacked. And what was the result? Nivelle bust himself behind half a million French soldiers in a couple of hours against concrete and wire set in the chalk and stunted fir-trees of the Champagne. If Nivelle had had his way, Haig would have been put under him, and been ordered to bust us against the Hindenburg Line, in one mass attack in depth. No, I am not an admirer of Mr. George from Criccieth!" 'Spectre' pushed over the bottle.

"Hear hear," said Phillip, thinking that Father would be pleased if he could hear that.

"You've got to have well-covered nerves to be a British Commander-in-Chief today. You've got to watch your step with everybody, from teetotal deputations who want to stop the soldier's rum to coves like Horatio Bottomley and George Bernard Shaw. You fix a date for an offensive, wanting to get on while the going is good, in fine weather, in other words; then you learn that the French north of Boesinghe aren't ready. So you lend them seventy thousand Chinese and other labourers to help make their gun emplacements. The French have over three hundred thousand, on leave, all the time now, you know, since the mutinies. God help us if the weather breaks, in this low-lying country, after we've tumbled it up with our guns. Yes, you've got to have a placid temperament to be the British G.O.C. in C. Have you noticed the shape of the Chief's profile? His forehead goes back in a straight line from his nose. My nose, and yours also, make an obtuse angle with the forehead, which is vertical to the ground. Haig's slopes back, like the Emperor Hadrian's. But consider the jaw! Tremendous strength and determination to hold on to what he believes to be right! The wide-spaced eyes reveal breadth of view, which means comprehension of the views of others. He is a good servant, and a good master, without brilliance, thereby lacking the defects of brilliance. The Chief has character, believe you me! His powers, in so far as he has to do what others want him to do, are extremely limited. In Paris, the Quartier General rules, and not the 'frocks', or politicians; in London the Imperial General Staff and the Commander-in-Chief are ruled by the politicians. I can tell you one thing, only you must keep it to yourself. G.H.Q. did not know until this morning whether or not the push was to come off, even though the preliminary bombardment has begun. Not a word about this to anyone, mind!" He poured more whiskey into his glass.

"Yes, the Chief was still in the dark, waiting for the War Cabinet to authorise the push. The P.M. very naturally doesn't want a repetition of the Somme, as I said just now. He wants divisions sent to Macedonia, and to Italy, for his side-shows. At the same time, Mr. George wants an omelette, made of Boche eggs, in the Chief's frying-pan over here, while fearing that the wrong eggs may get into the fire. Also, the Belgian coast must be cleared, declares Admiral Jellicoe, otherwise Tirpitz and his submarines will send us all to Davy Jones' locker. So the Chief, doing his duty to the Old Firm of Frocks in Downing Street, hands on this omelette idea, somewhat scrambled by now, from Plum, who sat too long in the sun on Messines Ridge, five hours to be exact——"

"I saw them, Westy. Plumer waited too long."

"He did. He certainly did! So the Chief says to Plum, 'I'm lending your frying-pan to the Fifth Army of the Fox, so that it won't happen again.' He doesn't exactly put it that way, of course, he says it with tact and friendliness. The trouble is, Plum knows the Salient like the palm of his hand; the Fox doesn't. Plum has the southern flank, from Battle Wood to Plugstreet. He's told to be ready to act offensively, north of the river Lys. 'I shall have three fronts', says the Chief, 'my left facing north-east, my centre facing east, my right facing south-east. I want to be able to break out of whatever front behind which the enemy reserves are not disposed to meet me, and so take him unawares.' At the same time, when he reads the Fox's plans, the Chief thinks of what the Old Firm of Frocks in London told him about going forward bite by bite. So the Fox has been told to go steady, and, at the same time, that the two objectives are, first the skyline about the village of Passchendaele, then the Belgian coast."

The speaker swallowed his glassful, and poured more.

"The Fox says, in effect, 'I shall want twice the number of divisions to do that, Chief', while Haig is thinking at the same time of what Jellicoe said about the alarming menace of German U-boats, while balancing it against what the P.M. said, and also what Pétain said about the state of the French Army, and how if the Boche knew what a state our gallant Allies were in they'd go through them so fast that there wouldn't be even a frying pan, let alone eggs to make it! And that's the theme of a novel I hope to write one day, to stand with *War and Peace*, bringing in all the causes and all the effects of a Great War that eventually brought the end of Christendom and let in the Barbarian."

"You mean the Germans?"

"I do *not* mean the Germans! I mean that what happened to the City States in Greece will happen to the European Christian nations. Europe is fighting now exactly as the ancient Greeks fought among themselves, until they destroyed their homeland, and the barbarian moved in."

"But *who* will be the barbarian after this war?"

"The spirit behind the mutinies in the French and Russian armies."

"But don't they want to stop the war?"

"That is the paradox. We want a third idea, Napoleon's idea: we want the United States of Europe. Today, that is only an idea. Tomorrow—but you and I, my dear Phil, have no to-morrow. We have the honour to be of the European generation that——" He stopped. "No!" His eye stared with pale blue brilliance. "*Courage, mon brave, courage!* The British never, never will be slaves! You, my friend, are at the cross-roads! Remember this: 'He who loses his life shall save it'. Put duty before self! That alone will carry you through to the end. He who *forgets* his own life shall enter into wider life! And remember, Phillip," 'Spectre' took his hand, "you have a friend who believes in you. Hell, I've had too much to drink."

Walking back to camp, while German bombers burred over-head, and flashes and crashes came from in front—events in the night made exhilarating by thoughts of Westy—Phillip felt a few spots of rain on his face. As though the rain was a signal, the eastern horizon flared up in a vast butterfly-flutter of light, as the British guns opened up in another phase of the preliminary bombardment.

Chapter 13

THE FOX OUT-FOXED

DRAGGING clouds broke into rain on the night of July 31. Some said it was due to the gunfire. Two nights previously the sections had moved up to Ypres in darkness made wan by the light of the moon in its first quarter, Phillip following with the limbers. Everything he had experienced in war so far was diminished by the sinister feeling all around him as he rode through the Grand' Place, despite the almost furtive activity among the ruins, where were hidden masked batteries of guns, including a 15-inch howitzer known as 'Clockwork Charlie' for its regular bombardment of Passchendaele station thirteen thousand yards away.

The town was partly surrounded by a moat, along one side of which rose massive red-brick ramparts, said to have been built in Napoleonic times. The years of German shelling had not destroyed them. Within the high walling were tunnels, lit by electric light, and sand-bagged against blast. Here with legions of rats lived Companies of West Indian labourers who filled shell-craters with rubble from the ruins, among other labouring jobs.

Although so much human life existed in the ruins, the spirit of desolation pervaded the place; its spirit was vacant and barren; nobody wanted to be there; the spirit of an unloved place was repellent with its smells of burnt cordite, mortar-and-hair dust, and chloride of lime. A psychical vacuum of lost life, old terror, and chronic hopelessness lingered in the crepuscular ruins. And yet, as one passed under the grey ragged walls of Cloth Hall and Cathedral, and came to the ruinous gape of the Menin Gate, just perceptible by the stone lions, couchant and pocked, on either side of the route, a faint illusion of life in the ruins called to one; for ahead lay nihilism. If, in the fossils of the town, life had floated in a void, now it had the steeliness of unendurable cruelty, which sought finally to deny life and happiness to all who moved above the ground, in any direction. One of many hundreds of thousands who had passed that way, Phillip proceeded, nervous animation of flesh and bone on innocent horseflesh because there was no alternative, while he remained unbroken.

The company guns were under the Divisional Machine Gun Officer for the barrage which was to begin with the assault. They were not to fire until zero hour. Aiming posts had been prepared, set up off the map, with direction by compass. Company battle-headquarters were in Paradise Row, at the far end of St. Jean, on the St. Julien road, five hundred yards behind the front line.

This was Major Downham's first time in with his own troops. While at Proven he had spent forty-eight hours in the line, attached to another brigade, but with no duties. He came back from that Cooks' tour, Phillip noticed, with a pack filled with souvenirs—shell fragments, nose-caps, German rifle cartridge-clips, a German steel helmet. These went into a parcel to be posted home to Downham *père* at Tulse Hill, in the purlieus of the Crystal Palace, together with shirts and other underclothes to be washed. A pair of long woollen pants was wrapped around a dozen ounce-packets of various brands of ration tobacco, and a box of Belgian cigars. "That'll kill Downham's old man all right," remarked Pinnegar. "Serves him right for having such a son."

Phillip returned from the battle-emplacements in Paradise Row beyond St. Jean and the rattle of a thousand wheels on the cobbled Place to the transport lines near Vlamertinghe, where the mill had been made into a Casualty Clearing Station, its walls hung with white sheets, its inner spaces lit by electricity revealing white operating tables and equipment as in an operating theatre in a London hospital. New sidings had been made from the main railway line, with names in the Flemish idiom—Bandaghem, Dosinghem, and Mendinghem. Areas for cemeteries had been wired off, and neat rows of graves prepared by Chinese labourers. Deep dressing stations had been made nearer the line, notably one in circular form, with tiers like an amphitheatre, under the Menin road, that straightness of fear which for three years had been under observation of enemy guns lifelessly between its fractured tree-stumps, revealing by day patches of pink mud, like the sores of the dead, where bricks had been tipped into shell-holes.

Phillip had taken up rations and heavy boxes of S.A. ammunition on Y/Z night, although it had been arranged with Downham that he and Rivett should take turn and turn about. He felt that he could not trust the job to Rivett. The sergeant's daily letters to his mother, exaggerating the nightly bombing, dangers just escaped, and general violence of life around him, showed that he was still very windy inside. And he was good at routine work, and reliable. If he got into real danger he might very well go sick, and a dud sergeant be sent up from the base to replace him, when it would be goodbye to the old free-and-easy life by day.

Phillip told himself that he had the best of the bargain, three to six hours every night taking up limbers, and more or less free during the day.

He slept through the opening barrage, which was at 3.50 a.m. By the time he was up, and had had breakfast, prisoners began to come down to the cages. Walking wounded, too. They told of success. Yet the steady rattle and crackle of small-arms fire told a different tale, he thought. These wounded had been hit on or near the first objective, which had been 200–300 yards across no-man's-land. The barrage had been tremendous, a wall of crashing smoke and flame, lit by thermit flares and oil bombs lobbed over by trench mortars. One man told a strange tale of figures following behind the assault waves, unwinding broad pink tapes, laying them carefully among the grasses and old shell-holes of no-man's-land grown with rushes. They didn't stop at Jerry's front trench, where upheaved brown earth made almost a straight line against the grass of no-man's-land, "as though it had been measured off by a chain, sir". Asked what the pink tapes were for, the wounded man said they had looked pink in the light of the bursting oil bombs, but were white. He went on to say that they were to mark the up-and-down tracks for the infantry and Yukon-pack carrying parties. There were parties of the Engineers carrying finger-posts, like those on the roads at home, painted white with black lettering. They had been made a proper job of. After a cup of tea he limped away, full of optimism, saying that Jerry had had it this time.

"He means he has, sir," remarked Nolan. "He's got his blighty all right. They'll be clearing the hospitals at the base of all cases. The Alleymans aren't fools, they knew what was comin', and have prepared accordingly. The fighting isn't started yet, to my mind."

Phillip was always happy in the presence of Nolan. Nolan had been for more than one joy ride with him, replacing Morris. Nolan seemed to reciprocate the feeling of companionship, for he always volunteer'd to take the place of any man on the roster who had gone sick—as some drivers did occasionally, especially those who, Phillip deduced from their letters, had some sort of complications at home. It was no good taking your mother or your wife or sweetheart to war with you, which seemed to happen when things were one-sided, not truly right between you and your mother or girl. That caused anxiety, and anxiety undermined a man and made him a prey to fearful thoughts. He had made a discovery! Talismans, too, showed fear. Some men carried little Bibles in their tunic breast pockets, or lucky charms, including crucifixes. No, he must not think that. And yet, Mother had given him that crucifix, which had been in the top drawer of his bedroom at home ever since he had returned from Loos in October 1915. In 1914 he had felt so anxious about it, it was part of Mother. Now he felt easier because it was safe at home, and would comfort Mother, because he had worn it, if he was killed. Not that he thought he would be killed; but it was no good trying to avoid your fate by taking all sorts of precautions, such as a bullet-proof vest, a miniature breast-pocket Y.M.C.A. Bible, or

three volumes of Francis Thompson's poems tied round the
stomach! If you were going to be killed, you would be killed.

A good breakfast with a couple of stiff old-man-whiskies made
all the difference to a point of view. And lighting his pipe,
Phillip went away to enjoy a few moments quiet reflection in the
red, white, and black "sentry" box, which he regarded as his
most valuable possession in France. Several other officers had
asked about it, including the C.R.E. of Division, a Staff Colonel
with grey hair and mild paternal appearance. Should not the
sentry box, he enquired, have been left for the Salvage Corps to
collect? All enemy stores, he explained, automatically became
Crown property. G.H.Q. Routine Orders were clear on this
matter. He added that it was probably a unique specimen: the
only sentry box with the Imperial Colours to be left behind in the
retreat to the Hindenburg Line.

"Sir, with all due respect, I fancy it is an Imperial latrine!"
said Phillip, at attention.

"Oh," said the C.R.E. "That's another matter."

A message was brought by runner from Pinnegar, saying that
company H.Q. had gone forward through Wieltje taking left fork
of road through the village for the St. Julien road. They were at
VENHEULE FARM, at a stated map reference.

After this came another message from Major Downham,
ordering him to be at the old company H.Q. in Paradise Row at
8 p.m., where he would receive further instructions. *Acknowledge*,
the message ended.

Phillip wrote in reply, giving time, code number of unit, and
reference number, *Message Acknowledged*.

No further news came from the line. He wanted to go to
Divisional headquarters to see the Operations map outside the
A.D.C.'s room in a canvas Nissen hut, but he was in command of
the company cadre, which meant standing by for messages either
from Downham at St. Jean, or from Brigade. He had seen such
maps during Messines, coloured lines of objectives stuck with pins
on which were paper flags, marking the advance.

At flare light he set off through the Grand' Place. Guns were
now firing among the ruins. Soon he realised that the attack had
not gone far, since enemy shells were womping around the Menin
Gate. Lines of transport accumulated. Military police stopped
any attempt to turn away for another route. They moved on,
halted, moved on again. It was like a relay race, going through

the last ruins before the Ramparts at intervals, drivers whipping their beasts.

Someone had copped it, he saw, as he urged the drivers through. Most of the shells were now falling forward, along the Menin road. They trotted up the Frezenberg road, turning left-handed by a large notice-board at Potijze marked Savile Row, with a direction arrow to St. Jean. At the end of the village were the old company headquarters in front of Wieltje. There the company sergeant major was waiting with a runner, to show them the way. "Major's a bit anxious, sir, about the ammo. coming up. So he sent me to fetch you. The sections are very low, sir."

"How did the attack go?"

"Rough, sir. The Brigade got over the Steenbeek, but had to come back out of St. Julien. Enfilade fire from a line of pill-boxes held them up, they say."

He led up the left fork of the road through Wieltje, bumpy with tipped bricks. Its flat raggedness was blanched by guns firing among the ruins.

"Jerry's been strafing a bit tonight, sir. I fancy a lot of stuff's coming from way up the Menin road. Looks as though the attack's been held up on the right, same as 'ere."

"Held up?"

"Yes, sir. The Brigade's been held up on the Black Line since this morning."

Phillip had seen a map of the objectives: there were six positions, each with its system of outposts, trenches, communicating *allees*, and lines of concrete pill-boxes. The first four positions were heavily wired—and marked on the map with primary colours: Blue, Black, Green, Red. The Red was called by the Germans Flandern I. Behind it stretched Flandern II, along the crest overlooking the Salient. Flandern III was on the plain below, covering the towns of Roulers and Menin. After that, open warfare. It was said that the Red line was the final objective for the first day; then a pause to get the guns up, before going on to Passchendaele by the end of the week.

Giant finger-flashes were playing the piano of hell behind the distant Gheluvelt plateau.

"Yes, it looks as though the Alleyman has foxed the Fox with his dummy battery emplacements, sergeant-major."

Hardly had they crossed the old front line when a shell rushed down in a shriek beside the leading limber and he found himself falling sideways, the mare still under him, until its legs were above him. Fortunately she rolled away and he could free his other leg. He lay inert, thinking he was hit, but when the mare began to scream and struggle, fear made him roll clear. The sergeant-major helped him to his feet. By flash-lamp he saw that the mare had a leg smashed at the knee. The tendons were cut, too.

"You'll have to shoot her, sir."

Scraping mud from his hands, he shot between the eyes; and went on beside the sergeant-major, over the grassy road through no-man's-land.

"There bin a lot of horses killed here today," said the sergeant-major. "King Edward's Horse in particular. They got near the Steenbeek, then 'ad to dismount and run for it. Cavalry's worse than the tanks for this sort of fighting."

At the old German front line there began a new road of timber baulks. The sergeant-major said this had been built immediately behind the assault by labour battalions. From the road smaller duck-walk routes branched off, marked by white tapes and posts driven into the ground.

"What was the barrage like?"

"It was dark one moment, sir, then it was suddenly shrieking crimson. All our faces was red, as we went over. I never seen anything like it."

Phillip imagined rows of umbered faces, staggering figures casting long shadows in a tremendous fantasy of fire. He wished he had seen it.

The uneven baulk road led into a raggedness of brown earth asprawl with German dead.

"The infantry went through Jerry's outpost line like a dose of salts, sir. They didn't take no prisoners." He imagined them swearing and sweating through torn wire after fleeing distraught creatures, to bayonet them in kidneys, or when they kneeled with hands upheld in surrender by upward butt-strokes smashing jaws: acts of jack-out-of-box cowardice. Poor little Jack-in-the box toy of long ago, Christmas present from Father, too square to go in his stocking, where was it now, with its funny little painted red face?

"But I reckon Jerry sucked us in after all, sir. He'd pulled out most of his infantry, and kept them back for the counter-attack. I reckon Jerry caught the Fox with 'is trousers down, then!"

"What happened?" A matey feeling came between them, and

the sergeant-major lapsed into his pre-promotion easy way of speaking.

"'S' afternoon, without warning, swarms of Jerry battalions come over the skyline. Cockchafer Brigade, some said they was, big men. We could see where they was getting to because they was firing lights from pistols, and aeroplanes with them flying up and down low like, strafing our outposts with their machine guns. Then at 4 o'clock, didn't it just come down cats and dogs! Cor, it might 'ave bin Bank 'Oliday at 'ome, for all the weather cared. Some of our infantry I seen wadin' up to their knees where the Steenbeek broke over its banks into shell-'oles. Jerry got stuck, too, coming down. We got them taped all right wiv our Vickers, cor, a proper slaughter it was! 'Cockchafers' or July Bugs, we buzzed them old dumbledores all right! The time was just six o'clock. I looked at me watch and noted the time, for it was the time arranged for opening up of the barrage. Cor, didn't it 'arf wallop down on Jerry! A proper 'arf a mo' Kayser we give them. They turned and 'ooked it for 'ome very soon. But on other sectors it looks as though 'e got 'is own back. Here's company headquarters, sir!"

They stopped beside a scattered brick heap marked by a white board with map reference. The sergeant-major pushed aside a blanket, and went down into a concrete shelter.

Major Downham came out with him. "Why are you late? Where the hell have you been? Our night-firing barrage should have been laid on by now! Come on, don't stand there! Get a move on! My men in the line are waiting for the belt boxes!"

A shell screamed down; he hurried down the steps of a German concrete cellar-shelter, leaving the warrant officer standing there in silent sympathy, as boxes of S.A.A. containing 160,000 rounds were unloaded for the men at the belt-filling depot in one corner of the shelter.

Major Downham's last words to Phillip were, "Tell Pinnegar I want him. Tell him to come at once. I've got to send in my returns to Brigade."

"Very good, sir. Goodnight, s'ar major. Lead on, Nolan."

The front line now ran north of the Steenbeek, recrossing it in front of St. Julien. The guide beside him said it had been captured that morning, but the boys had come back because of flanking fire from the pillboxes on the banks of the stream. They walked towards what looked like a stationary barrage. He began to feel watery, and tried to stop himself working his jaws. He spat violently at his weakness, anger rose in him against mother-face thoughts. He set his jaw and thrust forward, to hell with everything as he spat at the smoky red bursts of shrapnel.

To the right, a few miles away, tremulous piano-playing fingers had changed to a flight of butterflies with wings overlapping one another, trembling and blazing in radiance above the row of lily flares. In intervals of the uproar thin cries of wounded men lying out came through the nictitating darkness. The shell-fire in front ceased, and a swarm of machine-gun bullets pitter-patted into the ground. By the slow sound he thought they had been fired from extreme range, and deduced that the Alleyman was taking no chances of a night attack.

He saw longer stalks on the flares as they moved over the edge of the rise, and then what he imagined, from a memorised picture of the contour map, to be the shallow depression of the Steenbeek at St. Julien before him. The wooden road gleamed wide enough for two lines of traffic. Was he awfully late? Where were the other convoys? A sentry stood at a fork where it branched, according to the signpost, to Kitchener Wood.

"Oo are yer?"

"Machine-gun transport."

"Pass, machine guns. Any more coming?" Phillip saw he had a battle-police armband. Before he could reply Nolan's voice said, "'Ow d'you like so'jering for a change, copper?"

A flash-light beam was directed upon Nolan's box-respirator in correct position across his chest, the flap undone. The beam moved to the rolled gas-masks of the mules, correctly fastened to their brow-bands.

"Officer present!" said Nolan, sharply.

"Are we all right for Venheule Farm, corporal?"

"Just below the dip down, sir. Jerry's bin droppin' mustard gas. Nasty stuff, sir. You want to be careful not to get any on your hands or face. Burns badly, sir."

"Thank you, corporal. Are we the last of the convoys?"

"No, sir, the first I've seen tonight."

"Right, lead on, Nolan."

Soon they were in full view of the line below, marked to left and right of the shallow Steenbeek valley by diminishing lines of flares. The luminous butterfly-wings still rose to the zenith above the Menin road, where ruddy splashes and sparks revealed the fall of British shells among the German batteries on the Gheluvelt plateau. The tempest of hell! Nearly a thousand nights had passed since he had been in the woods beside the Menin road, with Cranmer and the others of the 1st Brigade; and never *for one moment*—except on that first Christmas Day—had the massed feeling in the Salient ceased to be the feeling of men lost in hell. Why, why, *why* was it all happening? But *why, why, why?* had raced through his head many times before: there must be a reason. It was like the dog trying to understand why sounds were coming out of the gramophone horn on the label of the twelve-inch record sung by George Baker in his deep bass voice:

> *Myself when young did eagerly frequent*
> *Doctor and Saint, and heard great argument,*
> *But evermore came out by that same door*
> *Wherein I went.*

Rain lashed down over the battlefield.

"Christ, we've had a time," said Pinnegar, by the light of a candle, which showed the cracked grey walls. "I've never known anything like this on the Somme." His grimy face was swelled, the eyes bright with contained shock. Opening one of the bottles which had been brought up, he splashed whiskey into his enamel mug, and said absently, "Have a drink."

"You drink, Teddy, you need it."

"Cheerio." He gulped, spluttered, and choked. Phillip struck him on the back. He recovered, drew a deep breath. "That's just what I wanted! Help yourself!"

They sat down on a pile of empty belt boxes; the carrying parties were taking filled boxes and rations from the limbers, under the eye of Pinnegar's staff sergeant. The pill-box had a steel door above three steps going down below ground level. "It had a direct hit from a nine-two how. It's cracked, as you can see. Jerry's got it taped, you mustn't stay long. Have you seen the bloody Sharpshooter? What did he say?"

"He wants you to go and see him at once, as he wants to send in his reports to Brigade."

"*His* reports! That's my job, or supposed to be. My God, he's a swine! He sits in his cellar and sends me chits all day. He's supposed to be here but he's too windy. So he remains where I'm supposed to be, at the reserve dump at K4 and passes on messages from Brigade to me. He hasn't once been round to visit the sections! I'm virtually commanding this company. He's the most bloody awful —— ——pot I've ever had the —— luck to serve under!" Having cursed Downham, Pinnegar looked less shiny about the eyes.

"I hear you knocked hell out of the Pomeranian Grenadiers, the Kaiser's Guards!"

"The Welch did that, going over! But we broke up the counter-attack. I reckon our barrels are now practically smooth bores! We fired off all our belts. I thought some of the water-jackets would burst, they boiled all their water. The rain had some use, after all."

"'Cockchafers', weren't they?"

"So I heard. How many boxes did you bring? Good, we can do with some extra ones. Did you leave eight thousand rounds per gun at K4?"

"I left ten thousand per gun."

"Splendid! We'll need 'em! Well, I must go round the sections. This rain's mucked things up for the tanks, quite apart from the fact that our preliminary bombardment ruined the ground for them. I suppose Downham didn't say anything about when we're going to be relieved? Anyway, we'll probably have to stay here when the Brigade goes out. It's lost a hell of a lot—nearly two thousand men, I reckon, from what I've gathered."

On the way back they passed a slow, continuous double line of limbers occupying all the board track, so Phillip turned off after cursing the leading officers responsible and managed, with the empty limbers, to get back over the craters, two hours later, to K4. A cold and wet sergeant-major was waiting for the empty belt boxes. "There's bin a spot of bother, sir, over some of the S.A.A. boxes you brought up. The belt-fillers said the cartridge rims were marked 'J' and 'T', which ammo has been officially condemned as old and liable to be faulty, in a G.H.Q. Memorandum. It was repeated in Company Orders last week, sir."

"Surely it isn't all dud stuff?"

"No, only some boxes, sir."

"Thank God! I'd better see the C.O."

"Sir," he said, before Downham could speak, "the dud boxes must be the extra ones I half-inched off the Brigade rear dump. I didn't stop to look, wanting to get it up quickly. I drew the proper amount of 'K.N.', and counted the boxes myself. Eight thousand rounds per gun for belt-filling, and a further three thousand five hundred per gun for Pinnegar. In addition, I've got eight thousand five hundred per gun of 'K.N.' at the transport lines, as well as a further four thousand five hundred rounds loaded and covered up in the spare limbers, ready for any emergency. I've brought back the empty belt boxes.''

"Where have you been all this time? Chin-wagging, I suppose?'' The Sharpshooter looked at his watch. "It's two and a half hours since you were here!''

"We ran into transport coming back, sir. We were first up. They were in two lines, taking all the board track. It was not easy going, over the craters.''

"Anyway, you've wasted the best part of the filling party's time, bringing that dud stuff. Why the hell can't you come into line with everyone else?''

Which line, the front line? Phillip asked voicelessly.

Rain, rain, rain, rain—for the first four nights and three days of the battle joined north and south of the Menin road. The German guns on the Gheluvelt plateau, with their alternative and dummy emplacements, remained master. The British gunners suffered casualties almost as severely as the infantry. Divisions which had lost half their effectives, as they were called, remained in the line, to go forward into machine-gun and field-gun barrages again and again, amidst tumbled and upheaved woods which were obstacles against tanks, like the shallow depressions made into lagoons of mud, by the attacking artillery.

Limbers could not move, except on the baulk tracks, and known roads in which rubble was continually being tipped at night, only to be flung up and away once more by the howitzers on the Gheluvelt plateau. Wreckage of horses, mules, their drivers and limbers strewed the tracks; for these winding routes, like the ribs of prehistoric snakes which had died casting their sloughs, were under automatic fire in bright moonlight all through the night until the vastness of dawn.

6 Mon   (Bank Holiday at home, ye gods!) As the s-m said, it is Bank Holiday weather out here; but where are all the carts, vans, traps, dogcarts, brakes, waggonettes, coster's donkey shallows, gigs, tandems, floats of milkmen, even coal-carts which rolled out packed with trippers from the rookeries South of the River along the roads into Kent, to the pubs, having a fine old time tearing branches, smashing bottles, and setting fire to brakes of furze and fern on the commons? Some of them are in khaki; in fact it is the same raucous and destructive life, only enlarged into war turning everything dead nasty. The crowds are here, the smashings and the fires.

Sergeant Rivett, after one night taking up limbers, went sick.

Division is relieved; we handed over guns to our reliefs, but not what is left of transport thank God. Nolan a tower of strength. Yukon packs, band on brow of man carrying one, are now the order, and pack mules. There are as many duck-walks in 6-ft. sections twenty inches wide as lines on the palm of "Spectre" West's remaining hand, the tiny lines all leading to the cross-palm creases of the beeks, now lagoons of mud in the dirtiest, filthiest, bloodiest Martian paw that ever had the nerve to open under heaven and call upon God to agree that it is all as He wished. At night the battle-field is all hammering and banging and booming, the surface of it laced with water reflecting the dazzling and terrible lights of the sky.

7 *Tue*   Coy inspection including transport. Some dirty dog had pinched our bright chains, and I got badly strafed for the old rusty ones, which we didn't have time to burnish while in the line.

While he was drawing funny faces at the end of the diary Pinnegar came into his tent, gave him an O.H.M.S. envelope, and said, "I thought I'd bring this to you, and tell you that I think it's a bloody injustice, and I'm prepared to back you up in anything you may want to say to the Colonel, if he sends for you."

To Lt. P. S. T. Maddison
From O.C. 286 M.

I have to inform you, in accordance with King's Regulations, that your name was not included in a list called for today, of Officers for promotion. Acknowledge.

It was signed by Downham, and written in a copperplate hand, the name of the addressee omitted and filled in by Downham himself, so that the Orderly Room clerk should not know it, apparently.

"Thanks, Teddy. I'm not due for promotion, anyway."
Then, realising from what Pinnegar had said about seeing the

Colonel, "I suppose—if anyone isn't recommended for promotion, he isn't, I suppose—well—I say, does it mean I might lose my job? Or even my commission?"

"I suppose there's a remote chance that you might be shunted back to the infantry. It's nothing to do with me, I assure you. I've told Downham you're all right, but you know what he is. He ought to have stopped with his Underground Sharpshooters in Blighty, and would have done, too, if conscription hadn't come in, and all fireside shrimshankers automatically became liable for overseas. Can't you see your pal, and wangle a job on the staff? Town major, Railway Transport Officer, or something?"

"Teddy, tell me, are you letting me down lightly? Am I stellenbosched?"

"Where did you get that expression from?"

"Stellenbosch was the name of the town occupied by G.H.Q. in the South African war. I suppose I'll be sent down to the base?"

"All I know is that Brigade sent in a chit that we've got to send one officer, or give his name anyway, to attend a course for the new type of infantry tactics in attack, when we go out to rest. The idea is probably a sort of liaison between us and the footsloggers. So the Sharpshooter told me to send in your name. I shouldn't let it worry you, Phil."

After some more talk, a booted leg appeared through the tent flap, "Hullo, you old Tarbaby! You got a smack in the eye, too? Well, I'll leave you two to talk it over by yourselves."

Bright was anything but his name just then, he was down to grimness. He wanted Phillip to join with him in a protest to the Colonel. He had done his duty, he declared doggedly, he had stuck to his job and looked after his men. He——

Phillip told him what Pinnegar had said: wait to see what happened, if anything; section officers could not be spared, they were dying like flies——

"Or not like flies, Bright, now I come to think of it. D'you know, since the return of sunny weather, the flies have increased so fast that they drank the ink out of my fountain pen, which I left uncapped on the top of the pipe-stove, through the nib. Green Spanish flies as well as blue bottles, coming, I reckon, from Bandigem, Dosingem, and Mendingem."

"What the hell'r you yapping about?"

"Flies. I've been wondering if it will bring about an increase of swallows. About the other matter, I agree with Pinnegar. It's wait and see."

"Of course there's flies where there's dead bodies! And you're quite wrong about wait and see! That's what Asquith did, and where did it get him with Lloyd George? The boot! No, I'm not disposed to let the matter rest until I get the boot! I damn well demand an opportunity to state my case, that Downham spoke in a scathing personal manner about how I conducted my private affairs at home!"

Phillip suppressed laughter. To tar and feather the naked body of your wife's lover and then turn him loose like that, without even a hat, was rather a public way to conduct one's private affairs! "Well after all, it did get into the papers, Bright."

"And serve the dirty little skunk right!" Bright's jaw shot out, and he looked at Phillip in a way that made the other say, "Well, I didn't do it! Why look at me as though I did?"

"I speak how I feel! Always did. I'm blunt, I am! And I'd do it again if it happens again! What the hell is there to laugh about?"

"Oh, nothing really." Only the idea of a poor wretch, as Mother would say, trying to do it again while completely disguised in White Leghorn feathers, so that even his eyes were hidden!

"You're a soft silly fool, that's what's wrong with you, Maddison! You'd let anybody piss on you and not raise a little finger to defend yourself. Go on, laugh at me!"

"Have a spot of old man whiskey, Bright! I wasn't laughing at you, honestly, only at your idea of anyone defending himself against a liquid attack with a little finger raised!"

"You're a bloody fool! You'd laugh at anything!" retorted Bright, contemptuously. "And you can stick your whiskey where the monkey stuck his nuts."

And Bright, with jaw extended and face pale, pushed his way out of the tent.

Phillip poured himself a quartern of whiskey, and wound the gramophone.

The battlefield was covered with tanks abandoned in all positions. Some were reared up, with tracks dislocated; others were shot through and through, half sunken away in shell-holes, smitched with fire, tipped over, ditched, bellied, and

broken. Sergeant Rivett being at a base hospital, Nolan now
looked after the lines, an acting, unpaid, and rather reluctant
lance-corporal, "But I don't mind wearing a stripe for you,
sir." On August 8 there was a violent thunderstorm, to add to
the terrors of the night. Phillip again gave his men rum when
they had delivered the stuff, and so once more the string came
back in hilarious mood. It was Charlie Chaplin funny to see
someone slip off a duck-walk beside a mule slowly pumping
itself along, *sock-plug-splosh* of feet, to haul out of a shell-hole the
troglodytic driver the heavier by more than a hundredweight
of slurry. A communal pull at Phillip's water-bottle of 20%
over-proof rum helped to keep the feeling of all being in it
together. One driver had been killed, on the way up, by a shell.
At last the body, after several back slidings, was secured upon
a mule's back and tied by feet and hands under the mule's
belly. It was the only way to bring the body back for burial;
and the arrival at the lines after daylight caused some remarks.
Bright already was known throughout Division, if not Corps,
as the Tarbaby; now it was variously said that 286 Company
M had brought back a stiffy for their private corpse factory,
and (this spread farthest) because of a reward offered by rich
parents. The truth was that it did not seem right to leave
Daddy M'Kinnell in that lonely waste of mud and water.

Chapter 14

PHILLIP IS FOR IT

10 Fri	Buried M'Kinnell in graveyard at Kandahar. Nolan put on the cross of ration box wood he made, in indelible pencil, *Sleep on, dear Brother, take thy Gentle Rest.* One can never tell a man's soul by his outward appearance. Company relieved at night. Took 9 hours. Guns brought back for armourers.
11 Sat	Half quarter day. £10 from M.F.O. making my balance at Cox's £127-5-4. Attack on Gheluvelt plateau failed. Saw remnants of 7th Gaultshires coming back, had been in line a week already and were done up. Other battalions had been in for ten days, hanging on by eyebrows in watery shell-holes. Westhoek taken by R. Irish Rifles. Got tight.

12 Sun   Refitting. Collected four new donks. Three drivers arrived,
                  but we are still six short.
13 Mon   We are to go in again tonight. Have told Nolan to see
                  that Cutts stays back, on picket, and to help stitcher and
                  cold shoer, etc.

During the four days out of the line the company, one of nearly
fifty which had been in the battle so far, together with one
hundred and ninety-two infantry battalions, had no rest. New
arrivals had to be trained and instructed. At least the Machine
Gun Corps was a specialist branch; it was the infantry which
suffered when drafts made up of men recovered from wounds and
young conscripts out for the first time were poured, regardless
of regiment, into half-empty and quarter-empty battalions.
They were like hundreds and thousands, childhood sweets
consisting of minute coloured round specks, half an ounce of
which, poured into a twisted paper spill, had cost a farthing.
The poorest children bought them, because they lasted longest.
The way to eat them was to dip a wet finger-tip into the spill
and suck off the dozen specks that clung there. Now they were
alive, the hundreds of thousands, with divisional colours on
helmets, shoulders, limbers, waggons—among them the Watching
Eye of the Guards; Keyhole of 11th; Red-and-White check of
25th; Pelican crest of the Earl of Derby, the 30th; Red Dragon
of the 38th; White Diamond of 48th; the letters H.D. of 51st;
Red Rose of 55th; Shamrock of 16th; Bloody Hand of 36th;
Red Sword of 56th.

The old woman in her little wooden cottage near Cutler's
Pond had a long spoon for taking "hundreds and thousands"
out of the glass jar, to be poured into the spill, each one making
a tiny rattle on the side of the paper as it fell. A tiny rattle in
the spill-shaped shell-hole, one of a hundred thousand in the
Salient making up the Fight, as the Staff called it; and the long
spoon was dipped again, wrote Phillip.

14 Tue   Attack postponed. Took loads of duck-boards to Mouse
                  Trap Farm by limbers 7 a.m.—6 p.m. Saw "Spectre"
                  coming down from the line. Terrific thunder-storm in
                  afternoon. More rain in evening. Went up line with
                  weary pack-mules at 8 p.m. Moonless slipslop dark.
                  Shelling bad. Board tracks tipped, splintered, floating
                  in places. Lost 3 mules and two drivers (Winnick and
                  Snell).

15 Wed   Got back at 2.30 a.m. Slept as I was, all in. Awoke
6 a.m. heavy and cold, on groundsheet. Sent off limbers
with Nolan on duck-board fatigue, M.T. farm, as
yesterday. Changed, shaved, washed, felt fit. Went to
draw coy pay at Poperinghe and saw "Spectre". We
went to a service in a disused hop-loft, after he'd strafed
me for drinking too much.

? Poetry is love, and love is courage.

"No," 'Spectre' West said on that occasion, "I'm not going
to ask you to have another cognac. You'll spoil your liver if you
get in the habit of wanting 'just one more'. I know what I'm
talking about. Why d'you look at me like that? You're thinking
that it's the reformed poacher who makes the best game-keeper,
no doubt?"

Phillip laughed. "I can't keep any of my thoughts from you,
Westy. All the same——"

"No, it's not the same! You are not me, remember!"

"The violet smells to me as it does to you."

The pale blue eye glared. "Aren't you being a little impertinent?"

"I—I'm awfully sorry, sir. I shouldn't have said that."

"And I shouldn't have said what I said. I've been an usher,
you know, and had too many small boys to bear-lead. What
I mean is that you still have poetry. You are not petrofact, like
me. I see life as a waste land; you see the flowers. You have a
future. George, bring me the cognac, and a tumbler. And
coffee for my guest."

Coffee pot from chafing stand, then bottle, tumbler, and
siphon were put beside him.

"Now, tell me about your trouble," he said, filling his guest's
cup. Phillip felt sad beyond words. Did Westy know he was
going to die? He found it hard to speak.

"Well?"

"I'm all right now, thank you."

"You've reconsidered the matter, whatever it was?"

"Yes, I have."

"Good. We must all dree our own weirds. I think I know
what you wanted to tell me, but I wouldn't be able to do anything about it. It's a matter entirely between you and your
Commanding Officer. In the meanwhile carry on as you are now,
and bite on the bullet. I said bullet, not bottle."

"That's what I intended to do."

"As I told you before, you're by no means the only one who comes up against it. At all levels of life there is not only mis-understanding, whence misinterpretation, but what might be called un-understanding, or failure even remotely to understand. Nowhere are things 'too well'; and that's an understatement. But I know nothing. I'm a low form of brazen life, a mere collector of local data. This weather hasn't given anyone a fair chance, which is an understatement. I was talking to 'Meteor' this morning. The weather has broken all records for rain this year. It was fine in August 1914. One and a half inches fell in August 1915, and just under three in 1916. So far this month, we've had nearly five."

"May I ask about the war?"

"By all means. But I know very little."

"Why didn't we go for the Gheluvelt plateau first? From the stuff coming from that direction, I imagine it to be as bristly with guns as a porcupine with spines. If Messines could be taken, why wasn't Gheluvelt taken the same way? It's no farther on than the Oosttaverne line was, and last June we would have got there if the reserves had been ready at once to go in. Surely the high-ups learn by experience?"

"Now you're asking what everyone else seems to be asking! I'll try and explain. As you know, Plumer got to the Messines heights in one bound. But instead of thrusting on to the open Oosttaverne line beyond, he waited. Lest it happen again, the Chief handed the Salient over to Hubert Gough, his youngest General, and a thruster. But it was a gunner's job to scupper the German artillery, the Porcupine as you aptly describe it, behind the Gheluvelt plateau. Plumer is a gunner. Gough, the Fox, tries to outflank it. His idea was to break through in the centre and outflank the Gheluvelt plateau with its concealing woods and reverse slopes. So there is the tactical dilemma. While trying to outflank, Gough is himself outflanked. The Porcupine shoots its quills into the side of the Fox."

"But didn't Old Man Moonshiner anticipate this?"

"I do not follow you."

"Big Chief Firewater whose genie out of the bottle cures the 'aigue'."

"You horrible punster! Yes, of course the Chief knew it. But the Chief does not interfere with his Army Commanders, once he has given them the job. He can only give a directive. He approved the Fox plan, and so did Plumer, whose Staff knows every puddle in the Salient, which the Fox didn't. And told the Chief so. Gough arrived here only on the tenth of June."

"But couldn't the Fox have carried out Plum's used arrangements, and plans?"

"My dear Phillip, plans are more than printed words. Plans are the spirits of many human beings. And even if transference at all levels was humanly possible, or practicable, it would serve no purpose to ask a Fox staff to deputise for a Plum staff."

"I see." He waited; and said, "I wonder if you would advise me. I forgot to leave my cards when I came to lunch last time. I've got them here. Who shall I give them to? I've written on them. One for the General, the other for the General Staff Officer."

"I'll give them to the mess sergeant. You must be the only officer below the rank of General who carries cards with him in the B.E.F.! 'Mr. P. S. T. Maddison, The Gaultshire Regiment.' Thank God someone thinks it's a gentleman's war! Have you had them with you all the time?"

"I brought them back with me from leave."

"I'll see that they are put on the Green Baize Board. What else have you got in your knapsack, a field-marshal's baton? Now if you're fit, we'll depart to the 'Old House' in the Rue de l'Hôpital. I'd like you to meet a friend of a friend of mine."

Phillip did not ask questions about this mysterious destination. Was it a Staff building? Had Westy a job for him, up his sleeve? A surprise job, perhaps in Intelligence?

They stopped outside a tall grey house, on the door of which was a notice, *All rank abandon ye who enter here*. Inside on the wall was a painted hand pointing to the door, with the words *Pessimists Way Out*. They went up a wooden stairway, and then up another flight, and so along a bare wooden corridor. On the wall was another notice, *If you are in the habit of spitting on the carpet at home, please do so here*.

"Is this Corps Headquarters?" laughed Phillip. He wondered if he had said the wrong thing, for 'Spectre' West looked straight ahead as he climbed up some steep open treads, and so into a large loft with beams and posts holding up the roof.

Phillip saw that it was a chapel. From the king-post was suspended a chandelier with a ring of candles. Beyond, against one wall, was a red altar cloth, with green borders. Another red cloth, with gilt tassels, hung from a beam above the altar. The space before the altar was flanked by two massive candles

on wooden stands. Beside each was a bowl of flowers. A carpet
covered the centre of the floor. There were a few plain wooden
chairs and benches, and two shrines, one on either side of the
altar, below semi-circular windows. There was a lectern painted
white.

'Spectre' West was standing erect. His eye was closed. As
Phillip glanced again he saw tears running down one cheek.

With the air drifting in under the tiles came the distant
rumbling of cannon. 'Spectre' went forward and kneeled
before the altar. He stood still, looking up at the whitewashed
beams and purlins, stained brown where rain had dripped
through the tiles, and at the smooth bare boards showing the
holes gouged by the goat-moth caterpillar in the living trees.
Father had told him about the goat-moth when he was a child,
he remembered, how it fed on willow and poplar. The air
shivered with deeper undertones of heavy howitzers, pounding
away in the Salient. Then the sun came out behind a cloud, for
light shone whiter through the five semi-circular windows. Here
men had clumped up the steep and narrow stairs, borne up by
Hope, seeking solace at the verge of unutterable Darkness. He
thought of Father Aloysius, of Mère Ambroisine at the convent
at Wespaelar, where Mavis had been to school, and Mother
before her, and Mère Ambroisine had stroked his head and said,
He is a good boy, Hetty.

He stood still, unable to pray in words, hearing the sparrows
chirping on the roof, and the incessant rattle of wheels on the
pavé of the road below. He thought of Francis Thompson on the
Embankment, sleeping on the paving stones under Waterloo
Bridge, while his mind was lit by poetry, the spirit of God. He
had read most of the poems so many times that he knew them by
heart.

> *Pierce thy heart to find the key;*
> *With thee take*
> *Only what none else would keep;*
> *Learn to dream when thou dost wake,*
> *Learn to wake when thou dost sleep;*
> *Learn to water joy with tears,*
> *Learn from fears to vanquish fears,*
> *To hope, for thou dar'st not despair,*
> *Exult, for that thou dar'st not grieve;*
> *Plough thou the rock until it bear;*
> *Die, for none other way can'st live.*

Yes, it was true. The old self must die. He had always known it, but had so seldom acted it. He felt strangely glad that he was at the front. It was the only life; the only death.

Afterwards, 'Spectre' West said, "Do you know 'The Mistress of Vision'?"

"Yes, I was recalling part of it while you were in front."

"I wondered if you were when some of the lines came into my mind."

"How strange! And yet——"

"Now you know why I told you that you did not need whiskey."

"I'm sorry to be obdurate, Westy, but we don't get the kind of food we had for lunch today, in the line."

"I know, I know," whispered 'Spectre' West. "You don't have to explain to me. Obdurate means hard of heart; you will never be that. Obstinate, yes indeed! I'm sorry 'Tubby' Clayton is not here, you would like him."

"Who's he?"

"Gilbert Talbot's great friend. Gilbert was a Green Jacket, killed in the flame attack at Hooge. He was a son of the Bishop of Winchester, and a fellow of the quality of Julian Grenfell. The altar over there is his memorial. It's a carpenter's bench. This was a hop loft originally. Take care how you go down the steps. They're built close and steep for better foothold, while carrying up bags of hops. Now I'm going to take you to have a hot bath. Only mind you don't catch cold afterwards."

To O.C. 286 M, Battle H.Q.   14 August   8 p.m.
Sir,
    May I have four drivers from the Coy lent to my section please to replace casualties. I have only 16 drivers for 47 mules. This means that drivers on fatigue all day have to go up with pack-mules all night. The matter is urgent.
    I am informed that Sergeant Rivett is about to return from the Base.

P. S. T. Maddison
lt, 286 M.

In the night of 15/16 August, through a terrain of yellow clay underlying sand and patches of gravel—a hungry soil, its fertility maintained in peacetime by ewe flocks wintering on turnips in the rotation of corn, hay, roots—a terrain now liquefied, without drainage and become morass again, nine British divisions

struggled forward to the tape lines laid from Langemarck in the
north to St. Julien and onwards to Frezenberg, thence across
the Ypres–Roulers railway embankment to Westhoek and the
Nuns' Wood to Stirling Castle south of the Menin road: a
distance, as the tapes were laid, of ten thousand yards.

Before the march-up, there had been protests at Corps level
that the attack would suffer because "the concentration of
German batteries at the back of the Gheluvelt plateau had not
been mastered". Also it had been stated that many of the tracks
and duck-walks, by which alone the infantry dumps were to be
replenished, were destroyed. Moreover, the assault divisions
were far under strength, despite drafts of conscripts and men who
had recovered from wounds. And all the divisions in reserve
to the four attacking corps were now immediately behind the
line, in addition to the last two divisions in Army reserve. The
jar of hundreds and thousands was almost empty.

To the young Fox, with eyes fixed on the distant sky-line,
came three of the best divisions of Old Plum. They were "to
be held back for subsequent developments", which meant the
break-out and pursuit into the Plain of Flanders. The Fox was
still on the Black Line, with the Green Line, otherwise Flandern
I, before him; and beyond Flandern I were Flandern II and
Flandern III.

On the morning of 16 August, after a rainy night to St.
Julien and back, Phillip heard the barrage breaking beyond the
muddy tapes which almost were trodden out of sight by 4.45 a.m.
He had then been back at the picket line about five minutes.
At the end of ten hours with the mule convoy he was almost
beyond speaking power; but compared with the infantry, he
knew, the transport section had a cushy life. He could sleep,
sleep, sleep; and out of the rain.

To O.C. 286 M, Battle H.Q.　16 August　1.30 p.m.
Sir, 21t Bright parading with 16 reserve gunners forthwith.
　　Your G437 of 9.35 a.m. 14 Aug. states ' Rations tonight will be as
last night'. 18 bags of 5 (i.e. 90 rations) went up last night (plus
8 officer rations). Will bring this amount at 6 p.m. tonight unless
I hear by messenger to the contrary. You do not say RUM, I shall
bring it nevertheless. Sergeant Rivett has reported for duty from
the Base.
　　　　　　　　　　　　P. S. T. Maddison
　　　　　　　　　　　　　lt, 286 M.

Behind the Salient many stories began to pass among the soldiers who, after relief, slouched in utter exhaustion through the Grand' Place. Phillip, ever curious to know more of the war, ever a little apart from his fellows, because he was always remote from himself, made many notes of what he heard. How the South Irish division had advanced beside the Ulster division —Shamrock with Bloody Hand—both so thinly shaken out into line as to look like raiding parties. The South Irish, let down by their own artillery, fought until all were killed or over-run by the *Eingreif division* which appeared out of nowhere: for a man was less then two metres high, often no more than a metre indeed, as he went forward upright, striving to carry high above the mud his bayonet and rifle. And how the South Irish had not enough men to act as moppers-up, so that the Spandau machine guns in Potsdam, Vampir, and Borry Farms—almost solidified by concrete—turned round, after waiting to surrender, and shot them in the back, before the sparse survivors, clogged and staggering, returned after almost reaching the Green Line. Others, together with isolated Ulstermen, hung on in shell craters while the main counter-attacks passed beyond them. The British defensive barrage dropped where they lay, so that they had it both ways. And how the 56th Londoners were caught by a curtain of high-explosive shell from behind the Gheluvelt plateau as soon as they advanced among the unburied dead of many similar assaults. They got into the splinter and root heaps of Polygon Wood and Nonne Bosschen, but were surrounded, while the Germans set up machine guns in the northern edge of the Nuns' Wood and enfiladed a brigade of the 8th Division, which was shot to pieces on the very ground on which it had been shot to pieces on July 31, and from the same woods. The Divisional General before the attack had protested that the woods on the south-west of the Gheluvelt plateau must be cleared and held before the second northern assault could advance, but his protest was over-ruled, though endorsed and forwarded by the Corps Commander to Army; and so 8th Division history was repeated in the same place.

A strange remark was made to Phillip about this time. There was a sort of soldier tramp who lived in a cellar under the ruins of the Prison at Ypres. He was a cook, attached to the gunners. He had a grey beard, and wore a Belgian peaked black cap with sabots, ragged khaki tunic and trousers, and a greatcoat lined with sandbags. He muttered to himself and seemed to be mad, and what he said was, "We'll never get back to the bright side of the moon; no, never again, never again." Yes, Phillip thought, we are on the dark side of the moon, our living is utterly unknown to the people at home.

17 *Fri*   Fine weather at last. Drying wind. Pinnegar said attack to be done over again. Rivett took duck-board fatigue.

18 *Sat*   Sunny. New moon rose over Passchendaele like a thin gold spider-leg holding black bag of eggs. Rivett again on fatigue all day; I took pack mules all night.

The news from St. Julien, *via* Teddy Pinnegar, about the attack on 16 August wasn't too bad. The Au Bon Gîte, an estaminet made almost solid with concrete, which had held up the advance on July 31, at last had been captured by a really clever idea. An aeroplane had been sent to fly over it and machine-gun it exactly one minute before zero hour, while two specially trained companies of Green Jackets got close up to it and isolated it with smoke bombs. The garrison of one officer and fifty men surrendered to the next wave, said Pinnegar, without having fired, otherwise not a man jack of them would have got away alive.

"You know, Phil, I never thought much of Guardees"— (what does he know about them, thought Phillip)—"but I must hand it to Cavan, who although he's a lord seems to have some brains. He had the bright idea to establish armourers' shops just behind the tapes, all ready to clean rifles and Lewis guns, and then pass them on to the front lines, in exchange for clogged ones. Have you seen the latest type of prisoner? Most of them are mere kids, it's like robbing an incubator. They either surrender, or clear off as soon as they're fired at."

Orders were given, after the almost total failure of the attack of 16 August (except at Langemarck) for certain positions, at least, to be captured, with a view to a further general advance at the earliest possible moment by the Shamrock and Bloody Hand divisions. The brigadiers protested that their brigades, reduced to hardly more than a battalion in numbers, were exhausted; the Divisional Generals agreed; the Corps General told the Fox that he was unable to carry out the attacks ordered.

19 *Sun*   Passed 7 tanks outside St. Julien, now quarter-mile from German line.

20 *Mon*   Rode into Pop for a bath 10 a.m. and saw Westy, who said that tanks I saw last night had succeeded this morning at first light in capturing 4 pillboxes beside Poelcapelle road. First tanks to do proper job since 31 July. Tactics:—tank approach was hidden by smoke and right under creeping barrage (shrapnel) while heavies fired ahead of them. Gaultshires and others immediately behind captured Hillock Farm, the Cock-croft, Owl's House, and Triangle Farm. Tanks fired 6-lb. shells into letter-box slits in pillboxes, holding up garrisons until infantry went in and killed, or shot them as they ran out. German officer found hanged by his own men in the Cockcroft, before the garrison ran away. 5 out of 7 tanks got back. No prisoners could be taken, as sometimes surrendered Germans resume fight when Eingreif troops arrive. 200 killed from 4 pillboxes. Our losses 1 officer and 2 men killed.

21 *Tue*   Z day tomorrow. Fatigues all day. Drivers were exhausted when we set off again with eleven mule packs. Zero hour 4.45 a.m. Rained. Pinn said attack went well, advance 400 yds on wide front. We are now within 200 yds of Langemarck–Zonnebeke road, but not yet up to Green line. P. said D. had been up only once to visit sections in line since 31 J. Also Alleyman covers pillboxes with fresh mud every night.

23 *Thu*   Went up line in morning by myself. Saw many tram-lines and all sorts of tracks and wooden walks. Dreary desolation everywhere. A great dump of steel rails, gravel, and sand lies near remains of Langemarck station. Visited the sections with Pinnegar. Got back at 5 p.m. Slept 2 hours, went up again.

These brief entries gave hardly more than a hint of the nightly transport hell, in rain and mud, mules scrambling for duck-walks, breaking the wooden treads, kicking and floundering amidst uptilted sections, cursed and screamed at by the infantry, whose walks they were. The teak and beech-wood roads were afloat in some places, crashed by shells in others, while cries of wounded in the liquid morass under the Brock's Benefit (as it was called ironically) of SOS coloured rockets came with whimpering shell fragments. In his diary were no references to the wincing, sweating pulses of fear, the electric adder running down the side of his head, to the bottle of whiskey by day, the

rum shared with the muleteers at night, the pictures in the brain
of himself regrowing the woods, of levelling the banks of the
brooks and in clear water seeing roach moving in droves over
waving water-weeds, white flowers of crow's-foot on long bines,
the green tresses of Sabrina fair: the black rotting pictures of
himself fitting arms and legs to dismembered trunks, broken-
pink-vested: or raising the dead among the larks and the peewits,
or to the fancy that the ghost of Cranmer was helping him, of
Percy Pickering and Peter and Nimmo and David Wallace, all
differences forgotten, come together again; of Albert Hawkins
in new butterfly tie smiling at him behind the garden fence, all
the misunderstanding of blood and weeping resolved in sunshine
. . . black sunshine, rotting away the world.

24 *Sat*   Renewed attack for today cancelled. Rode into Pop at
11 a.m. and got new trench coat from Dados, old one
was left in shell-hole I fell into on 23. Saw Westy. He
has been up the line every day, for special reports to
G.H.Q. He said attack against Inverness Copse, below
Gheluvelt plateau, on 22nd went forward until met by
Eingreif counter-attacks. We held bits of it at first,
but not enough infantry to press home.

Alleyman attacked Inverness Copse again yesterday
with flame throwers and drove us back, we counter-
attacked, drove them back, then our artillery shelled
our infantry there all the morning. So they withdrew.
Alleyman holds wood again. Said Moonshiner went to
Plum at Cassel yesterday afternoon. Draw own conclusions, he said.

26 *Sun*   Rained hard at night. Limbers, horses, and mules
bestrew the verges of board road to St. Julien. Took
up, for 1 and 2 sections, small elephant iron shelters.
Another attack tomorrow down south (? Inverness
Copse and Glencorse Wood again).

About 2 a.m. on way home, passed many troops on
duck-walks going in. If they got to tapes at, say, 4 a.m.
they wd have either to stand in 2 ft. of mud for 10 hours
or lie down in it, zero being 1.55 p.m.

Mine is really a cushy life. I am warm while walking
(sometimes boiling hot) and warmth is life; and I can
sleep when I get back.

27 *Mon*   Rained 1.30 p.m., wind driving & very cold. At night
heard that infantry were unable to light smoke candles
(each had 3) for self-protection à la tanks on Poelcapelle

Road a week ago. Lost barrage and remained stuck in mud. Alleyman, waiting to surrender, took pot shots at them.

28 *Tue*   Gale blowing heavy rains across Salient. Clouds dragging. Coy relieved at 11 p.m. Arrived Proven 9 p.m. completely done in.

29 *Wed*   Broncho Bill reported arrested, & taken down to Base for court-martial.

PROVEN
30 August

Confidential

FROM Lt. P. S. T. Maddison
TO O.C. 286 M
Sir

I have to report that this morning L/Cpl (unpaid) S. Nolan came to me requesting that he might see the O.C. Coy. Reason he gave was desire to revert to rank of driver. I asked why.

He replied that Sgt Rivett appeared very dissatisfied with his work, and that as he (Nolan) was of junior rank he could not reply. L/Cpl (unpaid) Nolan said that Sgt Rivett "made the remark to him that things had been a complete box-up during his (Sgt Rivett's) absence at the Base".

I spoke to Sgt Rivett, who said that "from what (he) could see, things had been going from bad to worse during (his) absence". I reminded him that he was not in command of the Section, and that his allegation reflected directly on me.

I then called L/Cpl (unpaid) Nolan and he too appeared very dissatisfied, and still wished to revert.

I thereupon told both N.C.O.s that I would have to refer the matter to the C.O.

During the absence of Sgt Rivett (sick) L/Cpl (unpaid) Nolan has been of the greatest assistance to me. I gave him a programme of work, which was carried out in all details. He has splendid control over the drivers, and I believe they obey his orders with the greatest willingness.

If, through this trifling matter, L/Cpl (unpaid) Nolan is allowed to revert, the Section will suffer, as the men will know the reason, and it will not help the spirit of camaraderie which is essential in the difficult and wasting circumstances we have gone through recently, and presumably will go through again in the near future. I should, as a personal matter, be extremely sorry to lose L/Cpl (unpaid) Nolan. He is an old Regular Soldier of the 2nd Gaultshires, and was out with the Seventh Division in 1914. He has three good conduct stripes, and a Marksman's Certificate.

With all due respect, Sir, I ask that his acting rank be confirmed to full Corporal (paid) so that he can in future have the just reward

for his work, which will be mainly up the line. He will be indispens-
able if I become a casualty. I must add that Sgt Rivett is also good
in his sphere, which is that of senior N.C.O. in charge of the Transport personnel and equipment generally.

I have the honour to be,
Sir,
Your most obedient Servant
P. S. T. Maddison
lt, Gaultshire Regt attd. M.G.C.

When after a day this letter was apparently ignored Phillip
went to see Major Downham.

While he stood to attention, his C.O. said, "Sergeant Rivett
has asked to be allowed to hand in his stripes. I have refused to
consider it. I note that you sign yourself as belonging to the
Gaultshire Regiment, while in fact you have already been transferred to the Machine Gun Corps. Far be it from me to do anything to stand in your way, if you prefer the infantry, as apparently
you do. Now will you hand over your Section to Mr. Pinnegar,
and the Orderly Room sergeant will give you your warrant
to proceed to the course you've already been warned for, at
No. 3 Infantry Base Depot, Etaples, tomorrow morning."

"I'll leave my gramophone here, I think. If I don't come back,
would you like to keep it, and the case of records, Teddy?"
"Of course you'll come back, old man!"

"Thank God I've seen the last of that horrible little one-eyed
dorp!" exclaimed a captain opposite Phillip, as the train clanked
and jerked out of Poperinghe station. Looking across, he said,
"Don't I know your face? Weren't you with the London
Highlanders in September '14? I thought so! I'm on my way
to Blighty. With any luck I'll have a job in England for the
duration. Ministry of Information, Whitehall. Extra pay and
allowances and green tabs! Where are you going? Etaples? My
God, I don't envy you! I'd rather be in the line than instructing
at an I.B.D., any old day!"

At Hazebrouck the train stopped long enough for them to
share a bottle of champagne at the E.F.C. Phillip felt better.
He began to enjoy a copy of The B.E.F. Times, a local rag
produced up the line, said his new acquaintance. Some blokes
had scrounged type and a printing press from a shelled house
in Ypres, way back in '15, and had started The Wipers Times,

which became *The New Church Times* when they moved to
Neuve Eglise, then *The Kemmel Times*, then *The Somme Times*,
and now *The B.E.F. Times*.

Phillip said it was jolly good, and why hadn't he seen it before;
to be told that it was a Divisional paper only.

"Why doesn't someone at G.H.Q. get it printed and distributed all over the B.E.F.? I am sure it would go like hot
cakes!"

The B.E.F. Times had all sorts of queer bits of decorative
printing on its pages, long curling thistle leaves, and other
wigglywoggly bits. It was very funny reading too.

CLOTH HALL, WIPERS

Under Entirely New Management

The ventilation of this Theatre has been entirely overhauled during
the summer months.

SPECIAL ATTRACTIONS

Haig's Company in a Stirring Drama, Entitled:

PILCKEM'S PROGRESS.
William's TROUPE :—
"THE COCKCHAFERS"

in a humorous knockabout Scene.

Book Early.   Prices as Usual.

EDITORIAL. We must apologise to all our subscribers for the delay
since our last issue. What a lot has happened in the interim! Much
to rejoice and *plume* ourselves about, but also many old chums to regret
the loss of. That unfortunately must always be the way, but this
time there seems to be more than a fair proportion of the old brigade.
Much as we regret the loss of our old G.O.C. we cannot begrudge
his departure and well-merited honours. Also the loss is tempered
by the arrival, in his successor, of one of the ' Cognoscenti '.

H'm, thought Phillip. That must be Plumer. He was *cognisant*
of the Salient, as Gough wasn't.

There has been so much to write about since our last issue that one
is rather at a loss where to begin. Hindenburg has won a long series
of victories (vide Official German news), and we have met with many

repulses (vide occupants of many well-aired and commodious cages
in the neighbourhood of Vimy, Messines, and Vlamertinghe). However the war goes on, and we are putting our faith on the journey of
Ramsay Macdonald to Stockholm!!!

The Editor has just returned from thirty days of the best and
brightest. A lot of time he spent in London with the wind well up and
a crick in the neck, but otherwise only filled with wonder at the bare-
faced robbery which is rife. We should imagine that there are
many people who will be sorry when the war is over and they don't
all keep restaurants!

He wondered how Eugene was getting on, and if he had hit it
off with Mavis. Gene had not written since his return, although
he had written twice to Gene. Perhaps he and Mavis—but it was
unthinkable.

GREAT LABOUR MEETING AT DICKEBUSH

Flamsey MacBonald in the
Chair

Last night Flamsey MacBonald addressed a large and sympathetic
audience at the Town Hall, Dickebush. Powerful support was
given by Messrs. Grictor Vayson, Arthur Tenderson and a host of
other hard (working) labourites. Mr. MacBonald commenced by
saying that the war should be stopped (loud and unanimous cheering),
and said that if only they would send him to Christiania he would
see to it. (A heckler here suggested that sending him to hell might
help matters.) He said that he had the interests of the working man
at heart. (Loud and unanimous cheers from Grictor Vayson.) When
asked, " Who the devil asked you to look after the working man, why
not get on with the job yourself", Mr. Flamsey only looked pained
and surprised at the ingratitude of the working man who grudged
him his self-appointed task of doing nothing in the House of Commons
at four hundred a year . . . a whizz bang then fell within a couple
of miles. As all present had every desire to avoid any harm happening
to these modest delegates, a rush was made to the platform to safe-
guard them from danger. They, however, had already left, so that
the citizens of Dickebush were prevented from wishing them God-
speed.

He put down the paper. Father had got angry like that with
Aunt Theodora, who had wanted the war to stop two years ago,
and had been boo'd with others when she tried to make a speech
from the plinth of Nelson's Column in Trafalgar Square. He

must write to her, and ask how she was getting on with the *crèche* for babies in the East End, organised by Sylvia Pankhurst.

ARMY TERMS AND THEIR DERIVATION

G.O.C.—Gold or carrots. Owes its origin to the gaudy colours affected.

A.P.M.—Awfully polite men. Originated in the politeness with which these people bandy airy persiflage with Transport Officers.

Like Mr. Bloody Brendon, probably still having a bon time in his big dug-out at Neuve Eglise.

T.O.—Ticked off (See A.P.M.)

M.L.O.—Medals and leave often. Reason obscure.

Trench—So called from the trenchant remarks from those inhabiting them.

Oh, feeble, feeble!

Area Commandant—See dug-out.

Dug-out.—Of two kinds. The name originates in a habit of the early natives who excavated holes for themselves to avoid the slings and arrows of the enemy. Another kind is the erection in which Area Commandants dwell.

OUR SHORT STORY

There once was a teetotal Quartermaster.
(The End)

ADVERTISEMENT

THE WESTERN ADVANCE CO., HOOGE
(D. Haig, General Manager)

Makes ADVANCES AT SHORT NOTICE
Under Private Arrangement.
No Security.
Secrecy Guaranteed.
Principal Remaining till end of War
Agents in all civilised Countries

Wires—CUT.   Phone—1917.
Code—Bab.

SOMEWHERE IN—WIPERS

by

Cockles Tumley

(in his inimitable manner)

You can't imagine what I've seen. Neither can I! Stay, I will tell you. I've worn a tin-hat! I've eaten a tin of bully beef! I've talked to a general! I won't tell you what he said, but you can take it from me THE WAR IS OVER. I've been in the support line, which is much more dangerous than the first. I've been in the reserve line, which is much more dangerous than the support. I have been in Div. H.Q. which is more dangerous still.

And I have even been back to G.H.Q. I have discussed the situation with the soldiers themselves, I can't tell you what they thought of it. AND NOW FOR WHAT I HAVE LEARNT. I have learnt that there's a lot of meat in a tin of bully. I have learnt that an army biscuit is a hard nut to crack. I have learnt that a tipping duck-board needs no push. I have learnt that Belgian beer needs a good deal of bush.

Every German prisoner I spoke to said the same thing. I can't tell you what it is, BUT THE WAR IS WON. To use one of our familiar slogans I say, "Watch the Q.M.". I was having a talk with one of the Tommies who had answered the call of King and Country, and I asked him what he thought of it all. I can't tell you his answer, but it impressed me wonderfully. Well, I will write more next week when my head is clearer. I must go now and have my photo taken in a gas-bag and tin hat.

COCKLES TUMLEY

(Another trenchant article next week).

He had caught a glimpse of Horatio Bottomley in early July, at Poperinghe, a ridiculous over-fed figure in a frock coat and tin-hat, his pasty face large, flabby and level with the shoulders of the lesser Staff officers surrounding him.

LITTLE WILLIE.—"When will our heaven-protected troops thrust back the hordes that seek to enter our sacred Vaterland, Papa?"
BIG WILLIE.—"When their Rawlies cease from Goughing, and their Plumers Byng no more."

ARE YOU SHORT?

Or do you wish to

ENLARGE YOUR BUST?

As long as you are not too short to send us a five-franc note—we can add a cubit to your stature or to your chest measurement.

JUST WRITE AND TELL US WHAT YOU WANT AND WE CAN DO YOU!

Lord B—— says, "Six months ago I was rejected from the Boy Scouts owing to my poor physique—now I am commanding a battalion of the Guards."

> " If you want to fill your bust,
>   Buy our stuff you simply must.
>   If you're troubled with your height,
>   Take our dope—you'll be all right."

Write to:—
WINDUP & CO., WIPERS.

Chapter 15

MUTINY

There was a feeling of desolation in the Infantry Base Depots on both sides of the railway at Etaples. He sensed it at once. The men might have been prisoners of war, without the freedom, such as it was, of a P.O.W. camp. At least the German prisoners of war knew where they were. The fact that they were in a hostile country gave them some sort of resistance, if not resilience. But here in an I.B.D. the men did not know where they were. They had lost the only thing that held them together: the spirit of being "all in it together"; they lacked the friendly encouragement of their own junior officers, a spirit which was to be found only in a regiment.

The camps were surrounded by barbed-wire fences. Military police carried loaded revolvers. Sentries with fixed bayonets guarded the gates. Only 10% of each Depot was allowed out on pass at any one time. If you had been warned for reinforcement, the time allowed you, whether officer or man, was only between 2 p.m. and 5 p.m. of any one day. It was not damned well good enough! No wonder the poor devils had a pathetic faith in Horatio Bottomley—at whom *The B.E.F. Times*, written comfortably in the rear, had jeered! So had he himself, Phillip reflected. One lived and learned.

Near the Depot camps, occupying hundreds of acres of sandy soil, was the Bull Ring.

Here thousands of men daily received intensive training with bombs, rifle-grenades, Lewis gun and rifle fire, and bayonet practice. They passed finally through a series of assault courses, in and over trenches, past exploding shells (gun-cotton slabs detonated beside small tins of petrol), through water plashes and barbed wire. Urged on by instructor-voices screaming almost hysterically to simulate sufficient patriotic pretence (Phillip thought) in order to keep their safe jobs, the effect of these ex-boxers, ex-wrestlers, and cheap-jacks was more horrible than being in the line; for at least that was real. There was something damnable about a Base system which treated old soldiers, some with two and three wound stripes, as though they were rookies, expecting them at bayonet practice on the usual straw-filled dummies to show frenzy for blood—Gar'n, smash th' bastard! Gar'n, three inches in the throat!—right nipple—left nipple—groin—then the butt of the rifle crashed into—(voice dropping to a sneer)—"the right place to stop him having any more little Huns".

The brass-braided wound-stripers, half dead inside their heads, three-quarters of their courage expended with the deaths of old comrades, muttered quietly to themselves. Loos—Somme—Langemarck—they'd had enough. Keep the bullshit for the rookies, who do they think we are?

In one of the camps, passed four times daily, to and from the great arena of the sandhills, was the Punishment Compound, in full view of the marching columns which were called to attention as the leading platoons drew level with the gates and sentry boxes. Here Field Punishment No 1 was on display: men tied back to back along a taut picket line, their arms stretched to the limit. Those who sagged during the time in which they were spread-eagled—one hour in the morning, another in the afternoon—were checked by red-capped military police. The effect on the beholders was degrading. Phillip heard men muttering. There were stories of legs and arms being twisted, of screams from the cells at night, and punishment by open-handed blows of boxing gloves. The cells were dark, with tiny ventilation holes at the top, each little more than the size of a sentry box, so that a man could not lie down in his solitary confinement. The whole place was rancid with subdued anger, with an under-current of bitterness and despair making for sullenness: the idea, it was said,

was to make life there so bad that up the line would be cushy
by comparison.

The second-in-command of Phillip's depot was a very young
major called Traill. He had three wound stripes and a Military
Cross. The pale delicacy of his face was emphasised by dark wavy
hair. Clean shaven, gentle-voiced, Traill looked to be about
twenty years old. Seeing Phillip reading *The Oxford Book of
English Verse* one evening, he came and asked rather diffidently if
he might sit beside him. They talked. Phillip was delighted to
find a kindred soul; and his depression, which had persisted ever
since leaving the company, began to lift. Soon they were talking
frankly.

"Why do they let the men marching to the Bull Ring see the
Jankers Compound, and those poor devils doing F.P. No 1,
Major?"

"The G.O.C. is an old-fashioned type of martinet, and I
suppose feels it's a case of 'pour encourager les autres'. Anyway,
the A.P.M. is a bit of a sadist, otherwise a coward, and likes to
throw his weight about."

"What's a sadist?"

"Some people feel better, temporarily at least, by hurting
others. It excuses a deficiency in themselves, I suppose."

"I think I know what you mean. A bully."

"Exactly. Moreover, the men all know he has never been near
the front, and it doesn't help him to know that the men know it.
And because of his feeling of not being good enough, he is the
more determined to carry out, to the letter, the orders of his
martinet master. You may think this a bit fanciful, but that's
how it seems to me."

"No, I don't think it fanciful! I know someone else like that.
Two people, in fact. No, three!" as he added the image of his
father to those of Downham and Brendon. "No—four," as he
added himself to the other three.

"I know," said Traill, sympathetically, thinking that the sigh
was for the thought of men tied up on the picket line. "My dear
Maddison, I've spoken about it to the Colonel, and so has the
Padre. The answer was, 'Oh, one mustn't interfere in the Provost
Marshal's sphere,' and that's followed by, 'When you've
served as long as I have, my boy, you'll see the wood and not
just single trees. Force must be used with discretion against the
incalcitrant.' By the way, I suppose you know they've got
Broncho Bill?"

"So that's where they sent him!"

"Yes. He's waiting to be sent up the line, to be shot."

"You said just now, 'force with discretion', Major. Surely the point is that it is used with no discretion, if those undergoing F.P. No 1 are visible? It does no good. In fact, the reverse. And another bad thing is the way men are drafted to go up the line, regiments mixed up indiscriminately! Don't these dug-in base-wallahs *know* that it destroys morale? What is morale but the feeling to stick to your pals, otherwise pride in your own crowd? They don't do it with the Guards; if they did, the Guards would cease to be what they are, the élite. They *are* the élite, because they feel it, and so act it out!"

"I do so agree. By the way, how comes it that you're at an I.B.D., when you're M.G.C.?"

"I was told that it was a sort of liaison course. Though how a transport officer——" He stopped. "At least, that's what I was given to understand."

"Well—— Of course, I can't really say——"

Phillip knew then that Downham had got rid of him. He was for it again, with the infantry. Any old lot, O God.

It was a fine dry September, sunny and calm. One morning the columns from the depots arrived at the Bull Ring drill ground, and, as usual, after the officers had fallen out behind Major Traill, the parade was handed over to the R.S.M. That red-faced giant of a man gave the order, in his stentorian voice, "Take off your packs and fall in on your markers!"; but not a man among the two thousand odd left his position. Instead, individuals began to light cigarettes; some sat down; others started to whistle. Then to sing. Phillip had not heard the song since early 1915, and hearing it now was a surprise. It belonged to the Bairnsfather grim-humour period, now almost old-fashioned.

I want to go 'ome
I want to go 'ome,
I don't want to go in the trenches no more,
Where whizz-bangs and Johnsons they whistle and roar.

Take me back over the sea,
Where the Alleyman can't get at me.
Oh my, I don't want to die,
I want to go 'ome!

The regimental-sergeant-major roared out, "Fall in on your markers!" Ironical cheers came from the lines of sitting men. The R.S.M. came over to Major Traill. Meanwhile another song was being sung, or rather shouted, as it passed down the lines of idle men.

> We are the boys who fear no noise
> When the thundering cannons roar;
> We are the heroes of the night
> And we'd sooner —— than fight,
> Our girls against the wall!

Cheers came across the packed gravel of the sandy parade ground.

> When this bloody war is over,
> No more soldiering for me.
> When I get my civvy suit on
> Oh how happy I shall be!
> No more church parades on Sunday,
> No more asking for a pass,
> I shall tell the sergeant-major,
> To stick his passes up his ——.
>
> N.C.O.'s will all be navvies,
> Privates ride in motorcars,
> N.C.O.'s will smoke their Woodbines,
> Privates puff their big cigars.
> No more standing-to in trenches,
> No more plum-and-apple jam,
> No more shivering in the shell-'ole
> While the sergeant pinches rum!

"I'd like to have a word with my platoon, if I may, sir," said Phillip.

"I don't see why not."

From afar came a chant, swelling to a roar,

> We want Broncho Bill!
> We want Broncho Bill!!
> WE WANT BRONCHO BILL!!!

Phillip found his platoon friendly.

"That's quite all right, sir! Nothing to do with you, sir! The boys are fed-up, sir!"

"Well, I've just come down from Wipers, I know all about it."

"That's right, sir! Nothing personal, sir."

As he walked back, a motorcar with a brass hat drove up. It was the Commandant of the Etaples Administrative Department. After talking with Major Traill, he said, "The parade is cancelled. March back to your Base Depots in companies under their officers!"

He drove away. Major Traill passed on the order to the R.S.M., who told the sergeants.

"Parade is cancelled! Fall in your men on company markers!"

They marched back to the camp. There the men flung off their equipment, and began to move in mass to the gates. They passed the sentries and swarmed down, in good humour and some excitement, to the bridge over the railway. Phillip heard afterwards what happened there. Three military policemen were standing outside the white-washed hut which was the M.P. post. One was the sergeant. He had been a heavyweight boxer. The leading men stopped short of the bridge, which was small and narrow. The sergeant drew his revolver. "I shoot the first man who tries to cross!" Jeers and boos greeted him. A sergeant of the Gordon Highlanders shouted, "Why aren't you at the front?" and walked forward. The boxer fired once into the air. "Go back, or I'll let you have it next time!" he said. When the Gordon Highlander went on, the Red-cap fired at the ground. The bullet ricocheted and hit the Gordon Highlander, who dropped. Immediately the men rushed the bridge and the policemen fled, throwing away the red covers of service caps, their white lanyards, revolvers, and holsters into the railway cutting. One took refuge in the R.T.O.'s office outside the railway station. The R.T.O. was a captain with white hair and moustaches, a decrepit old man. He stood outside the door and said quietly, "Go away from here. Leave this man alone. I have put him under arrest; now go away, I have work to do." They respected the old cock's guts, and went on to the town, several thousand altogether. The officers were confined to camp in the Base Depots. Military pickets were formed, but held back from the streets. Phillip wrote notes in his *Army Correspondence Book 152* then played bridge. All kinds of rumours arrived. The estaminets were drunk dry. Some huts had been set on fire. A thousand bottles of whiskey had been taken from the E.F.

canteens, with wine and other bottles. Rumours grew wilder.
Broncho Bill had escaped. He had had a gun-battle with the
Australian officers who had gone among the mutineers to shoot
the ringleaders. They themselves had been shot dead. The woods
around the town were held by Broncho Bill's men. Motor barges
coming up the Canche estuary from Folkestone, with rum and
whiskey, had been looted. The civilian crews had been flung in
the mud. One had been found, head almost severed. Broncho's
Bill's jack-knife had been found beside the corpse.

In the afternoon volunteers among the junior officers were
called for to go down into the town, dressed in private's uniforms,
with tin-hats, to mix with the crowd, and try and spot the ring-
leaders: for it was evident, said the Colonel, who had been speaking to the General on the telephone, that the mutiny had been
organised, because the same procedure had been followed on all
the various training grounds.

Phillip volunteer'd. At the Q.M. Stores he insisted on an old
tunic, puttees, trousers, and boots. No new creased issue stuff.
He was not keen, he told himself, to bring any ring-leaders to
book; but only to see the sights.

He had been lounging about in the Place for half an hour or
so, when a motor car drove up slowly. In it was a Brigadier-
General. The A.P.M. was beside him in the back, and an armed
M.P. in front beside the driver. Both were without arm-bands
and red cap covers. The General got out of the car, and began to
address the crowd pressing in to hear what he had to say.

"Are you British soldiers, or are you——" he got so far as
saying when a corporal of the Northumberland Fusiliers pushed
forward and said, "It's no use your talking now, General. You've
done all the talking in the past."

"How dare you talk to me like that?"

"Now now! Take it easy, sir!" When the General seemed to
be getting angry, two men held an arm each. Phillip pushed
forward. He felt quivery, but also determined to step in if they
started to hurt the General.

"Are you British soldiers, or are you——" the General
repeated, when the corporal held up a finger, and said, "Put a
sock in it, General! I've warned you! The boys are angry, and
I'd be sorry to see you hurt, General! We don't intend to fight
any more. Get that straight! The sooner you sign the movement
orders, the sooner we'll all be back in Blighty. The war's over!"

"Are you British soldiers, or are you hooligans?"

"Now, General, we have nothing against you personally. We've been doing the fighting so far, and now it's over. We can all go home, if you sign the orders. I've told you—the war's over!"

More men were now pressing around the car. The two M.P.'s in front sat still. The look on their faces, Phillip thought, was put on to give the impression that they were with the mob. The A.P.M. sat as though indifferently in the back. A man said, "How'd you like a stretch, copper? We know all about you. Why don't you go 'ome and do some more scalpin' among the Red Indians? G'rrt, you bleedin' bully, you!"

The Assistant Provost Marshal was said to have served before the war in the North West Canadian Mounted Police. With his horn-rimmed spectacles he was hauled out of the motorcar and rolled in the dirt of the road. Meantime the driver and his mate looked straight to their front.

When Phillip got back to camp the order had come that all ammunition was to be collected and returned to the Ordnance Depot. He was in charge of No 3 Company and, changing his tunic, went at once to see his second-in-command, whom he heard, as he entered the door of a hut, saying, "My orders are that any man objecting is to be made a prisoner."

"Suits us, sir," replied an old soldier. The second-in-command, a new officer, was about to reply sharply when Phillip said, "Less to carry on a route march!"

"Yes, sir."

Cartridge clips were collected in mess tins. When this was done, the old soldier remarked to Phillip, "I never in my born days bin so insulted, sir, not to be trusted wiv me rounds! Why, sir, I got 'em off twenty to a minute wi' me rig'm'nt las' day October fourteen, no one didn't need to take'm off'v me ven!"

"Who were you with?"

"Worcesters, sir!"

"Then you helped to save Ypres! Good for you."

Traill said that the G.O.C. had telephoned to Montreuil to report that he was unable to depend on any unit for fire orders. There was a pause, then the padre said, "To be fair to our boys, Major, I think we ought not to rule out that there are Bolshevist agitators among the men, trying to stir up trouble."

"What, Russians in France, padre?"

"Oh yes. I was down on the Aisne front last April, visiting

some friends, and three Russian brigades were there. One was a Kerensky brigade, and the other two real Bolshies. All three were in Nivelle's disastrous offensive, and were the first to start trouble immediately afterwards. They refused to go into the trenches, and in fact did as they pleased; for there were no reliable French troops to quell them. In fact, it was said at the time that fifty French divisions were affected, or should I say, infected."

"We heard in May, I was down south then, in front of the Hindenburg Line, padre, that two army corps set out to march upon Paris."

"Oh yes, they did. It was common knowledge. The whole countryside was filled with roaming soldiers. Even German prisoners who had escaped were not apprehended. In fact, some got back to the German lines. Why the Germans didn't advance, I can't imagine. They would have got to Paris, with nothing to stop them."

"Exactly! That's why the attacks in the Salient never let-up, to draw the German reserves!" exclaimed Phillip. "Why didn't they let our fellows know? It would have made all the difference. I was in First Ypres, and we all knew the risks, and that's what held the old army together. Officers and men had a wonderful friendship, no saluting, no shaving, General Sir John French, as he was then, right up the Menin road, walking on foot, passing howitzers coming down, Haig right up there, too, I saw him myself! Lord Roberts died of pneumonia at the end of the battle and I know for a fact that many of the old sweats were very sad about it. 'Bobs', they called him, 'little ole Bobs'."

"It's a different army now," said Traill. "Some of the men here are new out from home, combed-out conscripts who have been in munitions since the beginning of the war, getting high wages. Now they don't like the idea of a bob a day."

"But do you really think this show here is organised, Major?"

"I only know that similar uprisings have been reported from Calais, Havre, Rouen, and Dunkerque."

"Yes, it does look as though there's some sort of organisation behind it, as the padre said. At the same time, the men, all mixed up like this, have been virtually prisoners, lacking all *esprit de corps*. They have been treated as cattle by bad drovers who are afraid of them. The General said this morning to a crowd in the Place, 'Are you British soldiers, or are you hooligans?' The answer is that they are not British soldiers. They are hooligans, because they have not been properly led. Why, what little hope or pride they may have had, has been destroyed by being mixed up, and then sent off to any regiment, any strange crowd! I don't blame the men, I blame the system!"

"I agree," said Traill. "In fact, I find it hard to have any enthusiasm for my job here. I've asked several times to be allowed to go back to my regiment, but unfortunately the medical board won't raise my category above B2. So I'm stuck. I was hit at the Butte de Warlincourt," he went on. "It was pretty grim there, but from all I hear it's worse in the Salient. Many of the chaps we've got coming in now were only slightly wounded on July the thirty-first, but they aren't like the wounded coming back from the Somme."

"Yes, there's been a change since the Somme," said the padre. "A very noticeable change, I should say. You spoke just now about cattle being driven, Maddison. Oddly enough, when I see the trains coming in, it recalls to me the sight of Irish cattle boats docking at Liverpool before the war, what with the mud, and other things. The night bombing hasn't improved matters, either. Why the authorities put the hospitals alongside the railway, I cannot imagine."

Late at night a detachment of troops arrived from G.H.Q. Montreuil. They were said to be guardsmen, but turned out to be London territorials. They bivouac'd beside the river, having first set up Lewis guns pointing up the rue du Pont.

"Wrong place, mate! Try up the Menin road! Jerry's waiting, don't disappoint 'im!" These and other good-natured taunts were shouted.

Later, other detachments of the Manchesters and Royal Welch Fusiliers arrived by train, some with white mud on them, as though they had come from the Arras front. Pickets were marched through the streets of the town. The H.A.C., having removed their greatcoats, began to wield picks, with which they prised up cobble-stones, and the packed earth underneath, for trenches. Hundreds of idlers watched, and shouted witticisms.

"Wrong army, aren't you, mates, in them Jerry coats?"
"Saturday afternoon soldiers!"
"Cor, what a bleedin' waste o' man power!"
"Write to *John Bull* about it!"
"Brought yer boats, and little old bucket and spade, dears?"
The idea was soon seen: they were entrenching to form a

bridge-head. Rumour said that their commander had an order
written by Haig himself, to open fire if necessary.

At an estaminet in the Boulevard Billiet on the river-front,
while Phillip was listening to the talk, most of it shouted, he
recognised across the room the face of Tom Ching and at once
felt alarm. He got back behind others. Ching's face was redder
than he had ever seen it, but the thick lips, outstanding ears and
rounded forehead were unmistakable. Yes, the brass shoulder
numerals read *Artists Rifles*. If Ching spotted him, it might be
awkward, so he got up to go out. At the same moment Ching saw
him and his mouth opened, then he cried out, "Hullo, Phillip!
It's me, Ching!" Phillip at once turned to get away. While he
was crossing the room Ching called out, "Hi, Phillip! Wait for
me! What's the matter? I've got something to tell you! Hi,
Phillip!" Inwardly cursing the persistent Ching, who never had
known when he wasn't wanted, Phillip was stopped by a wedge of
soldiers coming in the door. Ching writhed his way forward.
"You are Phillip Maddison, aren't you?"

"Go away!"

"But what's happened? Have you lost your commission?"

"Oh, do be quiet!"

"But, Phillip, I'm your pal——"

"Go to hell!"

Several looks were coming his way. He got to the door,
pushed his way through, and ran down beside the river, then up
another street. If he were caught, they'd throw him in the water
and let him drown. Curse Ching, why the hell was he always so
awkward and everlastingly saying and doing the wrong thing?
Thank God he had got away in time.

What could he report? He could only say that from what he
had heard it did not appear to have been a planned uprising,
but a spontaneous break-down among the men recovered from
wounds, and due to go back up the line without leave; in some
cases, after fourteen months' continuous fighting since the Somme.
What was the Staff about not to *know* this? What had anyone
below the rank of captain in the infantry to live for, if there was
no leave? Had the Adjutant General's staff at G.H.Q. absolutely
no idea of how the men *really* felt? Did they think they thought as
they themselves thought? The ruling classes had ruling ideas,
because they were on top and had a secure way of living, based
on money. What could the high-ups know of the deep, almost
hopeless suffering from winter weather and poor food? As young

officers they had been in little *fracas* like the North-West Frontier, Egypt, Sudan, and the Boer War. They were, literally, picnics, especially for the cavalry. Joy of battle taking them by the throat and making them blind, yes, that had been the feeling, from unbroken reserves of *élan vital* and *joie de vivre*, before the look in the eyes became remote, before the legs dragged mile upon mile to nowhere through the watery crater-zones. Had *nobody* told Haig? Was his world, the world of the great and rich, so utterly removed from the lives of the poor?

He felt deathly pale. There was no harm in all these poor devils mooching about. They thought they were sticking by their pals. Would it happen with them, as in the French regiments which had mutinied? One man in every ten selected at random, to be marched away and shelled in a cordon'd-off area, *pour encourager les autres. Encouragement*—a bitter, bitter jest! If only 'Spectre' West could speak to Haig. Haig would listen to him. But would he? Rawlinson, the Boar's Head, wouldn't listen before July the First. No, the best thing was to be killed, and the sooner the better.

He could not sleep, and saw the dawn without hope through the open flap of his tent.

After an early breakfast he was down again to the river-side, hoping to God that he wouldn't run across Ching again. How had the men fed themselves? He asked one man. He hadn't. So they'd be starved into submission! He felt a little sad about it; but put aside the thought as he followed the crowd of whistling, singing men from the Place down the rue du Pont to the bridge-head. There stood a tin-hatted subaltern, holster flap open. He had a clean-shaven rather full face, and looked around with almost theatrical unconcern.

"Where's yer moustache, Harry Tate?" cried a voice. "'Why won't the car go, Papa?'"

The crowd laughed.

"Come on, David Devant! Show us yer first trick! Where's old Chung Ling Soo?"

More laughter at the mention of well-known music-hall stars.

The subaltern drew his revolver, on a blanco'd lanyard, from the holster. Ironical cheers arose.

"Oo'd'jer think you are, Percy? Broncho Bill?"

"You wait till Broncho Bill sees yer! 'E'll give you pistol, you naughty boy!"

"Mind it don't go off, Percy! It might break yer wrist!"

"I'll shoot the first man dead who advances! And my Lewis guns will open fire at the sound of the shot."

He raised his hand. Helmet'd heads popped up out of holes in the *pavé*, waterproof capes were whisked off Lewis guns. The sight of the black tubular bodies was ugly and cruel. Cries of anger and disgust arose. A shrill voice from the rear shouted, "Chuck 'im in the river!" To which a deeper voice from a lance-corporal in front replied, as he turned away, "No! They ain't worth it!" The crowd thinned as little groups of men wandered off.

Pickets, armed with entrenching tool handles and tin hats, searched the estaminets. Drunks were arrested. A few were rescued but the anger had gone out of the protest, for that was all it was, Phillip told Traill.

"You know, Major, in spite of what the Padre said last night, I can't see that this is a planned job. There's no real organisation behind it. Surely, if there had been, the ring-leaders would have known enough to arrange beforehand to have special squads ready and prepared to seize the key points, such as the arms depot, the A.S.C. dumps of food, the water-supplies, and above all the telephone exchanges? It's a sort of inevitable protest which one heard everywhere up in the Salient after the sixteenth of August when the second main attack from the Black Line failed—most of them 'back to the starting tapes'."

"Yes, there was remarkable unanimity in the letters of the wounded—both the Padre and I had to do a lot of censoring, you know. Again and again the phrase cropped up—'It's been murder this time'."

The telephone bell rang. Traill listened; and putting down the receiver said, "Hospital nurses going on duty are reported to have been pushed off their bikes. That's serious! The order has just come to hold the prisoners in the Field Punishment Compound at all costs. There's been a raid there, and some of Broncho Bill's pals have got him away. Five hundred men with machine guns and a searchlight are on the way. All officers are to stand by, with all equipment including revolvers, to act under my orders. The men remaining in camp will be confined to their huts. Sentries will be posted, but without ball, and no bayonets are to be fixed. This is to minimise provocation."

When the new troops marched in, squads were told off to mount guns, dig pits, and put wire around the prisoners' block.

The searchlight and generating lorry were put on a flank, to sweep light in front of the first line of cells wherein men, sentenced to be taken up the line to be shot in their corps' areas, sat in solitary and narrow confinement. Rolls of concertina wire were pulled out, to complete the strong-point.

Darkness came. All was quiet, except for the cries of the condemned. Going round the huts—he was in command of a company—Phillip felt strained and unhappy. The cries of the condemned arose in the moonless night, with fists battering on the doors.

"For Christ's sake let me out! I ain't a bad'n!"

"Help! Help! Don't let them shoot me! I overslepp, and I were afraid to report late! Oh Gawd, please 'elp me!"

Other cries were roared out. Screams of despair ended in groans. Cries in the morass were bad enough; these were unbearable. He did not show himself until his eyes ceased to sting. It was time for dinner—bully beef and biscuit stew. No fresh rations had been drawn.

He sat at the top table, beside Traill, unable to eat. The meal, such as it was, had hardly begun when the mess sergeant came in and spoke to the Colonel. The Colonel looked serious.

"Keep your seats, gentlemen. Major Traill and Mr. Maddison, will you come with me."

The Colonel went first and met a crowd of men almost at the door. He had got so far as "What are you doing in my camp——" when a flash-lamp was put on him and a shower of sand caught him in the eyes. He went back inside. Major Traill, lighting his face with his own torch, so that it could be seen, said quietly, "Now, men, we're all as fed up with the war as you are, but this sort of thing can't do any good, you know."

Voices called out, "Make way for the 'major! This way, sergeant-major, old dear!" A little Scotty with half a bottle of whiskey cuddled in one arm came forward. "It's a' reet, sir! We're only goin' to let the boys out. We're sent by Broncho Bill, 'specially to ask that the boys be let out. Then everything wull be all reet, sir! You'll be all reet, sir! I'll be all reet! We'll all be all reet! Have a wee drappie, sir!" and the bottle was held out.

"No thank you," said Major Traill.

"Go on, sir, we've got naught against 'ee!"

"Let me drink your health," said Phillip. "Just a wee one. Now listen to me, boys. The authorities have got us all taped. Two battalions have come down from the line. This town is

surrounded. Soon there'll be no food, if we keep this up. Neither
you nor I nor anyone else can fight a system. We all know
the war's bloody awful. I was out, as a private, in 1914,
with the London Highlanders. We were all up against it,
and still are. But it's no good trying to push the war out of the
way——"

"Put a sock in it!" cried a voice.

"Fair do's, fair do's, let the gentleman speak!" cried the little
Scot. "Now, sir, I'm a mon, see? You're a mon, see? We're all
men, see? Even Jerry's a mon, like me and you. So what t'hell?"
He raised the bottle.

While he was drinking, a lilac haze arose from behind the mess
building, and with it shouts and booing. At once the crowd by
the open door began to surge away, with cries of "Up the rebels!
Get the boys out!" There were cheers and whooping.

The line of cells, behind flat spirals of wire, was lit up by the
fizzling, astigmatic blaze. The light was unendurable, eyesight
was stricken. Behind its impenetrable glare came the rattle of
brass-and-canvas machine-gun belts, and an order to lay on. A
barrage of cat-calls, cries, shouts, came from the mass of impotent
faces. Chalk was thrown.

After an hour the last of the wandering groups had gone.

The mutiny fizzled out. In the days that followed various facts
became known. Three junior officers, disguised as private soldiers, had been beaten up. The Commandant left, another took
his place. Courts-martial were set up. For days handcuffed men
sat on benches awaiting turn for trial. The corporal who had
accosted the General in the town on the first morning was sentenced to be shot, with two others. Many other men got sentences
up to twenty years' penal servitude.

There were identification parades. Phillip was asked to pick
out the Scots lance-jack who had offered him whiskey. He
recognised him first by the fact that he was standing somewhat
on his toes, apparently trying to increase his height—a customer,
surely, he thought, for the Windup Company. The rigid figure
stared straight to its front, and Phillip passed on down the line
without stopping anywhere.

The sergeant of Military Police who had accidentally shot the
Gordon Highlander was sent to prison for ten years.

An armed gang of Australians, led by Broncho Bill, it was said,
got away in time from the town. They robbed supply trains at

night, and hid in woods by day. Eventually they reached the old Somme battlefield, where in that immense and ruinous warren, now overgrown by long grasses, brambles and other weeds, shots were heard in the darkness; for they had entered the territory of other gangs, particularly one known as the International Battalion, made up of French, British, and German deserters, all bearded men. Cavalry patrols had been sent periodically to hunt them down in that vast golgotha, but without result.

There was a dog in the camp, a black retriever known as Windy Bill. It was the first to dash for the underground tunnels when it heard the growling engine notes of approaching Gothas. Squalls of shrapnel fire arose from around the camp. Bombs swished down. Screams arose from the canvas hospitals. One night on picket duty beside the railway, lined with tents and marquees, Phillip heard a dreadful noise behind one canvas wall, and peering in, saw that the beds were jumpy with epileptics having fits. Another night he was on duty in a listening post on a hillock, with signal lamp and whistle. But Windy Bill, who had attached himself, had keener ears. Lifting up his snout, Windy Bill gave the alarm, and then fled to his tunnel. Soon there was a general stampede for the three tunnel entrances in the slope above the mud of the Canche estuary, and the four entrances to dug-outs in the chalk of the camp ground.

A sickly sweet smell of iodoform and gangrene floated up on the night air, with the wailing cries of epileptics who now slept out at the edge of the shafts. Many were killed, together with some W.A.A.C.s and nurses. Thermit bombs were dropped, some marquees burned. He found he was yelling at the long black shapes circling against the veils of thin cloud around the moon. In the morning it was said that hundreds had been killed, and thousands wounded.

There were dances for the Base staff. Officers only were permitted to dance with the W.A.A.C.s. No dancing was arranged for the tommies, so they danced among themselves.

Phillip had written to 'Spectre' West, telling him where he was, and what doing, but with no mention of the mutiny. He knew that all letters were being scrutinised. No reply came. When the course was nearly ended he asked Traill if anything was known about his return to the line. Had anything special come into the Orderly Room?

"I am wondering if I am supposed to be going back to my M.G. company, sir."

Mindful of the report from the Signalling School, Phillip had determined to give a good account of himself, as Father would say.

On passing-out day extra charges of gun-cotton were blown for the new General's benefit. Louder cheers were yelled as jumps were made into shell-holes occupied by straw dummies with painted faces, after rifle-grenades had burst among them. Smoke bombs were tossed frantically into pillboxes made of wood, asbestos sheets, and painted corrugated iron, after masks had been worn for twenty minutes continuously, five of them in the gas chamber. It was all eye-wash: who could charge like that in the Salient?

The officers were told to report to the Orderly Room for further instructions.

"Lieutenant P. S. T. Maddison?" asked a sergeant, running his nail down a list. "You are to proceed to your unit at Poperinghe. There's a train leaving in half an hour for Hop-out." (Hopoutre was one of the branch rail-heads, with Dosinghem, Bandighem, and Mendinghem.)

He felt faint with relief, and went to the mess. Yet doubt remained, centred on Downham. In the ante-room there were letters from his mother, Mrs. Neville, Eugene, Nina, and 'Darky' Fenwick. He put them in his pocket to read on the way up the line; then stoked up with three more large whiskeys with soda; and having settled his mess bill, stuffed a packet of sandwiches and a bottle of red wine into his haversack, and said goodbye to the Colonel, Traill, and others. Windy Bill accompanied him to the station and then, with a wave of tail, trotted back to camp, to seek further excitement from new arrivals for the Bull Ring.

Part Four

'SPECTRE' WEST

Chapter 16

THE GREEN LINE

At Hopoutre there was no transport, so he left his valise in the R.T.O.'s office, where he found a message from Pinnegar, *I'll be in the Aigle d'Or, come there*. In the hotel, to his immense relief he saw a new Teddy wearing three small cloth stars on his shoulder straps. They hurried to one another.

"I'm awfully glad to see you, Teddy!"

"I came in to m-meet you, old m-man!" stuttered Pinnegar, his face beaming. "Come in and have a drink, and I'll give you all the news."

"Congratulations on your promotion, Teddy."

"Yes, Wilmott told me this morning to put up my third pip! I've got the company!"

Pop went the cork, out foamed *Veuve Cliquot*.

"Are you joking? Where's Downham?"

"Gone! Pushed off a week ago! I'm damned glad to see you back!"

"Downham gone?"

"Yes, thank God. We've seen the last of that swab! Cheerio!"

They drank. "But how did it happen?"

"I'll tell you in a jiffy. The point is that you're all right! Wilmott's set aside that report, you know, about not being fit for promotion. I knew Downham, given enough rope, would hang himself sooner or later." Pinnegar drank, and said, "Here's to us!"

"Where is Downham now?"

"Probably in England by this time. Sick. P.U.O. Louse fever! If he hadn't gone sick, I was going to report him. I put him under arrest, you know!" beamed Pinnegar. "Cheerio, old thing!"

"Cheerio, Teddy."

"It came to a head over Cutts," he went on, with an expression of complete satisfaction. "You remember Cutts? Well, we've had the Gothas over almost every night, and one scored a direct hit on a Nissen hut next to our lot. Cutts ran out, yelling his head off. When I arrived, there was a scene of complete chaos. I've never seen such an exhibition of wind in all the time I've been in France! Not only Cutts, but Rivett. He was bawling at Cutts, saying he was under arrest. I was asking what the hell he was doing when Downham appeared in his pyjamas, under his British Warm. He made a bee-line for Cutts, and burst out that he'd been sentenced to death once before for cowardice, and he'd get him court-martialled again. Can you understand it?"

"Yes, I can."

"Damned if I can! I told Downham to pipe down, and he turned on me, shouting, before all the men, that he'd put me under arrest if I wasn't careful! If I wasn't careful! I wasn't afraid of the swab. I—I wish you'd been there. Honestly, if any-one had told me, I'd never have believed it. While Downham was yelling at Cutts, Nolan was holding him up. Cutts was absolutely gibbering, poor sod, while those two combed-out Sharpshooters were behaving like a couple of raving lunatics!"

Phillip felt warm with satisfaction. "Go on, Teddy."

"As I said, I was bloody well fed to the teeth, so I told Down-ham to pipe down. Then he bawled at me, so I said I'd put a bullet in him if he didn't shut up. He said something about get-ting me shot for insubordination, so I put him under arrest. All this, mark you, outside a Nissen hut after a direct hit, men stag-gering out, covered with blood, arms dripping, crying and moan-ing—and all Downham could do was to screech at poor bloody Cutts! Can you beat it?"

Courage is a habit, it has to be grown from small beginnings, Phillip thought. Of course! A child had to be *encouraged* by its father! And all its school-teachers! *Thou shall*: not, *Thou shalt not!*

"Well, as I was saying," went on Pinnegar, filling the glasses, "that quietened Downham all right, and we went back to bed. I'd hardly got to sleep again when he came to me full of soft soap, told me he had a fever, had had it for weeks off and on, that was why he wasn't really responsible for what had occurred. Showed me a thermometer registering 106. Any bloody fool could have seen that he'd put the end on his cigarette! I told him straight that what he said cut no ice with me. He offered to shake hands, and forget all about it. I told him that if he was as ill as he made out, he ought to see the doctor. There's an American one now, you know, attached to Brigade. Anyway, I said, I'd report him if he didn't. So he saw the doc, and went down the line, and now I've got the company! How have you been getting on?"

Phillip told him; and then asked after the others.

"Bright went back to the infantry. He wrote to me the other day, and asked me to press for what he called justice. I didn't care much for him, and told him it was nothing to do with me. Old 'Lucky' has gone, too. He got splashed with mustard gas, and went into hospital with burns. We've had three new officers since then. Two more are due tomorrow. Cheerio!"

"Cheerio. Has the company been in any stunts, Teddy?"

"Only the usual stuff, night strafing when we were in the line. There's a big push coming off soon. We're for that. Plumer's taken over some of the Fifth Army sector, you know. About time, too."

"How's Nolan?"

"I was going to ask you about him. Would you like him promoted sergeant? Well, ask him when you get back, and if he's agreeable, I'll have it put in Orders right away. Morris? He's still here. Black Prince is all right, too. In fact I've been riding him. He's yours, when you want him."

"Thanks. How are the sections? Up to strength?"

"No. It's the same tale everywhere, half-trained drafts, about fifty per cent of what we ask for, coming in. The infantry's being messed about, too, from what I hear. Same old story—Jocks into riflemen, riflemen sent to kilted regiments, the bloody fools at the Base don't seem to care what happens to regimental *morale*, so long as they shove up the line any old lot. Anyway, Phil, you're back, that's something! I was awfully pleased to see your face again," he said a little shyly. "By the way, I told the Colonel I've no complaints about how you've done your job."

"Thank you. What about Cutts?"

"I told the Colonel about him, too. It's damn silly letting a bloke like that come anywhere near the line. Wilmott isn't a bad chap, when you know him, in spite of being a cavalryman. We had a frank talk, he says he'll always do all he can to help, that's what he's there for. Cutts'll probably be sent home, he's enn bee gee out here."

"What about the new push?"

"Plumer's going to have a smack at the Gheluvelt plateau, where all the Hun guns are."

"Pity he wasn't put in charge of that sector first go off!"

"I know."

"Have you had any rain up here, Teddy?"

"Damn all. The ground's pretty dry now, except in the areas of the beeks."

"If the weather holds there's a good chance of getting forward."

"You're right. The rear areas are simply stiff with guns. Many more than we had at Messines. Also they've run up a lot more light railways, and trams. The whole of the old battlefield up to the Steenbeek looks like a lot of old corsets, with tram-lines and duck-board tracks spread out in all directions. We've even got a traffic manager in front of one of the new bridges over the Canal. They shunt empty trucks there, fill them up with shells, and send them up the line again, just like any goods-yard."

"What about the Alleyman shelling?"

"Their guns have been playing merry hell among the working parties."

"Working by day?"

"Got to. Thousands of them, going on day and night. I saw your pal 'Spectre' West, by the way, and had a crack with him. He's a bloody good chap, isn't he? Asked after you."

"What was he doing?"

"Goes right up into the outpost lines, to see for himself what's happening. Reports direct to G.H.Q."

"I'm glad you like him, Teddy."

"He's the kind of staff officer I can see eye to eye with! Says he wanted to be a parson after the war! Can you imagine it? He told me, incidentally, that fifty German divisions so far had been brought up from down south, and most of them been smashed. All the same, I reckon we've had just about as bad a pasting as they have. How about another bottle? I've got half an hour before I see Wilmott." Pinnegar looked at his watch. "I've ordered our horses to be in the Square at five o'clock, by the way. They're bringing the Maltese cart for your kit."

Phillip ordered the second bottle, they toasted each other, and Pinnegar went on, "Yes, this time Plumer's running most of the show. Limited objectives. No more staggering on beyond the five to six thousand yards' range of the 18-pounders. Nor even beyond extreme Vickers-gun range. We're doing five barrages this time, to a depth of a thousand yards." He became reminiscent. "I remember our opening attack on the Pilckem ridge. On our left were the Cockchafers, the Kaiser's crack corps, you know. They were overwhelmed by our barrage, and the Welshmen scuppered what was left of them, taking five hundred prisoners. That was because the German tactics then were to hold the first position in strength. They soon adapted themselves to our barrages, withdrawing most of their men before the attack behind their pillbox line. Then, when our chaps had got forward, too far ahead of our field gun and emma gee barrages, they put down a barrage and reversed the process."

"Guns from behind the Gheluvelt plateau?"

"Most of them, yes."

"Well, supposing they let us take the plateau, and then reverse the process, their guns being already withdrawn?"

"I—I think there may be something in what you say. But surely the gunners will know about it? There'll have hundreds of aerial photographs——"

"Anyway, you will mention it to Colonel Wilmott, won't you?"

"If you like. Now I must push off. See you in the Square about five pip emma. Now look after yourself, don't go and get a——"

"Not me, Teddy!" said Phillip, before Pinnegar could say what still made him wince a little when others spoke of such things.

The idea to see 'Spectre' West, in whose presence he felt calm and sure of himself, became obsessive. He went to the rue de l'Hôpital, and *Abandon rank all ye who enter here.* Up two flights of stairs and into the hop-loft chapel. A service was being held.

While in the train, uncertain of his immediate fate—whether or not he would be ordered to the infantry on arrival—he had thought to send no replies to the letters from home, even to Mrs. Neville: to shut off all things of the life that was lost, lest he begin to hope again, and so break down under the test of battle.

Now, with feelings of optimism and even joy, he knelt down, and became clear and simple. He must write a cheerful letter to Mother. And be firm with Eugene, refusing to lend him five pounds, as asked for. But how could he be curt with Gene? Perhaps the Brazilian bank had not received the usual allowance from Gene's father. What was a fiver between friends? Gene owed him over twenty pounds now. What a thing to think about, while kneeling at prayer—or supposed prayer. He would send three pounds. That was settled. Now he must pray. But he could feel nothing. Others were going up for Communion. Young infantrymen, soon to be in action perhaps for the first time. Into that hell. Dear Mother, I hope you are in the pink, as it leaves me at present. The dead turned pink, or wax-rotten, after a week or two in water. Stop the brain thinking in terms of fear. Think of Father Aloysius. But Gene's face persisted. Poor Gene, he must live a very lonely life, an almost bare attic at night, that awful corset factory by day. Not much life for a fellow, alone in London, his only friends being ones he picked up. He would send Gene five pounds. Doris, too, would want some new clothes. He would send her five pounds, too. He must ask Mother to promise not to say where it came from. And five pounds for Mav—Elizabeth. Elizabeth was a better name, stiffer, stronger, like a Queen's ruff, or whale-bone corset. Mavis was like somebody slipping on wet yellow clay. Tears filled his eyes. He saw Father scoffing at Mother's tears. Sentimentality was a favourite word of Father's, in criticism of Mother—no, not favourite, a *desperate* word. Anyway, he was being what Mrs. Rolls would call *morbid*. Because he was half-tight? He felt too remote, too apart, to go up for Communion. He stayed in quietude, thinking of Mother—what could he write to her? But all he could think was that the guns were vibrating in the timber frame of the loft, and rocking the air against his ear drums. How strange, that once he had felt that gunfire was exhilarating— from a distance! It was terrible and utterly dreadful. If only he could become clear, and truly brave, like Father Aloysius.

Men were leaving, trying to tip-toe across the margin of bare-boards, their boots awkwardly clopping. One awkward little tubby man almost hobbled past, the rectangular bulge of a miniature Church Army khaki Bible in left breast pocket of his tunic. His mouth was half-open, his eyes slightly apprehensive. Phillip kept his eyes averted, for it was Tom Ching. But what could he have done, had he spoken to him? Ching was like an invertebrate parasite, he seemed to insinuate himself always. And he was lasciviously treacherous, as when he had told Detective-Sergeant Keechey that he and Lily had gone into the Recreation Grounds that night. Ching was a teller of smutty stories, while he rolled his eyes. What *was* it about Ching that made him repul-sive? Had he any decent thoughts? Always as a boy he had been —slimy. But *why*? Ching seemed to have a permanent, profound illness-at-ease. No one could ever help Ching, who would always be—Ching. What *was* it about Ching that made him so repellent? He didn't seem to be afraid. Perhaps he was; and being insensitive also, he couldn't explain himself to himself, and so know.

Damn Ching! And yet—poor Ching. That dreadful home, a palsied fat father, and mother with settled anxious face.

What to say to his own mother? What *could* he say to her, when he could only express what he really felt; and by doing so, only reveal to her that he was further and further alienated from what she used to *think* she knew of him? Neither Mother nor Father had ever wanted his idea of truth; it was quite beyond their narrow world. *Hush, Phillip, hush my son, you must not say such things.* Fear, fear, fear! Fear of Father, fear of her son being himself, or trying to be. He had started a score of letters to both parents; come to an inevitable petering-out in each; and torn the letters up.

Should he go; or stay? He dreaded being conspicuous, so he remained on his knees, until all were gone, and the padre only was left. It was too late to go, then. He must say something. He got up and said, "May I thank you for a beautiful service, padre. This is a wonderful place. I'm just on my way to rejoin my unit after fifteen hours in the train. Do forgive me if I seem a bit odd, it's because I've drunk a bottle of wine."

"I'd think it odd if you hadn't drunk a bottle of wine after fifteen hours in an army train! Some of you chaps who come here have had considerably more than a modest bottle of wine! Capacity, I assure you, is no qualification, or disqualification! We welcome all and sundry, publicans, sinners, and the righteous alike. Our intentions are good, but sometimes go the way of all good intentions! As an instance: Last week we had several, shall I say slightly unsteady, boys from the London Irish here, and so I asked them to make a rule to limit themselves to two pints of beer a day. They were very young, scarcely nineteen. One of them later sent a message from the guardroom of the Provost Marshal's office, asking if I would go and see him. He was very much frightened, poor boy, because he had been found drunk, and taken in. I asked him why he 'had the drink taken'. What do you think he replied?" asked the padre, touching the top button of Phillip's tunic. "'Well, Padre, I've always been a teetotaller, but I did what you asked, took two pints, and here I am'." The padre, a short, sturdy man, threw back his head and roared with laughter. "However, all was well! I reported myself to the boy's Commanding Officer, as an *agent provocateur*, and was let off with a caution! No case against the boy was brought, I need hardly say. Now, may I be of help in any way to you?"

"You have, sir. Very much. This is my second visit, as a

matter of fact. I came here with 'Spectre' West—I think you know him?"

"Yes, indeed. One of my best friends. What are you doing now?"

"I've been on a course, and was wondering if he was still about."

"Oh yes, he comes here now and again. Your name is?—Maddison. I'll remember it, and tell him I've seen you."

"Thank you, sir. Well, I mustn't keep you. And thank you again for making this oasis for all of us."

When Phillip met Pinnegar he asked him if he had spoken to Colonel Wilmott about the possible withdrawal of the German guns from behind the Gheluvelt plateau.

"He said it was elementary tactics to place a battery so that it could fire in enfilade whenever possible, and that every depression behind the high ground was probably stiff with Boche batteries. I got the impression that he rather thought I'd got a bit of a nerve to query whether the staffs of the Division and Corps know their jobs or not."

The sun had gone down when the company, followed by wheeled limbers, moved through the grey emptiness of Ypres. The day had been bright and clear, but clouds had closed upon the sunset. Sandbag strips muffled the grind of iron wheel-hoops upon sett-stones. Phillip was on foot: the minimum of transport noise was ordered. Marching men broke step, no smoking was permitted.

Having left the town, the ambling sections followed the Brigade sign-posted track, as rehearsed in the back area. Pack animals had another track; wheeled transport only was allowed on the roads.

For three weeks the Plum had had ripening weather, thought Phillip. Then, as darkness fell, it began to drizzle. By the time he got back to the picket line it was raining steadily, and he was wet to the skin. There seemed to be a curse on the entire offensive, for so far it had rained on every night before an attack.

At 11 p.m. in Lovie Château, Fifth Army Headquarters in the woods three miles north of Poperinghe, General Gough telephoned to General Plumer on Cassel Hill, suggesting that the attack be postponed. The senior General replied that he would

consult 'Meteor', as well as his Corps, and some Divisional
commanders.

'Meteor' having stated that there was a risk of thunder-
storms, otherwise fair weather might be expected; and Corps,
"that the ground was go-able", Plum informed Fox that the
attack should proceed.

At three o'clock in the morning Phillip was standing, in heavy
wet tunic, breeches, and boots, in his tent. In one hand was his
tooth-mug, in the other a whiskey bottle. Having half-filled the
enamel mug, he drank most of it neat; then choked, spluttered,
and for awhile could hardly breathe. Then, as warmth uprose
in him, he wound up the gramophone and put on *The Garden of
Sleep*. The light tenor voice, so sensitive and tender, brought
him to his knees, as he held his face close to the concave nickel-
plated amplifier, and closed his eyes.

> *O Life of my life, on the cliffs by the sea,*
> *By the graves in the grass, I am waiting for thee.*
> *Sleep! Sleep!*
> *In the dews by the Deep,*
> *Sleep my Poppy Land, sleep.*

Sitting on a copy of the *Daily Trident* spread on the camp bed
to keep the wet away, he had a party with the candle, gramophone, and whiskey bottle. But soon thoughts of the imminent
battle possessed him, with fears of disaster and death. If the
rain kept on the infantry wouldn't have a chance, despite
the supports and reserves close up behind them. Damn! Damn!!
Damn!!! Why did the rain always fall on Y/Z night? He
touched the canvas, to see if any drops would come through.
The tip of his finger glistened, and lifting the candle, stuck to
the top volume of Thompson's poems, he let the flame dodge
about with its black smoke around the place he had touched,
to dry it up, and perhaps seal it with a film of wax. No drop
bulged; he was pleased with himself.

Rain, rain, rain. The infantry would be held up again by
mud. All the five barrages would be of no avail. Each one of the
five moving curtains of fire was planned to bite into and rip up
everything that lay or moved within its limits of two hundred
yards. The first was a creeping barrage of shrapnel by 18-
pounders; the second was a combing barrage of H.E. from 18-

pounders and 4.5 hows, with instantaneous or "burst-on-graze", as well as delay-action, fuses. The third was by 240 Vickers guns, to keep German local-attack reserves in their shelters; the fourth was a neutralising barrage by 6-inch howitzers to fall among the German field-batteries; the fifth was by 60-pounders and heavy hows up to 15-inch, to fall upon the known *Eingreif* assembly places.

In front of the first assault the creeping barrage was to lift 50 yards every 2 minutes, then it was to slow down to 100 yards every 6 minutes to enable the successive leap-frogging waves to keep close behind it.

Six hours of rain at this rate would mean three inches falling before 5.40 a.m. The infantry would be shot down as they staggered knee-deep in mud.

At one o'clock it stopped raining. Crawling out of the tent, he saw stars. He was still in his wet clothes. If the fellows in the line were wet, he would be wet, too. Now he could have some shut-eye. Morris would wake him at half-past five in time for the show.

The candle guttered, the wick sank, and went out. He was aware of himself in a slough of sleep, Morris shaking his shoulder: instantly aware of everything, despite deep reluctance to move again, to be.

"Blime, you're still wet, sir. Here's a nice hot muggerchar, sir."

"No sugar."

"No sugar, sir. Like you like it, not strong."

"What's the weather doing?"

"'Olding off, sir, and misty, like. There was a lot of Jerry's guns strafing away at half-past four, looked like up the Menin road, on the Australians."

Phillip looked at his watch. "Five minutes to go, Morris."

"That's right, sir." Morris left the tent. "Blime, sir, what's this 'ere ticket? I never sin like it before."

Phillip went out. Four bright lights were as though stationary in the far distance.

"They're parachute flares! I saw one just like them dropped over London by a Zeppelin!"

Scissor-like flashes leapt upwards, well to the north and south of the four hanging flares. So the German batteries had been withdrawn from the Gheluvelt plateau! They were firing from the end of the sleeves of Prince Rupprecht's golden scarecrow.

God help the men on the tape-lines under that storm of shells!

"It looks as though they knew the time of our attack, Morris."

"That's right sir," replied Morris, as he went away for his own mug of tea.

The German counter-barrage was now in full flash and rumble. The minutes to 5.40 a.m. passed slowly: then the four gold studs in the sky were lost in the roaring light of two thousand furnace doors opening.

After that there was a vain attempt to sleep against the imminence of a possible call to go up the line, so he went outside to dry off. The guns were quiet. It looked as though the attack had gone through.

No cavalry appeared: squadrons would have to come past the station.

After breakfast he visited a battery in the city, behind the prison. There he learned that nearly all objectives had been taken by 7 a.m., after local counter-attacks had been smashed. Liaison with the R.F.C. was good, reports of *eingreif* divisions on the way were coming in. This time they would have to come within range of the 18-pounders. Good old Plumer, he bit off just so much as he could chew up.

In the afternoon he rode over to Brigade, where the staff-captain, or chief clerk as he called himself, had remained when the Brigadier and his major had gone up to their battle head-quarters. The staff-captain confirmed the success: all along the Second Army front the advance had gone forward to final objectives. Half the north-west slopes of the Gheluvelt plateau had been taken. Over two thousand prisoners were in the cages. The barrage had been such that German machine-gunners in some pill-boxes had been so dazed that they were found sitting beside unfired guns. Fifth Army had had some trouble on the left, otherwise the advance was going like clockwork, the support waves leap-frogging through the first waves, and the reserves well up.

Leaving the staff-captain's office, he cantered back to the lines, telling Nolan to deal with any messages that might come in. "I don't think it's likely that they'll want any supplies taken up until this evening. I'm just going to Vlamertinghe, will be back soon."

There was a Casualty Clearing Station in the boarded mill beside the road, and he wanted to ask questions. Inside the

lower rooms white sheets hung on the walls, and across the
ceilings. Two R.A.M.C. surgeons, in white aprons, smoked
unconcernedly outside. They had been at work on case after
case all day. A convoy of motor ambulances was arriving.
Lightly wounded men, more or less content, having had their
wounds dressed, were sitting in the shade of elms lining the road,
smoking and talking as they awaited transport to the trains.
Their faces were almost carved in earth by dried sweat-runs
through grime. He got into conversation with an officer with
a bullet through his shoulder; and at first did not recognise him
as Douglas of the London Highlanders, whom he had last seen
at Loos, two years before.

Douglas said they were well forward of their outpost line when
the German barrage followed the four parachute S O S flares.
He spoke at intervals, and at times disjointedly; but what he
said, in effect, was:

"The mist helped us. Our barrage was overwhelming, except
on some pill-boxes. It kicked up a lot of dust. We had some
trouble with the pill-boxes at Potsdam House, but managed to
clear them with rifle grenades and phosphorus bombs, by the
time the barrage was due to creep forward just after seven
o'clock. We got to our final objective. I've never seen so many
flies when the sun was well up. But what I remember most was
a feeling of amazement that I was free to stand up and look back
at Ypres in broad daylight. I'd never seen it before. It was like
being in a new world. I realised that I was looking at it as the
Germans had seen it for years, every detail clear in the low
morning sun behind me. I'm by way of being an amateur
landscape painter, I've spent several holidays in North Norfolk,
where it's flat and sandy, with spruce and fir plantations, not
unlike what the Salient must have been before the war. Yes,
it was a wonderful sight, the cluster of Ypres ruins, quite small,
grey-white, the colour of wood ash. I wish I'd had my paint-box
and sketch book with me, I could have made some priceless
wash-sketches for an oil-painting when I get home. It was a
priceless opportunity, and I've missed it now. Turner relied
on his imagination, but I can't." He looked bleakly at Phillip. "I
realised that I had no talent."

"Well, I should say you had no paint-box, Douglas."

He wondered if Douglas were shell-shocked: not so much
because of what he said, but because his eyes had a fixed shine
in them, which might have been pain and shock, together with

puzzlement, because the unrealisable had happened before it could be realised. But there was also dislike, very nearly resentment, in his eyes; and Phillip knew it.

Captain Douglas, attached to the Royal Scots, had had mixed feelings about Phillip since the early days in the same tent at Crowborough in Sussex. Five years older than Phillip, raised with care and affection, the modest and dutiful child had early gone to one of the finest schools in England—Christ's Hospital. There he had been good at both games and work, and had developed in a spirit that was an extension of a thrifty and dutiful home: unquestioned duty, accepting life as it was because the spirit of parents, friends, and teachers affirmed his own. He was a Scot, proud of his clan, without pretensions; he had grown in surety of himself, his parents, relations. Before the war he had worked in the foreign department of a City bank, and played rugger for the Harlequins.

He had never questioned the existence of God; he prayed regularly. And an hour before he was hit on that morning of 20 September he had gone forward alone under heavy machine-gun fire, scrambling from dry shell-hole to shell-hole, and finally rushing up to a square concrete hideosity with a three-inch splayed opening low on the ground, flung himself down and then, working forward to the very issue of death, thrown in a phosphorous bomb, which bursting amidst coils of choking white smoke set on fire woodwork and uniform material, thus forcing surrender of the garrison. After that, Captain Douglas, a bullet through one shoulder, led his company forward to the final objective, although enfiladed from Bremen redoubt on the left flank, where he captured more machine guns and prisoners. There he had looked back at the grey mortar, stone, and brick heaps of a mediaeval city, and felt a sense of unreality in the sight, mingled with regret, almost a sense of failure, that he had not his sketch book and water-colour box with him.

That night, in his diary, Captain Douglas wrote

> I am glad, for the sake of my two dear, anxious parents at home, that I have come through; and glad for the sake of my wife; but regret that I am no longer with the dear fellows who had come to look to me, for some things, at least.

Feeling, as on all previous occasions, that Douglas secretly disapproved of him because he knew he was at base a coward,

Phillip moved away among wounded soldiers, offering cigarettes, asking, "How did you get on?", and "How was it going in your sector?" There were the inevitable stories of disaster: the footslogger's war was seldom wider than fifty yards, sometimes horizontal maximum of six feet—if he was lucky. Advancing waves had been shot in the back from pill-boxes and dug-outs not mopped up. Dug-outs? In the Salient? He heard in the accents of Lancashire about a line of shelters connected by a concrete tunnel a quarter of a mile long. Near Schuler Farm it was, below the Gravenstafel rise, on ground sloping slightly away from the Haanbeek. He was asking questions when a figure with gaunt and bloodless face under a grime of dust and smoke thrust itself forward and in a high, overwrought voice cried, "What the hell d'you want to know for? You bloody f—g cavalry bastard!"

"I'm not in the cavalry, I'm in the Machine Gun Corps, major."

"Anyway, I don't like your face, whoever you are! And who the hell asked you who you were, anyway? And in any case, you look to me just like a bloody f—g war correspondent! Don't you look at me! F— off back to your bloody machine guns, you inquisitive bastard!"

Then, seeing the two wound stripes, he said, "You ought to know better, blast your eyes!"

"Quite right! Sorry!" He left.

Sunshine warmed the alienated Flemish land. Cannon fire swelled and died in prolonged node and anti-node of deepest bass notes as the *sturmtruppen* of the *Eingreif divisionen* moved down into the outermost curtain of flame and flying steel. Some, but not all, were seen by the men who were connecting shell-holes for defence, using German shovels, and ungalvanised barbed wire of a gauge thicker than the British galvanised wire—the ugly, rusty, murderous, sullen wire of the Hun, as it seemed to many, cumbered physically, constricted in spirit, restricted in body, foul and filthy with the servitude of their living. But not always servitude: there were moments of fun, even of joy—some smoked German cigars as they worked, and took swigs of German brandy. The stuff to give the troops! The body in motion soon lost the terrors of immobility.

The consolidations were done, wherever possible, on reverse slopes behind the outpost lines in shell-holes, to be out of direct observation.

High in the air dog-fights faintly rattled and groaned, as squadrons of scouts, lost to formation, dived and zoomed, went round in tight circles, side-slipped and fell spinning, rolled and dropped in falling leaf stunts—a sight so common above the brown and blasted battlefield, where even the worms were dead in the crater-to-crater areas, that few bothered to look up.

In the consolidations, lines of old trenches were avoided where possible, for these drew howitzer fire from batteries firing south-west from below Passchendaele on the left of the British line, and guns firing north-west from Tenbrielen, Zanvoorde and Commines beyond the Gheluvelt plateau on the right flank. These enemy guns were widely dispersed, and hidden within roofless houses, barns, and sheds. Before they were fired, smoke-screens were laid to hide the flashes.

At 5 p.m., while Phillip was checking the loading of limbers, three coloured balls, one directly above the other—red, green, yellow—broke in the sky, in the direction of the Menin road, and floated there. At once the British barrage opened up. Hardly had it died away when another trio of lights arose to the left, and again a great cauldron seemed to be bubbling.

"That's up by Langemarck," remarked Sergeant Nolan; while Cutts, heaving up a box of .303, seemed to have lost his strength. Nolan helped him, and said reassuringly, "The company will have got Jerry taped by the time we go up tonight." The thought of the Alleyman machine-gun barrage on the beech-slab circuit made Phillip feel weak, too; so he went away to his tent to have a drink.

Half an hour later the S O S lights arose on the right, this time up by Polygon wood, where the Australians were fighting. Twice again, at 6.30 p.m., and at 7 p.m., the trio of rocket lights sailed up, the barrage crashed down, "hammer and tongs" said Nolan.

In a clear sky the sun went down, casting a purple tinge in the brick-red rays; and with the day the battle, too, seemed to have spent its force.

When the pallor of flares arose along the horizon, transport wheels began to roll and dip on all the roads of stone, rubble and wood; gun-teams, with horse and caterpillar tractor, hauled out their cannon, for the next step forward.

Chapter 17

FLANDERN I, FLANDERN II

The company remained in the line after the first artillery shock-battle, or step, in the G.H.Q. term of under-statement. Every Vickers gun was needed for the barrages on the German approach routes, while the second step was being prepared. Infantry rehearsals in rear areas took place daily; while tens of thousands of Labour troops—white, black, and yellow—worked in the back areas. The casualties among the British Labour Corps, as they laid wooden tracks for approach and supplies over captured ground, equalled those of the infantry in the assaults. Nothing in the Ypres salient had ever been cushy.

The first Plumerian step had taken the third German, or Wilhelm line, north of the Menin road; but only the lower slopes of the Gheluvelt plateau to the south.

The second step, six days later, again succeeded in the north, upon lower ground where bombardment had broken the beeks. But while it captured and held all of Polygon Wood, it failed upon the Gheluvelt plateau on both sides of the Menin road. Here the ground rose almost imperceptibly to the village of Gheluvelt on its crest.

During this battle, which took place in fine weather on Wednesday the 26 September, under a crescent moon (as recorded by Phillip in his pocket diary) there "were persistent rumours of hundreds of thousands killed".

Perhaps the rumours were suggested by the dust clouds hanging over the battlefield like omens of doom. After the continued fine weather, all the upper Salient, except the areas of the broken beeks, was so dry, particularly the fine sandy leaf-mould of Polygon Wood, that high-explosive shells with instantaneous fuses burst without penetration: up went palls of detritus, to float in the hot gases ascending into the misty morning. This black cloud hung over the battle, visible presage of doom.

The Germans now had more machine guns in the mebus, or pill-box rows, and in shell-holes and cavities under deracinated tree stumps. In some sectors battalions fought to decimation. From Ypres, and the camps standing thickly in the forward areas of reserve, S O S signals were seen to be going up, again and again, when towards noon the smoky mist lifted and the sun shone clear.

Phillip heard the rumours, one after another. So general was the feeling of pessimism, in contrast to the good news of the advance from the staff-captain at Brigade, that he put in Company Orders that evening a warning not to spread tales of disaster.

These Orders were written out by the C.Q.M.S. every evening, at dictation by the senior officer present. At six o'clock he ordered them to be read out to those men present in the camp.

"That's not what they're saying at the divisional dump," remarked Sergeant Nolan afterwards. "On all sides they are saying it's been a washout."

"Even the Aussies?"

"Well, no, sir, I can't say as I've heard it from any of them."

"Well, it isn't true, according to the staff-captain. I've an idea that it's been spread by the new drafts from Etaples, in for the first time. There was very nearly a mutiny when I was there, and many of the men, who were at the I.B.D.'s then, are now up here."

"I dunno, sir, I feel a bit fed-up myself, sometimes. Where's it all going to end? I don't see as how any side can really win this war."

So quietly had the attack been prepared, that the German Staff had thought that the British had broken off the battle. The attack came as a surprise to them. It was a stunning victory. But it was also a resumption of 'the battle for Passchendaele'. Both German and British troops had just about had enough. Rumours of disaster started to spread from the battle front and so down to the base; and by way of hospital trains, to Berlin— and London. Hundreds of thousands killed, said the rumour-mongers, tired of the war, on both sides. The French had gone beyond that condition; they had had enough.

Phillip was beginning to think that what people usually believed to be true was usually wrong. His intelligence, diverted by his upbringing, was beginning to assert itself against the commonplace, and commonplace ideas from which he had hitherto flinched. For he had been fortunate to find in Harold West both friend and mentor, one who made him aware of the possibility of a balanced outlook on all human actions. Major West had access to facts which were not generally known.

Thus, he told Phillip, while the "frocks" in Whitehall, "including the Prime Minister Mr. George", were saying that the Chief was "blundering on, losing hundreds of thousands of men in his stone-wall tactics", the facts were almost entirely to the contrary.

"The total number actually killed in both Second and Fifth Armies, that is, seven divisions, including the two Australian divisions fighting in the Salient on Wednesday, the twenty-sixth of September, was one hundred and eleven officers, and one thousand, one hundred and fourteen men. As for the Eingreif divisions, they are now being destroyed faster than they can arrive through the bottle-neck of communication into Western Belgium. London ignores this; it can only deprecate the 'terrible slaughter by Haig'; but if Mr. George could see it plain, he would realise the great advantage of the Chief's choice of Flanders as the battlefield area in which to carry out the Cabinet's instruction to destroy the German Armies! The enemy has got only two railway lines: *that is the whole point*! And in case you think I'm bloody-minded, let me remind you that I am not a soldier by nature, but a country parson."

After the attacks, and the counter-attacks, upon the ground beyond which the Germans could still hide their guns and the movements of their *eingreif divisionen* while looking down upon the British batteries and infantry, there was a pause. The late September sun had the glaze of ripening stone-fruit; but upon the earth, or that sector of scarcely twenty-five thousand acres which was the battlefield, its cornucopian virtue was denied. Europe had two ideas, Europe had two minds; Europe was sharing one death.

A week later, when the company was out at rest, the third step was taken, under a wasting moon declining to the west. It went forward along a tape line from the old junction of the Lauterbeek with the Broembeek in the north—where once the two brooks had met near the culvert under the embankment of the Ypres–Staden railway—to the high ground of Tower Hamlets on the Gheluvelt plateau just across the Menin road to the south. Rain had fallen the night before the battle, but not enough to stop some of the low trajectory German shells from bouncing off the ground when they struck. The wall of flame that was the British barrage moving before the assault passed over lines of German infantry which had been waiting for their own attack, timed to start ten minutes later. Neither side had known of the other's coming attack; first come were first to serve with the bayonet. Nearly all the Gheluvelt plateau was taken, and more than half the highest ground to the north between the Menin road and the village of Passchendaele, known as the Broodseinde Ridge.

But drizzle was the fore-drift of heavy showers of rain. On 7 October both Army commanders wanted to step, or thrust, no more. The Second Army troops had reached the original British trench line of October 1914, along the ridge. It had lain in front of the road from Becelaere to Passchendaele and West-roosbeke. Australian soldiers digging near Broodseinde noticed darker patches in some of the shovelfuls of sand, with finger bones, and blackened fragments of rotted khaki.

On the morning of 9 October the fourth step was taken. Fifth Army troops were to capture that section of *Flandern I* which remained untaken north of Abraham Heights near Gravenstafel; those of the Second Army to the south were to advance along the Flanders ridge to Passchendaele village. The German divisions were battered and demoralised: now for the possible knock-out, before the reserve divisions could be brought up on the single-line Belgian railways.

Four British divisions waited to entrain fifteen miles behind Ypres, whither the railway had been brought. The Cavalry Corps stood by, ready to exploit a break-through; while rain continued to fall steadily.

The day after the fourth step had been launched, two men, each with a long stick in his hand, were walking on one of the many duck-board tracks lying parallel to the Wieltje–Frezenberg road, alongside which was an almost continuous row of 18-pounder field-guns. Both wore thigh-length rubber wading boots, and mackintosh drivers' capes which covered their box-respirators, revolvers, field-glasses, and haversacks. The senior of the two, whose diminutive scarlet gorget patches on the collar of his ranker's tunic were concealed under a woollen scarf, carried, in addition, a map-case.

"I don't see how the infantry can possibly move in this weather, Westy. Must the attacks go on?"

"One thing I'd have you know, Phillip, is that the Chief remembers the fact that the Germans made a crucial mistake on the last day of October, 1914, when they chucked in their hand at the very moment when they had his First Corps on the move down the Menin road. That was the only occasion in this war so far when a battalion of Guards, the Lilywhites, broke, and some of their men threw away their rifles and left the battle. But you were there, and will know more about it than I."

"I think it had happened just before we went up the Menin road. But I do know that the Germans thought the woods behind us were stiff with reserves, also that our fifteen-rounds-rapid was from *automatische pistolen*, because one told me so on that Christmas Day. He said *they* had no more reserves, and as we had so many, the attack was stopped."

"I hadn't heard that." 'Spectre' West looked around him, at the brown waste land occluded by drizzle, and said, "If only the Chief could have had his own way, and attacked up here last May, instead of down south, as demanded by Joffre . . . the Messines mines had been ready, you know, for the attack in 1916, only the French insisted, then, that we should attack north of the Somme. So Third Ypres was put off in 1916, and again last spring. With the result that everyone can now see—only everyone, as usual, will draw the wrong conclusions. Now we must get a move on."

Cold squally rain began to drive into their faces.

They reached the transverse one-way limber track across the Pilckem ridge, and turned north to the St. Julien road. "I want to have a look at the batteries in the Steenbeek valley."

The teak track, nine feet wide, was in places aswim in the slipslop watery top-mud of the 6-, 8-, and 10-foot crater zone of the southern end of the Pilckem ridge. It lay behind what once had been a farm lane: the farms were now pill-boxes—Rupprecht, Uhlan, Jasper, Von Hugel—which had been captured on July 31.

Howitzer batteries, one beside the other, now squatted on the line of the original lane, between which and the teak track lay a light railway, with sidings for shell dumps.

"How goes it?" asked 'Spectre' West, his scarf opened to show his red tabs to a battery sergeant-major.

"Still on the first objective, sir."

The teak planks, 2½ inches thick and 9 feet wide, were scattered like the empty shucks of great insects caught, sucked out, and rejected by other squat insects within these webs of the dark side of the moon. A flash of light, a tremendous thud, a tearing sound in the sky: another 6-inch howitzer shell began its parabola eastwards.

Shattered limbers, with dead mules and horses, lay continuously beside the track. Now they were descending to pale gleams of water out-numbering the tippings of brown earth before them, upon which lay the track, like the flattened ribs of some prehistoric serpent. A sort of trestle bridge, which had been built to carry the track over the swamp, was broken and upended. Direct hits on it had scattered the wooden causeway. A notice said that cocoanut matting had been laid to the right of the trestle posts, two feet below water level.

'Spectre' West was one of three 2nd-grade General Staff Officers attached to Operations (A), G.H.Q. Each of the three majors understudied a Lieut.-Colonel (G.S.O. 1), commanded by the Brigadier-General who was Director of Operations in the B.E.F. Major West, who had been given a free hand where to go, had authority to visit any headquarters of any unit from infantry battalion and artillery brigade to Army. He had immediate access to any commander, from lieutenant-colonel to general.

He had been called various names during his travels, not all bestowed with good humour. They included G.H.Q. Spy, Ticket Inspector, The Tout, and The Bagman. He had a Vauxhall car with driver, and could come and go as he pleased. His job was to find out what was wrong, to hear and discuss ideas for correction, and to report what he had seen immediately on return to Advanced G.H.Q., which occupied about a score of railway coaches, fitted up as offices and living rooms, in a railway siding near Dunkerque, on the Belgian coast.

Some of the field guns on the west depression of the broken course of the upper Steenbeek, roughly marked by stumps of shattered willow trees, were unable to fire. Sand-bags or rather mud-bags filled with stone chippings had been laid on a double layer of faggot bundles for the foundations of the gun-pits. Upon each foundation two platforms of beech planks, one nailed crosswise upon the other, had been laid. But each kick-back after firing shook faggots, stone-bags and double-deck down unevenly, taking wheels and trail with them, until axles were aswirl. One gun had water lipping at its muzzle.

"The blasted Staff give us impossible jobs because they

never come anywhere near the line, but live a life of ease at the base," said one gunner subaltern, bitterly. "The barrage was bound to be a bloody wash-out when the rains started again. Look at my bloody guns! I ask you! What possible bloody sense was there in ordering an attack under these conditions?"

"What was the barrage like?"

"Weak, spluttery, no bloody good! We couldn't get our guns up, so we had to fire at extreme range."

"Six thousand yards?"

"That's right. And Passchendaele church, the infantry's objective, is nearer seven thousand yards."

"Had you not forward positions prepared?"

"Well, would we be here if we had? I ask you!"

"I am asking *you*," replied 'Spectre' West, smoothly. "Why did you not get forward?"

"Can't you see for yourself?"

"Yes, that is what I am here for."

Hairless, coagulated heaps lay around. Roughcast with mud, the horses lay where they had fallen, having lost the will to live.

"Here's the major!"

"Good morning," said 'Spectre' West. "I am from G.H.Q. How are you managing about ammunition supplies?"

The subaltern stared in amazement. A staff officer from G.H.Q.! Ye gods, what had he said?

"Well, it took our chaps fifteen hours to get here last night from the waggon lines, sir. We lost nine mules on the way. Some sank out of sight. We have to wash the shells in water before we can attempt to use them. I'm only at half strength, and working double shifts, anyway, or was, without reliefs. You can see the quality of our hotel accommodation." He pointed with his staff at a heap of straw floating inside a baby elephant shelter. "But that came up too. I mustn't forget that." He indicated a civilian hip-bath perforated by shrapnel. "*That*, sir, is a luxury. It is not a bath. It is intended for a bed. I understand there is to be a further issue of Beds, Bathtub, Officers for use of, One."

'Spectre' West threw back his cape, in order to pull out his Field Message Book 153. With pride Phillip saw the gunner's face unstiffen as he saw the seven wound stripes above the black hand, and the ribands of D.S.O. and M.C., each with a silver rosette.

Holding the book in the crook of his left arm, 'Spectre' West made some notes. "I'll do what I can, but I am an observer only," he said.

"Thank you, sir. Are you going to cross the Steenbeek?"

"I must get over somehow. I want to get into Passchendaele if I can manage it."

"Well, the best of luck to you! I'll show you the way."

It was 10 a.m., and the rain had ceased.

The three went back along the cocoanut mat, which had been laid from the teak track and gave some sort of foundation under the knee-high slop of mud.

"I think you'll find it passable, sir, if you keep to the cocoanut matting," said the gunner major.

Phillip waded in, to make sure that it was safe for Westy. Slowly he lifted his feet, one after the other, against the suction of mud above the layers of cocoanut matting, while prodding with his stick. Troops and pack mules passing that way had churned the pug, so that passage was through a sort of canal. "I think this is the best way," he called out, and the next moment sank to his waist. "It's either part of the original bed of the beek, or I'm in a shell-hole," he said, as cold water ran into his waders. It took about two minutes to move a yard, when he found the mat under his feet again. However, he had found the way.

They sloshed on to a duck-walk, while guns cracked around them, firing along a row of pillboxes. Half a mile ahead howitzer shells were droning down, raising inverted umbrellas of mud. "Our old friend Jack Johnson," said 'Spectre' West. "That must be at Kansas Cross." He looked at the map. "The Zonnebeke–Langemarck road should be in front of us. And that upright mark on the sky-line is Passchendaele church tower. We must get a move on."

The duck-walk was marked by a taped row of posts, on which hurricane lamps were hanging. Within sooty glasses flickers of flame could be seen. Other duck-walks were similarly posted. Phillip lay on his back on the walk, and emptied his waders by holding up his legs.

On these narrow ribbings of wood, carrying parties, some with Yukon packs with a band on the forehead, were slowly trailing forward. Others carried 18-pounder shells in sandbags. Stretcher-bearers in groups of four struggled against being rooted among the shell-holes: desperate, haggard men, with faces the hues of mud and smoke. Walking wounded, who had collapsed, sat head-down on the wooden path. Old German dead were lying about, swelled and waxen of face, in contrast to the recent British killed. It was always a startling sight, that of British soldiers lying dead. Although the Germans in *feld-grau* were men, too, there was no feeling from them. What was the difference? Was it the sharp-cut tunic collars, the eight buttons, the red cotton, or worsted, of the shoulder numerals? Or the sometimes shaved head, a slightly repulsive pink under the pork-pie cap? Or the knee-high leather boots? Or was there racial antagonism, deep down, quite apart from the war, as between members of the same family, his own for instance? What was it about the German dead that made him feel indifferent? The red of blood, the red of shoulder straps, the red piping of the pork-pie cap, contrasted with the modesty, the almost stupidity of khaki . . . if only he could think clearly and definitely about even one thing. And yet—the tremendous courage of the infantry, to keep on, despite this fearful horror! He himself would never again be able to stand a set attack. Almost worse was the exposure, the sleeplessness, life without horizon. He had a tent, and a stove, comparative safety, and a warm bed. It was easy to feel no fear under such conditions. But these poor sprawled and tumbled dead—had they got beyond fear, beyond pain? Lines from *The Mistress of Vision* recurred in his head.

> *When thy song is shield and mirror*
> *To the fair snake-curlèd Pain,*
> *When thou dar'st affront her terror*
> *That on her thou may'st attain*
> *Persean conquest: seek no more,*
> *O seek no more!*
> *Pass the gates of Luthany, tread*
> *the region Elenore.*

They came to Kansas Cross, and turned left-handed behind a line of field guns along the site of the old road. 'Spectre' West's destination was a brigade H.Q. at the Green House. This was sign-posted. Picking a way by tape, they came to a blockhouse around which troglodytic figures lay in a shapeless row. Mud had been clawed from these wounded men awaiting with the patience of death for ambulances, which were held up until the beech-slab road was laid from Zonnebeke.

The Green House lay below the Gravenstafel ridge, out of

direct observation of the German posts. Inside the massive concrete and steel blockhouse, with its smell of phosgene, stale smoke, sweat, and putredinous scatter of blood and brains and hair on bomb-pocked floor and walls, the Brigadier sat at luncheon with his brigade-major, intelligence officer, and a doctor. When 'Spectre' bent to enter the doorway, squeezing through the low space made smaller by a steel door buckled against the lintel, the Brigadier was about to cut into a cold partridge on a tin plate with wooden-handled French knife and fork. He had already offered to share this delicacy, out of a parcel from home, with his two officers, but they had politely refused.

Putting down knife and fork, he greeted the two newcomers curtly, for he was annoyed to be disturbed, after the emotions of the past forty-eight hours without sleep, mental relief, or physical ease. He was fifty-six years of age and had been wondering if he was about to be stellenbosched.

A couple of tommy-cookers, round tins of solidified spirit, were heating enamel mugs of coffee.

"What do you want?" he demanded, as a salvo of shells howled down and burst at Kansas Cross.

"I am from G.H.Q., General. I am Major West. I have come to hear the worst."

"How d'you do. Well, you've come to the right place. Sit down. May I offer you some bird?"

Phillip kept a straight face; it sounded like the bird, except that regular officers didn't speak like that.

"Thank you, General, but we have had our lunch. I am sorry to intrude on you, but my concern is to get the facts back to my Chief as soon as possible."

"Which side are you on?"

Again Phillip made his face blank. Did the old boy think they were German spies?

"O A, General."

"Oh, you're one of Jack Davidson's spies. Well, if you'll excuse me, I'll get some tuck down my throat. My intelligence officer will tell you what you want to know."

The captain with blood-shot eyes spoke slowly, with breaks to smooth his forehead with a hand. The march-up had been late, owing to some of the taped and lantern'd duck walks being shelled, as well as crushed and dislocated by mule packs. It took place in the total obscurity of a rainy night, without moon or stars. In places the laden infantry had lost direction. Some, stumbling apart from their platoon files only so much as a yard, had sunken helplessly into shell-holes and been drowned. The survivors had gone on, each man holding to the knapsack of the man in front, to arrive at the tape line, after more than fourteen hours' continuous going, in no condition for the fight. Some had arrived after zero hour. Those who, emerging from the lines of pill-boxes captured five days previously by other troops, had tried to follow a weak and fitful creeping barrage, but failed. Many of the shells of the barrage had fallen short among the little groups trying to wind a way round shell-holes lipped with water. The H.E. shells, which formed a fair part of the barrage, buried themselves deep in the mud and so limited their effect. Without proper guidance from the barrage, the infantry had come up against belts of new wire, thirty yards in breadth, and been shot down where they stood, unable to lie down because they were fixed to their knees in mud. Their Lewis guns were totally useless, they got clogged.

"I can offer you café-au-lait," said the Brigadier, with a sign to his batman.

The doctor said that some of the wounded had later managed to get back to the pill-box line from where they had started. These pill-boxes were now overfilled with wounded who had received no attention since they had crawled into shelter the day before. Other wounded men were still lying out.

"Where are the stretcher bearers, doctor?"

"A few are still on their feet, sir, but most have worked themselves to a standstill, during forty-eight hours without sleep or rest."

"How many do you consider are wanted, to get in the wounded on your brigade front?"

"Owing to the state of the ground, four reliefs will be required to carry a wounded man on a stretcher to the dressing station under Hill 40 near Zonnebeke station. They will take up to four hours for the double journey, provided the rain does not increase. There are about two hundred stretcher cases."

"When you say four reliefs do you mean each relief to be four men?"

"Yes. Sixteen bearers to get a stretcher to the dressing station."

"And two hundred stretcher cases?"

"Yes, sir."

"What about German prisoners?"

"There were, and are likely to be, none."

"You'll need about a thousand men." 'Spectre' wrote in his book. Then, "Before I go, I'd like to know exactly where the new wire belts are. I'll make some notes, first, with your permission, General."

He wrote down the map reference, then giving the book to Phillip, said, "Write at my dictation, if you please."

Of Flandern I yet uncaptured. Ravebeek waist-deep morass 30 to 50 yards wide. 300–400 yards east of morass on line Wallemolen—Cemetery—Wolf Farm—Wolf Copse—to Bellevue spur; thence Duck Lodge and Snipe Hall belt of continuous low wire 25–40 yards wide. Behind this belt mebus chain further protected by new apron-fence wire. Main resistance comes from m.g. teams concealed in shell-holes untouched by artillery fire and hard to detect. Reserves from division put in unaware of this wire by BACON failed, but troops were held back by HAM on Gravenstafel spur. Situation static 1.45 p.m.

"Thank you." He signed the notes, and they went out into the rain.

After a visit to another brigade H.Q. 'Spectre' West made his way, followed by Phillip, along the Zonnebeke road, for about a mile. Timber baulks were being laid beyond the dressing station at Hill 40. Behind the rise they turned left-handed, past the ruins of the station, and made directly for the line. Tired bullets buzzed and sighed down. The ground, which was sandy, and made fair going, had been in enemy hands less than a week before; German dead, fully equipped, even to hairy cowhide packs, lay everywhere, some still holding bayoneted rifles. They were the *sturm-truppen* of the 4th Reserve Guards division whose attack on 4 October, set for 6.10 a.m., had been boxed up by the Australians who had attacked at 6 a.m.

"Where are we going, Westy?"

"I am going as far as I can go without being shot. Do you wish to turn back?"

"No, *mein prächtig kerl!* How about a spot of lunch?"

"Not for me. This is the Roulers railway embankment." He looked at his map-case. "Just north of Nieuwenmolen railway crossing, at Tyne Cot, the Germans still hold the Flandern I position. The Second West Pennine division holds this sector, and I want to see how far they have got." He did not say that the fifth step, planned to be taken in less than forty-eight hours, was based on the assumption that the wire was non-existent along Flandern I, and that the last line of *Mannschafts-Eisenbeton-Unterstände* (*mebus* to the Staff, pill-box to the fighting soldier) had already been captured.

The railway entered what had been a cutting, but now was a prolonged mounding of earth like a scar, strung with wild loops of half-buried rusty wire, in the slope of rising ground to the sky-line. A German trench crossed the cutting. This, said a notice, was *Daring Crossing*, the Red Line. The trench had been deep, and revetted with posts and rough basket-work of willow, but the bombardment of the previous week had smashed, buried, and upturned most of it. A muddy twisted tape lay along it. They must now be close to the front line, thought Phillip, following behind 'Spectre' West. Did he know where he was going? If the attack the day before had failed, wasn't this still the front line? As though the same thought had come to him, the older man stopped, and looked at his map.

"So far as I can make out, we are about three hundred yards from what was the front line yesterday before the attack. I think perhaps instead of going on up the cutting, we should strike north-east, along Flandern One, until we meet with our fellows."

This entailed a scramble over the yellow sandy soil, on top of which was a clear view of a straight road with tree-stumps and broken cottages along a line which ended at a tower startlingly high. There in front was Passchendaele!

'Spectre' West studied it through field-glasses. "It looks as though it was once even taller," he said. "I wonder if the bells are buried below in the rubble, or have they been taken away. They found Messines bell, you know, the big tenor, and Plum presented it to the mayor. Well, we must get on."

Following up the German trench, they came to an out-post in a shell-hole. "Is this the front line?"

"One on'm," replied a Lancashire voice.

"Do you know who is on your flank?"

"The man in charge. Over yon." He jerked his head.

"Where are the Germans?"

"Doan't know, chum."

"Have you seen any?"

"Aye, some's about."

"Why are you here, and not going forward? The way seems clear."

"Officer told us stop 'ere."

"Where is he?"

"Doan't know, chum."

"A second-line territorial division, first time in action," said 'Spectre' West to Phillip.

A tin hat bobbed above the rim of a shell-hole twenty yards away. "Hullo there! Keep down, I say. You'll give the position away. Who are you, the relief?"

'Spectre' West walked over. "Halt! Stay where you are! I've got you covered!" Two rifles were raised out of the shell-hole.

"You should be looking for the enemy. Where are the Germans? What is holding you up?"

"We were ordered to remain here, sir, after withdrawing this morning."

"Why did you withdraw?"

"We got about half a mile forward without much opposition, then emma gees enfiladed from Defy Crossing over there." He pointed to the right. "Then we saw field guns being turned round. We couldn't deal with them, owing to the Lewis guns being clogged, and they were out of range of rifle grenades. When they fired at us over open sights, the order to withdraw was given. Since then, we've held this line."

"Has there been any firing?"

"None in front of us, sir, since this morning."

"Get your men out of shell-holes and come with me."

Strung out in file, a score of men under their young subaltern followed 'Spectre' West along the road. It was passable, and gave some sort of cover from the débris of tree trunks and stumps. Most strangely, there was no firing on the ridge; but from the north-west, in the unseen lower ground, came intermittent machine-gun fire. After going forward about eight hundred yards they halted, while 'Spectre' West looked at his map. He said to Phillip,

"If we had two battalions, we could clear the Hun out of the pill-boxes along these spurs from behind," pointing to the map which showed indentations in the contours of higher ground rising from the swampy areas of the Ravebeek. "So far, it looks as though the Hun has taken his troops from the ground here to reinforce his mebus groups. We'll go on, and see what happens. In file, ten paces between each man."

After another half-mile they halted again. He beckoned the Lancashire Fusilier subaltern to his side.

"In front of us should be the Flandern Two position. I want you to deploy your men, one half-section on the right of this road, the other on the left, and move forward in extended order fifty yards behind me. Do not fire unless you are fired on first. This is a reconnaissance, not an offensive, patrol. I shall go on ahead, down the road. Phillip, will you come with me."

The trench was not held. It was unwired. The tower of the church was now large. To the right Phillip could see, over the rubble of cottages and houses lining the road, a countryside of green fields and woods. It was strange to see, even a couple of hundred yards away, grass and hedges. It was rather ominously quiet. Perhaps the village was already held by units which had taken the pill-box line overlooking the Ravebeek? Perhaps Passchendaele was taken at last? How strange, and yet so ordinary.

They entered through the ruins of the village proper. Nothing happened. The church was a great pile of bricks, out of which arose the peppered tower, with holes in it, through which low-trajectory shells had entered, some to burst on impact, others, with delay-action fuses, to pass through.

"We are now about a mile in rear of the Flandern One position," said 'Spectre' West, looking at the map, "still held by the Germans. Yet here we are, through the Switch Line, Flandern Two, which comes back at right angles from Flandern One, north of Fürst farm on the Bellevue spur. The Second Anzac Corps, with the First East Pennine and Second West Pennine divisions, is more or less back on the starting tape." He marked the map. "Between them and Flandern One is a new belt of wire, then a fence of new apron wire around each pill-box in a line of mebus still occupied by the enemy." He wrote in his message book; closed it.

"We must go back and report the situation, as soon as we can. We must not be seen, lest we advertise the fact to the enemy that there is a gap in his line. I think we should remove our helmets, too. It is known by Intelligence that there is at least one fresh division, the Sixteenth 'Iron', on the way here, if it hasn't arrived already at the mebus line from the Ravebeek to the Poelcapelle-Westroosebeke road." He pointed to German positions marked on the map in red, and the approximate British line in blue. "Right! We shall now withdraw down the

road, in single file. Bring in your men, will you, Mr. Dixon?"
He folded his map.

A moment later Phillip cried, "No——No——!" but warning
came too late: upon the whistle, in the platoon commander's
mouth, a blast was blown, while he looped an arm with his
fingers on his tin-hat, the sign of recall. "Keep quiet, you fool!"

The patrol had crossed Flandern II and the 58-metre rise—
the highest ground on the ridge—and was about to leave the
road to go direct over the crater zone to Keerselaarhoek cemetery
when a machine gun opened up from the direction of Defy
Crossing, and by the direct crack of one bullet 'Spectre' West
knew instantly, before he could think, that he was hit.

He was a shadow looking down at his body on the ground.
With calm remote wonder he thought, *poor little body*. He was
distantly aware of other figures speaking but could neither see nor
hear them. This phenomenon was outside life. The shadow of
himself dissolved, and he was suspended in pale blue serenity
above the body he saw lying far below, as though asleep. His
entire being was remote in the thought, *That is not me*. He saw
only the cratered ground, no other figures.

Kneeling on the wet sand, Phillip said, "Where are you hit,
Westy?" which afterwards he thought rather a silly question.
No reply. The pale eye stared as though unseeing. "There's a
hole there, sir," said one of the men, pointing to the top of the
cape. Phillip unbuttoned it, kneeling by a face the hue of tallow.
His brain felt clear, his determination was without inner flurry.
He opened the tunic, there was a tear in the cloth above the
M.C. riband. Pulling away the field dressing, he gave it to Dixon
to hold. Then opening the shirt he saw a similar tear in the vest
beneath, stained with blood. The vest had to be slit by a clasp
knife, and there in the white flesh was a puncture through
which a bubble of blood swelled and subsided irregularly. It
broke, there was a sighing sound, and Westy's eye was opening.

"Don't try and speak, Westy! It's only a little wound, through
the top part of the lung only. You'll be all right!" To the others,
"Lift him up, gently now. Gently, gently! No, don't open the
field dressing yet. Keep it clean. Keep his arm down."

"I can't get his tunic off unless I lift his arm, sir."

"Then cut the tunic. Take your time. Slit it gradually.
Well done!"

The wound was small at the back. He felt a surge of joy. "The bullet went clean through!"

"The trouble may be internal bleeding, sir."

"Have you done any medical work?"

"A little, sir. In the Boy Scouts."

"Good man! Yes, lucky it's the top of the lung; though, as you say, it may be bleeding inside. Can you hear me, Westy?"

'Spectre' West moved each arm and leg in turn, and the knowledge that he was able to move them gave him impulse to say, "Where am I hit?"

"Just a slight puncture below the collar bone. I'm going to put on a dressing."

He made a muddle of it, and was going to try again when the helper said he knew how to do it. Phillip watched him passing the dressing bandolier-fashion around the shoulder. When the tunic was buttoned again, he said, "It'll be growing dark in an hour or so. Then we'll get you down, Westy."

His face less ghastly, 'Spectre' West said, "Listen carefully, Phillip, until I have finished speaking. Take my marked map in my map-case just as it is and do not open it. Take my field message book. Keep both dry. Go at once to the Town Major of Ypres, in the old prison, and ask for my driver. Tell him to take you immediately to Advanced G.H.Q. and there report to OA——"

"Where is that, Westy?"

"I asked you not to speak. The driver knows the way. If you do not find him, get a car and go at once to Westcappelle railway siding. That is about twenty miles west of Ypres, near Dunkerque. Ask for Colonel Firling, of OA. If he is not there, ask for Brigadier-General Davidson, of OA. Explain what you have seen, and what I have told you. OA—Operations 'A'. Now go."

"Shall I help get you back, first?"

"Go, damn you! Go!"

"Right, sir. I'll see you later." Then to the platoon commander, "Detail men to take Major West to the first-aid post. And send back a report that Flandern Two is unoccupied. Everything, in fact. Good luck, everyone. Au revoir, Westy."

"Go!"

Voiding thought on what would happen when he got out of the shell-hole, his mind set on his mission, he slithered into an adjoining hole, then rolled over its sandy lip into another. No

clakkercrack of emma gee—jubilation—up the old Bloodhounds,
—come on Cranmer!—fancy me, Phillip Maddison, carrying
dispatches to G.H.Q.——

With no interruption, filthy, hot, and wet with sweat, he got
through the cemetery, with its tangle of rusty iron spiked fencing,
monuments, and marble-chip flowers, and passing through the
out-post line, reported to a company commander about the patrol
600 yards N.W. of the cemetery. The captain had tired eyes.
Khaki figures closed round him.

"Who are you?"

"G.H.Q. Special Reconnaissance, attached Operations."

"How do I know you're not a spy?"

"Don't be such a —— fool! Do I look and talk like one?"

"Where have you come from?"

"Passchendaele. One of your platoons under a subaltern
called Dixon came with us, under orders from Major West,
G.S.O.Two, G.H.Q. He's lying out six hundred yards away,
over there. Will you please send a stretcher as soon as possible.
Now I have to get back with my report. Make way!"

Chapter 18

MOUSE TO LION

Darkness had fallen before he reached the area of wooden
tracks and walks; then, abruptly, a thousand guns opened up.
He could not see for light. He lost all sense of direction. If
only he had a prismatic compass! Again he thought how he had
scorned compass exercises at Heathmarket in the summer nights
of 1915, because "they didn't have them in the trenches".
Bloody conceited fool he had been then! A compass, of course,
would be no help to find a way across the watery morass, but it
would at least indicate in which direction lay Ypres. He tried to
imagine Westy's map, with the shape of the British line marked
in blue. Diminishing stalks of flares were discernible on three
sides, in the crashing seas of light. But where lay Ypres, where,
where, where?

He waited, telling himself not to flare up, but to remain calm.
Now, calmly to think. Was he facing a practice barrage by the
Second and Fifth Armies; or a German barrage to catch reliefs

and working parties? If the German guns were blazing into his eyes, then he had gone in a circular movement and was back on Passchendaele ridge, looking down upon the Flanders plain. In which case he was done for.

Damn that for a tale! He tried to imagine a map of the Salient, but it was no good. He nearly closed his eyes to limit the reflection of the flashes. Presently he thought that he could determine two kinds: one, white, stabbing, brief; the other, yellow, bulging, fluttery at the edges. White stabs of guns, yellow fans of howitzers.

As the barrage fire gave way to a slower bombardment he thought he could recognise a pattern in it. The field-guns appeared to be firing from a line across his front. This would fit in with his mind-map: for the heavier howitzers lined the roads out of Ypres, because they could not be hauled across the crater-zone; while most of the 18-pounders were along the west bank of the Steenbeek. Through eyes almost closed he tried to flash-spot the lines of fire. Yes, three main orange-flash lines, diminishing back—howitzers along the three main roads out of Ypres: Poelcappelle–St. Julien–Wieltzje: Frezenberg–Potijze: Menin. He was pleased with his calmness.

Yes, the flashes had a time pattern. He imagined the field-guns almost wheel to wheel, rocking on platforms just off the timber cross-tracks linking the three main roads up and down from Ypres. He was facing west.

The next problem. He knew the general direction: now for the particular one. Which track could he follow, and how could he find it without getting bogged down? If he went down an UP walk, and met exhausted troops, he wouldn't stand a chance. Pushed off, or even stepping off, he was sunk. He felt suddenly grey and weary. If only he had brought whiskey in his water-bottle. But Westy having gone on the waggon, he had, too. Pull self together, no good giving way. A five-mile walk lay before him, that was all. Ration and work parties using duck-walks would soon leave them vacant. So an UP walk would be the same as a DOWN.

He sploshed on to find one, feeling in front with his stick, advancing cautiously about a yard a minute against the suck of mud. This told him that he was already below the sandy Brood-seinde ridge. Steady now. While the slow bombardment continued, at least he would be able to see ahead through the red shadows of the night. Why red? Shells swooping overhead and bursting in front. The Alleyman must be retaliating.

He came to the head of an UP duck-walk, and waited there
for the muffled clatter of working parties to pass. Then away,
away down the corduroy path, in jubilation. He had no certainty
of where he was, until he realised that the glimmer of flares was
behind his back and over his left shoulder. That at least confirmed his mind-map: for the line turned back just before
Gheluvelt, which village was at the far end of the plateau, now
almost entirely taken—with no Alleyman guns captured. Suddenly, in the midst of bric-à-brac thoughts, in which the main
roads or wooden routes below him were serpents breathing yellow
fire and the cross-tracks were snakes scintillating in every scale,
he found himself among mounted men, mules, and limbers.
Zonnebeke! He was as good as home, he thought, as he set off
down the board track.

Thenceforward the way was hindered by a double line of
limbers glomerated with pack mules. There were descents into
holes between beech slabs, striking knee and thigh. At a cross-
track he lost direction, and trying a short cut was nearly
bogged down in what later he decided must have been the
Hanebeek in Sans Souci valley. Somehow he got back to the
Frezenberg board-road, wildly grateful to God for his luck. Once
on the beech track it was fairly level going, and when daylight
came he had passed most of the howitzer batteries east of the
ramparts of Ypres.

The Town Major was not yet in his office in the prison building. He had a billet in the Ramparts, said the corporal turned
out of bed. He said he knew nothing about a Major West's
driver. "We get hundreds, sir, coming and going. But the
Major may know."

"It's extremely urgent. Will you get in touch with him
immediately?"

"He's not on the telephone."

"Then send a runner, why not?"

The corporal smiled. "You don't know the Major, sir, like I
do. I couldn't very well upset his routine, sir. Sharp at nine pip
emma, he'll be here."

"But I can't wait two hours. I have to get to G.H.Q. I am
supposed to have a car waiting here for me, or rather for my
superior officer, who has been wounded. We got into Passchendaele yesterday afternoon."

"It's not really anything to do with me, sir."

"Will you inform the Town Major at once that the deputy of Major West, G.H.Q., is here, and urgently needs to get to Westcappelle."

"I'm afraid you've come to the wrong place, sir. I can't help you. This office deals only with area billeting, and matters like that. We're under the Area Commandant."

"Will you get him by telephone, then?"

"Well, sir, it's hardly my——"

"Ask at once for the Area Commandant. It is extremely urgent."

After some buzzing of the box, and much holding-on, this authority was apparently obtained. He went forward to take the transmitter, but the corporal said, with hand over mouth-piece, "Just a minute, sir, they're fetching 'im——" and turning his back, went on listening.

"Yes, sir. This is Town Major Ypres' office speaking. I have here an officer just come in who says it's extremely urgent that he gets at once to G.H.Q. He wants a motorcar to be placed at his disposal. He says he expected a driver to be here."

The corporal seemed to be listening to someone at the other end. It took over a minute. At last he said, "Very good, sir," respectfully. Then turning to Phillip, "Would you mind giving me your name and unit, sir?" Phillip did so, and the corporal repeated the words over the telephone.

After a period of silence, while the corporal listened again, Phillip said, "What's happening?"

"I was told to hold on, sir."

More time passed; then he heard the corporal say, "Very good, sir," as he put back the receiver.

"They're going to see about it, sir," he said to Phillip. "Right away."

"Who were you speaking to?"

"Someone in the Area Commandant's dug-out, sir. They said would you wait here, and they'll try and arrange transport for you right away."

He sat by the stove, half-asleep; then the corporal was saying, "You're pretty muddy, aren't you?"

"Yes, it's pretty thick up there."

The corporal had been ordered to "play up" to the caller, keep him there, until the Military Police arrived.

"Care for a wash, sir?"

"Thanks." Phillip took his revolver from the holster.

"Have you a bit of four-by-two I can clean this with?"

"I'll get it cleaned for you, sir. And how about taking off those gum boots, and letting me give them a dry? Your tunic, too, could do with a clean."

"Good idea! I suppose you haven't a spare pair of eleven-size boots, and some puttees, knocking about? I'd let you have them back."

After pulling off waders, he removed webbing equipment and tunic, slinging them on the table.

"I could dry your breeches too, sir, if you like."

Thoughts of a "Commend Card"—'this Non-Commissioned Officer showed commendable resource in depriving an armed deserter first of his boots, then of his revolver and breeches'—made the desk-soldier somewhat tremulous. "I can manage a pair of pants, and a pair of issue trousers, if you care to try them on."

"Thanks."

Phillip was sitting by the stove, resisting sleep, when the door opened and two redcaps came in, revolver in hand, followed by the A.P.M., who said as he pointed with his leather-covered short cane, "You're under arrest. Stand up, and put up your hands! You'll be shot if you attempt to escape."

He stood up, clad only in issue grey-back shirt with pink woollen pants from waist to ankle, and held out his hands with a gesture, half weariness, half amusement. Dear old Brendon, true to form.

Questions followed. Major Brendon realised that a false alarm had brought him out of bed. This fellow had nothing to do with Broncho Bill's little lot. And having recognised Phillip, he assumed the slightly amused, patronising manner of former acquaintance.

"So you want a motorcar, do you? To catch up with your unit, what?"

"No, sir. To get to Advanced G.H.Q., Westcappelle, at once. To give a message, and report."

"Really. And you've been rolling in the mud, to make it more convincing, what?"

"I don't understand, sir."

"Don't you? Well, let me help you to understand. You've been on the spree, and you've got the wind up because your unit is due to leave camp this morning, so you thought you'd chance your arm for an army taxi, to get back to camp in time."

"No, sir. I knew of no move when I left early yesterday morning, to go up the line with Major West. I had permission for the day off from my C.O., sir."

"Who is this Major West?"

"G.S.O. Two, OA, G.H.Q., sir. He's a friend of mine, I went up with him."

"What for?"

"A sort of holiday, sir."

"So you chose to spend your spare time going up the line, eh?"

"Yes, sir. Also I wanted to be with my great friend, sir."

"How did you come to know a staff officer at G.H.Q. well enough to go for a holiday with him up the line?"

"I first met him at the battle of Loos, sir."

"Really. And you expect me to believe you?"

"It's true, sir."

"How far did you get, while on this holiday up the line?"

"Into Passchendaele, sir."

"You mean the village itself?"

"Well, the ruins, sir. Then, on the way back, Major West was hit. He ordered me to go at once to Westcappelle. I was to call here and ask the Town Major for his driver. Major West's driver, that is. I imagine that the driver would be billeted somewhere, while waiting for him."

"It sounds an extremely unlikely story to me."

"Sir, time is getting on. Will you please consider ringing up Advanced G.H.Q. at Westcappelle, and ask for Brigadier-General Davidson? He is Major West's chief."

"Oh, I don't doubt that you've got the names right, but all the same I don't believe you. As far as I'm concerned you're a deserter, and I'm going to keep you under lock and key."

"But it's my duty to get to Westcappelle, sir!"

"You can keep that story for the Area Commandant."

"Sir! With all due respect, I make a formal request to you, before witnesses, that you telephone to Westcappelle, and explain that when Major West G.S.O. Two, attached OA, was hit, he handed over his information to me. Also that when I left him yesterday evening, he was lying in a shell-hole four hundred yards north-west of—of—of——" His voice broke, and tears fell.

He recovered himself at once, and wondered if it would help to convince Brendon if he showed him the message book and map case—which he had kept in his haversack, slung over his shoulders like a valise to keep out of the wet on the way down. But Brendon would be likely to take them to the Area Commandant, and so waste valuable time. The whole point was, as Westy had said, new wire had been put up in front of the Bellevue mebus line; and also around each pill-box, to keep phosphorus-bombers and rifle-grenadiers beyond range. The frontal attack planned for tomorrow morning would not have a hope, with howitzer shells burying themselves in the mud. The only way was round the flank, isolating the German garrisons in the pill-box line by getting behind them, on the higher ground.

"If only it wasn't you," said Brendon, not unkindly, as he sat down opposite Phillip, and opened his cigarette case. "You were a harum-scarum sort of chap at Heathmarket, and hadn't the slightest idea of anything."

"I admit that, sir. My only soldiering, such as it was, had been at the front."

"Sarcastic, eh?"

"No, sir. I meant in the way the R.S.M. of the Lilywhites, when we came up to reinforce the First Brigade, during First Ypres, in the woods off the Menin road, said, 'It'll be a good thing when all this is over, and we can get back to real soldiering'."

"Good for him," said Brendon. "That's the spirit! Well, I'll tell you what I'll do. I'm going to take you before the Area Commandant. I'm inclined to believe part of your story. Now get properly dressed and we'll see General Ludlow."

"It's General Davidson, sir, of OA."

"General Ludlow is the Area Commandant."

Brig.-General W. R. Ludlow was out when they got to his headquarters. "You'll have to wait until he returns."

"But I have urgent information, sir. Why can't I be allowed to telephone?"

"I might have believed you, if you hadn't gone too far, and put in that bit about getting into Passchendaele village," said Brendon. "You see, I happen to have read the latest situation report! No! You'll stay here, with me, until the General returns. I'm putting you in charge of an officer, who will be responsible for your carcase. Tell my groom," he said to the sergeant, "to bring round my charger now." He went to the lavatory.

When the horse arrived, Phillip said to the groom, "I'll just try this for the major a moment," and vaulting into the saddle, kicked in his heels, and galloped away.

While he was cantering along the grassy verge of the road to
Dunkerque, the Commander-in-Chief, at his H.Q. in Montreuil,
told a meeting of war correspondents that the failure of the battle
of Poelcappelle two days before had been due solely to mud.
"We are now practically through the enemy's defences," he said.
"The enemy has only flesh and blood against us, not 'blockhouses'; they take a month to make."

His first feeling was of dream-like strangeness that he was
where he was, his voice was hardly of himself, with the thought
that they must see through him as nothing. His former belief in
himself as someone above the ordinary ruck left him. He was
quivering with the long ride, following the exhaustions of the
previous night. He answered the Brigadier-General's questions,
wondering if some were traps, because the Colonel had asked
almost the same questions already. They must be testing his
truthfulness.

"A yard in *ten* minutes, did you say?"

"Yes, sir, that is what the Brigadier in the Green House said
to Major West. 'Some of my men in the Ravebeek below Bellevue
took ten minutes to advance a yard, and were sitting ducks'."

"And Bellevue is now wired, you say?"

"Yes, sir, belts of wire twenty-five to thirty yards deep."

"In front of the mebus line?"

"Yes, sir. Well in front of the pill-boxes. *And* the pill-boxes
themselves are wired."

"In addition to the twenty-five–thirty-yard belt?"

"Yes, sir."

"Show me on this map."

Again the points were gone over. Then, "Have you had any
sleep since yesterday morning?"

"No, sir."

"When did you last have some food?"

"I think it was the day before yesterday, sir."

"I'll have some sandwiches sent in at once. And some coffee?
I think I must ask you to dictate immediately a report of what
you've told us. Colonel Firling will take you to the next coach,
where you will be undisturbed."

The idea of dictating harassed him. He felt he would have
nothing to say. He was taken into an office, everything like new,
polished, neat, exact. A table with pens, roll-blotter, new nibs,
pencils, erasers. Blue pencil, red pencil. Thick foolscap paper

embossed with the Royal Arms, and in small black raised letters,
G.H.Q. France.

"I'll send in a stenographer. Is there anything else you want?
That's the door, should you want to wash."

"Sir, would it be possible for me to write my report? It won't
take me long."

"By all means! I'll leave you to it. Ring this bell if you want
anything. I'll be in the next coach. Come in when you've done,
will you."

Sandwiches came in, with a bottle of beer, corkscrew with
stag's-horn handle, polished tumbler, and table napkin. *Chicken*
sandwiches! He wolfed them, swallowed Bass' Pale Ale.

What he wrote he did not know: his pen moved fast over paper.
At last the account was written, signed, and taken to the next
coach, to be typed. Colonel Firling invited him to sit down. He
spoke about Westy, calling him Harold. He was surprised to
know that the Colonel knew about the Lone Tree business at
Loos. Then a half-bald major with large grey eyes and prominent
teeth came in, wearing an R.F.C. tunic without wings, and
Phillip was introduced to him. His mind did not take in the
name, but the Colonel called the newcomer Maurice. He had
some aeroplane photographs. The Colonel looked at them
through a magnifying glass. Then he passed one to Phillip, and
stood over him in a brotherly way while he looked at it. The
chief points were marked by arrows in Chinese white, with names.
He saw *Passchendaele, Flandern II, Keerselaarhoek, Augustus Wood,
Tiber Copse,* and others.

"Can you indicate just where you were when Harold was hit?
This was taken while you were writing your report. The glass
makes the detail plainer, I think."

He peered through the lens.

"You said about twenty men made up the patrol of the
Lancashire Fusiliers of the 197th Brigade. As you will see,
there is no appearance of any casualties. Of course they may
have been taken prisoner. On the other hand, they may have
got back to our lines. If so, we should be hearing before very
long."

"But the congestion, sir! The wounded are lying literally
wound to wound, and hundreds more outside trying to drag
themselves under cover!"

"If Harold hasn't lost too much blood, he might have walked
in, don't you think?"

The Brigadier-General returned. "Do sit down," he said genially. "I was most interested to read your report. You must look at it, Maurice," to the R.F.C. major. He went on to ask Phillip about his service; and on hearing that he had fought with the London Highlanders at Messines in '14, said that the regiment had done as well as any troops in France.

After his report had been typed, he read it through and signed the top copy with a signature that didn't look like his own. What he had said was pretty awful. Rifles useless; Lewis guns useless; wire-belts too broad to bomb across; wounded left out to die; hundreds brought in to Kronprinz and Waterloo regimental aid posts when barrage opened on morning of 9th; four hundred men wanted for stretchers on 146 Inf. Bde. front alone; weak, erratic barrage-fire; effect of counter-battery work nil; bayoneted rifles stuck in ground to mark wounded quivering in the gusts. Cries for help coming from all over the watery wastes below Wallemolen, Bellevue and the knuckles of the Passchendaele ridge. While half a mile above, on comparatively dry ground, on either side of the crest lay the equivalent of a private road, a deserted road, a road lying unclaimed by both sides, who were stuck either in concrete or in black mud, intent on old tactics which had confirmed the battle almost as an immovable object struck by an irresistible force. The way on the afternoon of 10 October to the Ridge had been open, behind the deadlocked lines, the one in concrete within barbed wire, the other rooted in swilling mud.

What *had* he said?

"Perhaps you'd like to lie down and sleep before dinner? I'll show you your quarters. Your division is now on the way to join Third Army. We'll send you down tomorrow, to Arras, by motor."

Towels, shaving kit, two hair-brushes; somebody else's pyjamas laid out on the bed. Stove glowing. Wash-hand basin; shelf of books. What did the Staff read? Kipling, Scott, "Old Luk-oie", Sommerville and Ross, Nat Gould, and *The New Pepys Diary*. He fell asleep with *The First Hundred Thousand*, by Ian Hay, which was about the battle of Loos but nothing like it.

The kindness of the easy-going, beltless senior officers in slacks, who called one another either by pet or Christian names. Their simpleness. They seemed to have no feeling as they discussed, almost casually, subjects other than that of the war. Of course, no "shop". But the odd thing was that when he had spoken they had listened to him, despite the return of his stammer, voice thin, hollow, hesitant, no good. The R.F.C. major had a stammer, too, and seemed almost a little foolish, in a clown-like, gentle way: large ostrich-egg-shaped face, almost protruding eyes and teeth while he balanced a glass of port wine on his bald patch and talked about Russia and Russian writers, only two of which Phillip had heard about—Tolstoi and Tourgenieff.

They all listened when he gave them his account of the Etaples mutiny, but his stutter returned with the dread twisty feeling, as he sat on his hands, as he began to feel hollow again; and his words petered out. One part of him was not in the least surprised when the R.F.C. major turned to him as their coffee cups were being filled and said, "You must write a book about what you have seen one day, when all this is over"; but another part was amazed that anyone on the Staff could say such a thing. No wonder Westy was happy among such men.

A sergeant-orderly came in. He felt a shock when he said to the Brigadier-General beside him, "The Commander-in-Chief has arrived, sir."

A quarter of an hour later, as he was smoking the second half of his cigar, he had another shock when the sergeant-orderly returned, to say, "Sir Launcelot's compliments, sir, and he would like to see Mr. Maddison now." For he realised that this was the Chief of the General Staff, referred to by the others as "the Professor".

He felt he could not get up. If he tried, he would fall. He put down the cigar, and waited for giddiness to pass.

The Brigadier-General said, "I expect you still feel rather tired after your night out, but you will find the Chief sympathetic, although he does not speak very much. He will in all probability ask you to elaborate your report, and you will find him a good listener. Shall we go?"

"To Sir Launcelot, sir?"

"Yes, he will take you to the Chief."

The Chief! The Commander-in-Chief! Sir Douglas Haig himself!

The feeling was almost that of going over the top in daylight, as he followed the Brigadier-General to another coach, before which sentries were marching up and down in light cast by arc-lamps. They were challenged; a pass-word was given and accepted. They entered a coach.

The C.G.S. had a long oval face and a moustache, seen in the light of a green-shaded lamp. He got up and said, "Hullo, Jack." Phillip was introduced, then left with the General with the star and crossed swords on his shoulder straps. The General had his typed report, on which, in blue pencil, were the initials D.H.

"The Commander-in-Chief wants to see you."

Phillip followed him through a door straight into a room where stood the figure known from a thousand thoughts and a hundred newspaper photographs, astonishingly not so tall as he had imagined, but looking at him without a smile, grey moustache brushed down and away below a straight nose dividing a face that, he thought, was very clear and straight of look on the right side, and kindly, even gentle, on the left side.

"Mr. Maddison, sir."

"Good evening, Mr. Maddison. Will you come here." Phillip came to attention, bowed slightly without realising it, and walked across a carpet with a shield woven into it to a map occupying a large part of one wall of the coach.

"Now will you show me where you went with Major West."

He did so, while a feeling of calm came over him. Dissolved was the figment of the great Field-Marshal. This man beside him was *safe*. It might almost have been Father, without the life-narrowing that Father had suffered. This father-like man was simple, and good like Father. Calm and at ease, he traced the route up the railway cutting, through the cemetery, and across no-man's-land and the road running through fallen trees to the square tower of Passchendaele church.

"It seemed to end the road, being bang in the middle of a straight perspective, sir. We got there without a shot being fired, and found the village unoccupied. The time was almost five o'clock. Major West said that with two battalions and machine guns we could have cut off the garrison of the mebus line from here"—pointing at Wallemolen—"to here"—east of Hamburg.

While the journey had been gone over in words the Field-Marshal had remained attentive and silent.

"Now will you tell me what you overheard when with Major West." When this was recounted, the Field-Marshal said,

"Now will you tell me what you yourself saw."

A feeling obstructed him: that this fatherly man, so strangely unlike the Famous Figure he had known, was more like Father than ever. Under the calm quiet scrutiny upon himself he sensed a feeling that made him doubtful, a little afraid of what he had written in his report.

"Sir—if you please, sir—I——"

"You may speak freely."

"Well, sir, I saw something of the effect of our machine-gun barrage about a hundred yards south of Passchendaele village. There was a German cemetery there, with wooden crosses, all of them 'Here rests in God an unknown German soldier'. The cross pieces were nearly all broken off about two feet from the ground, where bullets had clipped them almost in a straight row." He went on hurriedly, "Well, sir, about the terrain. The going is not so bad on the ridge, on the sandy ground, but down below it is, well, dreadful. This is not a personal complaint, sir. In fact, sir—you see, sir, it has been all right for the transport and carrying parties, because we've had something definite to look forward to every night, that is, sir, getting back to some sort of home. We knew that after a few hours we would, with luck, get back to where we could sleep. But the men going up, in slow single file, holding to one another in the darkness on the duck-boards, or across where they have been destroyed by shell-fire, take as much as fourteen hours to get from the Pilckem ridge to the Gravenstafel. I—I think they feel that they have no hope now, sir. No hope before, during, or after an attack. The mud around the old beds of the beeks is nearly up to a man's waist. And if he can get forward, his rifle or Lewis gun is useless. No hope if wounded, because he cannot crawl even into a shell-hole. In any case, sir, the shell-holes are now filled to within twelve inches of the broken rims. In fact, they connect, sir."

The Field-Marshal was silent, his gaze resting upon Phillip's face.

"All to whom I spoke, sir, said 'It's murder'. These were the rank and file, and the junior officers. I think some thought I had some sort of say in the matter of stopping the attacks, sir," he said, trying not to give way. "My ob-observations, sir, are that I heard that phrase again and again, but not as a complaint, sir. It was accepted. It was different at Etaples, when I was there for an Infantry course, last month. I must apologise, sir, if I give offence."

"I asked you to speak freely."

"Well, sir, I think that's just about all."

"Thank you, Mr. Maddison." The Field-Marshal opened the door for him. "Good night."

"Good night, sir!"

He felt exhilarated, he was free, he had crossed over the shadow line, left forever the old life. For him, Phillip Maddison, a Field-Marshal had opened a door. He thought of Father, who had always tapped on his bedroom door before entering, out of politeness, even when he had come up to cane him. But why was he crying?

While Phillip had been eating his dinner in "OA" mess, New Zealanders and Australians were taking over the sector between Bellevue and the Staden railway cutting. These troops cursed the departing "eh bah goom bastards" for leaving their own wounded lying out where they had fallen. The hardy Corn-stalks, unsoftened by a lifetime in bad air of factory, shop, and counting house, set themselves to bring in as many as they could. Four hundred bearers from one brigade of the New Zealand division were put in to clear the Second West Pennine wounded.

They were exhausted at the hour before dawn, following upon the difficult walk-up from the Pilckem ridge, but they recovered after a meal of salt beef, hard biscuit, and chlorinated water.

At 5.25 a.m. Phillip, lying awake between strange white sheets, heard distant reverberation; covering his head with a blanket, he abandoned himself to thinking about Lily, and Westy, almost twin souls.

The New Zealand division, on the right of Second Army, was at that time floundering to the attack opposite the wired pill-boxes between the Wallemolen and the Bellevue spurs. Between them and the Germans were the swamps of the Ravebeek.

The 3rd Australian Division was on their right, in the positions recently held by the Second West Pennine. It was almost the same plan of attack for the fifth step as that which had failed three mornings before. On the left of Second Army New Zealand engineers had laid, during the darkness, five coconut-matting tracks across the morass of the Ravebeek, hidden by the drizzle which turned to luminous fog the light-balls of the Germans, fired from their mebus. About zero hour, 5.25 a.m., the wind became stormy and brought drenching rain, through which the infantry struggled up the slope to the line of pill-boxes, which they had

known since the night before to be protected by deep wire en-
tanglements. There they tried to cut paths through the wire
with hand clippers, under heavy enfilade fire from pill-boxes.
The second and third waves joined them. Within a few hours
100 officers and 2,635 other ranks had fallen, among them
soldiers who had got through the 30-yard-thick wire-belt, only
to be shot against the apron tangle surrounding the 5-foot-thick
concrete pill-boxes.

After breakfast, Phillip said good-bye, and wearing a greatcoat lent to him by one of his hosts, seated himself beside the
driver of a staff Vauxhall. The hood was up, rain drove across
the green meadows and ploughed fields, shutting out the view,
which anyway would not be very interesting, he felt, as they drove
along the road to St. Omer. The destination was Arras, by way
of Hazebrouck and so to the mining area around Bethune, with
its desolate memories of Loos, when 'Spectre' West had been
wounded.

It was later he learned that the 9th Australian Brigade on the
right had got up the slopes of sandy ground, and, having suppressed machine-gun nests in shell-holes, had gone on astride the
Passchendaele road almost to the ruins of the village, where they
found some survivors of the Second West Pennine Division, under
a wounded staff officer with a black patch over one eye, who had
formed some sort of strong-point there. They were firing at
Germans retreating from the Wallemolen spur across the highway, beyond the ruins of Passchendaele.

When a runner brought back a message, at 10.50 a.m., that
the 9th Australian Brigade was holding the high ground above
the line of pill-boxes where the checked New Zealand troops
were lying, the Major-General commanding the 3rd Australian
Division at once decided to make an enveloping attack—a
right hook, as he put it—with a reserve battalion of one of his
brigades, in order to pass Passchendaele village. He was stopped
by order of the British Lieutenant-General commanding the
2nd Anzac Corps, who had made plans for another attack to take
place at 3 p.m. that afternoon, in the manner of the frontal
assault which had failed three days before, and again that
morning.

During the lapse of the four hours to 3 p.m. the Australian
troops on the crest holding the Flandern II position were being

pasted by German field-guns firing over open sights and by
machine guns and snipers. Left in the air, and facing annihi-
lation, the Australians withdrew, taking what wounded they
could across rain-swept wastes almost to their starting tapes:
whereupon the Corps plans for a frontal assault were cancelled.

By that time Phillip had arrived at Arras. 286 M was at
Wailly, at a training camp about three miles beyond the town.
Deciding to find his own way there, and look around, he ended
up at the Officers' Club. Suddenly life seemed blank, the war no
longer interesting. Mooching about the town, he heard semi-
musical noises. In one of the patched-up buildings a band was
practising. GRAND RAGTIME HOP TONIGHT ALL
WELCOME. After a drink with some gunners in the Club he
decided to take a room for the night, and accept their invitation
to dine. Afterwards they went to the dance hall. The only
"women" present were dolled-up female impersonators from
one of the local concert parties. The dance was not a scrum, as
he had imagined it would be, but taken seriously, with a Master
of Ceremonies blowing a whistle for each dance to start off, and
commands to "take your partners, gentlemen!" The female
impersonators were almost frighteningly real, with yellow curls,
stuffed bosoms, rouge, and scent. They were sometimes coy, at
other times leering. He had a half-turned-inside-out feeling,
dimly like the rough-and-smooth nightmare feelings of childhood. Or was it the stuffy atmosphere, the brassy noise, the
smell of sweat and greasy bully beef. Making his excuses to
the gunners, he walked back through a ghost town to the
Officers' Club, and went to bed, feeling lost that he was not
going up the timber tracks, into the glittering wastes of the
night.

In the darkness, a little more than forty miles to the north of
where he lay between rough brown blankets, twelve hundred
more stretcher bearers were arriving on the Anzac front to help
bring in the wounded to the bloody dressing stations known as
Kronprinz, Waterloo, and Spree. With sandbags tied round
knees, waists, and forearms, these men went out at first light to
the wire-belts which could be seen so clearly from the Gravenstafel ridge. No shots tore across the ragged brown slopes, white-
pocked with water, bestrewn with bodies drowned and drowning,
some broken and bled out, others still crying for help.

A wound is not always felt when it is received; but in the hours which follow pain can so consume the spirit that a man's life becomes elemental longing to be safe; while pictures in the mind assume such anguished need for mother, wife, friend, little children, or even to be allowed to die in the country of his birth, that his piteous cries sometimes dissolve even the iron constriction of war. Thus it was some of the Germans arose from their shell-holes, and having carried back their own wounded, moved down to their wire, and even came through it in places to help tend their enemies lying there.

Chapter 19

FLANDERS SANATORIUM

"Where did you get to, you old devil?"

Having heard, Pinnegar went on, "I had the wind up, I can tell you! I knew of course you'd gone with West, but wondered if I'd be strafed by the Colonel for giving you permission. I bet he's curious to know all about it, since the telegram came from G.H.Q.! Probably thinks you're a spy! I'd give a month's pay to have seen Brendon's face when you pinched his horse! Who did you see at G.H.Q.? Anyone in particular?"

"No. I just gave in the report, they sent me back, and here I am. What's happening?"

"Oh some bloody training for a raid the infantry's going to do. To keep them keen, said the Brigadier. Keen! They'll never be keen again. What we need is a couple of month's rest, down in the South of France. What a hope! Only senior officers get there, and then only if they have the right connexions. It's just the same as in peace time, it's all a matter of privilege."

He thought that if Darky Fenwick had said that, Teddy would have called it socialistic tripe. But Teddy had been through a lot since those days in the Angel hotel at Grantham.

"What do I do, Teddy?"

"There's nothing particular, Phil. The usual routine fatigues. Nolan has carried on quite well in your absence."

"Do you mind if I go for a ride? I feel a bit stale."

"I don't care what you do. More Cook's tours? Only don't be away too long. I mean, I think you ought to come back at night. I'm hoping leave will start again soon; it might do when we've done the raid."

On Black Prince, but without his groom, Phillip spent the days in riding about the old battlefield areas. He followed the road through Mercatel, which had been behind the German lines until the retreat to the Siegfried Stellung in March, and so to the Bapaume road. Along it to Ervillers, where Sergeant Rivett had written his graphic description of the three balloons being shot down; and so to Bapaume, now a shack town, with a double-gauge railway and great dumps. He had lunch at the Officers' Club, where he heard that a great tank and infantry school was to be set up at Albert. Most of the shot-up tanks had been salvaged from the swamps of Third Ypres and sent for repair, and then for use at the school. New tactics would be practised, for the final Great Push in the spring.

There were stories, also, of camouflaged watering-points being laid to within a few hundred yards of the front line.

He returned by way of the road to Cambrai, riding down as far as Beaumetz, then turning left-handed, crossed downland country grooved with valleys between Mory and St. Leger, and so to the site of the camp where Jack Hobart and the others of the original company had trekked, coming into green country after the winter ruination of the valley of the Ancre. There he dismounted, and stood still, pierced by memories of All Weather Jack, now lost for ever with other scenes of that happy springtime in Clover Valley. No, not lost: it lived on in his own memory, at least. It added to his life.

"The Brigade is now training with tanks," said Pinnegar, a few days later. "It's going to be some raid, in my opinion. The Brigadier's going home. Wonder who we'll have. I saw Byng today; he came to look on. You know we're in Third Army now, don't you? Have you seen the paper? There's been a hell of a drive through the Italians, at Caporetto. According to the German wireless, they've taken over a hundred thousand prisoners and three hundred guns, and have the whole bloody lot on the run. I suppose we're to do a show here, to give the Germans the idea that it's a proper push! A fat lot of reserves it'll draw from Italy!"

Orders came to move. In column of route, the company marched away at dusk, taking the Bapaume road. They bivouacked that night in Clover Valley, near the source of the

Sensee river. There they were ordered to remain during daylight, under cover of the camouflage concealing limbers and tents, the horses and mules already being scattered, each tied to its picket peg, near what cover was available. At dusk another move south, passing through Bapaume shortly after 9 p.m. and then following a track over an open rolling plateau for some miles. The night was quiet and slightly misty, with only occasional gun-fire. They crossed over the broad-gauge railway line beyond Bertincourt, and at last, weary and hungry, halted to bivouac among gloomy trees, from which, throughout the night, large drops fell upon the taut canvas tents.

The shut-in feeling of the night vanished with the sun shining down the rides and groves of a forest which covered several miles of open chalk country not unlike Cambridgeshire. Jays cried among the great oaks; holly and hornbeam, with coppery leaves still unshed, grew among the undergrowth. The screeching of jays was heard, and Pinnegar declared he had seen a squirrel.

"Cunning little beggar," he smiled. "It dodged me round a tree playing hide-and-seek for some minutes. The Flying Corps used to call this wood Mossy Face," he went on, as they lunched off glassed tongue, French bread, tinned butter, and mango chutney. "It's the shape of the ace of spades from the air. The Germans had an aerodrome in the clearing over there."

They made friends with an American doctor attached to the brigade holding the outpost line, which faced the Siegfried Stellung. The doctor asked them into his dugout to have a high-ball. Along one wall two rows of partridges were hanging by their necks from nails driven into the chalk. Each bird had a label on it, with a date.

"I guess I like my birds to hang for ten days, no more, no less," said the doctor. "I have respect for the life I have taken, sir, and consider it a dooty to treat what these birds have to give me, first as objects of sport, and then as objects of the culinary art, in an ethical manner. Does that seem strange to you, sir?"

"Not in the least, sir," replied Phillip, thinking that the doctor was ragging him. "I'm a bit of a taxidermist myself, when I'm at home."

"Is that so? Have you read Thoreau, young man?"

"No, sir, but I have read Frezenberg."

"And who is he, may I inquire?"

"Frezenberg Ridge, sir—a philosopher of nature. He wrote a book called *The Pond*, and lived mainly on boiled sea-weed."

"Wale, what d'yer know! Frezenberg. I will read his book. Meanwhile, I must express my regrets that your highball has no cracked ice, sir. Let me fill your glass."

"By all means. I like this kind of whiskey, sir. Is it American?"

"It sure is, sir. Old Crow Bourbon! Shipped under order by General Pershing himself, I guess."

Phillip brought Pinnegar with him the next time he visited the doctor's dug-out. Having been shown the partridges, Pinnegar winked at Phillip, to prepare him to observe the cunning way by which he intended to wangle some of the partridges for the mess.

"We've got a French chef from the Carlton in our company. Will you honour us at dinner tonight, captain? The chef is an expert on hashing up bully beef, if you don't mind such ordinary fare."

"Now, don't you want me to let you have some of these birds? I would be honoured if you would accept what you require, plenty more where these came from. How many boys to share the feast? Seven? That's swell! I will instruct my man to take your French chef seven of these birds shot by me on these French fields. I am honoured to know that a French chef will treat them with the respect doo to them."

"I'm afraid," said Pinnegar, "that I can only offer you Scotch with them."

"Now see here," replied the doctor, "I have some genuine chateau-bottled claret, Chateau Lafitte, '08. We will drink the wine that your Gilbert Keith Chesterton was anxious should not be diluted by water. You know the poem, I guess—in the Flood, Noah said, 'I don't care where the water goes, so long as it don't get into the wine'. I heard your Chesterton give a talk at Princeton, in '09. He was a great chuckling man. Sure, that's fixed! I will be honoured if you guys will drink Chateau Lafitte with me. Wale, I'll be seeing you boys tonight. I'll have the birds sent round by my orderly right now."

When they had left the dug-out, Pinnegar said, "A damned nice fellow, don't you agree? No bloody swank about him, like most Yanks. You know that story about the doughboy walking into a pub in Piccadilly and asking for a beer, then complaining it was flat. The barmaid said, 'I'm not surprised, we've kept it three years for you.' What's the matter, old man?"

"I think I had too much of that whiskey."

"You'll be all right. Don't forget to tell the doc. tonight how you pinched the A.P.M.'s horse!"

"Oh, damn that for a tale!"

Orders were issued that no working parties, or groups of men more than two in number, were to be seen within the Daylight Line. This was an area roughly two miles behind the British outpost line, much of it under observation from the Siegfried Stellung.

This great German fortress consisted of three lines of trench-systems, each with its front, support, and reserve trenches, all heavily wired. It was about 5,000 yards deep, and between the trench-systems were zones of battle. The main resistance trenches were sited on reverse slopes, out of sight of attacking troops, who would thus appear, to the Germans, on the sky-line. Acres of wire, making salients, some hundreds of yards deep, lay before the main system, with batteries of machine-guns sited beneath ferro-concrete cover, to fire down the sides of the wire-salients.

The trenches were 12-ft wide, and 18-ft. deep, with sloping sides to stop tanks. Deep underground shelters ran for miles beneath the trenches.

Phillip was sent for by the Brigade-major. A young officer was in the dug-out, looking to be about his own age. He had a round face, almost chubby, a small dark moustache, and wore a Burberry. Phillip got a shock when the Brigade-major introduced him to the newcomer. "This is the Brigadier."

The Brigadier was most friendly; then he sat back and let his Brigade-major talk.

"You have been on an infantry course at Etaples, haven't you? How would you like to be an instructor at the new Infantry-cum-tank Training School at Albert?" When Phillip did not reply, the Brigade-major said, "Well, think it over. Discuss it with your C.O. Or anyone else you like. No hurry. I hear, quite unofficially, of course, that you did a Dick Turpin ride on one of the Provost Marshal's staff horses to Westcappelle. How did you get on?"

"Very well, sir. I had to borrow a horse, as the motorcar was otherwise engaged."

"But you managed to get to Westcappelle?"

"Yes, sir. I spent the night with 'OA', and the next morning was brought here by motorcar."

"All very hush-hush, I suppose?"

"Well, sir, I was only a messenger boy, really."

"Is 'Spectre' West all right, d'you know?" asked the Brigadier. Another shock: on the left breast of his tunic was the maroon riband of the Victoria Cross, beside the white-purple-white of the Military Cross.

"I haven't heard yet, sir."

The Brigade-major said, dismissing him, "Well, think about that instructor's job at Albert. No need to make up your mind for a week or so. Ask your pals' opinions, if you like."

"Very good, sir."

He asked Pinnegar about it. Did they want to get rid of him? He felt he did not care much, if they did. But what was the idea?

"Give you a rest, I expect, Phil. After all, you've been out here, off and on, since 'fourteen."

He felt depressed. Perhaps they had heard about his drinking. They might even send him home, to help train a Young Soldiers' battalion. Eighteen-year-old boys, like himself in 1914. There was no life at home.

It was now dull and misty weather, between autumn and winter. All was quiet on the Western front. Third Ypres had ended, with the capture of Passchendaele by the Canadians.

Well within the Daylight Line dumps of baled hay and 4-bushel sacks of oats were being made at night, all of them carefully camouflaged. Also, mysterious shallow pits were dug in darkness, and concealed by day. If these were for batteries, where were the guns?

"It's all a huge bluff, in my opinion," said Pinnegar, "to make the Germans think we're going to attack. How the hell can we, with damn-all troops, *and* against the Hindenburg Line?"

One day Phillip went round the trenches with him. They were built up with sandbags, carefully and strongly wired; sumps under the duck-boards; deep shelters, all kept tidy. From one fire-bay he saw Germans walking about behind their trenches, easily within rifle range.

"Isn't there any sniping, Teddy?"

"Not so far as I know. Suits me."

They walked above and beside the communication trench. The grasses were wan and grey, with thin docks and starved-looking burrs; but here and there beside the trench grew tussocks of cock's-foot, blue-green, where passers-by during the early spring had urinated. That showed what a Garden of Eden it was, he thought.

Covey after covey of partridges flew up, with whirring wings.

At night, noises of the German light railway engine drawing trucks from Ribecourt to Havrincourt, behind their front line, could be heard distinctly. Occasionally a flare arose, and made a cocoon-like haze in the distance. Wood owls were now calling among the bare trees, softly, with bubbling cries, as though the young birds of that year were finding their mates, with whom they would remain until mustard gas or shell-fire did them part. But it was not England, he thought, dreaming of springtime days with Desmond over the Seven Fields, the woods around Fox Grove golf course, and farther into Kent, on bicycles. It would never again be the same England.

The days were misty, leaves fell laden with moisture, there was no wind. Still no official news of an attack. The gun sections were in their emplacements, life was the same from day to day. Except that, according to Pinnegar, lots of badgeless officers were constantly going round the trenches, wearing tin-hats covered with brand-new sandbag material, and brand-new tommy's tunics.

"Obviously staff wallahs! Their moustaches alone, and those ill-fitting tunic collars, would give them away, even if they'd left their walking sticks and Thermos flasks behind!"

Field guns were moved forward at night, to just behind the front line. They lay silent under camouflage. He heard something said about sound-ranging and battery boards, and thought that these must be data of range and direction prepared "off the map", since none of the guns had registered.

Pinnegar continued to scoff, saying that the idea of an attack was a huge bluff. Some of his "odd-looking wallahs" who went round the lines, usually at night, carried apparatus that was obviously nothing else but disguised cinema cameras, he declared. And the letters on their badges, F.S.C., although they said it was Field Survey Company, were more likely to be Field Salvage Company. He wouldn't put it past Lloyd George to have sent them out to survey the old iron which would be lying about when

the war was over, hundreds of millions of tons of it. There would
be a world shortage of steel for years. He was born and bred in
Birmingham, he wasn't bluffed! The war wouldn't last for ever,
and when the Germans cracked, they would crack suddenly, and
then—steel! The collection of freaks and long-haired Weary
Willies in uniform were only disguised old-iron merchants!

As a fact, they were flash-spotters and sound-rangers. With
telephones, directors, telescopes, buzzers, and wiring schemes between two and sometimes three points, flash-spotting of enemy
guns was taking the place of orthodox registration. Flash spotting
depended upon the simultaneous recording of the flash, as the
shell left the muzzle of the gun, at two or three stations at the
end of a measured base.

Sound ranging, which was more intricate, depended on the
time-record, made on a cinema film from three or more stations,
of the spread of the sound-wave of discharge. Adverse conditions
for sound-ranging were a contrary wind, and possible confusion
of shell-wave with gun-wave; mist and fog prevented flash
spotting.

The invention of the Tucker Microphone made it possible to
discriminate between the records of several batteries firing at
once, while by observing the shell-bursts and noting the time of
flight the calibre of a gun could be deduced.

Thus German batteries were being located, so that they could
be accurately swamped by counter-battery shells at zero hour;
and the British batteries doing the job could remain silent until
the moment of assault.

The new Brigadier became known as the Boy General. He
was said to be twenty-three years old, the youngest General in
the British Army. His substantive rank was lieutenant in one of
the two regular battalions of a North Country regiment. He had
held all temporary ranks to lieutenant-colonel, before getting a
Brigade.

Riding into Bapaume one day, Phillip went to the Officers'
Club, and saw the Boy General there. And to his surprise, the
General recognised him, saying with a smile, "I hope you won't
steal my horse this time, Maddison!"

"Not while I've got Black Prince, sir!"

Then, moving away, he felt awful. The General would think
he was familiar. Ought he to apologise? Oh, why had he been
such a fool as to answer like that?

286 M.G. Coy B.E.F.   14 Nov. 1917

Dear Mother

I am writing this in an Officers' Club somewhere in France. I must apologise for not having written much during the past three months. I hope all is well at home. Will you give my love to everyone, and say I'll write when I can. I expect you've seen by the papers what's been happening, more or less, out here. Personally speaking, no news is always good news.

Will you please order, for every day until further notice, a copy of *The Times*, from Hanson's in Randiswell? *I do not want any of them posted to me out here*. Will you please keep them for me, meanwhile look at the Roll of Honour every day and look for the name of Major H. J. West, D.S.O., M.C., which may be under (a) The General List, (b) General Staff, (c) Gaultshire Regiment (which you will find under the heading of Infantry). He may be listed under Captain H. J. West, or Major, or possibly Lt.-Col. (He is the one I told you about, whose parents keep, or used to have, The Grapes tavern in Lime Street, in the City. But I *do not* want you or Father to call there, or at the War Office: just look in *The Times*, please). If you see the name, which may be under Killed, Wounded, Missing, or more likely Wounded and Missing, will you then cut out the whole Roll of Honour of that day, and post it to me without delay? I do hope the foregoing is clear.

We don't hear much out here, once we have moved away from former associations. This is all I can say at the moment, for reasons you will no doubt understand.

I have heard neither from Desmond nor Eugene for some considerable time now. Leave may begin shortly, but I do not know for certain. I saw Ching twice during the summer, or late summer, once when I was on a course, and another time just before he was going up the line; we didn't speak, as I only had a glimpse of him. There are many hundreds of thousands of faces out here, and it is rare to meet anyone you knew in the old days. Now I must do some work. Black Prince is still going strong, and everything is pretty cushy.

Yours affectionately,
Philip (with one "l ").

Also love to Father, Elizabeth, Doris, Mrs. Feeney, Gran'pa, Aunt Marian, and all who ask after the donkey boy—real donks this time!

Having signed the addressed envelope, as self-censor, and posted it, he sat down to look at the papers. Bonar Law, whoever he was, had asked for and got without discussion a new vote of credit of £400,000,000 for the war. The National Debt,

whatever that was when it was at home, was now £5,000,000,000.
It had been £648,000,000 at the outbreak of war. I suppose I've
got some of it in my bank, he thought, with satisfaction.

> The scene in the House of Commons, as Bonar Law made his
> speech with rapidity and remarkable lucidity, in a matter-of-fact tone
> of voice, and with only half a sheet of notepaper to aid his memory,
> was most striking.
>
> Never has there been seen in the House of Commons so many
> senior members. It was truly a gathering of the Fathers of the Nation.
>
> The young and the strong must continue to go forth and try to
> make the crooked straight by brute force, despite the suffering to
> themselves and sacrifice of life.

What utter tripe, as Teddy would say. He threw down the
paper.

While he sat there, two officers began talking a couple of
yards away. One spoke about the "sloppy discipline" he had
found in the line when his battalion had taken over.

"Huns were apparently allowed to stroll about behind their
trenches, in full daylight. I soon altered all that. I organised
the battalion snipers, and waited until a score or more of Huns
were sunning themselves openly. My men got some juicy targets
—forty-two entries in the Game Book the first two days."

Bloody fool, he muttered. It was what Teddy would call
robbing an incubator. He moved away to another chair, and
tried not to think about it. "The Game Book". "The only good
Hun is a dead Hun." But they did not understand. With sinking
feelings he recalled what cousin Willie had told him about the
German officer after Christmas 1914 sending over a message one
night, asking them to keep under cover, as their machine guns
were to fire at midnight during a staff inspection.

But it was the same spirit almost everywhere. In the paper
was an account of a row in the House of Commons, over a motion
in favour of peace by negotiation supported "by a minority of
only twenty-one", among them being names he had heard Aunt
Theodora, when a Suffragette, speak of as "lights in darkness"—
John Burns, Ramsay Macdonald, Charles Trevelyan, James
Thomas, "the railwaymen's secretary", and Philip Snowden,
who

> has none of the ingratiating manner of Ramsay Macdonald. Wholly
> unconciliatory, his bitter jibes and defiant expression when referring
> to what he is pleased to call "Die-Hards", arouse only contempt.

Bitter jibes were no good, even in the mind; it led to game-booking the game-bookers. One must try to be generous about people and their faults. Often the faults came from matters that were not their own fault. How magnanimous Lily had been about Keechey, who had cold-heartedly seduced her. To forgive was to be forgiven. He sighed; and was about to take up *The Bystander* when he saw, in one of the armchairs, a familiar red face under unbrushable sticking-up short fair hair. Cox, of all people! The last time he had seen that almost blistered face was just before July the First, at Albert. Cox had told a lie, claiming to be senior to himself, and thereby, as the supposed second-in-command of the company, had dodged the attack, remaining behind with the battalion cadre. Cox was now pretending not to have seen him, judging by the way he held his paper still. So Phillip went over to Cox, and mimicked Cox's former manner of addressing himself, saying,

"Hullo, you one-piecee bad boy! What are *you* doing here?"

"I might ask you the same question!"

"Oh, I'm just mucking about. And you?"

"Hush-hush, old boy. Mustn't say."

"As a matter of fact, Cox, I was wondering if I'll take a job at the new Tank and Infantry Liaison School at Albert."

Cox pretended to splutter. "What, another instructor? My dear One-piecee, almost everyone I know has been asked to instruct at that bogus school!"

"Well, as it happens, I *have*, Cox."

"Shall I tell you how? You were specially sent for by your Brigade-major. Your Brigade-major specifically asked you to talk over your prospects with your friends. My dear One-piecee, I do assure you that it is the main subject of conversation at the bar over there this very moment!"

"Then what's the idea?"

"Softly softly catchee monkey! 'Les oreilles ennemies vous ecoutent'. Comprenez? I see you do! But hush! Play the game, One-piecee! Don't let the side down. Wait here. Drink perpends!"

Cox returned, carrying a bottle and glasses.

"Now, my dear One-piecee, I'll let you into something *not* planted out by Intelligence, Third Army. If you repeat it, I shall deny it. I am relying on you to be more discreet than I am. In any case, you can draw your own conclusions."

"I don't quite follow you——"

"You will. First of all, I owe you an apology, One-piecee, for claiming seniority to you in the company under Bason."

"Oh, I've forgotten all about that, Cox."

"No you haven't! But I'd like you to know that the reason why I held back was because my missus was going to have a baby. Anyway, my transfer was due any moment."

"Yes, you told me at the time."

"And you thought I showed the white feather, didn't you?"

"Not until you accused me of showing it! Then I knew *you* were windy, to be quite frank!"

"How d'you mean?" The old sun-scorched irritable face, part eclipsed by eyeglass, looked at him sourly.

He knows I know he's a funk, thought Phillip. Putting on an ingenuous expression he said, "Well, if a chap thinks too much of his mother's feelings for him, or his wife's, as the case may be, he's bound to feel pretty awful inside. Death literally stares him in the face. His bowels turn to water. The thing to do then is to take more rum with it, to dilute the water. I knew that when you taunted me, it was because you'd been taunting yourself, until it was unbearable. So you passed it on. At least, that's how I see it."

"Have you heard of Confucius, One-piecee?"

"Vaguely."

"Well, read Confucius, when you get the chance. Chin chin!"

They drank. "What's your hush-hush about, Cox?"

"Chains."

"How d'you mean?"

Cox lowered his voice. "It may interest you to know that the whole of Great Britain has been scoured during the past two months for a certain weight of chain. Two thousand fathom, to be exact. But we got 'em!" Cox with his boiled red face and sandy eyelashes had a Mongolian stuffed-pheasant glass-eye look. Was he bottled?

"It means nothing to you, One-piecee?"

"Frankly no, *mein prächtig kerl!*"

"Thank God! I nearly let it out!"

After the third bottle, he did let it out.

"Swear on your honour to God you'll keep it dark? You know the Tank Central Workshops at Teneur? You don't? Then you're more damned ignorant than I thought, One-piecee. Teneur is where I've been working with my company of Chinese coolies. We've been on the go, day and night, for the best part of

a month. What for, you wonder. I'll tell you. Making enormous
faggots! Or fascines, as they call 'em. Each containing seven
dozen faggots of straight brushwood, held together by chains
hauled tight by two tanks, each pulling against the other. At
one time we had eighteen tanks on the job. Result, three hundred
and fifty fascines—each a solid roll ten feet long, and four and a
half feet in diameter."

"What are they for?"

"Wouldn't you like to know?"

"How much does a 'fascine' weigh?"

"Well, it takes twenty of my coolies to push one along the
ground!"

"I think you're sprucing!"

"You'll find out, all in good time, you one-piecee bad
boy!"

18 Sun	At 5.25 a.m. Alleyman opened up on our outpost line just inside the wood and raided. Sergt and 5 men taken back.

3 p.m. Secret O.O. from Bde said Zero day for Raid
20th. Wood crammed with new arrivals, including our
div. infantry. Pinn. said he knew two days before, when
secret O.O. were given him personally by Bde-major.
RFC been over daily, to spot any poor camouflage.
Cavalry Corps standing by. Under Camouflage; also
whole Brigades, 'within a stone's throw', said P. in
hollows and ravines completely covered over.

4 p.m. Ger scout came over, hedge-hopping, was shot
down by Lewis gun. Said lost his way, thought he was
over Arras.

7 p.m. Tanks came into woods. Bloody row, clankings,
crews shouting etc. What hopes of secrecy. Some had
Cox's ' fascines ' on top, for tipping into deep trenches.
Each tank had its own canvas ' stable '.

11 p.m. Pinn says our trenches are to be flattened, to
allow tanks to go straight over. Also armoured cables
laid to Bde h.q. Another Alleyman raid, one man
pinched. Will he split, is the great question.

In the wood were many tanks under canvas covers, over which
string-netting tied with bits of black and green cloth was spread.
Pinnegar explained to his officers what was to happen. A Raid
on a wide front, to penetrate the Hindenberg Line, led by tanks
each of which had a special function. There were supply tanks,

to tow sleds in line; tanks with chain grapnels, for pulling up belts of barbed wire. First to go over were the Advance Guard tanks. Each one had two Infantry tanks working with it. Leaving its tracks through pressed-down wire, it was to turn left at the enemy trench and shoot up any opposition, thus protecting its pair of tanks following with the infantry.

The pair of Infantry tanks was to make for a special place in the German main trench. There the left-hand tank was to drop its fascine. This was done by dipping its nose while release-gear was pulled. Having crossed the wide main trench, it was to work left-handed down the trench parados, to get any "late sleepers" coming up from dug-outs. While they were "put finally to sleep", the right-hand tank of the Infantry Pair would be making for the second line. There, in a similar main trench, it would drop its fascine, cross over, and work down left-handed as before.

Meanwhile the Advance Guard tank would have gone over the two main trenches and, keeping its own fascine on its neb, make for the third line and "bonk the bloody thing in. Then we come up, and emplace our guns for barrage fire for the second phase of the advance".

Phillip made notes in his diary.

19 Mon   Heard that G.O.C. Tanks is to lead them flying his flag. Looks like rain. Usual battle weather. Two yellow and red flags to be thrown out by fascine-dropping tanks; infantry will stick them in to mark borders of bonked faggot for others following.

Infantry in three groups. Trench Clearers, who carry small red flags to mark tank-paths through wire, then mop up dug-outs, etc.; Trench Stops, who catch what bolts from tanks (a la ferret); Trench Garrisons, who stay in captured trenches (and meet any counter-attack, tho this 'eventuality is not to be discussed'). Pinn. said nearly 400 tanks, and 96 infantry batts. going over. Plus all cavalry. Some raid!

Special parties to lift wounded out of the track of tanks.

10.45 a.m. Pinn said Z hour 6.20 a.m. (Sun rises 7.27 a.m.)

German prisoners, who said a raid was expected, called this sector ' the Flanders Sanatorium '. They also said they heard our ' caterpillar tractors hauling heavy guns into wood ' last night. As Westy once said,

' The staff knows damn-all, unless you or I tell them'.
Still, RFC says no tank tracks visible anywhere.

Returning with limbers tonight, passed scores of tanks
going to their forming-up lines. They went like snails,
in bottom gear, engines almost idling. Two hundred
yards away I couldn't hear them, so had a shock, finding
myself suddenly among the dark shapes.

Tank wallah told me earlier spoof orders had been
hung in Secret No Admittance office of 1st Tank Bde at
Arras, and spoof maps, plus bogus plans. But nobody
pinched them!

20 Tue   Alleyman barrage opened up at 4.30 a.m. Feared
worst in this shelter, where stove burns cheerily. Wrote
last letters, just in case.

5.15 a.m. Gunfire stopped. False alarm.

After the sergeant and five men captured in the German raid
on the Sunday night had been interrogated, as a precautionary
measure reserve machine-gun batteries had been moved to behind
the third line of the Siegfried Stellung.

Two hours before dawn of 20 November, after examination
by senior German officers of the British prisoners taken forty-eight
hours previously, an urgent warning was sent down to all units
to fit armour-piercing bullets into every third place in all machine-
gun belts. But time was getting on; and it was not long before
some of these messages, half copied out, were to be found lying
in abandoned battalion headquarter dug-outs.

Chapter 20

VICTORY

While the German warning was going over their telephones,
350 tanks, having rolled and bundled their camouflage nets,
started to move forward, while many aeroplanes flew low over
the lines. Roaring of engines filled the dank darkness. Ten
minutes later, in the murk of first light, infantry followed behind
the leading tanks; and as they walked into no-man's-land a
thousand hidden guns opened up. The reverberation of this

tempest of light was riveted by the combined noises of as many
Vickers machine-guns streaming their nickel jets into and over
the Siegfried Stellung.

General Sir Julian Byng's Third Army was about to occupy
the Flanders Sanatorium.

"It looks as though Haig has done it at last, sir," said Sergeant
Nolan, at 7.30 a.m.

From the Brigade Observation post had come news that tanks
and infantry had reached the first Hindenburg position. Smoke
and mist had obscured early telescopic vision: now the morning
was clearing. German prisoners came past, under escort. They
were middle-aged men, some with beards, and very young
soldiers of the 384th Landwehr regiment—the equivalent of
second-line territorials. They said that the attack had been a
complete surprise. Walking wounded followed.

After an early breakfast Phillip led his pack mules down
through the wood. Sergeant Nolan was to lead them, to his
disappointment. But Pinnegar had been firm. No more Cook's
tours. The donks were loaded with ammunition, water, oil,
rations; unladen donks were to carry the guns and tripods.
The Brigade was timed to leave the wood at 9 a.m. The young
Brigadier had been given a distant objective, beyond Graincourt,
a village about 8,000 yards behind the German front line. The
Brigade was to advance beyond the village, take the wooded crest
of Bourlon Wood, and hold the approaches into Cambrai until
the cavalry arrived.

There was half an hour to go. News came in that the Germans
themselves had been preparing to make an attack from Havrincourt the following morning. Villages behind the first line had
been full of storm troops. Now they were either dead, prisoners,
or had run away. While the company stood by, field batteries
passed at the gallop, one following another, to take up positions
beyond the German front line.

A message came through that the Brown Line—the second
Siegfried position—had been taken.

"I can't believe it, Phil! There's a catch in it, somewhere.
You'd better get back, and get ready to follow on. Our brigade's
going through now. Cheerio! See you later."

"Good luck, *mein prächtig kerl!*"

On the way back, he saw from higher ground an entire division
on the move, three brigades in line, each battalion in column

of route. It was a tremendous sight. He felt really keen about the war for the first time. It was the strangest feeling: he really had passed the shadow line.

"It only wants the bandsmen in front of each battalion," said Morris. The drivers cheered when Phillip told them the news. "We'll soon be back in Blighty now, sir!"

As the day grew brighter, he could see tanks crawling up and down the chalky lines of trenches, dragging wire behind them, and rolling it up. Long strings of pack mules passed, dozens of them. Shortly after 10.30 a.m. he could see, through his field-glasses, tanks and infantry about Marcoing. Then, farther on, as weak sunlight spread over the grey-green landscape, he could see tanks moving up to the crest of the Flesquières ridge, the equivalent of the Passchendaele–Broodseinde ridge in Flanders. Four hours to take—not fourteen weeks!

It meant the attack had got through the whole of the Siegfried Stellung, into open country beyond. The Intelligence Officer said, "I doubt if Division and Corps will believe it!"

Apparently confirmation of this staggering fact was required; for no cavalry appeared.

In the meantime, something had happened on the Flesquières ridge. Shells spouted like waves breaking on a distant coral reef; thin black columns of smoke drifted from burning tanks. Three—four—five on fire were counted. Obviously a German battery had been missed, and was firing over open sights as the tanks appeared on the sky-line.

In the foreground, clusters of men could be seen at work making roads. Other groups were laying a light railway; and carrying forward armoured cables to advanced brigade-head-quarters—all as planned.

In the early afternoon the cavalry appeared, squadron after squadron trotting over the grass to the south. They went down out of sight, then reappeared moving in files over the cleared German trenches. Soon they dismounted, and the horses were led back, under cover. Was it as at Monchy-le-Preux, in the April attack, he wondered.

After them came cyclists and motorcycles with sidecars in each one of which sat a gunner facing to the rear with a Vickers gun— the first troops of the Motor Machine Gun Corps he had seen. They bumped away down into the lower valley.

When would the order to advance come? Drivers were sitting

on horse-rugs on the ground, happily playing nap and solo
whist for sous and centimes. French civilians, driving cows and
pigs, and carrying bundles of clothing, appeared stoically in the
British lines. A message arrived from Pinnegar, saying he was
going forward to his new battle H.Q., and would send a message
later where to take further ammunition, water, and oil, which
were to be brought up by limber.

"Where are our donks?" he asked the senior driver, a lance-
corporal.

"They should be back by now."

It was 3 p.m. Not much light remained.

"I don't like the look of all this," he said to Morris. "It's been
too cushy. What's behind us, to carry on? They called it a raid,
didn't they? That's what it'll turn out to be, in my opinion."

At 3.30 p.m. he left L/Cpl. O'Flynn in charge, and rode
forward with Morris to the company headquarters which had
been marked on his map the day before. It was in the second
German line.

Remembering the congestion and muddle of the transport
during the first night of Loos, he must reconnoitre the way before
darkness fell. Followed by Morris, he cantered through the
wood and down the clearing to the old front line.

It was a strange feeling to be riding upon a new battlefield,
hardly damaged by shell-fire, passing German dead strewn
everywhere, the wounded still among them, some sitting up,
others lying back, in patient silence awaiting their turns for
stretchers. Everywhere rusty tangles of wire had been lugged
about, and left in untidy heaps. The firing trench was hardly
blown in anywhere. Hares ran about, stopping to peer with
ears taller than the grasses. A few shells droned down and spouted
blackly, "just to show there's a war on, sir", said Morris.

They crossed the deep and wide main trench of the first line,
upon a wooden bridge just completed. Ahead lay the ruinous red
village of Havrincourt. The pre-war road to it, crossed by the
lines, had been cleared of fallen trees by hundreds of pioneer
troops and was now being filled in and levelled. A concrete
shelter sunken into the road, with splays a foot above ground
level, was about to be blown up.

An extension of the Canal du Nord, with tunnels running
under hills, was being built at the outbreak of war. Part of the
works, abandoned in August 1914, was the *Grand Ravin*. This
was marked on the maps as possibly a formidable obstacle.

Running from south to north, it crossed the Havrincourt road. The tanks had feared it, as the unknown. But all had gone well: six fascines, enough to fill the *Grand Ravin*, and covered by chalk, gave enough stability for a staff motorcar to wobble its way over, pushed by half-a-dozen cheerful pioneers.

Phillip dismounted, and leaving Black Prince on the road with Morris, went to look for Pinnegar. A Vickers mounted forward of the trench parados drew him: yes, it was 286 M. The new H.Q. were in a deep dug-out, which had flowers painted on the wooden walls below. By candle-light and flash-lamp book-cases and pictures were visible on the panelling. The officers' rooms leading off from the corridor connecting the main assembly rooms—lined with tier upon tier of bunks—were furnished with carpets, tables, brass-and-iron bedsteads with sheets, pillows, and woollen rugs. No wonder the Alleyman called it a Sanatorium!

A gunner led him along a corridor, past a canteen. Broken bottles lay on the floor, and spilled liquids. There was a bar, with looking-glasses behind shelves on which bottles and cigar boxes still stood. A battle-policeman was on guard, beside a row of candles. It looked as though some of the moppers-up had mopped up more than prisoners. No doubt there would be a celebration party, too, among the red caps later on.

"In there, sir!"

"Thank God!" said Pinnegar. "I thought you were never coming! Have you got the limbers?"

"Not with me, Teddy. I came to——"

"Why the hell not? We're waiting to go up to Bourlon Wood, and we can't very well carry our bloody guns and belt boxes, can we? Didn't you get my order?"

"Only to stand by with limbers, skipper."

"That was Z 9. Didn't you get Z 12?"

"No, sir."

"But I sent it half an hour after Z 9, telling you to come at once, with all transport! Didn't you get it?"

"No, I didn't."

"But you've come here!"

"I came because I'd had no orders, and it will soon be dark. What's happened?"

"The usual balls-up. Division ordered the Boy General to stop getting forward from Graincourt, until our flanks were secured, but the Boy was right up with the foremost infantry, and went on with some tanks he'd got hold of, and bloody

well took Bourlon Wood! Now he wants all our guns at once.
My God, I thought you'd have the sense to know something like
that would happen!"

"I wanted to do it, but thought for once I'd obey orders! However, I'll go back at once, and bring up the pack mules, *and* the
limbers! It will take—let me see—I can get back in half an hour.
Then the return—nearly five miles—if there isn't any hold-up,
it will take us at least another hour to get here. I'll be on the
Havrincourt road between half-past five and six pip emma."

Why hadn't he followed his hunch? Orders anyway took
hours to arrive during a schemozzle. It was Loos all over again.
The German line open, the wave spent.

Timeless rainy darkness upon congested track lit by gun
flash and glare of bursting shell. Wire tripping and entangling,
tearing at hand, puttee, and tunic, mules in chalky mud fetlock
deep often kicking against barbing pain. Had the guide lost
direction? Questions about the way to Havrincourt caused one
explosion, a screaming flow of curses out of the darkness in front
when a driver replied to "Who the hell are you?" with an
innocent, "94673 Driver Gordon, sir."

Apparently some harassed colonel was under the delusion that
the transport belonged to the Gordon Highlanders of the 51st
division, "who hadn't the guts to attack the Hun holding out
all day at Flesquières, although there was no bloody wire and
no f—— trenches or supports behind them! And for f—— miles
on either flank and f—— miles behind Flesquières there was not a
f—— Hun to be seen!! Call yourselves soldiers, and Highlanders
at that? You're the scum of Glasgow, you haven't the guts to
attack even from the rear, and now you have the bloody im-
pertinence to tread my men into the mud with your b——
f—— mules, God damn you to hell!!!"

Phillip had listened to this exhausted-man tirade while pushing
Black Prince forward. He said, "I am sorry to disappoint you,
sir, but this is the Two Eight Six Machine Gun Company of
the East Pennine division."

"Then why the hell didn't you say so at first? This driver
said he was the Gordons!"

"His surname is Gordon, sir. I wonder if you could tell me
if this is the way to Havrincourt?"

"It was when I was there half an hour ago, but whether or
not it's there now don't ask me! Where d'you come from?"

"Where you're obviously going, sir."

"Where the hell's that?"

"Stellenbosch, *mein prächtig kerl*!"

He moved away into safe darkness, laughing with an imaginary Mrs. Neville as words floated after him, "You're a bloody fool, whoever you are!" Another of the many chance acquaintanceships of the Great War was ended.

The infantry was exhausted. The cavalry had come up late. The headquarters of the Cavalry Corps were still thirty-six miles away. The initiative was lost. So were many of the communications. Tanks had crushed the main cables; iron hoops of wheels of field-guns and limbers, entangled mules and horses, had broken the slighter wires of buzzer and telephone. Mounted orderlies and runners had been too slow. Carrier pigeons were half-trained, bemused by noise, subdued by the cold weather; wireless was not used properly because it was not understood. A steel spring had been transmuted to lead.

All day the German garrison at Flesquières, near the five tanks knocked out by a wounded German gunner officer serving the gun himself when all his crew were killed, had held to their re-entrant while knowing that British troops had gone miles past them on both flanks. They were in the air; they stayed because it would be useless loss of life to go back over open ground, enfiladed from two sides.

Because of the gap in the British advance, older Generals advised caution. The G.O.C. the Highland Division did not comply with a suggestion from the G.O.C. East Pennines that he should attack across the East Pennine front, but *behind* the Germans at Flesquières. He required the help of tanks, he said. So the lead weight dropped. The East Pennine General ordered his foremost Brigadier to remain where he was, at Graincourt on the left flank, far ahead and almost to the Cambrai road. This Brigadier, who was the Boy General, "saw no reason why the order should deflect him from the attack of his immediate objectives". Two dismounted squadrons of King Edward's Horse, inspired by the V.C. commander who had gone up to be with his foremost troops, joined the advance, and reached the long straight cobbled road which led to Cambrai.

Darkness had fallen when reinforcements were heard coming up. A platoon of the Duke of Wellington's was resting beside the road. The step was crisp and uniform; could these be the Guards?

But as the column came near, coal-scuttle helmets were seen against the stars, instead of the more usual pudding basins. Some of the patients of the Sanatorium, from Flesquières, were escaping.

The new patients lay still, fags concealed in practised palms; the company passed; then a party of toughs joined the rear of the column and jumped on the backs of a *feldwebel*, a *hauptmann*, and one other. Cries, shouts, screams as Lewis guns rattled. Fifty Germans were killed, and thrice that number taken prisoner.

At 10 p.m., when 286 M arrived, fighting by bomb and bayonet was going on in the trenches west of the beet-sugar factory beside the Cambrai road. By midnight all sixteen of the company's guns were emplaced: seven around Graincourt, nine covering the gap to the sugar factory a thousand yards away.

It had been raining for seven hours.

The company headquarters were under the church. Going down to see Pinnegar, Phillip came to a sort of crypt. Brick pillars supported a vaulted roof. On the floor hundreds of men were lying asleep.

Below the crypt several stairways led down into the chalk. They were steep, and timbered as usual, but had about double the usual number of steps. At the bottom was a gallery, lit along its length by electric bulbs diminishing in the distance.

It was a maze of turnings and doors, and almost asphyxiatingly hot, with fug of tobacco smoke, sweat, paraffin vapour of Primus stoves, and burnt cooking fat: an atmosphere horridly quivering with the pulses of the diesel engine driving the dynamo in one of the rooms. The vibration seemed to be pumping the stomach, by way of the ear-drums.

Going up and down corridors, trying to find Pinnegar, he came upon the engine room, getting a sickening shock when a door opened and two Germans came out, carrying red-banded boxes. A momentary shock: this was no subterranean invasion, but a clearing of charges of ammonal, many boxes of it, that had been hidden behind the boards of one wall of the little room adjoining the engine-house. The two German engineers had been running the plant for some months, it being divisional headquarters. The R.E. officer superintending the removal of high explosives told Phillip that the old Hun had apparently not overlooked the chance of the place being captured some day, for there were two hundred kilograms of ammonal hidden under the catacombs.

"Was there a time fuse?"

"No. The detonator was connected direct to the main switch, or what anyone would reasonably take to be the main starting switch, wired to the batteries. It was damned fortunate that the Boy General got here first, and ordered the two Huns to carry on with the lighting arrangements, for one of them said, in effect, that if that was so, he might as well point out that what looked like the main switch was a starting switch, at least not for the engine alone, but for the end of the war as far as everyone around was concerned. They added that if their services were going to be retained by the new board of directors, they thought it their duty to show the Herr foreman where to dig for the explosives. They were able to show the precise spots, under floors and timber casings of walls, since they had buried the stuff there in the first place!"

Phillip felt sick. It was like being in the boat to Ostend, *Pieter der Konig*, going to see Mavis at the convent at Wespaelar. There was the same steady shiver of the engine through the walls, and the thud of shells or guns coming down from above was like the bows lifting up and plunging down into big waves. He looked for a lavatory, there must be one somewhere, but how would they get the stuff away. Pumping perhaps—pumping: *his* damned heart was pumping in his ears and pumping water into his mouth.

Round one corner he heard horrible singing, as two soldier servants washed plates and cups in a bucket of steaming water, while smoking cigars. He opened a door, and saw a Madame Tussaud's scene—one that would have made Teddy livid—an elderly Brigadier sitting in a crimson plush armchair, a round pedestal library table upon which his booted legs rested, a fire burning in a white tiled stove on which flowers were painted, a shelf above it with looking glass, before which stood a French carriage clock, its pendulum visible behind the glass case. On the walls were oleographs of the Kaiser, the Crown Prince, and Field-Marshal von Hindenburg; while spread upon the table was a large-scale map of Bourlon Wood printed in German.

"What the devil do you want?" cried the Brigadier-General.

"Sorry, sir, I thought this was the lavatory."

He returned to the little room adjoining the engine, and in the chalk cavity behind the ripped panelling found a convenient place. After all, exchange was no robbery!

"Where shall I place my picket line, Teddy?"

"Christ knows. I don't. It's up to you."

"I think the best place is in Havrincourt. There's probably water there. Well, cheerio. I'll be up in the morning, to see you."

The drivers had three days emergency rations: one tin each of bully beef, Maconochie stew, and pork-and-beans; a pound and a half of biscuits in a linen bag, and shares in tins of butter and plum-and-apple jam. Someone got a fire going behind a wall standing amidst the ruins of Havrincourt, facing away from the enemy—although flares were going up on either side as well as in front. Phillip uncovered the rum jar, and poured about a quart and a half into the steaming dixie of tea boiled with sugar. A cheerful timeless binge followed. The convoy had got through. Soon drivers were creeping on hands and knees to sleep beside bales of hay and oat sacks overlaid by tarpaulins.

Unable to sleep for cold, he went to find out what was behind a light glimmering in the remains of the Havrincourt château. Gun-flashes revealed two motorcars standing outside, with the stencil of a bantam cock. With luck he might find somewhere to sleep. It was the 40th Divisional Headquarters. To the two sentries by the door he said good-evening, and walked inside, to see faces around a table on which stood German beer-bottles winking with candles. The General was looking at a large map. Men with red tabs were writing on pads, on their knees. The conference seemed about over, for soon message books were being shut, armfuls of maps collected and tied in bundles. He went away into the night and as he waited there he heard one of the officers asking where he could find a pole, or a stout stick. He helped in the search, thinking it wise to say who he was, in case the sentries were suspicious; and hearing the tank officer ask about the way to Graincourt, said that he had just come from there, and would direct him. He was asked about headquarters of brigades, and told them where his own were, under the church; and with white bundles of maps for the next attack slung on a clothes' prop, the officer and his orderly set out. Phillip returned to the château, and tried to sleep under the table of the empty conference room, but it was too cold, he was wet, water squelched in his boots when he got up to swing his arms. His head ached, from the extra rum he had drunk.

21 *Wed*   10 a.m. attack on Bourlon Wood and village failed. Rations etc. to Graincourt. Pinn said lots killed. Tanks

arrived late. Guns couldn't all get up, only one road, and that axle-deep in mud.

22 *Thu*   More attacks on Bourlon, which is slight rise dark with leafless oaks in distance. Many low-strafing Alleyman aeroplanes about. Bombs and m.g. Hard scrapping around Crucifix in Bourlon Wood. S O S signals not replied to. Pinn said the new rifle-grenade " rocket "— bursting with 2 red and 2 white balls—is n.b.g. They get muddled with R.F.C. contact flares—white for infantry, red for cavalry.

Haig and staff officers were riding about Flesquières ridge in morning, watching Bourlon Wood through field glasses.

23 *Fri*   Div. relieved 1 a.m. by 40th (Bantam). Into hutments Havrincourt Wood. Saw Yank doc. at Dressing Station, he very popular, no swank, and sympathetic. On fatigue, carting road material, all limbers. Tracks as bad as Ancre valley. Only one good road, pavé Bapaume–Cambrai, ½-mile-hour progress. 40th Div. attacked Bourlon Wood. Failed. Rain intermittent, wind cold, sky overcast.

Tanks in Bourlon Wood; and Fontaine village, 2 miles from Cambrai.

Our scout planes flying low, strafing Alleyman. Many shot down.

All transports working on roads, 8 a.m.–10 p.m.

"Yes, it is wonderful news," said Richard, on the Friday morning at breakfast. "I wonder if Phillip will be in this?" He held open *The Daily Trident*, with its black headline of CAMBRAI VICTORY! "We have, according to the report, made an advance four to five miles deep with hundreds of tanks on a front of ten miles, taken thousands of prisoners and a great number of guns! Listen to this, Hetty! 'Our tanks might have been waltzing through the Hun barbed wire.' Thank heaven that the powers that be seem to have stirred their stumps at last!"

In Head Office there was quiet satisfaction all the morning. Then at midday something extraordinary happened. Mavis, going upstairs to the Luncheon Room, heard noon striking, as usual, from the clock of St. Paul's Cathedral. The Head Messenger, returning from Lloyd's, said that the carillon of St. Paul's Cathedral was playing a tune. "I last heard that when Peace was declared, at the end of the South African War, sir," he told Richard and others in the ground floor Town Department. The news spread. Could the Germans have surrendered? Paul, the tenor bell, was heard striking noon. The manager of the Department went into the street, as the cathedral clock was striking noon. Immediately afterwards they heard Great Paul, the tenor bell, booming. The sonorous echoes were followed by the full peal of twelve bells; immediately afterwards, at the signal, all the City churches followed with wildly clashing noise. People were coming into the streets, waving hands and handkerchiefs, half the Town Department went out, leaving Richard working at his desk. He wanted to follow, but tears were dropping from his eyes. Mavis ran down the mezzanine iron stairs, overcome by the general feeling. On the pavement she thought of Albert Hawkins, who had been killed, O, long ago; she prayed silently for his soul; she thought of her mother, alone in the house, poor Mother . . . but she would have Mrs. Bigge next door, and also Gramps and darling Aunt Marian. Poor Doris, she would be thinking of cousin Percy, killed over a year ago now; poor Aunt Liz and Uncle Jim, what could Victory mean to them? It was all wrong, these people could not possibly understand. Nobody really understood, Phillip by now was probably tipsy, with his safe job. Still, it would make Mother happy, she doted on her donkey-boy, mothers always did care more for their first child than for the others. She could not bear the cheering, it was awful, why waste time, she was having first lunch at twelve o'clock, there was nothing really to rejoice for. And going back into the office, she saw that old Journend was crying, and Father was blowing his nose loudly. He would! Soon it was over, and she was back at her desk, working away under green-shaded electric light.

24 *Sat*	Bourlon Wood taken by Bantam division. Great news. Cavalry going through tomorrow. Haig issued Special Order of the Day, thanking all ranks. "Capture crowns a most successful operation." Working all day and half night on roads. Wet through. Wish I'd kept my waders and long thick woollen stockings. Squelch squelch squelch. Three Alleyman Guard *divisionen* reported to be at Cambrai.
25 *Sun*	Our Guards division at Bourlon. Cavalry came up. East Pennine relieved Bantam in Bourlon Wood, at night. Very eerie, going up through trees with mule pack, to edge of Bourlon village. Sweated hot. Saw

stragglers, incoherent. Three mules died by m.g. fire.
Driver Gordon wounded. Cold and raining.

26 *Mon.* Fine and bright. Heard that Byng himself is now
i/c Bourlon attacks. Our batteries shelled to hell.
Alleyman can see every flash etc. from Bourlon.

"Bourlon village to be captured without fail tomorrow." The Guards div. and ours to attack side by
side. Feel rotten, slight headache.

The wood sinister, snipers are everywhere, no definite
trench lines. Trees cover about a square mile.

This morning saw G.O.C.'s Guard div., East P,
and Corps arriving at Havrincourt for conference in
my "bedroom" of last Tues. night. Then Byng's car
arrived, and then Haig and staff rode up.

After a short while Haig came out, and rode across
to the Flesquières ridge.

The Field-Marshal had said that "no further offensive operations could be attempted, but that he was satisfied that the plan
for the 27th offered every chance to secure the main object,"
which he described as "to capture and hold the best line for
the winter". Thereupon he left.

The General commanding the Guards division objected to
the plan for the 27th. The advance of the Guards would be
"exposed to artillery fire from the high ground north of Romilly,
and also from behind the Bourlon ridge and the western out-
skirts of Cambrai. The objective to be reached was 1,800
yards; he had only six battalions available for whole operation.
The assault upon Romilly was essential to the attack to secure
the Bourlon ridge".

In effect, he said, the Guards were asked to make a salient
out of a salient: and if resources were not sufficient for this
attack, it would be advisable to withdraw from the low ground
and establish a main line of defence upon the Flesquières
ridge.

The Third Army commander decided that the attack must
take place as planned. He was aware, he said, that the London
division, then in the Achiet-le-Petit area, represented the last
of the reinforcements he could expect, and that, "whatever
the fortunes of the morrow, the Third Army's offensive must
be brought to an end".

Thereupon orders were issued that the object of the Guards,
with 12 tanks, was to "gain all the ground from which the
enemy can observe our batteries, and to take the village of

Fontaine". The East Pennine division was to attack in line
with the Guards, to secure, with 20 tanks, the northern part
of Bourlon Wood, and the village.

Snow was falling when Phillip, following the company, left
Havrincourt for the Cambrai road. It was congested with
traffic, being the only hard road leading to the left sector of
the battle. The German machine-gun barrage hissed over
and down. Copper-sheathed bullets with steel cores sometimes
struck sparks from the cobbles. They passed the wreckage of
waggons and horses. Shells growled down in front, near the
sugar refinery. He suggested to Pinnegar that they turn off
the road, and follow one of the parallel tracks, but Pinnegar
replied that the snow would have covered most guiding posts
and all the tapes. Shrapnel burst redly in front.

"I'm fairly sure I know the way, Teddy."

"We'll go by road and risk the shit flying about."

Two figures stood by the brick-and-iron ruin that had been
the sugar refinery. The arrival of the company was checked
by the Brigade-major: the Boy General said, "Well done!
Keep going!"

29 *Thu*   Attack on Bourlon failed. Two companies of Grenadiers wiped out at start, only sgt with 6 men getting
into Fontaine. One company of Scots Gds, sent to join
them, shot down. Sgt took command and reached
sunken road from Cantaing, and held on until ordered
to retire. Coldstream enfiladed but some reached
Fontaine. Irish Gds on left went through Bourlon Wood
and dug in on fringe with both flanks in air. Our Bde
at first lost in darkness among trees, but reached village
(Bourlon) where hand-to-hand scrapping. Attack called
off in afternoon by Byng. E.P. div. to be relieved
tonight by 2nd N. Midland.

The relief on the night of 29/30 November. Thousands of
gas-shells falling. Yellow-, green-, blue-cross shells plopped
down. Soft swooping noises, almost gentle, like sighs, followed
by the slightest of pops. Angry buzzings and hissing among
them—the enemy machine-gun barrage. Rotten-egg smell:
phosgene, with its delayed action on the heart——

"All drivers to put on their animals' masks! Look slippy!
Then your own."

The whole area was being drenched by gas. Stifling hot mask of box-respirator. Goggle glass steamy. Damn, why not anti-dimmed by paste? Impossible to speak, rubber teat in mouth.

Shells screamed down on the road. Wheel fragments flying, screaming horses. He lifted his mask. "This way, this way!" Better the suck of mud on track than splatter-flesh-blood on road. To get away, get away, get away, teeth ground with the thought of get away.

No more shells. Safe to lift mask, and sniff. Must have done a mile in masks.

"Halt in front! Five minutes' breather. No smoking."

He plodded back to see Pinnegar, at rear of column.

"Where are we, Phil? How far from Graincourt?"

"It should be in front, Teddy."

"Oughtn't we to get back on the road?"

"It's frightfully congested at this hour. The relief of the Guards and ourselves will add to it. I know the way."

"How far is Demicourt?"

"About two and a half miles past Graincourt."

Demicourt, about half a mile behind the old British front line, was the Brigade assembly area. There they were to rest before going, with the remains of the Division, to refit in a back area.

"The men are just about all in, sir," said the sergeant-major.

"Yes, for Christ's sake get a move on!"

After half an hour he had doubts about being on the right track. Where was Graincourt? How could he have missed it?

Continuing onwards, they came to an unfamiliar wood. Beyond and below sloping ground lay the dark mass of a village, revealed by a line of distant flares. O God, where were they?

"Don't look like Graincourt to me," said the sergeant-major.

"Nor to me."

"Then where the hell are we?" asked Pinnegar.

"I don't know, Teddy."

"Well, you should damn well know! For two days and three bloody nights we've been fighting your *prächtig kerls* the Alleymans, while you've had damn-all to do! I told you Demicourt on my message, couldn't you bloody well have familiarised yourself with the route by daylight?"

"We've been on road-making fatigues all day, skipper, and only returned half an hour before leaving to meet you."

"Who the hell cares?" shouted Pinnegar angrily. "Couldn't
you have left Nolan, and gone off to find the way? What the
hell d'you think you're here for? To go on bloody Cook's
tours, like a bloody war correspondent?"

The sergeant-major said, "I think that's the Bapaume road
in front of us, although this don't look like Graincourt, sir."

"But those flares look like it, Teddy. Jerry's lines go parallel
to the road, below the sugar factory. We must have come in a
wide circle."

"Then what the bloody hell'r we arguing about? Lead on,
for Christ's sake." They crossed a small stream. Phillip could
not remember any stream around Graincourt, or the Bapaume
road. But the line of flares was the same. With a shock he
realised that the moon was in the wrong place.

The moon, two nights past the full, had risen about 8 p.m.
Out of the *east*. The German lines below Bourlon ran *west*
of the Bapaume road: they were an extension of the Hindenburg Line going up to Bullecourt and Arras. He felt giddy.
Was he ill, his mind become unreliable? The road in front
was straight. It must be the Cambrai–Bapaume road. Perhaps
he had a temperature. He had been in his wet things for over
a week. The sooner he was bloody dead the better.

Passing by the village, they moved across grass, and down
a gentle slope, to the road. It was trenched on the near side.
They were challenged. "Who are you?"

"Machine Gun Corps. This is the Cambrai road, isn't
it?"

"That's right."

"Thank God! Which way is Boursies?"

"Never heard of it."

"It's just behind our old front line, about half-way between
Bapaume and Cambrai."

"Then you're right off it, old boy. This is the Cambrai–
St. Quentin road. It's not healthy to move on it, the Boche
is less than half a mile away. His patrols are probably a couple
of hundred yards off."

"Oh hell. Our chaps are dead beat."

"About turn is your only hope. And the sooner the better.
The old Hun¯has got some pretty hot mortars opposite, and
we've had a Special Alert Warning."

He fought against panic. What would Pinnegar say? No:
the point was, how to get back.

"If I can make Havrincourt, I'll know where I am." When Pinnegar came up, he said, "We're a little off course, skipper."

"Havrincourt isn't far, come into my cellar, I'll show you on the map," said the unseen speaker. In candle-light he was revealed as a captain of the Queen's regiment. He pointed out the position on a map.

"We're here, at le Quennet farm. If you go on the road, it's a bit tricky as far as the fork at Bonavis farm. The old Hun has got it taped by his mortars. The right-hand fork will get you to Gouzeaucourt. You'll have to be careful all the way until you've got past Steak House and the Hindenburg support trenches. From there onwards it should be fairly plain sailing, for, as you can see, the line runs south while your road to Gouze-aucourt lies south-west."

"But that's a hell of a long way to go! My men are just about done in!" cried Pinnegar.

"I'm afraid I can't suggest anything better."

"Well, thank you very much," said Phillip.

"Not at all. I'm afraid I can't offer you a drink——"

Pinnegar, no longer angry, thanked the Queen's captain, and the convoy went on, iron bands of limber wheels rattling loudly on pavé. But no shells came over.

Half-way to Gouzeaucourt the gunners were crying weary. Pinnegar said he'd had enough, so they turned off into a village which had some walls standing, and there bivouacked. Having seen that the mules and officers' horses were tied to limbers, and the drivers under tarpaulins, Phillip followed Pinnegar and the section officers into a dug-out. Taking off his wet clobber, he put on pyjamas, which were in his haversack ready for the camp at Demicourt; and getting into a bunk above Pinnegar fell asleep.

Noises of bumping hovered on the verge of consciousness; noiseless shouting seemed to be going on for a very long time. Then he was aware of being in a bunk, of Pinnegar's face looking up at him with the light of an electric torch, of the sergeant-major talking to him. Then a voice bawled down the stairs, "They've broken through! They're coming! Jerry's broken through!"

Throwing trench-coat over pyjama jacket, with an arm through one sleeve, he followed Pinnegar and the sergeant-major up the steps: hesitated in a rush of thoughts: scrambled

down again to grope for his boots, which were not where he
had pulled them off. He felt shivery, his eyeballs ached. Where
was Barrow, he thought, irritably. Barrow had taken away his
things to dry them, also to sew a button on his breeches.

No Barrow. No boots. No breeches. No shirt. No tunic.
The rattle of a Lewis gun came from almost immediately outside. With shaking fingers he buttoned his trench-coat, and
carrying tin-hat and revolver holster on webbing belt, went
up the stairs, telling himself to be calm, to remain calm, *not
to panic* if Germans were near, but to drop belt and tin-hat
and stand still, with arms raised. He saw it happening apart
from himself, and felt no fear, only calm anticipation. If he
was shot, he was shot. Let it come.

Outside it was grey and misty. Many aeroplanes were flying
low, about a quarter of a mile away. Bullets cracked. Figures
were moving through the ruins. Tin hats. Farther off, a line
of advancing Germans. They appeared to be firing from the
hip. Enemy 'planes were flying low, machine-gunning. Dozens
of them. He ran bare-footed up the cobbled street, and saw,
with tremendous relief, the mules already hooked-in to the
limbers. Field-guns were firing in the ruins. Infantry, some
without rifles, hurrying down the street.

Sergeant Nolan was waiting. "We're just about hooked-in, sir."

"Good man, oh, good man!"

"They say the Alleyman's got flamethrowers, but they won't
have carried them things so far. Best get out, sir."

"Have you seen Captain Pinnegar?"

"Gone to see to the sections, sir."

Pinnegar came back, looking grim.

"We'll have to get back to the reserve line, wherever it is.
From what I hear, the outpost line had been overwhelmed.
Look at that lot!"

Panic-stricken faces were passing, among them an officer
striding on alone.

"Let's get a move on! Trouble is, no bloody ammunition.
We left ours in Bourlon Wood, for the relief."

Phillip remembered the map of the night before. "There's a
station at Gouzeaucourt, Teddy. We might get some there.
There's bound to be a dump of sorts. Shall I take the limbers
there?"

"It's as good a place as any."

"I'll see you at the station!"

"Righto. Lead on, for Christ's sake. Better make for the road, though these bloody Hun scouts will strafe us, I suppose."

Barrow appeared, flushed and panting. "I've got your clobber, sir!"

"Shove it in a limber! Are you ready, Nolan? Turn left just before the straight road. You know—the one we came down last night. Better still, keep off it, keep a parallel course, about a hundred yards short."

They got down without trouble, and found a train standing in a siding of the Decaville light railway built before the battle, when Gouzeaucourt had been about two miles behind the British lines. Its iron trucks were loaded under tarpaulins. The A.S.C. officer was clean-shaven, and wore pince-nez spectacles. He was saying that he could not allow any unauthorised removal of food or ammunition, when Pinnegar drew his revolver and said, "That's my authorisation! If you don't bloody well get out of the way . . .! Come on, get a move on, s'ar-major, get the limbers filled!"

"I must ask you to give me a receipt for the stores you're taking," said the A.S.C. officer.

"You'll be able to give it to the Boche, who was just about up to our field-gun batteries in Gonnelieu when we left half an hour ago!"

The A.S.C. officer looked bewildered. He went to the telephone, while tins of biscuits, boxes of Maconochie, bully, butter, and whiskey were put in the limbers, together with bombs and S.A.A. The A.S.C. officer came back to say that the line was dead. He looked anxious. He was saying that five heavy batteries of howitzers were in Gouzeaucourt when an engine was heard coming down the track. A great rattle approached, enveloped in steam. Waving arms were seen as the train rushed backwards into the station. The trucks were filled with elderly men. An officer standing up in the last truck shouted as it passed, "Germans! Coming down!" The train swayed past, going south, at its maximum speed of about ten miles an hour. It was soon gone over the skyline.

"Better fill a couple of belts," said the sergeant-major.

While this was being done, Pinnegar took the officers into a shed, where they filled their bottles with whiskey and water. "May as well let the men have a swig," he said, giving each section officer a bottle. Small loaves and tins of butter had already been dished out.

Drivers' carbines were hauled from limbers, magazines charged. Half a dozen belts had been filled when engine-steam was seen again at the top of the cutting. The train was returning to the station. Hardly had it stopped when the pioneers jumped out, and made for the village.

"Look at them, the ragtime army," said the sergeant-major, a stocky little man with a big dark brown head, as he munched bread and butter. One of them heard and shouted in a broad West Country voice, "They'm zwarmin' through Gosh Wood, maydeers! The man in charge a-roarin' and a-bawlin' in Jarman 'Zurrender!' 'a crieth! You'd bestways start sparkin', maydeers!"

"Closin' time! Jerry'll be 'ere in 'arf a mo'!" cried another.

"What do you feel about a receipt now?" said Pinnegar, whiskey-jovial, to the A.S.C. officer. "Of course, if it will make you happy I'm quite prepared to give you one for the whole bloody train." Dot-like figures were now to be seen at the top of the cutting about a thousand yards away. Bullets began to buzz. "How d'you reverse this thing?" he went on, peering at the engine dials. "Like this?" He pulled a couple of levers.

Steam expanded, wheels raced. The train began to move back towards the sky-lined German dots.

"That will keep them guessing," said the sergeant-major, stuffing the last of half a loaf into his mouth, followed by butter scooped from a tin with his forefinger.

As far as could be seen, little groups of men were hurrying westward, down the road from Gonnelieu to the north-east, and crossing rising ground to the west. Explosions reverberated, as dump after dump was blown up by the Engineers. Warmed by whiskey and water, Phillip began to enjoy what was happening. Yet he was trembling: he realised that he was still half undressed.

286 M helped to hold a line in an old British trench running across the high ground beyond Gouzeaucourt. The Vickers guns covered open ground from a wood about half a mile north of the Peronne road to Revelon farm, a distance of nearly two miles. The defence was organised by a Brigadier-General who had lost his brigade. He had just had time to get out of his dug-out headquarters not far from Gonnelieu; and with clerks, cooks, and various stragglers had made a stand in Gauche Wood. Then behind him, he said, the Boche had come down in trucks drawn by a light railway engine going full-bore. The Boche were

dressed in khaki and wearing battle-bowlers and so obviously windy that he tried some of his German on them; whereupon they reversed the engine and went back the way they had come.

"Unfortunately we were out of ammunition or we'd have got the lot," he said to Pinnegar. "It only shows you, one can never trust a Boche." Then turning to Phillip, and looking at the pyjamas, "Where have you come from, the Ritz?"

"Oh no, sir," replied Phillip, playing up, "I always fight like this!"

The General roared with laughter. Pinnegar's gift of a bottle of whiskey had made him happy, too.

The line was held; an attack stopped. The Germans went back. Pinnegar produced some food with another bottle of whiskey; and best of all, the General told them that the Guards division was on the way from Havrincourt wood, to stop the rot.

Phillip took his transport section to lower ground near Havrincourt Wood a couple of miles back. There he was told by a rueful Barrow that his clobber had been left behind when the limbers were cleared to take ammunition boxes; so he wound a spare pair of puttees round his feet and legs, before returning on foot with Morris to the line. The best part of a bottle of whiskey and water had given him a sense of invulnerability, the shivery feelings had gone. His eyes still had the stinging feeling, otherwise he floated.

"It's a good thing you fellows managed to lose your way last night," said the General. "Your guns couldn't have appeared at a more opportune moment, as far as I am concerned."

By the rumble of bombardment behind them, the Germans were still attacking along the Bapaume road. "It was obvious that they would try to drive across the base of our bite into their Siegfried Stellung," the General continued. "Both Division and Corps repeatedly warned Third Army that the Boche would return the compliment, but I suppose Army reserves have gone to Italy, after that affair at Caporetto."

Battalions of the Foot Guards were forming up outside Havrincourt Wood. Phillip, sent back by Pinnegar to supervise the filling of belt-boxes in preparation for supplies that night, watched them getting into artillery formation. The sun appeared in rents of low cloud. Strings of pack mules were taking up Vickers guns and ammunition, for the barrage before the counter-attack.

Behind the Guards were gunners of some of the siege batteries which had been left behind in Gouzeaucourt. Other units, which had broken in retreat, were being collected and re-formed. The most amazing sight was the appearance of the Guards themselves, both officers and men. They had been relieved only the night before, after the fighting in Bourlon Wood; yet here they were on parade with boots shining and puttees free of mud, trousers and tunics neat, wooden casing of rifles brown with oil polish. Amazement changed to pride as he saw them advancing in diamond formation: watched them doubling out on the sky-line into extended order as they came under fire. He followed with others as the hammering of machine guns laying the barrage seemed to serrate the day: saw them pass through the old trench while others there, including some Americans of the 11th Engineer Railway Regiment, rose up and joined them: and hastening forward, under the machine-gun barrage, the attack went down the slope into Gouzeaucourt—where later the supply train, only partly raided by the Germans, was available for the Guards, whose quartermasters duly gave the A.S.C. lieutenant receipts for all supplies removed from the trucks. Nothing could have been more convenient; it fed the division for the next two nights and days.

As for the engine and trucks Pinnegar had started on its southern journey, they were reported to have passed, driverless, through Epéhy without stopping; the train continued on to Villers Faucon, where the engine ran out of steam. For the remainder of its time upon the 60-cm. line it was known as the Ghost Train.

286 M went back that night to Ribecourt. The senior lieutenant-colonel of the Brigade was in command, the Boy General having been killed during the heavy assault of the Germans debouching from behind the uncaptured Siegfried Stellung north of the bulge.

The colonel was curt about the absence of the company. What had happened elsewhere, he said, was not his concern. There was no excuse for not having made every effort to get to Ribecourt the night before. The Brigade had been ordered at noon to move to Lock 7 of the Canal du Nord, to support another Division, and the 286th Machine Gun Company had been found wanting. The Divisional Commander had called for a report on the matter. The discipline of the Machine Gun Corps generally

was considered by the Third Army Commander to be unsatis-
factory. It was realised that the Corps was new, and had expanded too rapidly for a proper esprit-de-corps to be properly
cultivated; but now discipline was to be enforced.

Pinnegar was asked to read the acting-Brigadier's report, and
to sign that he had read it. When he came to tell Phillip, his
eyes showed hurt under their anger.

"Why didn't you tell him it was my fault, Teddy?"

"Why should I? I was in command, wasn't I?"

"Then I shall!"

"Not with my permission."

"Then I'll apply in writing to be allowed to see him."

"What bloody good would that do?"

"It wasn't your fault, it was my fault."

"Why split hairs? What the hell can they do? Only send me
back to the school at Camiers, and take away my third pip. Or
even send me home."

"Stellenbosched?" Phillip started crying.

"What the hell's the matter with you? I don't give a hoot, I
tell you, now the Boy General's gone! He was a bloody good
man. He'd have understood. We helped at Gouzeaucourt, didn't
we? I'm quite happy about going back to my regiment. Don't
let it get you down, *mein prächtig kerl*! Let's have a drink."

"I won't, thanks, Teddy."

"Aren't you well?" He put a hand on Phillip's forehead.
"You've got a temperature, old man. How d'you feel?"

"Oh, not too good." More tears.

Pinnegar made him see the American doctor, who diagnosed
"Perdoxia unknown origin".

"Skrimshanker's fever, doctor."

"Wale, I have never heard a louse called that, young man.
You are feeling mean, I guess?"

"Yes, I am, rather." He wondered how the doctor knew
about Pinnegar taking the blame. "But Teddy wouldn't let me
see the Brigadier."

It was explained that mean in America meant poorly.

"I'll send you down to Casualty Clearing at Edgehill, outside
Albert, young man, with a recommendation to the Colonel there
that you have a long rest in Britain."

"But I'm not really ill, doctor!"

"Don't you want to go home?"

"Not very much."

"Is that so? Wale, I guess that attitude is most unusual. Haven't you any young ladies you want to see?"

"No, doctor." More tears.

At last the doctor got it out of him. "So your girl was killed, and you want to avenge her death. Now see here——"

"No, not that exactly, doctor. If I had been true to my great friend, who loved her, Lily might not have been there when the aerial torpedo fell."

"Oh ho, I get it now, young man! But you must not assume responsibility for God, no sir! If that dear girl's time was come, nothing you or anyone could do would have averted it. When the Lord calls, each one of us must answer alone."

Phillip looked suitably receptive to the idea, without being able to accept such an aspect of God.

"Now don't worry your head about what is beyond you, young man. You have had a long, long time out here, I guess, and what you need is a long, long rest. And be kind to yourself. Relax those taut nerves of yours. I am going to send you right down to Edgehill so soon as your man-servant has brought your pack."

"Mayn't I go out to see my friends before I leave, doctor?"

"No, sir, you will stay right here! One hundred and three temperature is not to be fooled with. You will go with the next convoy to Edgehill, and I will say goodbye for you to Teddy and the boys."

"Thank you, doctor."

He could write to Teddy, to Nolan and to Morris; but nothing could be done about Black Prince.

Chapter 21

COMUS & CO.

3rd Gaultshire Regt.
Landguard Fort, Suffolk.

Dear Teddy,

I am posting this to the Birmingham address you gave me, to be forwarded. How and where are you? I've wondered a lot, since I left the coy. Here things are much the same. I was sent to Mrs Greville's hospital at Polesden Lacey near Guildford, but managed to get out after a week. The Board gave me 3 months' Garrison B duty, and 10 days' leave which were somewhat dud, as I saw none of my old pals. My best news is that 'Spectre' West is not missing as we feared, but wounded only, and back in England.

The first thing Phillip had done on arrival home was to ask where *The Times* copies were; and on going into the front room he saw a neat pile of newspapers on the table, and on the top a list, written in the clear and careful handwriting of his father, containing all the casualties in both the Gaultshire Regt. and the General Staff for the past six weeks. At the bottom of the Gault-shire list, on two sheets of foolscap paper, was the word FOUND in large letters, and the entry

Captain (temp. Major while seconded to the General Staff)
H. J. West, D.S.O., M.C.

He sat down beside the aspidistra in its brass bowl, and cried.

Hetty saw, with pity that she tried to conceal, that he had a thin, staring look. She tried to tell herself that on no account must she question him about his doings in France. She was alarmed by his later manner, after he had refused a cup of Benger's Food. He was so silent and restless, going from room to room, to see if everything was the same, and finding it the same, appeared to be unable to bear it. He could settle at nothing.

At last she said, "Are you sure you are all right, Phillip?"— stopping herself just in time from calling him "dear". "Is anything the matter?"

"I think I'll go down and see Mrs. Neville."

"I did hear Mrs. Feeney say that Desmond is home on leave, Phillip. He's got his commission; something to do with anti-aircraft guns."

"How did Eugene get on with Mavis—or should I say Elizabeth?"

"Oh, I don't think she saw him after that one time, Phillip."

"I didn't think he was quite her sort, Mother. So she saw him only once?"

"Yes, dear. He took her to the Coliseum."

"And then wanted her to go to his flat?"

"Your sister Mavis—oh dear, what am I saying—Elizabeth didn't say, Phillip. It was a long time ago."

"I think I'll go next door and see Gran'pa and Aunt Marian."

"Yes, do, dear. I am sure they will be most pleased to see you."

Afterwards she saw him sitting on the first seat of the Hill opposite, where so many times, looking from the verandah of her bedroom, she had seen all the children playing happily in the summers of long ago. Was he hoping that Desmond or Mrs. Neville would see him? For he had not gone down the road after seeing Papa.

Elizabeth—she *must* remember never to say "Mavis" by mistake —was the first home that day. Hetty asked her to be very very careful what she said.

"He's in the sitting-room, playing the gramophone."

"Father's, or his own?"

"Father's, Elizabeth. His own was lost in France, he says."

"Yes, and if Father comes home unexpectedly, he'll blame you!"

"Now, Mav—I mean Elivabif—oh, what am I saying——" She laughed, the mood swiftly changed, she felt like crying, but said gaily, "Go down and see your brother, Elizabeth, and do be nice to him, won't you? He isn't very well. I'm just going to make some dripping toast; it will help keep out the cold."

Mavis saw Phillip sitting over a glowing coke fire. "Hullo, how are you? Haven't you put on a lot of coke? Father will say something if he sees that! Coal and coke are awfully hard to get now. Didn't you know? There's no need to stand up. I know very well you don't think much of me!" She felt distress. Why didn't he say something? "Well, how are you? Can't you answer, eh?"

"Quite well, thank you. How are you?"

"Aren't you pompous! Well, you don't look well! In fact, you look ill! Is anything the matter with you?"

"I've had a touch of trench fever."

"I hope it isn't catching! Well, go on playing the gramophone, I shan't tell Father! I'm not that sort, you know!" Tears came into her eyes. She went out as abruptly as she had come in, and he heard her calling out as she went upstairs, "Mother, hurry up with my tea! I'm hungry. Nina is coming on leave this evening, and I promised to meet her at the station."

It is quite like old times in London, now that a few of the Gothas which used to lay their eggs on us at Proven come over and play hickaboo.

He had been returning from a long walk around the darkened streets—unable to face Freddie's Bar or the Gild Hall—hurrying past the ruins of Nightingale Grove with clenched hands and ruinous thoughts—and was approaching the Fire Station when he heard whistles, and then past a stationary, empty tram came the tinkle of a familiar bell, and there was Father bicycling slowly down the street, blowing his whistle. Upon his chest was slung a white placard, printed with red letters

POLICE NOTICE—TAKE COVER

He followed the figure in the now empty High Street, while guns began to open up for the apron barrage protecting Woolwich Arsenal. Soon bits of shrapnel were coming down.

"Take cover! Take cover!" called out an urgent voice. Phillip recognised 'Sailor' Jenkins, standing under the railway bridge by the Conservative Club. Bowing shoulders, hands in pockets of driver's coat, he replied in a Cockney voice, "Don't get the pushin' wind up, chum," as he slouched past.

Richard had come home, put on arm-band and steel helmet, stopped only to swallow a cup of hot water (the tea in the pot had been made too long, and he must look after his "nervous stomach") then down to Randiswell Police Station on his Sunbeam, and so on duty. No longer an upright figure, a little bowed after nearly forty years of office life, he pedalled on at the regulation pace of eight miles an hour, regularly blowing his whistle, while fragmentary thoughts passed through his mind—relief that his son was home again; bewilderment, scorn, and anger at the idea of Lord Lansdowne, whose letter to *The Times* asking for a negotiated peace had been referred to in *The Daily Trident* as "the white flag of surrender", being ready to betray his country; depression that the great victory of Cambrai, for which the bells had been rung, had turned out to be a defeat, with hundreds of guns lost, thousands of prisoners taken, and no doubt as many killed. Someone had blundered; and according to the *Trident*, that someone was in a very high command.

Shrapnel fragments rained down, tinkling on paving stones, clattering on slate roofs, and wood-block roadway; some falling with whizzing noises, some like little sighs, even moans. He pedalled on.

Phillip saw his father returning from the Obelisk, and was glad that he was all right. The white blur passed. He looked for a coffee stall, but it was not in its usual place. Food scarcity,

he thought, and went home by way of the mill in the lane called
Botany Bay, with its rows of little houses, and so to the Hill, in
darkness and silence.

> I saw that chap Ching I told you about, one night. Somehow he
> had heard I was home, and called. He is now a civvy, with 100%
> disability pension in the offing, he told me. Apparently he swung the
> lead very cleverly. Pretended to be mad with shell-shock, and ran
> at his colonel in the trenches with a bayonet, crying "There they
> are, the Germans!" They sent him down the line; and knowing that
> real shock is accompanied by temperature and faster heart beats,
> he chewed and swallowed cordite, and got away with it. Said to
> me, "If I'd have run at a sergeant, I'd have got jankers for insubor-
> dination, and had to stay in the line, but I worked out that no-one
> would rumble me if I went for the C.O. when he came round with
> the Adjutant." I shook him off by jumping on a bus in the High
> Street. He can't bear himself, for some reason; always was a hanger-
> on, even as a boy, never knew when he wasn't wanted. But who am
> I to talk?
>
> Well, Teddy, I didn't see any shows on my leave, at least not the
> ordinary kind; I went once with my people to the Old Vic, and saw
> *As You Like It*, which I suppose was "the stuff to gie 'em" of those
> times. Personally I begin to enjoy Shakespeare. Then, at the end
> of my leave, I got a notice from a brass-hat Captain *for* Lieutenant-
> colonel, *for* Adjutant-General, who had the honour to be My Most
> Obedient Servant, curtly ordering me to report forthwith to the above
> unit, and here I am, on my first night, having signed out for Mess
> Dinner six hours late, because I can't very well go in in field boots,
> though I have taken off my silver-plated racing spurs which merely
> tickled Jimmy the Mule so that he used to stop when I was trying to get
> him to jump in order to enjoy more scratching upon his hairy hide.

From the dark cavern of Liverpool Street station Phillip had
gone to Ipswich, then by slow branch line to the terminus of
Landguard Fort, where he arrived in darkness. As he was finding
his way along a road suddenly it was lit up by clusters of Very
lights rising above rifle and Lewis gun fire and the gruff coughs
of hand grenades. For a moment he sweated; then realising it
was a night assault practice, walked on until he came to sea
glimmering in pale rushes upon the shore. He went along a row
of terraced brick houses, at the end of which were dark shapes of
hutments. On his left was a fort-like house, standing on turf at
the shingle edge.

He reported to the Orderly Room. He was posted to "C"
company, and told to share a billet in No 9 Manor Terrace with

a subaltern named Allen. If he went to the Officers' Mess across the barrack square and enquired of the mess sergeant, he would be given an orderly to show him the billet.

"Mess dinner is at seven thirty. It's Guest Night," said the assistant adjutant. "Have you got your kit with you?"

"It was lost in France. I only heard yesterday that I was to come here, and so haven't had time to see my tailor for infantry knickerbockers."

"The breeches are all right, but you'll need ankle boots and puttees for parades."

"Very good, sir."

No 9 Manor Terrace had a cast-iron gate which had not yet been taken for salvage, because it was rusted open on its hinges, and more or less unshiftable except by blows of a sledge hammer, explained the orderly, as he pushed open the front door, to reveal a floor hair-light down a passage. His guide went in, a servant came out of the end room and showed him a bedroom with a small fire in the grate, and lit by a gas-mantle, under which sat a young officer reading at a three-legged table. He stood up, putting down his book, hesitating whether or not to say good-evening. In his fatigue Phillip mistook this attitude for aloofness, and after a pause gave the other a curt good-evening.

"Good evening, sir," replied the young officer.

The servant waited. Then he said, "Have you got a camp bed, sir?"

"No."

"May I lend you mine?" enquired the young subaltern, gravely.

"No, thank you. I can sleep on the floor."

"In your valise, sir?" asked the servant.

"I have no valise."

"Right, sir, I'll soon fix you up!" He spoke in so cheery a voice as he left the room that Phillip felt ashamed of his curtness.

"Do sit down, sir, won't you?" said the junior subaltern, offering his chair, as the door closed.

"No need to call me 'sir'. I'm only a lieutenant. Just been turfed out of the M.G.C. That's why I'm in this get-up," he said, as he took off his driver's coat. "My name is Maddison."

"Mine is Allen." The chair was placed forward.

"Thank you, Allen. What's the book?" as he sat down and stretched his legs.

"Oh," hesitatingly, "Euripides."

Phillip saw that it was in Greek. "My only acquaintance with Greek is through the *Smaller Classical Dictionary*. Have you been here long?"

"A fortnight."

"Cadet Battalion?"

"Abbreviated course at Sandhurst."

"Oh, a regular."

"Well, yes—for the time being."

A series of jangling bumps came through the walls, followed by scrapings and a blow on the door, which opened, to admit two soldier servants with an up-ended wire-bedstead. The new batman explained, "I thought I'd borrow Major West's, sir, as he went up on leaf s'afternoon."

"Major West? With a—with a—you know—wounded—lost a hand, and one eye——?"

"That's right, sir. The major told me to fix you up with any-thing you wanted in the meantime like. I'll bring in a table and chair, sir. I've already got a spare harticle."

When Allen went to the mess, Phillip, who had returned there to sign off, sat in the room and read the newspaper he had bought for the journey. Among the items was an announcement that the Army Council had approved the issue of a watered rainbow silk riband to be worn by all members of the British Expeditionary Force who had served or were serving in France or Belgium up to and including 14 November 1914, when the First Battle of Ypres had ended. The riband would shortly be available.

He read the item several times, and felt a glow, but the glow lost its warmth when he thought of Baldwin, Cranmer, and all the others. . . . He opened the new copy of the Oxford Book which he had bought on returning home, and copied out one of the poems in his letter to Pinnegar.

> *They told me, Heraclitus, they told me you were dead,*
> *They brought me bitter news to hear and bitter tears to shed.*
> *I wept as I remember'd how often you and I*
> *Had tired the sun with talking and sent him down the sky.*
>
> *And now that thou art lying, my dear old Carian guest,*
> *A handful of grey ashes, long, long ago at rest,*
> *Still are thy pleasant voices, thy nightingales, awake;*
> *For Death, he taketh all away, but them he cannot take.*

It would hardly do for Teddy, who would think he was blotto; so he threw the copy in the fire, and went outside. He sat on the shingle, in the roar of the waves; and coming back again, walked towards the hutments. Music of a brass band was playing somewhere. Of course, it was Guest Night. He had cut Guest Night, he supposed.

At half-past eleven Allen returned.

"Thank you for letting me use your chair."

"No, no, please sit down! I'm just going to bed." Allen undressed, washed, cleaned his teeth, knelt to say prayers, and was winding up his watch when there was a tap on the door. A senior subaltern stood there. "My name is Sisley," he said to Phillip. "Will you come with me?"

They went together down the terrace to the camp. "I thought I'd have a word with you," said the other. "We can talk best in the card-room, now the bridge-players have knocked off."

I'm going to get a ragging for cutting Guest Night, thought Phillip. How events in life repeated themselves! And always due to his own faults. It was the spirit of a man's life that recurred, for events had no assembly upon him, as it were, apart from a man's own pattern in life. Death was outside that pattern. Well, he would face whatever was coming, quietly. Nothing really mattered. No excuses!

"The others have gone to pull Father out of bed," said Sisley, stepping back before the ante-room door. Was someone going to spring upon him, a scrum? Phillip walked in; the room was empty. "We won't be disturbed in the card room when they lug in Father. He always goes to bed early on Guest Nights, which is a bore, when he is wanted to play the piano. Do you play, by any chance?"

"I'm afraid not."

"What will you drink?" Sisley rang the bell. With the order he said, "And ask the mess sergeant for the sandwiches, will you?" When the tray came, he raised his glass to Phillip. "Here's luck! Do help yourself to sandwiches. Now I'll come to the point. Some of us here know that you've had bad luck, and we want you to know that you're among friends." He raised his glass again, said "Good health!" and swallowed the rest of his whiskey and soda.

Phillip could not speak. He just managed to drink.

"We know," went on Sisley, "how well you did at Loos after

'Spectre' was hit. He had bad luck, too, before July the First, you may remember." More drinks arrived. "Now get outside these sandwiches. We appreciate your reasons for not coming into mess tonight, although had we known in time, we could have fixed you up with a pair of slacks."

"Well, thanks very much, Sisley."

Voices without, door barged open, half a dozen subalterns coming in, lugging a large amiable figure with the droll face of a clown. A red grenade on his sleeve showed "Father" to be the Bombing Officer. He looked like a farmer; but when he had given, after repeated demands, his patter on how to sell a gilded brass watch at a Fair, Sisley told Phillip that was how "Father" had earned his living before the war.

Followed a sing-song around the piano, Father vamping on the keys. When the assistant adjutant arrived, Father got up, swallowed his beer, said "Thank God for small mercies", and departed. The newcomer sat at the piano, the sheet music of *Roses of Picardy* having been placed before him. He sang in a sweet tenor voice, reminding Phillip of the singer—who was it now? what was his name?—over two years ago at Grey Towers, Hornchurch—what *was* his name?—he had become engaged to the C.O.'s daughter, and was killed on July the First. What *was* his name? It worried him that he could not remember. Was his brain going? What *was* the name? He could hear the voice, see the face, the smile, the brushed-up Kaiser-moustache. He tried desperately to remember. He had sung *Rosebud in my Lady's Hair*. There were no roses in Picardy, only poppies, most of them in no-man's-land. Francis Thompson, doped with laudanum, on the Embankment, broken boots and all, sleeping at night on a newspaper, under the arch of Waterloo bridge, and writing his poem on the poppy by day, when not holding horses' heads for a copper.

> *The sleep-flower sways in the wheat its head,*
> *Heavy with dreams, as that with bread:*
> *The goodly grain and the sun-flushed sleeper*
> *The reaper reaps, and Time the reaper.*
>
> *I hang, 'mid men my needless head,*
> *And my fruit is dreams, as theirs is bread:*
> *The goodly men and the sun-hazed sleeper*
> *Time shall reap, but after the reaper*
> *The world shall glean of me, me the sleeper.*

In June the periscope showed a level red of poppies fringing shell-holes, wire, and the emptying uniforms of the dead. Roses in Picardy, Flanders, or Artois! Christ, what civvy-songwriter rubbish! What did they know about the truth? Then came the old and hopeless longing for Lily.

> *She is waiting by the poplars,*
> *Colinette with the sea-blue eyes;*
> *She is waiting and longing and sighing*
> *Where the long white roadway lies . . .*

He was too old for them; he who had known Lily in the gas-light among the yews of St. Mary's churchyard, long ago. In their eyes, unfocused from the present, was still the dream of hope. If only he could feel like them. Arms on one another's shoulders, warm with comradeship, buoyed by mutual esteem, they lived in the words and music—brother officers, come together for a cause in which few could now believe, but which had been made into something greater than themselves—the spirit of a regiment, the instinct of service one to another, the selflessness of love. If he could not live for them, he could at least die with them. He fortified himself by thinking of the two lines from *The Mistress of Vision*:

> *When thy song is shield and mirror*
> *To the fair, snake-curlèd pain——*

On Christmas morning there was church parade. He wore infantry knickerbockers made in the town, with new brown boots and Fox's puttees. From the tailor, too, he had got a piece of the new watered rainbow riband of the Mons Star, sewn on his left breast. Two-thirds of the battalion not on leave marched with the regimental band to and from the parish church. On the way back they passed the pier, and the last houses of the town, and came to a row of beach huts behind an asphalt promenade which ended the watering-place. Beyond was the brown ridge of shingle. On the ragged horizon of the North Sea was visible a tiny lightship. Approaching the camp, companies were called to attention: and then, six feet above the sea's edge, a Camel single-seater scout flew past, the pilot waving a hand. Eyes remained to the front, arms swinging in unison, boots breaking upon the road rhythmically. At the head of the column, behind the drums, *rat-a-plan-plan—rat-a-plan-plan—*

walked the tall, bearded figure of the Colonel. Then the fifes ceased to shrill; *boom-boom-boom* of the bass drum: brass music of regimental march arose in frosty air, with glints of the sun upon the drum-major's whirling stick.

By tradition, the officers were invited to the Sergeants' Mess before luncheon. The Colonel, the first cousin of the Duke of Gaultshire, six feet four inches tall, famous oarsman and once a Viceroy, genial, blue-eyed, spoke to every sergeant in turn. He appeared to know every name, to remember every personal detail—village, wife or mother, family history. Moving among the sergeants, the Colonel spoke to every man. Likewise he seemed to remember the name of every officer, and all that previously had been replied in answer to his genial questions. It was said that when, in his quarters within Fort House at night, he dictated letters to his secretary concerning his Estate, his Grand Mastership of Freemasons, and other public affairs, he wrote private letters upon his knee at the same time. In the Orderly Room, dealing with defaulters, he never raised his voice, but spoke quietly, with impersonal ease, in the same tones with which he praised others on occasion—always detached, remotely paternal, equable. The spirit of service to thousands of acres of land and nearly a thousand years of English history was in his blood.

Phillip watched the amiable Viking figure, with the full blue eyes—a caricature of whom by Spy he had seen on the walls of Flowers' hotel—drinking a pint of beer with the Regimental Sergeant Major. This was another, if not majestic, certainly terrific figure with three wound stripes, Military Cross, and Distinguished Service Medal. And when he talked with the sergeant he had spoken to at Charing Cross station fourteen months before, Phillip began to feel really at home for the first time in the war, and trills of joy moved in him as he told himself, These men are from the countryside that my mother and grand-father belonged to, and still belong, and now I am with the Gaultshires!

And yet—with a pang—I have come with an adverse report—all in the Orderly Room and the mess must know it by now: and through my fault entirely Pinnegar has been sent home, too, in disgrace.

Under the green baize board, to which Orders and other notices were pinned, there was a table, and on it a thick leather-

bound book containing photographs of officers of the Regiment.
Looking through it, he saw 'Spectre' West, as a second-
lieutenant, standing before a painted roll of scenery. He looked
very young, but with the same expression of directness under his
high white forehead. The flat service hat looked strangely old-
fashioned. The photograph had been taken in Gaultford, the
capital town. Allen had told him that West had been a junior
master at the school, when it had grown from the county grammar
to a public school. Allen had been at the school, where he had
won a Classical scholarship to Balliol. He hoped to go up when
the war was over.

An envelope came, addressed to Lieut. P. S. T. Maddison, to
report to the Orderly Room immediately. Thumping heart,
drying mouth. *Resigns his commission, the King having no further
use for his services.*

Phillip had spent a week drilling with others on the square.
The Colonel asked him how he would move a platoon, without
halting it, through a gateway from one field to another, when it
was advancing in line towards the gate. The Colonel had a
little sketch of the gateway, the two fields, and the platoon in
line.

"What order would you give your platoon, Mr. Maddison?"
Phillip could not think. He remained silent.

"Would you not mark time, Mr. Maddison?"

"Yes, sir."

"Then what would you do?"

Silence.

"Your men are marking time, Mr. Maddison. How to get
them through the gate?"

"I would form fours, sir."

"What then?"

"I would order left turn, then forward march, sir."

"Surely 'Forward march' is a cavalry order, is it not?"

"Yes, sir."

He could not remember.

"Your men are still marking time, Mr. Maddison."

"I would order, By the left, lead on, sir."

"Yes, I think that would get them through. That will be
all, Maddison."

"Thank you, sir."

The assistant adjutant later told him that a favourable report
had been returned, with his dossier, to Eastern Command,

together with the C.O.'s recommendation that he be gazetted as attached to the 1st Battalion.

"The *first* battalion?"

"You served with the first at Loos, surely? But you'll probably remain with us here until your next medical board in March. By the way, you're down for four days' Christmas leave on the thirty-first."

Happily he returned to the ante-room. A full moon was shining over the parade ground; first warning had been sounded. He was looking at the book of photographs when the electric light was cut off. Derisive cheers came from the bridge-players, with loud calls for candles.

Passing through the immovable iron gate, he saw chinks of light through the shrouded windows of the front room. Could 'Spectre' be back? It was a shaking thought. Quietly he pushed open the front door and crept past to his room, where Allen was reading by fire-light. The borrowed bed was gone; in its place, a faded green stretch of wood and canvas. He went out to see his servant.

"Mr. Oliver-Jones, when he went out, gived it to me, sir," said the batman. "He told me to sell it if I wanted to."

"How much d'you want?"

"Would ten and a kick be too much, sir?"

"Too little! I'll give you a pound for it."

"Very good, sir. The major was asking after you, sir. He's in the front room now, sir."

Back in his room, he sat down on the little beer barrel, with a cushion on it, which his batman had scrounged from the mess sergeant. Allen went on reading. Phillip remained still, deeper entoiled. The front door opened; there were greetings in loud voices. Evidently a party was going on in 'Spectre's' room. He felt he could not face them.

"I think you are expected," said Allen, at last. "Major West has just returned from an Investiture at the Palace. He looked in here about half an hour ago, and asked for you."

Phillip forced himself to go. Entering, he saw faces in candle-light around a central figure sitting back to the door, tunic off, trousers rolled to the knee. Although faces were turned to the newcomer the sitting figure did not move.

"Good evening," said Phillip. 'Spectre' appeared not to have heard. Over the sitting man's shoulder he saw white and nobbly feet standing in a tin basin filled with steaming water. He noticed particularly the big-toe joints, which stuck out, so that the toes themselves appeared to point inwards. Too small boots in childhood! Dear Westy. Perhaps he was as shy of the meeting as he himself had been; the thought released warmth, and bending down, he put a hand over the older man's hand, and squeezed it gently; whereupon 'Spectre' screwed round his head, and looking round his nose with his one eye, exclaimed, "Hullo, you horse-thief! How are you? Stand in front of me, and let me look at you! No, don't look at those barnacles!" for Phillip had glanced at the new tunic hanging on the wall, to see a second silver rosette upon the D.S.O. riband. "What adorns your manly breast is worth all of them put together!"

A seat was found; and then 'Spectre' asked Phillip to tell him what had happened after he had left him on that rainy afternoon.

All seemed to be listening intently. The warming whiskey made it seem all a joke, which amused him the more his hearers laughed. He imitated portly Brendon, while someone re-filled his glass, and another gave him a lighted cigarette. He added bits about Broncho Bill's exploits in repeatedly stealing the A.P.M.'s breeches. "So I thought it was about time someone pinched his nag, to save both Broncho Bill and Brendon further trouble!"

"Now tell us what you did at Westcappelle."

"Everyone there was awfully decent. Among other things, they sent aeroplanes to photograph the sector east of the cemetery, to try and find you, Westy."

"Now let me tell you something! It wasn't aerial photography to which I owe my life—not that it's worth a damn—but I owe it to the finest General to appear in this war, apart from the Chief. I mean Monash, of the Third Australian division. If he'd had his way on the eleventh of October, we would have taken Passchendaele a month before it fell to the Canadians! Moreover, it was another Jew, one of his Brigadiers named Rosenthal, who got on the Ridge behind the Belle Vue pillboxes on the eleventh, and believe you me, never were figures so welcome! So when any of you ever feel like damning Jewboy profiteers in this war, chalk up against it John Monash, and the Third Australian division!"

When I was alone with Westy—he asked to be remembered to you, by the way—he said, "The slums have died in Flanders. And it is the descendants of those who in the old days were sent in hulks half-way round the earth by England, for protesting against bad working conditions, or for stealing a sheep to feed their starving children, who were among the first to come to the help of England." He rather talks like that now: the G.H.Q. attitude, I suppose.

Anyway, we're going to spend New Year's Eve together in London, in the same hotel where I once went with Jack Hobart.

The night before they went to London the band played in a marquee adjoining the dining room. Pink-shaded electric lamps lined the table-centres, faces glowed with laughter and talk. The Bandmaster came in just before the King's health was proposed, to stand beside the Colonel with a glass of port, afterwards sitting down to smoke a cigarette.

In the ante-room there was singing, and later still a sort of scrum started, one side trying to roll up the leader of the other side in the carpet, with cries of "To the incinerator!" The struggle twisted itself as far as the card-room, where a young lieutenant-colonel, a famous cricketer known as "Johnny-won't-hit-today" roared out, "Stop that bloody row!" but nobody took any notice, until the electric light went out, and someone shouted in pretended rage, "You bloody Gothas, go home, damn you, go home! Candles, Candles!"

The fun ended just before midnight with the assistant adjutant singing *Roses of Picardy*, which quietened everyone—only the juniors were left then. It was sung in candle-light. Then "Father" Andrews brought in what he called his trumpet-violin, an affair of cat-gut which extended tautly over a cigar-box, from the other end of which protruded part of a brass motor horn. Playing with a horse-hair bow, he made comic noises, until Sisley, muttering "You have no soul", took it from him, seated himself on the edge of a chair, held it between his knees, and drew from it such plaintive and tender notes of *Danny Boy* and then of *Waley Waley*, that the only other sound in the ante-room was of distant anti-aircraft guns.

On New Year's Eve Westy and Phillip were in the train to London.

"Flossie said she remembered you. But she says that of every-one. What she does remember is who, among her rows of photo-graphs, has been killed. It gives her a romantic feeling to say, 'He was killed', and 'He was shot down in flames'. The place is becoming a crush, as more and more people discover it."

"Perhaps all the rooms will be booked, Westy?"

"Flossie keeps some back for her friends. Anyway, I booked a couple when I was in London."

Phillip was about to ask how Westy could have known that he would be at Landguard; but thought that possibly he had invited him when one of his other friends couldn't come. So he said, "It was great luck for me to be sent to the Gaultshires, instead of to the Prince Regent's."

"Well, I remembered what you told me about having a bit of trouble with your C.O., so I asked 'Nosey' Orlebar to keep an eye on you."

"Thanks very much!"

"Nothing to thank me for. There's been far too much mixing up of regiments, which destroys esprit-de-corps. Among strangers a man feels that he belongs only to himself; in a regiment, to his friends. Every regiment ought to insist that it look after its own. It just wasn't possible during Third Ypres; it would have needed organisational resources that weren't available. Tell me how you came unstuck at Cambrai."

"I lost the way down from Bourlon Wood, when we had to wear box respirators. Wouldn't have happened if I'd had a compass."

"Where did you get to?"

"Right down on the other flank, by the Escault canal, instead of the Canal du Nord. So the guns weren't available when the counter-attack came from Moeuvres next morning. However, they came in handy for 'Vincent's Force', at Gouzeaucourt."

"I've been reading *War and Peace* again in hospital, and have come to believe that there's something in Tolstoi's theory of war. All impulses recoil upon themselves, thus carrying their own collapse. By the way, I met a friend of yours at Flossie's, who asked to be remembered to you." He added casually, "Sasha."

"I wondered if she was still about."

Dare he ask about Frances? But Westy would then know that he was wondering if Sasha . . . Change the subject. The Colonel.

"I remember Spy's cartoon of Lord Satchville in the smoking room at Flossie Flowers', Westy. Dark blue cap, tall and bearded, large blue eyes, holding an oar. I suppose pink ties were the thing in those days?"

"It's a Leander tie."

"For rowing?"

"It's a rowing club."

"How is Frances, Westy?"

"Very happy when I last heard of her. She was married in the autumn."

"Oh, I see."

"Somebody in the Indian Army. He's now in Palestine, I'm told. Now I'm going to get some sleep. We shan't get much tonight."

At Liverpool Street he said, "We'll get a drink at home. You remember my parents?"

They took a taxi to Lime Street. The sitting room was laid for tea. How like his own mother Mrs. West was; but more composed. Mr. West, judging by the photographs on the walls, had been a regular army sergeant: pill-box cap, cut-away jacket, tight trousers with a stripe down them, big moustache. There were many photographs, including two young men in khaki, apparently Westy's young brothers.

After tea, Mr. West went upstairs with Westy, and Phillip was left with Mrs. West. She seemed eager to talk about her son.

"He always talks about you, Mr. Maddison."

"Please call me Phillip!"

"May I? Harold always speaks of you as Phillip. So we know you already, you see! He is very fond of you."

"I can't think why!"

"Oh, don't say that! He says you are a very loyal person. He told us a lot about you when he came back last time. You took his message, didn't you?"

"That was easy, Mrs. West. And apart from that, any of us would do anything for Harold. He's a wonderful man!"

"Yes, everyone tells us that. Even as a boy, Harold was always very considerate to others, not like most boys. He was like another father to his little brothers. So kind and patient. They loved him dearly."

Phillip was silent.

"You look tired, Phillip. Would you like to lie down a bit?"

"Oh, I'm all right, really."

"Are you sure? Well, I won't fuss. Yes, Harold was always all that his mother and father could wish for. And as I said, always so good to his brothers. There they are, up there." She pointed to a family group. "Yes, he was the kindest brother to our two little ones. He used to take them out whenever he came home from Christ's Hospital, and kept it up when he was at the University."

"They're in the Army, too, Mrs. West?"

"Yes, they joined up when the war came. We lost them," she said, gently.

"Oh, I am so sorry."

"They were in the Post Office Rifles, and were together when it happened, when the shell fell in the trench. It was at Hill Sixty—you know it, perhaps?"

"I was never there, but of course I've heard of it."

"Have you any brothers, Phillip?"

"Only two sisters."

"How nice for you! Father and I had only boys. I expect you are very fond of them?"

"Yes, Mrs. West."

"You're going to see them this leave, I expect?"

"Yes, we live only a mile or two out, near the Crystal Palace."

"Nice and high up! Father and I are looking forward to retiring after the war, but I don't want to go too far away from my friends. I'm a proper Cockney, you see. But Father, he wants a garden. It's in his blood, he was born in Gaultshire. So we thought of looking for a cottage not too far away. Harold wants to take Holy Orders, he told you, I suppose?"

"Yes, Mrs. West."

Why did he feel a little disappointed? Was it because Westy now seemed to be almost an ordinary person?

They dined at the Café Royal, and went to see Teddie Gerard in a *revue*; Phillip's former attitude towards 'Spectre' West was recovered under brighter lights. With recovery came a new feeling, that Westy must be extraordinarily gentle, under the rather gruff manner. And what a marvellous understanding of children he had! One day, Mrs. West had said, she had taken Harold and his youngest brother to the Guildhall, where the faces of Gog and Magog the giants had terrified the little boy, so that he said again and again when he got home that they were coming to take him away, and was afraid to go to bed. So Harold had made a model with clay and painted the ugly face, and then given his brother a hammer and told him to break it up.

"I thought when I first saw you, how like you were to Harold when he was younger, only your eyes are bluer, Phillip."

Seek from fears to vanish fears,

One day poetry would have to shatter the old fears of Europe; a Blakian mental fight.

Exaltation gave way to exultation, that he was in such a wonderful gathering. He had seen Sasha, who had almost run to him to take his hand and call him darling. At first he had pretended to be cool, wanting to hurt her a little. She had taken his arm, and hugged it; seen someone else, held up her hand, whispered "We'll meet later—darling! Don't forget!" and dashed away through the dancers. Later—her smooth body, so gentle and girlish in the darkness. This time it would be different. Westy was talking to some of his other friends, round a table, bottle in ice-bucket—he strolled happily through the throng.

In the centre of a group a man was talking to a most beautiful girl, with fair hair and blue eyes. Her face was vaguely familiar. Where had he seen it, on a photographic postcard of famous actresses? She was not like Lily Elsie, or Gladys Cooper, or Zena Dare. Who could she be? She stood face to face with her companion, a short man with a rather large head, but he had such a direct, clear look that the oversize head was not remarkable after the first glance. He had a little moustache, and wore the uniform of a cadet officer. What were they talking about, and why were the others listening? Moving closer, he heard that they were speaking in poetry to one another. This was exciting. He pushed his way nearer, and recognised the Indian Maid's Song from Keat's *Endymion*. The Cadet said:

> "*Whence came ye, merry Damsels? whence came ye,*
> *So many, and so many, and such glee?*
> *Why have ye left your bowers desolate,*
> *Your lutes, and gentler fate?*"

The beautiful girl, who was staring delightedly at the cadet's face, replied:

> "*We follow Bacchus! Bacchus on the wing,*
> *A-conquering!*

Bacchus, young Bacchus! good or ill betide,
We dance before him thorough kingdoms wide"

He: *"Come hither, lady fair, and joinèd be*
To our wild minstrelsy!"

She: *"Whence came ye, jolly Satyrs! whence came ye,*
So many, and so many, and such glee?
Why have ye left your Bushey haunts, why left
Your nuts in oak-tree cleft?"

He: *"For wine, we follow Bacchus through the earth;*
Great god of breathless cups and chirping mirth!
Come hither, lady fair, and joinèd be
To our mad minstrelsy"

Phillip knew the poem; they were jumping over the lines, picking pieces to suit themselves. There were tears in the eyes of the girl as she said,

"Like an own babe I nurse thee on my breast:
I thought to leave thee,
And deceive thee,
But now of all the world I love thee best.
There is no one,
No, no, not one
But thee to comfort a poor lonely maid;
Thou art her mother,
And her brother,
Her playmate, and her wooer in the shade."

"That's very pretty, dear," said the voice of Flossie Flowers. Hardly had she spoken, when another voice with an exaggeratedly genteel accent said, "All the same, y-ew can't beat Robert W. Service!" The voice, the manner, the attitude, the appearance of the man seemed out of keeping with the rest of the crowd. He was noticeable because he was the only one in fancy dress. He wore a white wig tied behind by a black bow, and there was so much lace at the sleeve-ends of his dark velvet cutaway jacket that he had to hold up his right arm and wiggle it before he could grasp the glass which he had left, after a sip, beside a potted palm. His kilt was a pattern of large yellow and red chequers, like the stockings he wore with buckled shoes.

"I said, y-ew can't beat Robert W. Service!"

"Who are you?" asked Flossie Flowers, turning to stare at the speaker. "How did you get in here?"

"I came here to meet my uncle, Miss Flowers. You know him, I think I'm right in saying, Miss Flowers!"

"Your uncle? Who's yer uncle?"

"Don't you know, Miss Flowers?"

"No, I don't! I don't know your uncle, and I don't want to know 'im, whoever he is. The sight of his nephew is enough. Now, dear," to the beautiful young woman and her escort, "you two turtle doves get on with your piece. And if you, in that ridiculous outfit," turning to the aggrieved young man, "interrupt again, I'll have you put out!" Her face became mottled; her first nature had overtaken the façade of refinement. "I can do without your sort in my 'otel!" She walked after the retreating Prince Charlie.

"Let's flee to Eighty-eight!" Phillip heard the girl say, and with a pang watched the two moving away.

Looking around for 'Spectre' West, he saw that he was with Sasha. She was holding his arm, as though caressing it. He heard her say, "No, darling, of *course* not——" and thought that they had been talking about him. It was a shock. He had been feeding on the idea of her coming into his room later that night. Well, he was glad that it was Westy she preferred. This time it would not be like Desmond and Lily. Should he leave at once? He knew no-one. Standing irresolute, he overheard talk between the playwright and another man.

"Rough diamond, Freddy."

"More like the top, or should I say *bottom*, of a lemonade bottle, Hugo."

"The rot's started, Freddy. This pub never had fairies in before. Not that I'm agin 'em. But not here, what?"

"Flossie's gettin' a bit rough, Hugo. Who is his uncle? Looks like a Grouse and Claret. Or would you say a Jock Scot?"

"Looks more like a Parmachene Belle to me, Freddy."

"Parmachene Belle! Sounds like a Mason-Dixie railway engine. Good title for a musical, 'The Parmachene Belle.' Where did you get it?"

"It's the name of a Canadian fly, Freddy."

The playwright called Freddy shot his cuffs, and squared his shoulders. He was wearing a dinner jacket, like many others, obviously soldiers, on leave.

Miss Flowers came up. "Wonder if the flycops put in a nark,

Freddy. Let's have a little drink. Lord Streaky 'as made too much money, so why shouldn't the soldier boys drink his health on New Year's Eve?"

"Who is the Parmachene Belle, Flossie?"

"Him? I dunno, Freddy. Oh Gawd, here he comes again. Let's take cover in the cellar, boys, and have a little drink."

Prince Charlie, with wretched eyes, came up.

"On my word of honour, Miss Flowers, you *do* know my uncle!"

"Well, tell us his name, dear," she simpered.

"I've been trying to tell you, Miss Flowers. Willie Clarkson!"

Flossie Flowers guffawed, and said, "There's no such bloody man!" She took his hand, continuing in her society voice, "All right, I wasn't serious. Willie's my dearest friend! So you're his nephew, well well! Of course, I remember now. You're part of a trapeze act at the Coliseum aren't you?"

"That's right, Miss Flowers! The Three Macs! I also recite!"

In her cockney voice, "Yes, Uncle Willie told me you did, only keep it dark. There's only two people allowed to recite 'ere, and you're not one of them. I can take this nonsense"—shaking the hairy sporran with her hand—"but not the Green Eye of the Little Yellow God stuff. Oh hell, what's the odds? What's your name? Bobby? You're all right, Bobby. Well, about Uncle Willie. We all love him, so don't be hurt by this little story. When he'd come back from Buck House after fixin' up Royalty for charades—you know the story he tells—George Graves kidded him up that he was to be knighted. Uncle Willie *was* in a state! It was a shame, really, Bobby! Uncle Willie expected a call any moment, and after awhile when it didn't come he got George Graves to try and find out what was holding it up. George comes back and says that H.M. was waiting there, sword drawn all ready, and taking practice jabs at the curtains, just like Hamlet. 'Send for the man, whatsisname, that actor feller,' says H.M. 'But first tell me his name, so I don't fix upon him some other pore innocent, inoffensive bastard's name for the rest of his natural.' Jab, right through the arras! 'Come on, what's the feller's name?' 'Willie Clarkson, Your Majesty,' replies Gold Stick in Waiting. 'What name did you say?' asks His Majesty. 'Willie Clarkson, sir.' 'Willie Clarkson?' shouts the King. 'Are you trying to be funny? There's no such bloody man!' And with that he swishes the sword back in the scabbard and goes off in a rage. 'There's no such bloody man!'"

"It's just a gag, of course!" laughed the exaggeratedly genteel voice of Bobby. "I don't believe a word of it, so there!"

"Well, enjoy yourself, Bobby. But no gettin' off in my 'otel! Or out you go! See?"

Poor little creature, thought Phillip. So that was a fairy. Then they did actually exist. The fairy was biting his lip, his hands clenched.

Depression became black. He did not know anyone, either. He looked for Westy and Sasha. People at tables were in parties, laughing and talking happily. He went out into the street. It was nearly midnight. A black police van was waiting round the corner.

Wild cries echoed down the ravine of the street, alcoholic yells of abandon to happiness—for the moment. From afar came a shriek. His stomach turned acid by inferior wine, he thought wildly of the loneliness of life, of Eugene perhaps in his flat all alone. He had written to tell Gene that he was back; but nothing further. And his own home? Father, Mother, the girls, waiting up in the sitting-room, for the stroke of midnight—the sherry decanter already taken from the mahogany cupboard below the book-case with the Gothic glass front. Father solemnly filling the little glasses three-quarters full—then looking at his watch—"Well, I think we are almost in the New Year, Hetty"—and rising out of the armchair—"Here's to your very good health, all of you——" Mother saying, too quickly, "And absent friends—including Phillip! We mustn't forget Phillip——" "I was not forgetting Phillip. I was about to propose his health——" then everyone raising the little, rather heavy, old-fashioned, ornate cut-glasses, and sipping.

He looked at his watch—ten minutes to twelve; and over-coming a desire to walk away, returned to the hotel, remembering that he was Westy's guest.

The dance room across the courtyard was crowded. To his surprise he saw that the band was changed—five negroes now sat on the dais, playing a foxtrot. One of them, the drummer, struck a suspended cymbal with his stick. And then, with arm upraised, his ebon electric energy demanding attention, he laughed gutterally and cried, "'The Black-eyed Susans'!"

Cheers greeted the announcement; and squeaky, brazen din began. Moving past the dancers, he saw Sasha at her table, with 'Spectre' and others. He pretended not to see; but to be still searching. Then she got up, and was coming toward him, holding

her jewelled vanity bag. Still he pretended not to see her, until
the last moment, to prolong the feeling of being wanted by her.

"Darling, you look so utterly lost! Where have you been?"

"Oh, I went outside for a bit."

"We've been looking for you. Come and join us, it's nearly
the New Year. Isn't it thrilling! A *new* New Year! All our very
own, to do just what we want to with! I'm rather tipsy, darling,
I've had too much champagne!"

She took his arm, he went gladly. Her legless husband, sitting
there, greeting him with a smile of splendid teeth. He looked
keen and bronzed of face, as though he had been in the sun.

"Rollo's just back from the Riviera! Isn't he splendid?"
Rollo moved his wheeled chair, pulled another up beside him.
"Come and sit down, Maddison. It's just about midnight."

The band stopped. Scattered cries and clapping were lost in
cheers. *Boom-boom-boom* on the big drum.

"I guess thar's one min't t'go, la's gen'mn!" cried the band
leader.

A circular line began to form around the floor. People got up
from tables to join in. He wondered about Rollo in the wheeled
chair—should he remain with him—but of course, Sasha was
taking him. He hung back pretending to watch with interest.
"Come on, darling!" He hastened forward; but seeing Westy
standing by the wall, moved to stand beside him.

"Hullo, Westy."

"Where did you get to?"

"I went for a walk outside."

"Have you had any supper?"

"Not yet."

"You'll be lucky to find anything left at the buffet."

"I'm not hungry, thanks."

A prolonged roll on the side-drum, followed by bump-bump-
bump-BUMP! of the big drum, the nasal voice of the band
leader throwing into the room, lariat-like, the curving phrase,
"I guess this is it, la's gen'mn," with smiling flash of teeth; then
taking up his trumpet, he blew a long high blast which shaped
itself into *Should Auld Acquaintance Be Forgot*, while hands were
held out to make a chain around the floor.

"Come on, *everybody*!" cried Flossie in her society voice, as she
led "Spectre" West into the throng, followed by Phillip. The
wheeled chair made for them—he crossed hands with Rollo,
pretending not to see the outheld hand of Sasha, hurting himself

a little while wanting to hurt her by keeping away from her. She linked up with Westy. He imagined her in Westy's bed, but was unable to see in his mind what Westy would do; was he, too, "an icicle, whose thawing is its dying"? Was he still faithful to Frances, *because* she had not been able to return his love? Yet if he could yield to Sasha, she ought to be lovely for him.

He swung his arms, holding to 'Spectre' West's wrist beyond the black hand, and to Flossie's fat hand, hard with rings, on the other, making up words for the song.

> *Should auld acquaintance be forgot*
> *Then blast my bloody eyne,*
> *O take a cup too many, boys,*
> *But don't fall in the Rhine!*

Cheers, yells, rattle of hunting horns; pop of corks everywhere. Drink to the New Year. Victory! To hell with D.O.R.A.! The man with hairy hands, wrists, ears, and nose called Hugo, drinking a toast with Prince Charlie, who looked coy and yielding. The Negro band bombilating away, the leader grating out *You Great Big Beautiful Doll*. Freddy saying to another man, "Hugo'll get a whopping big bill from Flossie, although all the wine he's had, six bottles, came from 'Streaky' Southbend's bin. Just like the old bitch. She sent me in a bill last October for a hundred and twenty pounds. I didn't pay it, and a month later for a hundred and forty, although I didn't come here once after I'd got the first bill. So I paid the first one she sent in, and she let it go at that."

Phillip remembered this conversation when, a month or so later, he got a bill for £37 for "Cocktails and Wine".

Sometime later on a snake was formed, of men holding on to the shoulders of the one in front if a man, and to the waist, if a young woman. The snake went up the stairs, and into the bedrooms, hauling out any would-be sleepers or courting couples. Two doors were burst off their locks by Hugo's shoulders, angry complaints smothered by cries and laughter. From room to room the snake went, from floor to floor, except the garrets which were the servants' quarters. Then out into the frozen street, just to show the fly-cops, as Flossie called them, where they got off.

"The fly-cops are always trying to pinch me," she said, her Cockney voice released by drink. "Go on, everyone, let 'em try and pinch you for loiterin' and accostin', the flat-feet!"

Many went back, to avoid the cold; about a score went on, to find a lamp-post with a ladder-bar at the top. There was a bet on: Hugo had laid a level pony with Valentine that Prince Charlie could swing a complete circle. Valentine, apparently, did not know about the trapeze act at the Coliseum. At last a suitable lamp-post was found in a cul-de-sac, near a tree. There Prince Charlie removed his wig, jacket, shirt and vest, and swarmed up in little more than his kilt and stockings. He reached the cross bar, launched himself upon it, and began to swing. The swings were about level when Phillip noticed the black van drawing up at the entrance of the court. Two policemen got out, and watched.

Everyone under the lamp-post looked at the swinging figure.

"Three hundred degrees," announced Hugo.

"The question is, will he whirl?" said Freddy.

"Three hundred and twenty degrees—keep it up, Bobby!" cried Hugo.

Grunts seemed to tear the swinger. Up one side almost to the vertical—a pause——

"Three hundred and forty degrees. You'll do it, Bobby!"

"Oh dear, he's almost *en déshabillé*!" exclaimed Freddy, with an assumed lisp. "How shocking! Indecent exposure, my dear!".

The kilt was almost an inverted parachute.

"Goodness gracious, I hope he won't catch cold, Hugo!"

The rise; first showing his front almost vertical, then his back. The kilt was on the point of collapse when the police officers came down.

"Move along," said one. "Don't you know there's a war on?"

"Keep going, Bobby. Three hundred and fifty degrees, old boy!"

"Come along, get a move on!"

"Wait, constable, wait, dear boy!" said Freddy. "The great question is—will Colonel Parmachene-Belle be able to make it, as the Yanks say? Don't forget it's adding to the gaiety of nations, and therefore to the war effort, officer!"

"Are you trying to be funny?"

"All my life, alas, I am trying to be funny, officer," said Freddy. "I must send you some tickets for my play. Good God, can you beat that? Three months on the Western Front, just home on leave, and as fit as a fiddle! The war's as good as over, officer!"

Cheering broke out around the lamp post. As though frozen, the swinger remained inverted, exactly upright, on balance at 90 degrees to the ground, while his eyes stared down at the police. At that moment searchlights opened up, in the reflected light of which the white figure, clothed from the waist downwards by the kilt, was clearly revealed.

"We've seen enough," said the policemen. Names were taken; and Colonel Parmachene-Belle, carrying an armful of clothes, was pushed into the Black Maria. Hugo and others went to bail him out; Phillip slipped back to the hotel.

Sometime later he went up to his bedroom, leaving the noisy throng below. He was in bed, with the bed-light still on, wondering if he dare go in to see 'Spectre' in the adjoining bedroom, when Sasha, wearing a dressing-gown, came in. "Oh, darling, I've found you at last!"

She sat on the edge of the bed. "Where have you been?" He told her. "You looked so surprised when I came in. As though you'd seen a ghost."

"I thought that perhaps you'd——"

"Given you up? Oh, Phillip, how little you know women."

"How is Rollo?"

"Sleeping blissfully, the babe. You look tired, my lamb. You're shivering. You're cold! I must warm you." She got in beside him, turned over, and looked at his face. "You have such a gentle mouth, darling. Are you still thinking about Lily, that saintly person?"

"I think of her sometimes, Sasha."

"She would want you to be happy, darling. The dead are not jealous, I am sure. A little curious perhaps—faintly curious. They know, I believe, in some remote way, that love is the same in life as in death."

"Yes, Sasha."

"Darling Phillip."

"Sasha, have you seen Westy?"

"Not since I said goodnight to him downstairs, darling."

"I was wondering about you and him."

"Of course, how natural! I love Harold, but I am not much good for him, darling. He's *quite* locked away. And so desperately sad, deep inside. Don't be too sad for your friend, darling. You're not too deeply sad inside, are you? You mustn't be. Lily loves you, and wants you to be happy."

He felt a hypocrite. Lily was poetry, which was beauty, and truth; but it was not of Lily that he had been thinking all the evening. And yet now that Sasha was beside him, he was thinking of Lily.

"You sighed, darling. I'll leave you to sleep."

"Don't go, Sasha."

"Very well, darling. Now sleep—and do not worry that dear head of yours." She turned off the light.

There was another switch, for a central light, by the door. When this opened, and the light was switched on, 'Spectre' West was seen standing there.

"Oh. I beg your pardon," he said distinctly, before switching off.

Sasha called out, "Hullo, darling!" as she turned over to reach the switch of the bed-head lamp. "Phillip and I were just talking about you. Were your ears burning, darling? Oh don't go! Darling, look! I'm in my dressing-gown!" She followed him through the door. He heard her say, "I was just coming, darling, cross my heart, but dropped in to say good-night to Phillip, and found him shivering with cold——"

She came back a minute or two later, and said, "I suppose I am the Scarlet Woman of Flowers' hotel after all."

"Is that what he called you, Sasha?"

"Oh heavens no! Someone called me that once—who was it —Lord Something—one of the new ones—'Streaky' Southbend, the Golden Grocer. I suppose I am a bit that way, if one comes to consider it in the light of Methodism."

"Where did Harold go, Sasha?"

"Back to his room. Only he's locked the door. I don't think I *quite* deserved that, darling."

"I ought to go to him."

"No, leave him alone, darling. I'll go and calm him later on. He's such a poor lost child, really. All you soldier boys are lost children."

She got in beside him, and bent over to kiss him. He felt a tear fall on his forehead. He lay tense, thinking of Westy. What would he think of him? Had he come between Westy and Sasha, as he had between Desmond and Lily? He must go to Westy. He lay still.

"You hold on to your ideals, darling," she said, kissing him on the cheek. "I love you dearly, you are so sweet."

He lay unhappily still, until he heard footfalls along the

passage. He got out of bed, pulled on slacks and tunic, and in bare feet hurried to Westy's room. It was unlocked and empty. Returning along the passage he put on socks and shoes and ran down the stairs. The night porter was in his lodge, stirring a cup of tea beside an open bottle of saccharine tablets.

"Have you seen Major West?"

"'Im as just went out? With a black patch over one eye?"

"Yes. Is he coming back, d'you know?"

"All 'e said to me was Good night and a 'Appy Noo Year, as 'e give me a dollar. Took 'is 'aversack wi' 'im, so I reckon he's gone, sir."

Phillip went back to find Sasha. The bed was empty. He dressed, and went after Westy.

Devon.
May 1957–May 1958

Printed in Great Britain
by Amazon.co.uk, Ltd.,
Marston Gate.